I0710498
ENEMIES
PIPER LAWSON

For every girl who'd bring a damaged billionaire to his knees...
And decide she liked the view.

PART 1

BEAUTIFUL ENEMY

CHAPTER 1

Rae

The man across the arrivals lounge in Ibiza is abrasively beautiful. The kind of attractive that could rip you in two.

Which is exactly what seeing him does to me.

Wearing a dark suit, cut close to his strong body, he carries himself with a confidence no man should possess.

No one is that right, least of all *him*.

The man in the lounge turns, calling out to a woman across the room. He's handsome, but I realize he's not the man I haven't been able to get out of my head for the past two months.

This man has dark eyes, not electrifying blue ones. He lacks the crisp British accent that reeks of boarding schools and privilege. Plus, I don't have that feeling in my gut, as if the ground is vibrating beneath my feet.

"I'm sorry, Miss Madani." The baggage clerk's bright voice drags my attention back to the counter. "Your bag was tracked from New York to Heathrow but hasn't shown on the system since."

Her words settle in, and a knot forms in my chest. "That's not possible. I need that bag."

"If we can't deliver it to you in twenty-four hours, you will be reimbursed up to five hundred euros."

I press the heels of my hands to my eyes.

Barely sleeping on the plane, then stumbling onto the next after stopping to brush my teeth and collect a Starbucks grande to get me through customs and the transfer is catching up to me.

I should've known it was a bad idea to put everything I owned in that bag.

Including my pills.

Someone bumps me from behind, and I glance back to see a string of five women in matching white minidresses. The woman at the front of the bachelorette train that was on my plane is wearing a crown and sash, and the train hollers about "one last time."

I'm the only one here *not* looking for a party.

"I understand this is disappointing. A young woman like you, I bet you had your vacation wardrobe chosen." The woman takes in my black tank top and ripped jeans as if I'd do better to start from scratch.

"I'm not here on vacation." I shove a chunk of dark hair out of my face and feel for my crossbody bag, the computer nestled inside.

Thank fuck.

I wonder what she'd say if I told her the truth. That I'm here because I set my career on fire standing up for what I believed in and every venue that was fighting to finger me two months ago is dodging my calls.

When I leave the baggage area, the low-grade throbbing in my gut won't quit.

The company that hired me said they'd send a ride. Sure enough, by the doors is a huge man in a linen suit with graying hair. He holds a sign that says "*L. Queen.*"

"That's me." Professionally, at least. "You can call me Rae."

"No baggage?"

"I wish. What's your name?"

"Toro, señorita."

I fall into step with him as we dodge tourists and head out the double doors.

"Looks like everyone's here to party," I notice.

The people pouring out of the airport are ready to dance and drink and party their cares away.

"And you?" Toro asks.

"I'm here to help them."

I grin and slide my sunglasses onto my face, the warm air washing over me. It was spring in New York yesterday, and now it's summer in Spain.

The ocean breeze washes over me as Toro shows me to a Mercedes limo and holds open the back door.

"I'm riding up front."

Before he can argue, I pull on the passenger door and lift a book off the seat—*Eat, Pray, Love.*

"This your throwback book club pick of the week?" I set it on the dash, and my lips twitch as I cut him a look. "Don't get me wrong, I read it. Upper-middle-class blond chick searches for purpose after her divorce. Found it as relatable as you probably did. Some of us don't need an international journey to find ourselves."

I fasten my seatbelt as he pulls out of the spot.

"Then what are you doing here?"

I shift in my seat under his suddenly curious gaze. "Dream come true. You mix in Ibiza, you can work anywhere."

But this gig isn't just my big shot...

It's my last shot.

I'm twenty-four years old, and if I don't crush this residency, I might never get another chance to do for a living the one thing that makes me feel alive.

I've wanted to make electronic music since I first put on headphones in front of the computer my parents got me after a traumatic sophomore year of high school.

DJing connects me with an audience in a way that's safe and intimate at once. Unlike other performances, they don't come to watch me.

They come so I'll move them.

There's no better trip.

But the industry doesn't exactly welcome new people with open arms. I've fought with everything I have to get where I am.

Or at least where I was two months ago.

"You came alone," my driver says as we pull out of the airport, and I arch an eyebrow.

"You'd be surprised what a woman can do without a man, Toro," I tease.

I can't imagine being serious enough about a guy to have him travel with me for work.

I'm not blaming my viewpoint on divorced parents. More like every time life has gotten hard, I've found myself alone.

People leave fast when having your back costs them something.

"I have a grown daughter I haven't seen in some time. She is independent like you. That is why I'm reading the book. My wife said our daughter enjoyed it, and I would like to understand what she likes."

It's so paternal my chest tightens. "She's lucky you take an interest."

"I'm sure your parents are very proud," he says, and I swallow the hard lump that rises up my throat without responding. "I will take you to your accommodations."

"Would you take me to the club instead? I need to check on some specs." Besides, there's nothing I'll do at the villa except stress about my bag.

Toro palms the wheel like a caress. "*Debajo*. It means below."

We pass another venue on the beach side of the road. The sign marking the entrance to the outdoor club is huge, and I watch it in the passenger mirror, a shiver starting in my chest and leaving me tingling all the way down to my toes.

"That's La Mer." I sit up straighter.

People plan their entire vacations, their entire years, to join the party at one of the biggest clubs in the world.

"I'm going to play there someday."

Toro laughs. "No woman has." He shrugs at my curious look. "My daughter is into EDM."

I slide my sunglasses down and smile, feeling my ribs expand with possibility. "Tell her I'll be the first."

Debajo is housed beneath a resort, a fact I forgot until Toro parks around the side of the hotel and walks me to a back entrance.

The underground venue used to be popular but has seen better days, but it still picks up crowds on the long weekends in the summer—like everywhere else on the island.

Toro speaks to security in rapid-fire Spanish, and they let me in.

"Call when you are ready to go to the villa," he insists, pushing a card into my hand as I sling my crossbody bag over my shoulder.

When he's gone, I turn to survey my space.

Everything is industrial, black and chrome. Bars along either side and the stage at the far end of the floor. Booths surround the dance floor. A catwalk overhead wraps around in a balcony and cuts over the middle of the floor, partially obscured by a low, black wall—probably VIP booths.

Two guys work behind the bar, readying it for the evening ahead, while another moves boxes with a cart. None acknowledge me. Capacity is supposed to be two thousand, not that it pulls in that many now.

Still, it's nicer than I expected, and for the next month, this place is mine.

Tonight is the start of something good. I can feel it.

"Damnation."

I jump at the female voice before a woman straightens from behind the setup of boards and sound equipment on stage.

When she spots me, her eyes narrow. "Doors don't open for another twelve hours."

"I'm not a tourist. I'm mixing tonight. Raegan Madani. Little Queen," I go on, supplying the stage name I picked years ago because of its similarity to my given name and because it gave me a persona to build on.

The woman's cropped blond hair has a little gray, but she's midthirties, slim, and wearing a green sundress. A shrewd elf with a tan. "Leni. I run the club."

"And you're American," I say, noticing the accent.

"Hawaii. Big Island, born and raised."

I take the stairs to the stage, then turn to survey the sleek, black Pioneer media players flanking the latest mixer. A lifetime of dreams turned into switches and dials that put power in one person's hands.

"It's had a makeover," she says, noticing my appreciation. "I'm taking over from the previous management long enough to get her on her feet."

"Her?"

"Every club is a woman. Don't think a man could hold this much passion or euphoria. Or this many secrets. She's had a rough patch, though." Leni pats the board but her knowing gaze lands on me. "Must sound familiar."

I bristle, hands gripping the strap on my bag tighter.

"Calling out the head of Echo Entertainment on social media for everyone to see was a dumbass move," Leni goes on.

"A woman was assaulted at their venue on a night I was playing. No one at the club or the organization took responsibility. Harrison King owns the company."

"You knew the woman who was assaulted?"

"Does it matter?"

Too many people ignore women they don't know. I needed to look out for her, even if it was after the fact.

"Let me guess—since then, the clubs that were knocking down your door won't touch you."

I lift my bag and set it on a free spot. "This one did."

I pull out my notebook computer and peer into my bag, remembering my costumes were also in my checked bag. Shit.

"Was it worth it?" she asks.

"Yes." My gaze flicks to hers. "People need to be held responsible for their actions. I don't care how much money Harrison King has. Or how pretty he is. Or how big his dick is."

Her slow grin is feline. "You're the only one. Paparazzi stalk him. Models throw themselves at him. He built an entertainment empire most moguls on their deathbeds would envy, and he did it without a gray hair in sight."

I shiver. From sleep deprivation, not from remembering what it felt like to stand a breath away from that man.

"Rumor is he's hiding out now," Leni replies. "Maybe you hurt his feelings."

"That would require him to have feelings."

Leni smirks as she holds out a network cable. I lift the lid of my notebook and hit the power key, but the battery's dead.

"I'll never play another of his clubs for as long as I live." I pull the laptop's power cord and adapter from my bag. Before I can reach for the power bar across the desk, a smooth, impossibly male British voice comes from overhead.

"That's a shame. Because the contract you signed says that, for the next month, you're mine."

CHAPTER 2

Rae

*H*arrison fucking King.

The man himself appears on the catwalk in one of the VIP booths, wearing tailored pants the color of sandy beaches and a white button-down shirt that skims his broad shoulders and muscled chest.

Every inch of his form screams wealth and privilege. His hair is perfectly trimmed, the dull burnished gold darkened to a warm brown in the low lights of the club.

A strong, straight nose and square jaw compete for attention with his firm lips.

He must have a decade on me but looks as if he could make the Olympic swim team without breaking a sweat.

Our first and only confrontation is forever imprinted in my memory. When I approached the billionaire stranger at the wedding reception of two musicians who are mutual friends, I had been riding high on righteous anger. Anger I'd kept in check during the actual wedding—to spare my friends—and unleashed soon after with the help of a few drinks.

I don't make a habit of hating people, but this man makes me rethink that stance.

"What the hell is going on?" I demand.

Electric blue eyes, not unlike the neon sign outside, bore into me.

"You signed a contract to play my club."

He starts toward the stairs, taking them with leisurely strides until he reaches the main floor.

"It wasn't yours when I signed the contract." I would have noticed if his company, Echo Entertainment, had been on the documents.

"Not my problem you can't keep up with the industry."

The staff behind the bar have snapped to attention. They didn't look up when I arrived, but now, they're hustling to wipe imaginary spots off the surface while sneaking furtive looks at the man before me.

Harrison crosses to us, stopping in front of the stage. His shirt is open at the collar to expose a tan throat, the muscles flexing lightly. His mouth curves to reveal a smile as perfect as it is cold.

I whirl to face Leni, who lifts a shoulder as if anticipating my accusation.

"Listen…" she starts.

"Leni." He holds up a hand, cuts her off without so much as a word.

Arrogant prick.

I slam the cover of my notebook and slide it in my bag before shouldering it. "I'm not playing your club," I toss at the man in front of the stage. "Not tonight, not ever."

I stalk down the steps and head across the dance floor.

I make it across the club, then yank on the door.

It doesn't open.

Desperation rises up the second I feel him at my back.

"I'm disappointed." That smooth voice is inches from my ear, close enough his breath tickles my skin. "I've been anticipating this since our first meeting."

I spin around, my nostrils flaring as I stare up at his infuriatingly gorgeous face.

How could I have mistaken the man at the airport for Harrison King?

No man on earth has his intensity, his charisma.

"A woman was assaulted at my gig in LA," I bite out, angry with both of us now. "My gig at *your club*. Your booking agent didn't give a shit. No one at corporate returned my calls demanding an explanation. When I finally got to you, you didn't give a shit either."

"When you confronted me about it at a mutual friend's wedding, you mean."

He says that like it matters.

"If you think I have time to personally care for everyone who sets foot in a building with my name on the deed," he goes on, "you underestimate the size of my empire."

I lift my chin. "If you can't protect the people you serve, you have no right to one."

His throat bobs, a flicker of surprise flitting through his eyes.

Even kings have vulnerabilities.

I try the door again, realizing the lock is on. After turning it, I yank the door open, grab my bag, and run past the confused security guard on the other side.

In the parking lot, I'm breathing heavily as I pull out my phone to call Toro. I need to get out of here—out of this man's presence.

At my resort, I can figure out what the hell to do next.

A ringtone sounds, but the call breaks before Toro answers.

Shit.

I scan my surroundings, my gaze landing on the busy road.

"You have an exceedingly low opinion of me," King calls from behind me as I head for the street, searching the horizon for a cab.

"I'm surprised you care what my opinion is."

His expression flickers with emotions I can't read before he slips into aristocratic arrogance once again. A resting asshole face if I ever saw one.

"I trust your attorneys looked at the terms for failure to fulfill your contractual obligations," he goes on.

The wind blows my fallen hair into my face, and I set my bag down at my feet to shove it back with vicious hands.

"Thanks to you," he drawls, "one of my top-performing venues became the worst overnight. You will recover what you cost me. For the next month, I own you. If you try to leave, I will sue you for every dollar you own. I will take your computer"—he picks up the bag at my feet, and I tense—"your music. Every scrap of clothing in your wardrobe and on your body."

Each word lands on my chest like a brick.

Breathing is hard. We're outside, but it's as if the greedy asshole has consumed all the oxygen.

"What. No response?" he chides softly.

I'm usually the type to rebel with silent resistance, but I refuse to go down without a fight. There are too many bullies in this world.

"If it takes litigation to get a woman naked…" I snatch my bag from his hands. "Your game needs work."

His mouth twists in disbelief.

Before he can respond, the horn of a car honks and a cab pulls over to the side of the road.

I reach for the back door of the car, my heart still thudding.

"If you try to leave, I will sue you for every dollar you own. I will take your computer. Your music. Every scrap of clothing in your wardrobe and on your body."

Even as the car pulls away from him, I can't kick the sickening possibility he's right.

For the next month…

The man who ruined me owns me.

CHAPTER 3

Rae

When the cab pulls up to the sandstone villa perched halfway up a winding road and sheltered by a lush hedge of greenery, I can't help but appreciate its beauty.

Judging from the size, this villa is more like a boutique hotel than a resort. When I enter, backpack in tow, a woman looks up from where she's vacuuming. I don't spot a concierge or front desk, so I approach the woman.

"I'm supposed to be staying here tonight." I reach for my passport, but she stops me.

Her face brightens as she clasps my hand between both of hers. "*Sí, señorita*. I am Natalia." Her voice is warm and welcoming. "I will show you your room."

She leads me up a staircase and down a hall with doors on either side, half a dozen in total.

"This will meet your needs?" she asks as she opens a door.

I step into the room of pale-yellow walls, and beyond them are double doors opening to a balcony that overlooks the ocean. "It's beautiful. Thank you."

She nods before ducking out, closing the door.

The sight and the fresh scent of the water unlock my chest, a twisted knot wound tighter since my run-in with the devil himself.

I'm in another country without most of my possessions, and my only potential source of income is the man I hate.

But I know one thing—there's no way I'm playing for him. I'll walk into the sea first and never come back.

I pull out my phone, digging around to find the contract. His name's not on it anywhere, but that's not unusual for a large organization.

The amount I stand to lose by not playing has my stomach sinking.

I send the paperwork off to my lawyer anyway, asking how I can get out of it.

This gig was supposed to be my salvation. Instead, I'm being forced to play for the man I hate.

I'm used to traveling, but suddenly, I feel adrift.

I do a quick calculation of the time difference—six hours behind—before I hit a number on my phone.

"Hey!" Annie's panting voice comes through the speaker. "You caught me in the midst of my morning stomach pyrotechnics."

"Hardly seems fair Tyler's on tour and you've been hugging a toilet for the last two weeks."

My roommate from arts school and her rock-star husband are going to be parents in less than five months.

"Don't worry. He'll be making it up to me."

Her breezy tone has me shaking my head. I have no doubt she'll tell him what she wants. Or that he'll move mountains to give it to her. Their relationship is almost enough to make me believe in love.

"I was going to ask if you had a chance to lay down vocals for that track I was working on."

"I need one more listen before I send it over," she promises. "Now please distract me so I don't think about how every smell in our house makes me want to upchuck."

Her earnest plea makes my mouth twitch.

"I just got into Ibiza." I flop down on the double bed, which gives gently under my weight. The fabric smells fresh—not from-a-can fresh either. "But the residency gig isn't what I signed on for."

Telling her the full extent of what's going down might upset her or, worse, make her try to intervene.

I don't need her solving my problems. Both because I can solve them myself and because she knows what went down between Harrison and me.

We met at her wedding.

And Harrison King is a friend of her husband's.

As unlikely as it seems that the man who glowered down at me today has any friends, evidently Tyler Adams, a guy I went to school with and respect, met him on tour and they formed a genuine bond.

Annie makes a noise of sympathy. "If it's anything like doing a show on Broadway, it's exhausting and scary but rewarding too."

Doubtful.

"Where's Mr. Tall, Dark, and Broody?" I change the subject.

"Tyler's in Amsterdam this week. Since the honeymoon, I've been going into travel withdrawal. I heard Ibiza is beautiful."

My feet carry me out to the balcony. My finger trails along the sandstone half wall as I inhale the fresh air.

"Only if you're into fresh air, crystal-blue waters, beautiful people, and partying."

She laughs. "Hard to imagine anything could ruin that. You deserve it. I don't think you've stayed in one place for a month since college."

The problem with staying in one place is you get attached to it. You expect things of the people around you.

I learned early how dangerous and destructive that can be.

"Listen," I start, "I should let you go. But it's good to hear your childish enthusiasm. You want a souvenir?"

"Bring me back a good story and we'll call it even."

I click off and stare at the water.

Harrison's right about one thing—I can't leave without a plan. Right now, if he wants to go after me legally, I have no doubt he'd win.

Annie wants a story.

I might be young, but I'm not powerless.

I won't run from this villain.

Not without getting a few swings in first.

Harrison King might be the man with the money.

But I'm the girl with the mic.

A light knock at the door has me turning back toward the room as Natalia comes in, a perplexed look on her face. "Where are your bags?"

"The airline lost them."

Her eyes widen. "*Dios mío.* I can take you shopping, if you like, or send you to the best boutiques."

I cross to the middle of the room and look down at my clothes. I need something to wear tonight if I'm not leaving today. "Maybe not the best boutiques," I warn because that sounds expensive. "If I called them and told them what I wanted, could they send a few items over?"

"Of course."

"Including a wig," I say, setting my phone on the dresser and tugging out the half-assed bun I made on the side of the road an hour ago. "Blond," I decide.

If it's a strange request, she doesn't balk. "You should go to the beach. We also have a pool and a jacuzzi. Enjoy yourself before you have to work. You're too young to look so serious."

Inspired, I reach for my computer.

Natalia is right. Just because I'm here doesn't mean I can't enjoy myself a little.

Defiance flows through my veins as I send off a quick text to Annie with some lyrics for a new verse.

My contract says I'll play for Harrison King.

It doesn't say I have to do it nicely.

CHAPTER 4
Harrison

"We're here, *señor*." My driver's eyes meet mine in the rearview mirror as he pulls up in front of the club.

I straighten my suit. "Thank you, Toro."

"Are you sure you're ready?"

I frown. "It's a Thursday night like any Thursday night."

Except it doesn't feel like it. My body is humming, braced for a fight or coming off of one.

I shift out before Toro can open my door. He follows me around anyway, stubbornly taking the car door in his aging hands as I fasten my jacket.

"It's a new club. The renovations are only just complete. And new talent," he goes on as I start for the entrance.

I pull up, turning to cock my head at him. He only nods before retreating to the driver's side.

New talent indeed.

I head to the back door. Security stands at attention when they see me.

A man with a purpose is dangerous to the world.

A man without a purpose is dangerous to himself.

When I enter a room, it's to tell people what I want and make it immediately clear I'm going to get it. The faster they see that, the more painless it is.

My first acquisition was filthy and spare, cobbled together like the money I used to finance it. Now, I stride down a private hallway used for deliveries and talent, absorbing the fresh paint and shining floors with a grim satisfaction.

When I bought Debajo, everything was in disrepair, as if its name meant not only "beneath" but "forgotten."

It takes a particular eye to see what others miss. But for a man who looks beneath the surface, one who's as relentless as he is patient...

There is treasure to be found.

Now, the club is a cool kiss. An elegant reminder of how far I've come.

I wish my parents could see it.

The twinge in my gut sneaks up on me, lingering like the burn of bad whisky.

A budding actress who's rising to stardom makes her way toward me, coming from the direction of the club.

"Hello, gorgeous," she purrs, the telltale enthusiasm of alcohol lingering in her voice as she stops in my path with an inviting smile. "Haven't seen you stateside for way too long."

"You came to find me and enjoy my hospitality," I reply evenly. "So, my plan worked."

She slips her hand inside my shirt, and I smoothly withdraw it, my grip firm enough there's disappointment in her eyes.

A hundred men in this place would take her home tonight.

I'm not one of them.

I used to enjoy beautiful women, particularly ones who made a lifestyle of *being* enjoyed.

No more.

Not since I let myself believe one could stand at my side and be what I needed. Trusting a woman with my life, my home, my future, cost me far more than the years I invested in that relationship.

It won't happen again.

I straighten my shirt before I continue down the hall, making eye contact with the security guard at the end and nodding to him to keep an eye on her and make sure she doesn't find trouble.

I feel the pulsing music through the leather of my dress shoes before I hear it. I approach the door that leads to the club, then turn and take the stairs up to the second level. At the top, security opens the door. Pulsing music flows into me, through me.

The metal grate flooring creaks beneath my feet on my way to my private booth next to two other VIP booths upstairs. Below, revelers drink and dance to the opening act.

I pause, one storey up with a perfect view of the performers and the crowd.

I've been out all day but have confirmed with Natalia and Toro that my newest contractor intends to play tonight.

I knew she would see reason. She might be fiery, but there was no way she'd abandon this. I'd sue her fast enough she'd land on that curvy bottom.

The first time we met, at the island wedding of my friend Tyler, she was fury itself. Barely waiting until after the cake had been cut and the couple rode off into shining bliss to rain righteous hellfire on me.

I told her the same thing I'd tell anyone criticizing my business: Thank you very fucking little for your input.

Evidently, she wasn't pleased with my reaction.

A single social media post condemning my business caused the door income of my best club to drop by half overnight and spurred a bloody mountain of paperwork and hostile media inquiries my team had to deal with. Most of them made their way up to me and ruined a string of otherwise good days.

A small consolation was that she exploded in an equally destructive way.

My PR staff told me that while a few fans had applauded the move, many were ambivalent. More importantly, no club owner from London to Miami would touch her for fear she'd find fault with their operations.

Part of me envies her idealism. We were all naïve once, even if the last time I knew so little of the world I was still in knee socks.

"Whisky, Mr. King?" the upstairs VIP bartender asks, and I nod.

"In my booth."

"Sí, señor. You have a visitor."

Before I can demand who the fuck is in my private space, the bartender's gone. I round the corner of my booth and stiffen.

"Let me guess—half your renovation budget was for the club and half for whisky." The last person I'd expect is sitting in the booth in khakis and a polo shirt, nursing a drink.

"Ash. I didn't realize you were coming."

My brother Sebastian is a decade younger, and has a propensity to avoid me unless he wants to lay blame at my feet.

"Premier League has been over for a week." He flashes a grin. "Thought I'd raid the bar at your newest club."

"I've bought two more since."

"Yet you're still here. If I didn't know better, I'd say you were hiding."

Ash doesn't miss a thing. He's the smarter of the two of us, yet he plays professional football and I'm the one running a corporation.

"I'm not hiding. I'm relaxing."

His smirking gaze runs from my dress shoes up the suit to my tight face.

"You look positively rejuvenated," he quips. "When will you stop this relentless quest for acquisitions? When you own every entertainment venue in the world?"

I accept the thirty-year-old Glen Scotia whisky the bartender brings on a monogrammed napkin. "We'll find out."

"Our parents wouldn't want you to do this," he says.

My grip on the glass tightens. "You don't know what they'd want. You were a boy when they died."

My brother shifts out of his seat. He has the same hair and eyes as me, but he's a few inches shorter. He's made the most of what he's been given and is now a forward for the second-best professional football club in England since getting drafted out of uni last year.

"I thought you'd started to mellow when you were with *her*." My brother leans over the railing next to me. "You stepped back from the business. Started genuinely enjoying life a little. It was good to see, Harry."

I sip, and the smooth alcohol lingers on my taste buds. "Love is an illusion. I was a fool to think it was more."

The tabloids paint me as a richer-than-Midas entertainment mogul with no greater pleasure than adding to the piles of money I've made.

It's easier for me that they do.

Their needling over superficial flaws and supposed weaknesses doesn't bother me.

It keeps them from digging at the real ones.

The crowd below us is dancing, losing themselves in the music pounding through the speakers, reverberating off every wall.

"Leni texted this afternoon to say I should come down to see a show," Ash says over the music. "She also said a woman tore you a new one." His grin flashes white for a second before the club lights go dark.

The hairs on my neck lift in anticipation.

The DJs change over. It happens every night between the opening act and the headliner, but tonight, I feel it.

It's a tug in my gut, a thrumming in my veins.

It's why I came, though I'd never admit it.

The way she spoke to me earlier… No one challenges me like that.

She can't honestly think she'll get out of this deal. The fact that she's here means she's admitted the truth.

She'll bend to me, like everyone else does.

When the black light comes on, the crowd erupts.

She's on stage, her hair, trousers, and cropped body-hugging top glowing white before the lights change to a more normal range.

Out of costume, off stage, she's moody, seething. A girl who hissed at me like a cornered animal.

On it, she's vibrant.

Her clothes cling to her body in a way that draws attention to her curves but also lets her move uninhibited. A long, blond wig is a stark contrast to her warm skin and dark lashes, thick and lowered as she studies the computer in front of her with the intensity of a rocket scientist navigating a launch.

"Little Queen," Ash observes. "The name suits her."

I've always preferred women as careless as they are beautiful. But there's something about her that makes it impossible to look away.

"She owes me," I say at last, my voice gravel. "And even queens must pay their debts."

This arrangement is supposed to be strictly business, but the idea of seeing her admit she can't fight me is oddly appealing.

Fuck. I need to get laid if a naïve young American hurling insults at my decency and my empire makes my cock hard.

But I'm still watching her, trapped in the limbo she creates with her energy, her music, leaning in like a shameless voyeur.

She's the rebel girl every horny teenage boy at boarding school badmouthed, then secretly fucked his hand to at night while wishing it was her pussy instead.

I expect my brother to rip into me for being soulless. When I finally force my attention to him, he's watching her, as entranced as every one of the drunk and high patrons below.

"She's pretty."

Alarm coils in my gut. Before I can snap a response, or even decipher the layers of my reaction, the track changes.

Boys want a fight
Want to prove they're right
Let them scratch and hiss
Circle when they piss—

The words seep into my skin.

My gaze narrows on the DJ, and as if she senses it, she looks up toward our booth.

And in a move as graceful as it is deliberate, she flips both middle fingers.

Ash barks out a laugh, the genuine kind I haven't heard in far too long. "Fuck, Harry. I think I'm in love."

CHAPTER 5

Rae

"Hello, American," a male voice whisper-shouts as I yank off my headphones at the end of my set.

The man standing within earshot is my age and the kind of preppy handsome that sells Ralph Lauren campaigns.

I look at the security guard, who is facing the other way. *Not again.*

"Hey!" I shout at the guard, who finally turns back, spotting the man next to me.

"He's a VIP," the guard mouths.

Perfect. I should've known Debajo would be one of those places where VIPs get whatever they want.

"Don't worry. We're going to be friends." The man who approached me offers a blinding grin that's familiar and not. "That was quite the set. Have a drink with me."

"I'm not sticking around."

"Please?"

I could use a drink. Plus, I won't be able to sleep for hours.

With luck, I'll get to bed by six o'clock in the morning, stare at the ceiling for a few hours while waiting for a response from my lawyer, then drag myself out of bed midafternoon to do a little sightseeing and get my bag before catching a flight out of here.

"You're buying," I inform him.

Before heading to the bar, I stop in the bathroom, pop two ibuprofen, and wipe the sweat from my face and neck.

My new friend meets me outside. "Not going to lose this wig?"

I hold a strand up. "This is my natural hair color."

He grins. "I'm Ash. Now is when you tell me your real name."

"I don't think so." I settle in next to him as we head through the private backstage halls. Security lets us pass without comment.

"Damn it. It was going to seem natural when I called you Raegan, but I guess I can't say you told me."

I stop abruptly. "How did you—"

"Come on, blondie." He grabs my wrist and tugs me after him.

My real name might be on every contract, but I keep my personal life separate where I can. It's strange hearing not only my nickname, which all my friends use, but my full name.

"Wish I could hide out for privacy," he says, reading my mind. "I play pro football."

I scan his lean form. "Quarterback?"

He scoffs. "Proper football."

He holds the door for me, and I walk through into another world. There's a private bar, beautiful people lounging at tables, a poker game in one corner. The veneer of casual exclusivity is impossible to miss. Diamonds against crushed velvet. Wool suiting on faded leather stools.

My gaze lands on the table of men playing cards. One in particular has me stiffening.

Harrison King is wearing a suit tonight. He's impeccable. Not runway-model beautiful, but mafia-don ruthless. Sharp angles and unyielding planes. His strong face is sculpted into an intense study of the cards in front of him, the ones on the table.

Ash follows my gaze and snorts. "Don't let him ruin your fun. Just because he's a prick and he owns the place…"

I arch a brow. "I'm glad I'm not the only one who thinks so."

We head for the bar, and he orders me a cocktail.

"Harrison King stole my belongings," Ash goes on after. "Held my head underwater until I conceded. Told on me." There's a pause as I process each of these transgressions. Finally, Ash raises his glass, grinning. "He's my older brother."

"So, he sent you to make nice." I shouldn't be talking to anyone who shares an ounce of DNA with the man I loathe.

"Hardly. He'll be upset I'm talking to you."

I take a sip. The vodka soda is clean on my tongue, in my throat, as music from the afterparty outside drifts in.

"Then by all means, continue."

Ash barks out a laugh, blue eyes warmer than his brother's. "If you hate him, why are you playing his club?"

"A mistake. One I'm going to fix in the morning so I can get out of here."

"That's unfortunate. You should stay."

"Help the man I hate make money?" I scoff.

"I'm going to tell you a secret. You're making money too, Raegan."

"Rae," I correct, not because we're friends but because hearing my full name weirds me out. "Why do you care?"

He turns the glass in his hands. "Women have followed him willingly all his life. I think you'd show him there's another way."

"He wouldn't appreciate another way. The man treats women like disposable napkins."

"He proposed to the last woman he dated. They were engaged, until she ended it."

I cut Ash a surprised look. The idea of Harrison King having a softer side, of wanting to spend his life with another person, is hard to picture.

"I can't imagine what he did to deserve to get dumped." I don't hide the sarcasm, but I'm still processing the "engaged" part.

"He trusted her too much." My new companion's voice softens. "We date the people we think we deserve. Though he'd never admit it, my brother doesn't think he's worthy of better."

My attention drags across the room to the man in question, hating that those words make me question Harrison King's spot in hell.

I realize my mistake too late, because he's spotted me.

Harrison King rises from the table with the grace of a shadow. Now, he's headed this way.

I can't help comparing the two men. Their coloring is similar, a faint tan from the sun under dirty-blond hair. The same magnetic blue eyes. But where Ash's friendly, Harrison is cold. Cut from marble.

"Brother," Ash greets him as he arrives. "You're the only person in a suit at this hour." He nods to the rest of the room, where every other man has long since stripped his jacket off.

"I wear one because it's my club," Harrison replies.

I take a drink. "There are other options to hide the stick up your ass besides Hugo Boss."

"It's Brioni."

Ash cackles in delight. "I was telling our little queen how exceptional she was tonight."

"When my club is full, I'll praise her," Harrison states.

Ash turns back to greet a friend, leaving me and Harrison at the bar.

"Unfortunately, this was a one-night-only performance." I shift off the stool. "But I'm glad you enjoyed it."

"Not half as much as you did." He blocks my path. "I saw the way you lose yourself up there. In *my club*, which you seem intent on despising."

My body tingles, from his closeness and the intimacy of his words.

"It's a persona. Not me."

"You can't hide how it makes you feel. You've had orgasms less satisfying than what you experienced tonight."

Anyone in the crowd could tell I was having a good time. But the way this man watched me, the way he's watching me now, feels as if he sees under my clothes.

Under my skin.

The thrumming in my stomach streaks lower, between my thighs.

Laughter goes up from across the room, but I can't look away from Harrison King.

"You know nothing about my orgasms, and you never will."

I'm hot, and I pull the hair over one shoulder to leave the other bare. He follows the movement, attention lingering on my exposed skin and heating it like a filthy kiss.

"You told Leni this afternoon that you hated me no matter how pretty I was or how big my cock is, which means you've considered both."

My breath catches.

"That's why you're angry," he continues. "You hate me, but the thought of me gets you off. I might be a villain, but in your dreams I still slink into your room at night and make you come."

His voice strokes down my spine like a filthy whisper. That decadent accent he deploys like a weapon is obscene.

"The only thing I've thought about," I say, nodding to his belt, "is how you must be compensating for something to be this much of an asshole."

When my attention drags back up to his face, the expression scorches me alive.

A cheer goes up from behind us, and we turn to see Leni come in the door, lifting her hands. "You were great," she informs me with a grin, offering a high five. "See you back here Monday?" She looks between Harrison and me. "Unless the boss eats you first."

The man at my side growls, and Leni laughs.

I'm mystified by the dynamic, still remembering the way he shut her up without a word earlier.

When I reach for my phone, Harrison frowns.

"What are you doing?"

"Calling Toro for a ride."

"He's an old man who needs his sleep." He jerks his head at one of the bartenders, who reaches for a house phone on the wall. "A car will be here in five minutes."

He gestures toward the hallway, then follows me out.

The man is a ruthless billionaire. Incapable of compromise. Incapable of love.

Except he might be a villain to me, but he's not to Leni. To

Toro. To his brother.

I have a handful of friends now, but a network of people I go back with? People I trust and who trust me?

That sounds like make believe.

Security holds the outside door for us, the guard already nodding to me with familiarity. "Mr. King. Miss… Queen."

A half laugh is out of my lips before I step out into the cool evening. Harrison cocks his head.

"Cute couple," I drawl.

I catch his eye over my shoulder, and he huffs out a breath when he realizes I'm trying to piss him off.

"You're the one making this hard."

I rub my hands over my skin in response to the sudden chill—of the night air or his words. "Hard's the only way I know."

He strips off his jacket, and my gaze is drawn to the muscles of his shoulders and chest through the shirt beneath.

I'm distracted enough it takes me a moment to realize his intention as he closes the distance between us.

"No. Don't—"

I lift both hands defensively, but he drapes the expensive fabric around my shoulders and pulls the lapels closed over my chest before I can stop him.

"You'd probably like to freeze to death your first night." His closeness invades my senses, makes it hard to think. "If only to leave me in a jam."

"I told you, I'm leaving in the morning."

I start to shrug out of the coat, but he stops me.

"Keep it."

What kind of a man is fastidious enough to wear designer suits but doesn't care about giving one away to spare me a few moments' chill? Before I find a good answer, the cab pulls up.

As I drive away from Harrison King for the second time today, I finger the edge of the jacket.

I'm alone again.

The rush of relief I expected doesn't come.

CHAPTER 6

Rae

"Have you found my bag?" I press a hand to my face to stifle the yawn. It's noon, and I managed two hours of fitful sleep in the luxurious bed at the villa.

"Unfortunately not." The woman at the airline repeats the words I heard yesterday about reimbursement as I flop onto the bed and drop the phone next to me.

I stare longingly at the bedside table, where my bottle of pills would typically be. Instead of my belongings, the only way I've personalized this room is by throwing Harrison's suit jacket over the lampshade until I can figure out what to do with it.

After, I make a call to my attorney, who says there's no clear loophole to get me out of this contract and avoid the damages written in—which I never thought I'd be in a position to consider.

I'm stranded in Ibiza without options, my pills... even a damned razor.

The jet lag is messing with my head.

My workout clothes were in my checked bag, so I pull on my sneakers and the skinny jeans from yesterday.

One glance in the mirror over the dresser shows my hair is a mess of craziness. I yank it all up into a ponytail before I peer out into the hall. No sign of anyone.

When I reach the top of the stairs, rapid shouting in Spanish comes from below, ending with, "Get back here!"

Then I'm attacked.

A big, black dog with brown eyes barrels toward me, leaping. His paws hit my thighs, his lolling tongue licking at my arms.

I catch him awkwardly.

"My apologies, señorita. He loves people," Natalia calls up the stairs from the doorway of the kitchen.

The creature lets me set his paws back on the ground but continues to eye me as if I'm the only thing he's wanted his whole life.

"His master hasn't had time to take him out for his walk today. I was late finishing my errands yesterday, and…"

Probably because she went to get me clothes.

"Are you going for a walk? Would you take him? He's no trouble."

Guilt has me saying, "Ah, sure."

We never had pets growing up. My parents are both in tech— my dad left Tehran for computer engineering at UCLA. They've always kept long hours, and though their careers meant my brothers and I never suffered materially, a dog would've been one too many interruptions for their goals.

I take the stairs down as Natalia gets the dog's leash and fastens it on, meeting me at the front door with a grateful smile.

"You would like breakfast when you return?" Natalia gestures toward the kitchen. "And tea?"

I'm not used to being served by anyone, but my stomach

growls—probably because I haven't eaten in almost twenty-four hours. "Coffee would be great."

I take the dog out and let the sea breeze go to work on my brain.

Telemanco, where the villa is, isn't as busy as Ibiza Town. It's relaxed and stunning, and I could totally take a vacation here if I had the money.

As I walk, I use my phone to read articles about Harrison King and Echo Entertainment. Search engines keep insisting I want to know about his travels with his ex-fiancée, model Eva Nilsson. There are photos of them in cafés, on the red carpet, at charity galas, and even on the beach.

She's stunning, and I can't help noticing the way she beams at him.

Maybe Ash is full of shit. I don't see a woman who would've left. She looks utterly devoted.

Not that there's *nothing* to respect about Harrison King. He relentlessly built an entertainment empire, so he's clearly focused. But he's soulless.

It was easy to forget when those bottomless blue eyes were boring into me last night in the VIP room. For a moment, I couldn't help wondering how deep you'd have to fall to find something more in him, and whether it might be worth it.

A grinning old man descends on us, speaking to the dog. "His name?" he asks me after a moment.

I tuck the phone away, stalling. "Licorice."

The man looks surprised, but the dog barks agreeably. After a few more pets, we continue on our way.

"That was embarrassing," I inform the dog.

He cocks his head, lifting both ears.

After we're interrupted another few times, I realize walking the dog is not a way to get quiet time to myself.

So, I make a game of it and give him a new name every time.

"Costas."

"Siegfried."

"Roy."

I wind "Bowie's" leash tighter to rein him in as I scroll through my banking information on my phone.

I don't check it often because the only thing I need money for is a roof over my head and plane tickets from show to show, both of which are usually covered by the venue.

Still, the balance is lower than I'd like.

I scan through the recent transactions.

One automatic withdrawal from last month—rapidly approaching for this month—makes me curse.

I hit a contact on my phone, chewing my lip as I wait for the line to pick up.

"Hello, cousin," I say when it does.

"Hey." Rustling sounds come over the line as if Callie's getting out of bed.

Since we were kids, we had a running joke of greeting each other formally. Living a few hours apart, we'd mostly see one another at family events and holidays. We weren't allowed to have cellphones until high school, and we weren't supposed to use our computers to message.

Of course, we did anyway, but we kept up appearances to fool our parents.

Since high school, I haven't been close with my brothers or

parents. Callie's the nearest thing I have to family, and though we don't hang out on the regular, she's the one person who's stood by me since I was a kid when I needed it.

I picture her in the West LA apartment she shares with a roommate as I press the phone to my ear to pick up more sounds around her, clues as to her well-being. "Are you working this week?"

"Um, I'm not sure." More noises, as if she's moving around.

My cousin is normally upbeat and inquisitive. Her response makes me pull up, stepping away from the route so we don't get trampled by runners or tourists. "Listen. I'm calling because I might not have the money this month."

I hold my breath as I wait for her disappointment, or protest.

"It's fine," she says, her voice flat.

"You don't need it?"

"We need way more. Something we were counting on fell through. I'm not sure we'll make it this time."

Alarm has my hand tightening on the phone. "How much are you short?"

She sighs. "Twenty thousand."

Shit.

There's no way I have that kind of free cash, even *with* this contract.

"Can you get a loan?"

"I tried. We've just been served an eviction notice."

The sunshine is every bit as bright, but as the dog tugs me down the path, my feet are heavy as bricks.

"Your landlord can't kick you out, especially given the circumstances."

"He doesn't care. I'm going to be spending the next week

packing."

I've been trying to figure out how to leave Ibiza in one piece, but my chest aches when I think of Callie, the one person who's always had my back.

When I help her, it's because I want to and I can. Not because she asks.

"Don't pack yet. Let me get back to you."

When I return to the villa, I'm still trying to think of how to help Callie.

I step inside, the leash looped around my wrist. I stop to yank off a shoe.

Before I can, the dog bolts.

I trip each step as he drags me across the floor, up the stairs.

"Stop. Licorice! Costas! Siegfried! Roy! Bowie!"

He hesitates at the last word, and I manage to suck in a breath before he lunges again, nearly knocking me flat on my face.

He galumphs down the hall with me stumbling behind. The door at the end is cracked, and he sticks his nose in before shoving it wide and barreling into the room.

I barely notice the wood furniture and sunny orange walls of an office.

Especially when my gaze lands on the man on the phone, seated on the edge of the desk.

"Unacceptable. We had this solved last week." Harrison King is impeccable in dress slacks and a blue shirt that matches his eyes. Eyes that widen when the dog launches himself onto the man.

"That was the whole point of the deal," he bites out into the phone. "We invested in the renovations expecting a return. This is a multibillion-dollar business, not fucking child's play."

I stop in the middle of the room, the leash still taut.

"That's your job," he goes on. "I suggest you do it." Harrison stabs a finger at his phone, ending the call.

"Down, Bowie," I say belatedly. I don't know what Harrison King is doing here, but seeing the dog put his paws all over the expensive clothes is oddly satisfying.

Harrison's gaze drags up my body from my running shoes, a slow study. Judging from his drawn brows, it seems to leave him with no more answers than when he started.

"Bowie?" He shifts off the desk and crosses to me.

"I don't know his name. But he seems pretty rock and roll."

Harrison loosens the leash from around my wrist. The Rolex on his wrist glints in the light from the open windows.

"It's Barney," he says as he releases me. "And he's my dog."

Surprise slams into me.

"You and your dog are staying at my villa." I look around the office again, needing somewhere to focus that's not his unrelenting attention.

"No. You and your attitude are staying at *my* villa."

Horror washes over me.

I slept at this man's house last night? Walked his damned dog?

What kind of a controlling freak invites a contractor who hates him to live with him?

And skips the invitation, I might add.

"Why?" I blurt.

His gaze is chastising. "I decided it would be easier to keep an eye on you and ensure you complied with your contractual responsibilities. An impulsive decision I'm already regretting," he adds, frowning as he searches my face.

I could scream, but my attention drags back to his watch. I could probably pawn the thing and solve all of my cousin's financial problems.

Harrison King could snap his fingers and pay off the debt of a small country.

My mind spins as I concoct a plan that keeps me one step ahead. "About the contract—"

"I've told you, if you break the contract, I'll sue you."

"I want to renegotiate."

His mouth snaps shut.

"You've invested a lot in Debajo's renovations. Give me twenty-five percent of the door for the next month and I'll fill it."

He folds his arms across his chest, the blue fabric pulling across firm muscles. The way his eyes narrow as he clicks smoothly into business mode is as compelling as it is intimidating. "Because you can do things my PR firm can't?"

I match his posture. "Obviously."

I'm bluffing. Publicity isn't my strong suit, unless you count publicly going down in flames. But he doesn't need to know that.

"And if you don't?"

"I don't get paid. But when you make money, I make money."

Something nudges at my thigh, and I look down to see Barney inserting himself between us, tail wagging.

"Ten percent," Harrison replies as I bend down to scratch the dog's head.

"Twenty. And I'm moving to alternative accommodations."

"Fifteen, you stay, plus I get three requests of my choosing."

The evenness of his voice has my jaw dropping. This man acts as if he always gets his way.

"What kind of requests?"

"Any requests," he says impatiently. "If I want you to clean the pool using your thong as a filter, you will."

My hands fist at my sides. "I'm not a genie in a fucking bottle. Clean your own pool."

Harrison turns away. "Then there's no deal."

The dismissal is swift and brutal.

I don't understand his endgame. One more mystery about the already-confusing man before me.

But I know that what he wants is to put me in a corner.

"These requests don't involve other people," I say at last, and his head cocks.

"Only you."

The way he says those two words makes me shiver.

"Eighteen, plus your stupid requests," I counter.

His blue gaze is intense enough I feel my ribs crack.

We shake, and electricity runs up my arm at his touch.

He pulls away first. "I'll have my solicitor send a new copy of the contract. I expect your signature by the end of the day. Along with my jacket."

My head snaps up to meet his mocking expression. "You knew you'd get it back. That's why you gave it to me."

"It's Brioni." He says it as if it's an answer.

"You're unbelievable. Controlling, demanding, manipulative… No wonder your fiancée left you."

His fist clenches around the leash, and when he speaks, his

voice is dangerously low. "Be careful what you say when you still want things from me."

A knock on the door is followed by the housekeeper's immediate entrance.

"Ah, *perdón!*" she gushes when she sees us. "I see you and Señor King are getting more acquainted." She's either oblivious to the tension or ignores it. "I thought señorita would like to know her suitcase is in her room."

My heart leaps. "The airline found it?"

"No," Harrison intervenes. "The contents were spilled when we retrieved them, but I trust everything is there."

He found my suitcase when the airline couldn't. Through what, some kind of billionaire black magic?

Relief surges through me, though it's short-lived when I remind myself who's responsible for it.

His voice follows me to the door. "You may buy replacements for anything missing from your luggage and charge them to my account, with one exception. I do not tolerate my employees on drugs of any kind."

Son of a…

"And don't forget my jacket."

I sprint down the hall and unzip my suitcase, tossing clothes and wigs and toiletries out onto the floor.

The pill bottle is zipped into an inside pocket.

And it's empty.

CHAPTER 7
Harrison

My father used to say, "You can't control a man's thoughts, but you can command his actions."

That's what I'm intent on doing today in the office—forcing men's hands.

One man's hand in particular.

On paper, Christian Geroux owns Ibiza's greatest club.

In my mind, it's already mine.

I've wanted it since I was twenty-one.

Finally, I got word he's open to selling. I won't waste this chance.

But making headway amassing the greatest collection of entertainment venues in the world requires the right frame of mind.

I finish my outdoor workout before seven, ready to take on the day and already thinking about my meetings and strategies for my next acquisition.

I'm not thinking about the young woman I installed in my villa.

At the time, it seemed like a way to supervise her. I regretted the decision the moment she tripped into my office uninvited yesterday, towed by my dog like a water skier behind a furry yacht.

After acting as if she'd have cut off a limb if it would have gotten her out of the contract she'd signed, she flipped my deal and proposed a new one.

Negotiation 101. When you have all the leverage, there's no need to make further concessions.

But she caught me off guard, and I was curious what had changed for her since the night before when I'd set her in a cab with my favorite jacket around her shoulders.

The one I found swimming in my pool the next afternoon, the chlorine doing God knows what to the wool and the striped lining.

I ground my teeth together as I retrieved it with a cleaning implement, looking up to be sure she wasn't watching from her balcony.

Clean your own pool, she'd said.

She's nothing like the women I spend time with. She says she doesn't care for money or wealth.

Except she asked for a raise.

Which means, on one level, she's exactly like the women I spend time with.

Now, when I return to the villa after my workout, there's a sweater hanging on the back of a chair at the dining table.

My first thought is of payback. Dropping this into the pool and picturing her finding it there.

What the fuck is she doing to me?

I'm thirty-five years old, and I'm giddy with the prospect of ruining something of hers just to see her reaction.

The fabric is surprisingly soft as I lift it. A thin woven cover-up that's more feminine than I expect.

"What are you doing?" Natalia's voice makes my spine stiffen like a schoolboy caught masturbating.

I glance back to see her watching from the kitchen. I lower the garment, trying to forget the scent, warm and floral with something like vanilla beneath.

"Removing this from my dining room."

I start up the stairs to the open hallway that runs along one side of the villa, her sweater dangling from my fingertips like a limp rag.

Now, Rae's door is closed—it's midafternoon, and she's still asleep despite not having a show last night—but sounds inside have me frowning. Movement, shuffling.

Is someone else in there?

The possibility arouses dark thoughts.

First, she destroys my jacket. Then brings someone home to my house…

I crack the door, and my dog comes barreling out.

Light beyond the door beckons, and I peer inside.

She's alone in bed.

On her side facing the door, her dark hair is a wild mane around her head.

Her baggy T-shirt is twisted, pulling tight across her breasts, as if she was fighting sleep itself. Her lips are parted, her lashes a thick fringe that twitches against her cheeks as she dreams.

A rope tugs tight low in my gut.

Is there any time of day, alone or surrounded by people, when she finds peace?

I fold the sweatshirt and lay it on the dresser, taking in the belongings scattered around the room. My fingers itch to straighten the clothes and gadgets I went through myself when the bag arrived thanks to a call placed by one of my staff to the airline.

Denim. Off-label trainers. Cotton lingerie.

The wigs are curious. She owns as many of those as clothes, yet most women I know spend hours and thousands of dollars to try to replicate what her hair seems to do naturally.

There's no sign of the unlabelled pill bottle I found in her bag.

It had to have been recreational. No seasoned traveler would pack a necessary medication in her checked bag and risk losing it with a missing suitcase.

Drug use in Ibiza is practically a prerequisite, and I can't keep it out of my clubs. But I can keep it out of my employees, which was why I dumped the pills without a second thought.

Rae stirs, mumbling under her breath.

"What was that?" I murmur.

She repeats the single word, still sound asleep.

Adrenaline and dark triumph chase through my veins.

If she was mine, I'd shift over her on the bed, brush the hair from her face, and wake her slowly. The brush of a knuckle along the softness of her cheek. The press of my body against the curves of hers, enough to have her responding in kind even in sleep.

But she's not mine.

I won't claim another woman as mine again. I might take them to bed—not that even that idea has held much appeal recently—but I won't offer them my life, my heart.

Because those things aren't what they truly want and because they're nothing I can offer again.

She's here to fill my club and repay her debt.

I slip out of her room before she wakes.

The morning passes in a frustrating glut. The new initiatives at my clubs are taking time and money, and I'm being reminded what a headache acquisitions are as the man standing between me and my latest prize refuses to give a straight answer to my offer.

The club I'm seeking to add to Echo Entertainment isn't only a line item on a balance sheet.

It's personal.

Since my split with Eva, the tabloids accuse me of hiding out in my Ibiza villa.

I let them.

Perhaps there's been some self pity, but I'm laying the groundwork for the biggest deal of my life. I'm in control of a multibillion-dollar company, not a fool nursing a broken heart.

From this day on, every ounce of my attention, my money, and my influence will be devoted to winning La Mer.

When I jog down the stairs for lunch, the sight at the bottom has me swallowing an irritated groan.

The sweatshirt is back on the kitchen table as if I never took it upstairs.

I watch Rae from behind as she makes coffee, moving easily around my kitchen in faded jeans and an orange T-shirt that has slipped off one shoulder. Her hair is caught in a thick ponytail that lays over the opposite shoulder and has me remembering how wild it looked earlier as she talks on the phone and rubs her neck.

"When can I speak with him?" She takes a sip from her mug,

then makes a sound of displeasure. "I'm sure he's up to his ass in requests, but have him call me."

She hangs up, tucking the phone in the back pocket of her tight jeans.

"Boyfriend dodging you?" My slow drawl has the intended effect of scaring the ever-loving fuck out of her as she whirls to face me.

Most women find me appealing, but she seems to decide I'm barely worth sharing the kitchen with when she points at her mug. "Instant coffee should be banned. I pegged you as a sadist, not a masochist."

She turns her back on me before I can respond, rubbing her temples before sliding one hand down to her neck.

Withdrawal symptoms. My sympathy fades.

"I meant what I said about staying clean while you're in my employ." The sharpness in my tone makes Rae stiffen.

"Well, now that you've tossed my stash, I guess I'll have to. What exactly did that look like to you? E? Cocaine? GHB?"

"The newest craze is 2CB—"

"Is that what was in my bag?"

My gaze narrows. "I don't know."

"It's a headache. Not withdrawal." She nods toward her notebook computer on the kitchen table before dumping the contents of her mug into the sink. "Been bent over that for twelve-plus-hour days since I was a teenager."

"So, what, two years, then?"

The comment earns me side-eye as she puts a kettle on and fixes something else on the counter obscured behind her body. "I'm twenty-four. I've been doing this ten years."

I cross to her and press a thumb into the muscle where her shoulder joins her neck inside the wide strap of her bra, and she sucks in a breath. "What are you doing?"

Rae tries to twist away, but I don't let her. "It's a trigger point. Breathe."

"You are a sadist."

"Give me thirty seconds. If it's not better, you can call me whatever you want."

For once, she does what I say.

The muscle starts to give under my hands, and I rub a small, deliberate circle that makes her hiss.

I let my curiosity get the better of me. "So, you started at fourteen. High school dropout?"

"Got my GED at sixteen and finished early so I could work on music."

Determined.

"Plus, I don't sleep much."

I switch to the other side of her neck and dig in there. This time, she doesn't jerk away.

"You looked as if you were sleeping fine this morning."

She rips herself out of my hands, bracing against the sink and turning to level me with accusing eyes. "You were in my room?!"

"I returned your sweater. You're lucky it suffered a kinder fate than my jacket."

"And you stuck around to watch me."

"You talk in your sleep. Not my fault you were saying my name."

I'm expecting her to snap back at me, maybe even hit me, but her expression is shocked.

"I didn't." The whisper drags along my skin, and fuck if I can't help thinking how she'd sound whispering other things.

"You did," I promise.

Her throat works as she swallows.

A timer goes off, and she slips out from where I have her against the sink.

The knee-jerk disappointment makes me grimace.

I have no interest in her, not as a woman. But the rejection is still painful.

I turn to find her pouring coffee into a mug. She holds it out. "Real coffee. I bought it in town."

"There isn't real or fake coffee…" I take a sip, the flavors mingling pleasantly in my mouth.

Rae's face lights with triumph, her lips curving. "I told you."

Ash was right. She is really fucking pretty.

Especially when she smiles.

It's the first time she's beamed in my direction, because I would've remembered.

And it's a good thing. If her negotiation had opened with that, she might own my villa right now.

My chest warms, my cold heart thudding harder against my ribs.

"La Mer," she goes on, oblivious to my turmoil. "It's bigger than Coachella, than Vegas, than anywhere. Why don't you own it?"

"I'm working on it. The things most worth having take time to acquire."

She reaches for the mug, and our fingers brush.

I wanted to catch her off guard, but it's me who's rocked when the bolt of attraction has my abs clenching under my dress shirt.

Her eyes widen before she pulls away and heads for the dining table.

"So, how are you going to fill my club?" I ask as she drops into the chair.

I grab the wrapped sandwich Natalia made me knowing I'd come for it when I was ready before returning to perch on the edge of the table.

"I have to give them a different experience every time. Plus, I'm figuring out how to get on the right people's radar."

"Debajo isn't going to be the 'it' place," she goes on. "It's a basement. The place for those who don't want to go to the 'it' place."

"People like you? The rebels and outcasts?"

"I'll take that as a compliment."

"You should."

Her gaze flicks to mine, surprised.

"You're abrasive and petulant." I can't help going on. "But add a wig, a hundred thousand euros of sound equipment, and some strobe lights? A rebel girl can turn into a nightclub goddess."

Her lips part. "Goddess."

"I'm not referring to your looks," I say evenly, though the more I stare at her, the more I want to. "Goddesses aren't defined by their beauty. They're defined by their power. You have that, yet you react to the world instead of commanding it."

I don't know why I'm telling her this, but it's been weighing on me since the first night I saw her play.

Maybe I see something in her I recognize, the feeling she's been wronged and is trying—futilely, desperately—to set things right.

"Easy for you to say," she replies. "People wait for you to act. By the time I have a chance, they've already made up their mind about me. Already decided things that change my present and my future."

The earnest way she's watching me, like my words are sinking in, has my chest tightening.

"Learn to take your power and no one can tell you what to do."

Her dark lashes blink as she cradles her chin between her palms, inhaling slowly before letting the breath out.

"Well, damn. Thanks for the career advice, Mr. King," she says, deadpan.

Insolent. Instead of offering her the chance to play Debajo, I could've let her languish in the obscurity she brought on herself.

And she's repaying me with insults.

When her lips twitch in a smirk, a jolt of lust snaps down my spine.

I said I wanted to bring her peace.

I take it back.

I want to shut up that mouth that delights in insulting me, my cock, and the empire I've built. To watch those dark eyes cloud when I shove her back on this table, drag the denim off her legs and make her explode on my tongue.

It's the first I've wanted a woman this powerfully in months, the first I've pictured what it would feel like to take my pleasure alongside hers.

But it's attraction.

Meaningless. Harmless.

It won't control me.

I reach across her for the mug. The next sip I take is better than the first. "No. Thank you."

"For what?" Rae shifts back in her seat, wary.

It's my turn to grin. "For the coffee."

I head for the stairs, sandwich in one hand and mug in the other.

She's still growling when I reach the top step.

CHAPTER 8
Harrison

Security at Debajo is surprised to see me twice in four days.

I make my way to the private balcony, waving off the offer of a drink. After the week I've had, though, I sorely want one. Between meetings and business dinners, plus an overnight to London, I've barely been home enough to confirm the villa still stands. But today I did my business, worked out, put on my suit, and here I am.

In fact, I have a plan to advance my business agenda that will happen this weekend.

I told Rae to take her power.

It's about damned time I did the same.

The man who's been avoiding taking my calls about his club can't avoid me any longer...

He's hosting a charity gala at his home, and I'm invited.

On my way in, I checked the door with Leni—lower than Thursday.

I shouldn't be disappointed. There was no earthly reason to

believe a twenty-something woman could do what my PR team couldn't.

I'm listening to the opening DJ and entertaining a group of visiting businessmen from Australia in my booth when my phone buzzes in my pocket.

The letters blur at the sides as my eyes adjust in the dark.

Ash: Where are you?

Harry: Debajo.

Ash: I'm worried about you. We both know what day it is.

Harry: I'm fine.

Ash: High functioning human being fine or drowning your sorrows in expensive liquor fine?

I frown. Of course he's thinking about it too. Not even the French-press coffee—which I've been having the past three days— could snap me out of my melancholy this morning.

I don't respond, and another text comes moments later.

Ash: Speaking of problems, Christian's gala this weekend. Will Mischa be there?

Harrison: He had better not be.

I need to get important business done with our host.

Mischa Ivanov's presence would be more than a complication.

I'd rather eat glass than be in that room with my business rival—

both because the business I want to do is more easily conducted without him and because of the woman who's been publicly on his arm for months.

I shove the phone back in my pocket, feeling the change in energy in the club before I look up.

Rae is in the booth, and suddenly I get the "American Dream" theme Leni has been pushing all weekend on social.

Tonight my little American is wearing a platinum wig and a white halter-neck vest and trousers, like a girl-next-door Marilyn Monroe pinup. Except her hair is twisted and spiked.

Not a goddess. A monster.

An arrogant Medusa.

In a room full of people trying to attract one another, she's practically daring anyone look too long.

I shift over the railing, entranced.

When I brought her here, I did my due diligence. I wouldn't let just anyone play my club. But now, watching her play...

Her music lacks the echoing numbness of house tracks. It's melodic. Intimate.

I've only seen her a few times since the run in that left me drinking her coffee and imagining how she tasted instead.

But all of my suits in my wardrobe are accounted for and the pool hasn't acquired any new textiles to clog the filter, so I suppose that's progress.

I stay for the set, half listening to the men I'm entertaining while inwardly hoping Rae can weave the same spell on me that she weaves on the crowd.

I want to forget the things Mischa Ivanov has done. The things I said to my mother before she died. The vows I made after, that they wouldn't die in vain.

To give up every shred of my own expectations and lose myself in what this woman is creating.

After a few tracks, I look over to see her pressing a hand to her head like she did in the kitchen.

She said it wasn't withdrawal.

Whatever it is, I'm not taking chances.

I motion to security upstairs, pointing at the stage. "Get her water."

"Mr. King, I'm sure there's water—"

"I want a fucking line of them. Enough to hydrate a platoon."

He nods and speaks into his walkie. Moments later, one of the bartenders arrives at the stage with a champagne bucket full of waters on ice.

At the end of the next track, she glances at the waters, then back to her computer.

She transitions into a mashup, "Diamonds are a Girl's Best Friend" mixed with something R&B.

Then she looks up toward the catwalk and flips both middle fingers in the air.

The crowd erupts. They have no idea who she's calling out, but they get off on her defiance.

Perhaps I'd get off on it too, if I wasn't the one she was defying.

Despite the fact that she refused to eat with me the one time I took dinner at home, and barely acknowledges me when we pass in the house, I notice things.

She's terrible at taking care of herself. Lives on fumes. Doesn't go to bed until four or five—I was up one night and saw her light on—even when she doesn't have a show.

That might be fine for a group of college students on holiday, but for a professional who does this year-round? It's unsustainable.

By the end of her set, I haven't seen her touch the water. It's concerning.

"Bring her to the VIP," I tell security.

I'm waiting there, halfway through a poker game, when I feel the presence at my back.

But when I turn, it's security, alone.

"Señor King, she did not want to come."

I drop my cards and leave my chips where they are as I shift out of my chair with a nod to the other players—rich businessmen and VIPs all of them. I grab my jacket off my chair and shrug into it.

"Where is she?"

He doesn't immediately answer, and I take off through the halls.

She's still taking selfies with patrons.

Concern replaces my irritation when I see the fatigue on her face. Security shadows me, but I wave them off as I cut through the crowd to her.

"I told security to bring you back."

She glances at me but poses with her fan. "I didn't want to."

Frustration clashes with the other emotions inside me today— loss, grief, sadness.

"You looked unwell."

Her grin is as aggressive as her spiked hair. "Unwell? I tore the roof off your chic basement tonight, and you think I'm unwell?"

She shoves me out of the way and beckons for the next fan.

"Strange. A woman reamed me out recently—and publicly— for avoiding taking care of someone who was my business," I bite out as the fan takes a selfie, Rae muttering an apology when her hair nearly pokes the man in the face before he heads on his way.

I dismiss the small line of eager fans waiting, ignoring their protests as I grab my DJ's wrist and tug her after me toward the back door.

On the way, I snatch a water bottle off the bar and shove it at her chest.

When we're outside, fresh air washing over us both, she rounds on me. "I can't handle this tonight."

"Because I give a shit whether you pass out on stage or in the middle of a crowd?"

"You don't care about me. I saw you up there, hosting a dozen men exactly like you. All you care about is whether I'm making you money."

My summer home has turned into a hostile place. I'm walking on eggshells in a house with my damned name on the deed.

If I'm going to keep her around, it would be easier if she didn't think I was the devil.

"Follow me." I walk to my Ferrari Roma, then ball up my jacket and throw it in the rear seat as I shift into the front.

The seat molds to my body as I lean back against the headrest and wait.

Seconds tick by.

Finally, the passenger door clicks open, and she shifts inside. "Are you taking me somewhere to kill me?"

"Would've been far easier to do it in your sleep."

"You don't do things the easy way either."

I start the car and shift into gear and pull out of the parking lot.

"My parents died of an overdose. Both of them, the same night. Fourteen years ago. That's why I don't tolerate drugs in my business."

I grip the wheel tighter as I navigate the streets.

"I'm sorry."

Her voice is low, the contrition genuine.

"You didn't know?"

It was in endless media outlets at the time. They were senior executives at a massive international organization, plus visible contributors to a dozen charitable organizations in the UK and abroad.

"I would've been ten."

Fair enough.

She leans an arm against the window. "The pills you found were prescription. For anxiety. I haven't taken them regularly for months, but I like having them just in case."

Relief blurs with guilt.

"Why were they in an unmarked bottle? And in your checked bag, for God's sake?"

"Why not? I wasn't expecting the airline to lose my suitcase."

I navigate to a place I would know with my eyes closed, then I pull into the parking lot.

I shift out of the car and retrieve a bottle of Glen Scotia from the boot. "The first time we came to Ibiza, I was eleven. Ash was a baby. My parents bought a villa here when I was thirteen. I lost my virginity in that house."

Rae shuts the passenger door. "I hope she was well paid."

The laughter rips from deep inside my chest. I don't let anyone make fun of me.

Just this once, I allow it.

My companion shifts up onto the hood and turns to look out over the sand and surf. "They left it to you when they passed?"

I shake my head. "They would have. But their assets were tied up."

I take a long swig of whisky, the warmth scorching my throat like a welcome friend. Rae waves me off when I hold the bottle out to her.

"My parents didn't own nightclubs, but they managed real estate for a large Russian investor. When I was a teenager, they found out their employer was into… less than legal side businesses. They told him they wanted to go out on their own. Even purchased a venue under their own name."

My chest tightens. They were optimistic about the possibility of working for themselves.

"Their employer wouldn't let them. The project burned down, and the investigation ruled they had burned it down to collect the insurance. As a result, they collected no compensation. A few months later, my parents were dead of an overdose, but they didn't use drugs."

I feel her attention on me, the shocked stare. I don't know why I'm telling her except that I haven't fucking told anyone in a long time, and today of all days, I can think of little else.

"I vowed I would clear their name and rebuild what they'd lost—in my own way. So, when you say I only care about making money… you're wrong. I care about restoring their legacy. Putting right what should have been. I won't apologize for that."

The tightness in my throat, in my chest, won't release.

"This was my mother's favorite beach. We came every year for her birthday." I lean forward, brace my elbows on my knees. "I still do."

Rae shifts toward me, the moonlight catching the highlights in her hair.

"That's what today is," she says softly, and I nod.

Her presence shouldn't feel comforting, but it does.

Strange how the same woman can bring me madness and peace.

"So why bring me?"

I lace my fingers together as I listen to the waves crash against the shore, watch the lights of the city reflected in the distance. "This is a place to escape your demons. Or entertain them. You seem like a person who does both."

Rae shifts off the car, taking the bottle from my hand. She tugs off her shoes and tosses them back at me. I grab them out of the air so they don't land on the hood of my car.

I follow her out onto the sand. "Give me the whisky."

"Come get it."

There's only one other couple within sight on the beach, locked in a heated embrace. Her gaze lingers on them, and I take advantage, catching up and taking the bottle, then rewarding myself with a long drink.

"This is known as a romantic place," I inform her.

Rae rolls up her trousers and steps up to the edge of the ocean, her teeth flashing white in the dark. "So, you didn't bring me here to kill me. You brought me here to fuck me."

I chuckle. "You're a porcupine, and it's not only your hair. I wouldn't stick my cock anywhere near you for fear it would come back covered in quills."

Her low laugh ripples across the sound of the waves.

I'm starting to think it would be worth it.

I wonder who I'd find when I stripped away her clothes. The woman she is on stage, or the one in a T-shirt and jeans with a bottle of anxiety pills to keep her company?

Perhaps both.

I want to find out.

So fucking much.

I reach for the buttons on my shirt, undoing one after another. Then I toss the shirt at her head.

She catches the fabric, looking up in surprise.

I'm already working on my trousers, unfastening and unzipping them before shoving them down.

Her gaze lingers on my body. "Is this how you get women?"

"Let's find out."

I'm nostalgic and buzzed, and the way she's looking at me helps both.

The cool water licks my feet and ankles as I stop in front of her. "Admit you want me," I challenge. "I won't tell a soul."

She pries the alcohol from my grip. "I told you—the only way you'll ever get me naked is to sue the clothes off me."

My hands close over hers on the bottle. She doesn't let go.

I back into the surf, and her grip means she's forced to follow. "That could still be arranged."

Rae's lips curve in the dark as the water rises up her body.

It soaks her trousers. Her stomach. I don't stop until water reaches my abs and her chest, and I feel the tug of the undercurrent.

The exhilaration on her face is interrupted by shock when she notices the marks on my chest.

"What is this?" She nods to my pec, the mass of white lines there.

"Prison tattoo."

She looks up in alarm, realizing I'm joking when she sees my expression.

"It's a scar from boarding school," I amend.

Her brows tug together. "You let another person do this to you?"

"'Let' is a strong word. Boys can be cruel."

"Anyone can be cruel."

The water is up to her ribs, high enough it licks at her breasts when a wave rolls through, leaves her top stained and her nipples hard against the fabric when it recedes.

I want to trace the path with a finger.

Maybe my tongue.

"I didn't mean it."

Her words have me jerking my gaze up to meet hers.

"About your ex-fiancée and that you deserved for her to leave you."

I pull the bottle toward me and take a drink. "I thought I was in love. She was a spoiled princess. We wanted different things."

She takes the bottle back but not to drink it. It bobs in the water at her side, her grip on its neck assuring it doesn't drift away.

I reach a hand out experimentally to touch one of the spikes in her hair.

It's sharp.

"Your brother said you dated her because you thought she was what you deserved."

Her voice is low, but the words land in my chest as my hand

falls away.

She's young.

Too fucking young to ask questions like that.

My attention drifts down her body exposed by the water. Her lips, full and parted. Her shoulders, dripping with the sea.

It's all there on her face. The vulnerability she hides under sarcasm and barbs.

"On stage when you play, you're generous," I murmur. "Are you so generous when you fuck?"

Rae's eyes widen as she holds my gaze for a heartbeat. Two.

What I'm feeling is attraction, but it's more than that. It's reckless. A need no amount of money can solve, a question no woman but this one can answer.

She backs slowly out of the water, and my gaze sticks to her body even as she reaches the shore.

"What are you doing?" I rasp.

Rae bends toward the sand, every curve hugged by her wet clothes. When she straightens, something glinting in her hand, her slow smile catches me off guard.

"I need your keys, King. Because you're drunk and I'm driving."

CHAPTER 9
Rae

The car is built for speed, but I'm more aware of the man in the passenger seat than the roar of the engine. He's still distractingly naked from the waist up, his arm resting on the windowsill.

"Turn right," he says.

"I know."

"You're an insolent chauffeur."

"I'd be more pleasant if you rode in the back." I spare a glance for the impossibly cramped rear seat of the Ferrari.

My companion's grin is quick and surprised, but my gaze falls to the scars on his chest once more. Evidence of something I never entertained...

Harrison King is human.

I don't know what to do with that information, except wish I could forget it.

But I can't.

His parents died, suddenly and horrifically, and took everything he knew of life with them. He started over from nothing with only a vision of what might have been to keep him company.

I know how lonely it is to rebuild your world once it's shattered. I've felt the grief that comes with losing not only your security, but yourself.

We make it back to the house and park in front of the villa.

He reaches over me and hits a button on the car's dash, opening the trunk. I shift out of the car as he retrieves his bottle of liquor from the trunk, then I follow him up the steps to the front door.

At night, the villa is breathtaking. This entire place feels like a magical escape.

Harrison turns to me on the landing and holds out a hand. I place the keys in his open palm, and he closes his fingers so fast I jump.

"What are you thinking?" he murmurs.

"I'm wondering if you always keep a bottle of liquor in your car."

His eyes crinkle at the corners. "Only today."

We head inside, finding Barney waiting in the low nightlights of the kitchen. Harrison leans down to pat the eager pet before grabbing a lowball glass from the kitchen shelf and starting toward the stairs, glass in one hand and bottle in the other.

I don't think it's a good idea for him to drink more, or alone, given what this day means to him. "I want a sandwich," I blurt.

It'll keep him from drinking, plus put real food in his stomach in case he continues.

"You're asking the wrong man." But he pauses on the first step long enough that I try something crazy.

"Please?"

With a wary look, as if he's guessing what I'm playing at, Harrison relents and crosses to the fridge.

The dog makes a hopeful noise as the door opens.

"Natalia keeps the good stuff in here," he murmurs, pulling on a drawer.

"She hides it from you?"

"Used to when we were kids. I ate anything in sight for a few years."

He uses the fresh bread on the counter and serrano and hard cheese from the fridge to make two sandwiches.

Claiming seats on opposite sides of the table, we eat in silence.

This is the longest we've gone without sparring.

"Enjoying the view?" He catches me checking him out, and I swallow my bite and nearly my tongue along with it.

"Your brother's hotter," I manage.

Harrison lifts a brow.

"What? He's my age." I shift in my seat. "Unlike you."

Blue eyes cool on mine. "Don't let me stand in your way."

The comment shouldn't disappoint me. It does.

Tonight, he looked at me like I was more than means to an end.

It was unexpected and thrilling.

We finish our snacks, and Harrison offers the last piece of meat to Barney, who spins in a delighted circle.

"You don't strike me as the dog type."

"My brother bought him for me after Eva left." Harrison takes our plates and sets them on the counter.

"Said he was to keep me company," he goes on, "but I think he wanted to soften me."

We start for the stairs, Harrison gesturing for me to go first.

He's behind me, so close that if I turned, we'd be touching. His strong chest and arms, those unearthly blue eyes, his vile, gorgeous mouth.

"Did it work?" I ask over a shoulder.

The house is quiet except for Barney's soft whining from the floor below. As if he feels the tension from his spot on the rug by the door.

"You tell me."

When we get to the top, I pause and turn.

He's right there. Beautiful and messed up and filling my senses.

When I lift my chin to meet Harrison's gaze, we're breathing the same air. His mouth is inches away, his bare chest too. All that power carefully restrained.

"As a boy, I wondered if the people who are softest on the inside are hardest on the outside."

"Why is that?" I manage.

His eyes are deep as the ocean, guarded emotions swirling beneath the surface like rogue currents.

"Because they have to be."

I never claimed to be in exceptional shape, but as I pull up at the end of my run on Friday, I'm breathing heavily while Barney barely pants.

"I'm sending you some money," I tell Callie as I ruffle the fur on the dog's head.

I've played three shows in Ibiza and been paid for the first two. True to his word, Harrison cut me in—though the door was nowhere near enough to make a dent in the twenty thousand, which means I need to haul ass to fill the place the rest of the time I'm here.

"I would never have asked you if it wasn't—"

"I know," I say. "It's important to both of us. How is work?"

Her voice is instantly more enthusiastic as she talks about the young women she's met during the past week at an event she ran.

The past few days, I've been feeling better too. Working on social media, on my sets, and even meeting up with Leni to get ideas for how to draw more people to Debajo.

I'm more comfortable now that I have my belongings back.

Minus the pills. I still find myself looking over to the nightstand for them at least once a day.

"So, how are the guys?" Callie's voice drags me back. "Any hot locals or all tourists?"

I can't tell if it's the steep hill leading up to the villa or the memory of swimming with Harrison King that has my heart hammering.

The man who kept my mind whirring long after I crawled into bed Monday night, body still tingling from the sea and his presence and driving his car, isn't a tourist or a local. He's a globe-trotting billionaire who hides himself behind his thirst for conquering.

Are you generous when you fuck?

Under the half moon, far from the lights of Ibiza Town, the question floored me.

Not because of his hard body or physical intensity, but because he showed me a piece of his soul, then leaned in.

What he told me about his parents' deaths, how everything he does is devoted to building what they could've had...

I can't help looking at him through a new lens.

Which hardly matters because since that night, he's been avoiding me.

I'm sure if I pinned him down, he'd say he's been occupied with work and dinners out.

But Thursday morning, I was up earlier than usual and tripped into the hallway in my pajamas to use the bathroom only to run into him emerging in his towel, clean and unshaven.

He caught the fabric before it slipped too far, but I could see the trail of light hair from his navel downward.

If I thought the night in the ocean was dangerous, this was indecent.

He looked startled to see me awake, muttering about his showerhead being replaced in the ensuite while I tried not to choke on my own tongue.

When he didn't attend my show that night, I was disappointed.

The door inched up as a result of video streamed from the previous performance. I should've been relieved there was no moody owner to keep me from talking with fans and helping ensure next week's gig would be even bigger.

I wasn't.

Since the richest man I've ever met made me sandwiches half-naked in his kitchen, he's been dodging me like a high school quarterback who's dealing with one too many irritating crushes.

"Rae, you're not responding. That means there's a guy."

"He's not my type," I say as I reach the door of the villa and push it open, going for the dog's leash before my shoes. Lesson learned on that front.

"I'm everyone's type," a familiar voice calls from the living room.

"I know you took a hit to your career by standing up to King," she goes on, "but it speaks to the kind of person you are. You deserve a hot summer fling."

Guilt gnaws at my stomach.

Maybe I could stand to get laid. But I roll with guys more likely to sell their belongings for a ticket to an indie music festival than count the money from their international conquests.

Even if my body thinks the man would make a beautiful distraction, it's wrong. I'm here to do this job.

Not to fuck him.

After saying goodbye to my cousin, I hang up and cross to where Ash is stretched out along the couch watching sports.

"What is this place, the headquarters of the British Billionaires Club?" I mutter.

"Charming. But I'm a future member, not a current one."

His smile is contagious as he gestures to the couch next to him. I drop into the spot, still sweaty from my run.

"I told you you'd stay," he gloats. "I trust my brother charmed you into it?"

"Not quite. We came to a new agreement that worked for everyone. Why are you here? Don't you have a hotel?"

"I'm staying at a villa with guys from my club. Though once you spend an entire season with a bunch of pricks, you've had enough of them by the end."

"Then why did you come to Ibiza with them?"

Ash frowns. "One of the veterans is trying to turn the club against me. I had a reputation for being perfectionistic when I was drafted. It served me fine my entire life, but apparently teammates don't like my standards applied to them. It's like fucking secondary school all over again."

"This is why I never made friends in high school." When Ash starts to rise from the couch, I tug him back down. "People decide what they want from you. You have to show them they're wrong."

He holds out his coffee. "Try this. Natalia got it."

"Natalia didn't get it. I did."

Ash cocks his head. "Brilliant American girl."

Harrison walks in, looking between us. The tension on his face deepens. "You two are lying around all day?"

Ash puts his hands behind his head. "Just waiting for you to come and judge us."

His brother shoots him a look that could freeze an active volcano before glancing my way.

No sign of a thaw.

He's gone the next instant.

"It's not you," Ash says. "There's a charity gala event tomorrow night and major players Harrison needs to show face with."

Curiosity has me leaning in. "And he doesn't want to?"

"Only because his business rival might be there."

"The man your parents used to work for."

Ash shifts back to one end of the couch, surveying me with surprise.

"He told me he wants to build an empire to atone for what happened to your parents. What he thinks happened to them."

Ash nods, still looking impressed by my knowledge. "Our parents worked for the Ivanov family. Now their son has taken over the business."

"Harrison thinks they had a hand in your parents' deaths."

Ash flinches. "Wealth and power make people do strange

things."

I shake my head, trying to catch up. "Mischa and Harrison are the same age?"

"Two years apart. But they went to school together." Ash frowns. "This gala is a bore, but the host is a friend of the family." His expression brightens. "Come with me as my date."

I snort, until I realize he's serious.

"Can I wear this?" I gesture to my running clothes, and he barks out a laugh.

"Fuck no. It's black tie. I'll pick you up at eight!" he calls as I head to my room, taking down my hair and eager to shower off the sweat.

Before I can, my gaze flicks to the nightstand, and I do a double take at the bottle of pills there.

Same medication. Same dosage. Enough to last me until I leave.

What the…?

He's been avoiding me all week. No more.

I head down the hall and push in Harrison's office door without knocking.

He looks up from his desk, looking caught out but otherwise immaculate in a pale-green shirt that sets off his blond hair and slight tan.

"You replaced my pills," I say.

"I estimated the dosage based on the size of the ones I disposed of."

I turn toward his bookshelves. The fact that this man knows more than anyone about my weaknesses has my stomach clenching.

"Thank you. I like knowing they're there if I need them."

It's almost as if they're an artifact from a version of me that no longer exists but one I don't want to forget.

There are dozens of books, and I trace a finger along the faded spines before I pull out one in a clear plastic case. "*The Count of Monte Cristo*. A good man who lost his way on a path for vengeance."

"Vindication. Justice. There's a difference."

I open the cover and take in the date, my mouth rounding. "A first edition?"

"The first edition was published as a serial and in French. This is a second."

I nearly drop it in my haste to replace it on the shelf.

"Why did you let me pick it up? It's three hundred years old and could fall apart in a second."

"Beautiful things are made to be touched."

The softness in his voice sends shivers through me.

Like that, I'm rocketed back to the night on the beach. His words, his closeness, his intensity.

"I understand from Leni the door was up by a hundred last night," he goes on. "You'll need to do better if you want to profit from our deal."

I frown. "I see our truce is over."

"Were you hoping it wasn't?" He cocks his head.

I refuse to cop to anything where he's concerned. He'll make me pay for it.

"There's something about you I can't figure out."

"Only one thing?"

He ignores me and continues. "What changed from your first night in Ibiza to the next morning that made you renegotiate?"

I don't want to talk about this. It's personal.

But the man who told me about his parents dying two nights ago replaced my anxiety meds.

There isn't a clean line between business and personal with him, if there ever was one.

"My cousin co-runs a program for women who've experienced sexual violence. Their funding has been slashed by government cuts. They need help keeping the lights on for a couple of months, or they won't be able to keep providing services."

He blinks at me as if I told him I wanted to buy breeding rhinoceros and start a farm back in Orange County.

"That's very committed," he says at last. "But you can't take responsibility for everyone in this world. There are too many evils."

Conviction has me standing straighter. "No woman should have to endure sexual violence, and they sure as fuck shouldn't endure it alone."

He studies me long enough that I feel as if he's peering beneath my skin, under the layers of Little Queen or Rae which are fit for public consumption.

He shifts in his chair, his strong body reclining as both hands curl over the armrests. "There's a charity event tomorrow for the local environmental commission. Plenty of cynics like me and bleeding hearts like you."

"I heard. Ash asked me to go with him."

"Ash?" Surprise flits across his handsome face. Harrison rubs a hand over his jaw. "Tell my brother he can find another date. You'll go with me."

I laugh, incredulous. "What? Why?"

"I can want the company of an earnest young music producer in my employ. Who knows? Perhaps you can elicit business for your show next week."

I could promote Debajo, but that would mean being the date of this man I respond to when I shouldn't. Fancy clothes, booze, Harrison King looking like the god he is while he wraps Ibiza's in crowd around his finger.

Since my conversation with Callie, I can't help wondering what else he could do with those hands.

Harrison King might boast about his empire, but he has the goods to back it up.

Would he be as capable if he applied himself to a woman?

I know he would.

What I'm less sure of is whether he'd plow through her, demand she bend to his every need until she's so caught up in his storm she can't resist it...

Or whether he'd check his ambition long enough to learn and explore and test and play.

To step out of his need for power like I watched him step out of his clothes that night at the beach.

I swallow.

Spending a night with him would be more than a quick fix. I can't let him get under my skin more than he already has.

"I don't think so."

His gaze narrows as he folds his arms across his chest. "You don't *want* to spend an evening with me."

I cross to his desk, lift the letter opener off the blotter, and hold it out. "In case you need help scraping yourself off the ground."

But before I can turn, a hand closes around my wrist, hot and firm and strong.

"I said it would be more appropriate if you dated my brother.

That wasn't a suggestion."

"Really? You're so damned subtle it's hard to keep up," I taunt.

Bad idea.

His thumb brushes the underside of my wrist. Soft, deliberate.

My pulse leaps in response, and the letter opener clatters to the desktop.

"I need a date, and you owe me three favors," he drawls. I don't realize I've stopped breathing until he releases me again. "Consider this the first."

CHAPTER 10
Rae

This is a bad fucking idea.

I take a deep breath as I turn back to the mirror. The dress is the color of tangerines, ripe and lush.

It's cut high at the front, circling my neck like a collar. The back is nonexistent, starting above the top of my ass. The skirt has a high slit up one thigh, and the long fabric on either side ripples when I turn or walk.

Before I could ask Ash what to wear or browse shops on my own, the box appeared on my bed.

The sky-high wedge sandals that came with the dress are the same color as my skin. They're uncomfortable as hell when I fasten them around my ankles, but before I can decide whether to take them off, a knock sounds on my door.

"I understand most women consider tardiness a virtue, but I didn't expect it of you," comes the grumpy British voice from the other side.

I pull it open an inch, and my chest contracts.

Harrison King is breathtaking in his tux. James Bond come to life, with a hard body, sculpted lips, strong hands, and eyes that promise to steal your secrets and keep them for himself.

But it's the naked hunger on his face when he sees me, his gaze dragging over me like he's starved, that makes me want to turn around and slam the door.

"It's more Little Queen than me," I quip to hide the ripples of awareness.

"She's you. And this..." His gaze runs down my figure again. "This is definitely you."

His praise warms me. I don't need anyone else's approval, but knowing a man who's seen everything, done everything, could have anyone, gets simple pleasure from being in my presence is a high I never expected.

"You arseholes coming, or should Toro and I go on ahead?" Ash taunts from down the stairs.

When I start along the open hallway, Ash spots me from the foyer and dining area below and whistles. "Christ, Rae. If you're looking for a man tonight—"

"She's not," Harrison informs him.

I make it down the hall without incident, then trip at the top of the stairs. Strong arms grab my waist, my ribs, before I can spill down to the first floor.

"Are the shoes the wrong size?" Harrison murmurs at my ear.

"No. They're the wrong style." I go on at his confused look. "If I wanted eight more inches, I'd have asked for it."

"And I'd have given it to you," Ash declares, making me grin and Harrison glare.

Toro greets us outside. "Beautiful," he says, beaming at me.

"Thanks. I had the dress in my suitcase." I wink, and he laughs. "What about this car?" I nod to the vintage Rolls-Royce, a departure from the usual Mercedes, complete with a chrome ornament on the hood.

"Had it in my basement," he teases, and it's my turn to grin.

Since I arrived in Ibiza, we've found a handful of moments to talk. In the car, I learned Natalia is his wife and that they've worked for Harrison's family a long time. One day, when I found him working in the garden outside, I insisted he let me help him. In exchange, he told me about his daughter.

He misses her. It's clear from the way he speaks about her.

But he and Natalia enjoy taking care of the house, and Harrison and Ash are extended family to them.

Toro goes to help me into the back of the car, but Harrison holds the door first. I shift into the middle, Ash claiming the other side.

"This is cozy," Ash says pleasantly.

We're pressed tight, my shoulders brushing both of theirs. But it's Harrison's I'm most aware of, his body that makes mine tingle.

"So, whose place is this?" I ask, trying to settle my nerves.

"Christian Geroux. A businessman," Harrison states.

He looks as if he's going to say more but pulls out his phone and frowns at it.

When Ash leans forward to talk with Toro, I glance at Harrison's screen, doing a double take. "Whoa. That font is size a million."

"What are you talking about? It's barely legible."

"You need reading glasses."

Harrison presses his lips together and refuses to say more as we head to the party, his strong profile a dark outline against the lights beyond the car.

The idea he has a weakness pisses him off like a business deal gone sour. I smirk the whole way to the party.

The villa we pull up in front of is every bit as sprawling and impressive as the one I'm staying in. More formally designed and decorated, it's meant to be enjoyed by guests as opposed to the people who occupy it when the lights go out.

There are terraced gardens flanking a curved driveway, discreet security in tuxedos at either side of the door. Twinkling lights are just visible on some patio along the side.

We head in through the front door, staff immediately descending to offer us drinks. I'm distracted from the sudden surge of nerves by the gorgeous house, every wall filled with art, every corner with lush plants.

On the terrace, a hundred people are milling about. There's a six-piece band in one corner and a dance floor. Torches light the huge outside space, with recessed lighting on the inside.

"This place is incredible," I murmur to Ash.

"Christian had it built as his holiday home. He spared no expense. He never does."

Before long, people are approaching us—approaching Harrison mostly. When pressed, he introduces me as Raegan. No one calls me Raegan, but as unsettling as it is, there's something new about it on his lips.

I'd been expecting Harrison to be distant like in the car or confrontational like every other time, but he's the opposite. He stands close enough to steer me with a hand on my back, but his presence feels protective rather than controlling.

For a minute, I wonder what it would feel like to be on his arm for real. He's a king here, and not only in name. This world he plays in, he runs it.

The men he considers rivals must be formidable indeed.

One of the women smiles in my direction as Harrison and her husband, who's in media, talk global news and business. It's a strange vibe as she leans in. "Do you model?"

I choke on my drink. "Not lately."

"Ah. Harrison is a master at keeping beautiful women on his arm. But I suppose things change."

Her catty tone makes me stiffen. Next to me, Harrison glances over in the middle of his sentence. As if he didn't hear but sensed my reaction.

A hand on my back has awareness tingling up my spine.

"You know," I say to her, "I was reading a story last week about how this wine tasting club was served the wrong wine. Instead of a thousand-dollar bottle, they got a twenty-dollar one. And they gave it rave reviews."

"I don't follow."

"Quality doesn't come from a label," Harrison cuts in smoothly.

The fact that he was listening enough to stay on top of my conversation, not only his, has gratitude blooming in my stomach.

He leans in, brushing his lips against my ear. "Everything all right?"

"I can handle them."

"I know you can. But that doesn't mean you should have to." He squeezes my arm, a brief reassurance as genuine as it is surprising.

I'm not comfortable at large events. Unless I'm performing, where I have distance from the crowd, I prefer small groups with people I know.

When I stopped going to parties in high school, around the

same time I started working on my music, I figured my friends would understand.

They didn't.

The girls who used to invite me to things turned their backs on me.

When I tried to explain that I couldn't relax and enjoy myself, they froze me out.

Evidently our friendship was based on gushing over our older brothers' college friends, and getting drunk enough we couldn't remember what we did the next day.

Once neither of those things appealed to me, I stopped appealing to them.

Tonight, Harrison's telling me he knows I've got this. But in case I don't, he's got me.

It's that realization that has me pulling back. "I, ah, need to find a bathroom."

I duck out, feeling his gaze between my shoulders.

On the way, I get lost and run into a distinguished-looking man in his seventies.

"Good evening. We haven't met," he says, reaching for my hand.

I let him take it, press a dry kiss to the back. "I was just looking for a bathroom," I say when he releases me.

"*Bien sûr.* This is my house, and I can show you the way."

"Oh! Mr. Geroux."

"Christian, please." He graciously spreads his hands. "Make yourself at home. I do enjoy hosting, and I'll have fewer opportunities when I retire."

"Then why retire at all?"

"Because I have children who require me unlike any business. For some of us, it's a pleasure to build and acquire and possess. A game. For others, it's their life—they need to prove themselves, to redeem themselves."

Christian's eyes gleam. "My ventures are like my children. I will miss certain ones more than others. La Mer is a once-in-a-lifetime place."

My heart kicks. "You own La Mer?"

"For thirty years. You've heard of it." He looks genuinely pleased.

"It's exquisite. I've always wanted to—" I cut myself off before saying "play there." "Attend."

"You must while you are here. As my guest, before I sell to one of its many suitors." He hands me a card. "Give this to the men at the door, and we will let you in." He pats my arm as we arrive at the bathroom door.

But as I thank him and head inside, my head is spinning.

Harrison's here to see the man who owns La Mer, which can only mean one thing—he's here trying to buy it.

This is what he's been working on all week while he's been avoiding me. Judging by how big this deal must be, I bet he's been working on it far longer than that.

And what of his rival? Does the Ivanov family want La Mer just as much?

I know what it's like to have your past snapping at your heels, but it's bigger for Harrison.

If tonight is as important as it sounds, why did he go to such lengths to bring me as his date?

The only thing I can think is that I'd be a distraction for the other partygoers. A tacky novelty.

Except I remember the way his hand felt on my back. How genuine he sounded when he wanted to make sure I was okay.

Everything I learn about him makes me more confused, and more drawn to him.

I touch up my lipstick in the mirror, still surprised by the woman looking back at me.

She might not be a goddess, but she's different than she was two weeks ago.

I have a career again. A club that's starting to feel like mine, that's doing better thanks to me.

I have people to smile and laugh with.

And tonight…

I have a date with a man who's complicated and sexy and a worthy opponent.

Why not enjoy it a little?

My shoes are rubbing in all the wrong places as I head down the hallway, intent on finding Harrison.

His voice reaches my ears at the same time as the music far away. I can't make out the words, but I spot him in a corner, speaking to a stunning blonde. She's statuesque, like an old movie star with perfect hair and perfect curves.

It's her voice I make out first. "It's not the same without you."

When she reaches for him, laying a hand on his face—that coolly untouchable face—every thought evaporates.

I watch them for a minute, my chest aching in protest as he murmurs a response too low to hear.

For a moment, on his arm, I felt as if this world was mine too. To borrow, if not to own.

But seeing Harrison in a moment of obvious intimacy with the woman I assume is his ex reminds me I'm an outsider.

I don't know this man. I can't, and I shouldn't want to. Just because he's capable of being close with someone doesn't mean I should expect him to do anything other than hurt me or disappoint me.

I take off the uncomfortable shoes and leave them in a corner behind a potted plant. As I start down the hall, I run into Ash.

"You should've come with me, American Girl," he tosses.

"I shouldn't have come at all."

His grin fades as I grab a drink off a passing tray.

"Tell him I'm heading out," I say. "If he notices I'm gone."

Harrison

I told myself I wouldn't feel a thing the next time I saw her.

I was wrong.

"Do you remember how we used to lie out all day sunbathing in Monaco?" Eva asks.

It's not as if I still care for her, but the echoes of it fill my chest when I thought I'd burnt them out and remind me of something important.

I'm capable of caring.

"Where is your date this evening?" I interrupt.

"Singapore. Or maybe Tokyo." She waves a dismissive hand as

if his absence makes him unworthy of discussion.

I glance past her. "If this is your attempt to keep me from speaking with Christian—"

"Of course not! I hoped I'd see you tonight."

Her soft pout used to get to me, but now, in the hall where she's cornered me, I see only the manipulation beneath.

"Well, now you have. Give my regards to your new diversion for me."

I brush past her down the hall, determined to find Christian.

Though my primary purpose tonight is to pin down our host, I can't stop thinking about the woman who excused herself from my side twenty minutes ago and hasn't returned since.

As I pass impeccably dressed guests in tuxes and dresses in every color of the rainbow, my mind flashes back to my reluctant date handling herself in the den of rich vipers.

I'd half expected the seething sullenness she'd graced me with more than once, but in this exclusive crowd, she was both gracious and assertive.

It pleased me.

Everything about her tonight pleased me from the second she stepped out of her room in that dress looking even more stunning than I'd expected.

After spending my mother's birthday with Rae, I did avoid her for the better part of the week.

Not because she'd done something wrong—on the contrary, I was thinking about her too damned much.

But when I learned my brother planned to bring her tonight as his date, something inside me broke.

The same part of me that purred with satisfaction when I drew her against my side, caressed her back with my hand like it was my right.

None of it means anything. Not compared to the reason I'm here.

I force her from my mind as I reach the doors of the library, spotting my quarry inside surrounded by a circle of men.

"How good to see you, Harrison." Christian's gaze lands on me, and everyone parts to let me in.

I extend a hand, which he takes. That's their cue to leave, and they depart.

"Let me guess," Christian says, accepting a fresh drink from a waiter once the other guests have pulled the library doors closed behind them. "You're here to talk about football?"

"I'll leave that to my brother. No, I'm here to remind you that you're going to sell me La Mer."

He sighs. "Harrison... I've known you for two decades. Ambition has always been a strength. But as an old man, I'm telling you to find other things in your life. My children are my joy now. Did you meet my Sylvie?"

I mentally scan the faces from the party, vaguely recalling a pretty young woman who greeted us near the door. "Yes. Lovely."

"She is. My other children are settled, but I worry for her."

"The young have a way of surprising you. She'll find her way."

I glance out the window and spot the glowing orange dress, Rae's dark hair in waves around her shoulders.

It's refreshing to see her without a costume beyond the dress I chose for her.

But as she trips down the steps, alarm has my abs clenching.

Christian follows my gaze, making a sound of muffled surprise.

"Perhaps we should finish this conversation another time."

No. We should finish it now.

But as Rae reaches the curved driveway, my feet won't cooperate.

"One moment."

I head out to the hall, pushing through the crowds and ignoring anyone who tries to stop me.

Ash steps in front of me before I reach the front doors. "Don't."

"Don't what? Tell my date she should stay until the end of the party?"

"She said she wished she hadn't come."

A sharpened spear sneaks under my ribs.

I shouldn't fucking care what she thinks, but I'm angry. She said she'd come with me, and she's turning her back on me at the first opportunity.

I shove past Ash and take the steps two at a time.

"Raegan."

She turns, and I soak her in. This time it's not the way she looks in that dress, though she's stunning. It's the expression on her face—hurt and disappointment.

Words always come easily, but now I'm reaching for them. "What happened to your shoes?"

She blinks up at me, ignoring the question. "The woman inside. Your ex, right?" Surprise slams into me, but she continues. "You could've brought her. It looked as if she would've been more than happy to come with you. Or leave with you."

My mind races to process her frosty tone, settling on something as fascinating as it is improbable.

Is she jealous?

Raegan Madani? The woman who ruined her career to score a few points on me?

The possibility fucks me up in the best way.

"I get that the only reason you hired me was to play your club and make back what I cost you," she goes on, and her dark eyes are big enough to swallow me whole. "But you do not get to dress me up and drag me here and *use* me like this."

She points at her bare feet, and the red welts have me wincing.

"You should've told me the shoes didn't fit."

She shoves me, hard enough that I stagger. "I shouldn't have worn them at all! Your stupid favor didn't involve footwear. I came because I said I would, and I thought maybe you wanted me to come with you. Which is crazy. This is your world. These are your rich, entitled people. Enjoy them."

I didn't know I had the ability to hurt this woman. Even Eva, whom I thought I loved, proved to have an icy heart I could never penetrate. But this woman—this girl—who's so extraordinary on a stage and is so stubborn off it…

It makes me wonder what other good things she hides beneath her tough exterior, pretending she cares for nothing and no one.

"I didn't know she'd be here," I say at last. "She left me for Mischa Ivanov. My rival, the man I hate."

Her eyes widen with disbelief. "Your fiancée left you for the man who killed your parents?"

I nod. "She wanted a different kind of power than I offered."

The light from the torches dances along the curved driveway, reflecting in her dark eyes. Emotions collide on her face.

Compassion.

Hurt.

I wish we were alone instead of here at this party.

Fuck it.

I close the distance between us, take her face in my hands.

The surge of adrenaline when I touch her, when we lock gazes, is real.

The pull between us is real.

There's only one woman I wanted on my arm tonight. And since she left it, she's been missed.

A familiar car pulls up the drive, pulling into her peripheral vision, and Rae steps back.

She reaches for the door, but I slam it shut with a hand.

"Don't go," I bite out. "If I've made you feel less in some way, I'm fucking sorry."

I need her to understand how hard I've worked to get what I have, to keep it. That letting a person come between me and my revenge nearly cost me everything.

She pries my fingers off the door one at a time.

"Don't be sorry, Harrison. Be better."

As the car pulls away with her inside, I'm left feeling empty and frustrated in a way that has nothing to do with Christian and the deal.

CHAPTER 11

Rae

The next morning, there's a message on my social profile asking for an interview.

I message back:

> **If this is about what happened in the spring, I don't do interviews.**

There's a reply almost instantly.

> **I want to talk about your new gig in Ibiza. You're causing a lot of buzz. When can we meet?**

I've never done face-to-face interviews, which are outside my comfort zone because it's harder to control the conversation, so I tuck the phone away without responding.

I shift out of bed and trip over to the door, catching sight of my still-sprayed hair in the mirror. The makeup that didn't quite come off my face last night after the party.

The party.

It all rushes back. Playing Cinderella. Pretending to be part of that world.

And the feeling of seeing Harrison with his ex.

As I step out into the hall, I expect to hear him, but there's nothing.

His office door is closed, and so is his bedroom.

"Looking for Mr. Moody?" Ash calls from the dining area downstairs.

I lean over the railing. "Maybe. What're you doing here?"

"Got back last night to find our club's villa trashed. Tripped over bottles and naked tourists to come over."

I pad downstairs and eye the green smoothie Ash is drinking. "That looks disgusting."

"So do you." He ruffles my hair. "But last night, you were stunning. Everyone noticed." He pauses. "He left for business this morning."

"Oh." I try not to feel disappointed he didn't tell me. "For how long?"

"Who knows?" His eyes narrow. "But there's something in the kitchen for you."

I look where he's pointing to see a huge stainless-steel espresso maker.

"Shit. Does it do laundry too?" Up close, it's even more impressive, and I run a hand over the levers and dials before reaching for the instruction manual next to it. "He must have decided he likes good coffee," I say as I thumb through the pages.

Ash's snort has me looking up. "Yeah. He bought it for himself," he says dryly.

I set the instructions on top of the machine, spotting a Post-it note stuck to the stainless steel.

There's a number scrawled on it.

Eleven hundred thirteen.

It's the door from Thursday's show—up from eight hundred when we started. Two thousand is capacity, so while it's trending in the right direction, we're nowhere near selling out.

"Maybe he bought it for when he returns?" I wonder aloud.

"If that's what you think, you're daft." Ash is watching me with a grin and folded arms. "There's something going on between you and my brother."

I match his posture. "It's called a grudge."

"That might be how you both started, but it's not why you were upset last night."

"A month off from soccer and you're a shrink?"

He plows on, unmoved. "I was twelve when our parents died. Harry showed up at the door of my boarding school. You know the first thing he said to me?"

I shake my head.

"'No matter what anyone says about them, they loved you. That's all you need to know.'

"That day, everything fell to him, legally and practically. He kept me out of the investigation into their deaths. Dealt with their business interests dissolving. It didn't make him crumble; it made him more resolved. You can call him lots of things, but when he commits to something—someone—he'll see it through or die trying."

My chest aches as I think of Harrison, younger than Ash and I are now, being ripped from his education and confronting not only his parents' deaths but the fallout.

"I still hate him half the time," I admit.

"It's the other half that's interesting." He pauses. "While they were engaged, Eva tried to get Harry to step back from his business, supposedly because she wanted time together. Turns out it was so Mischa could get a toehold in markets where his business was strong.

"La Mer would be the final nail in his coffin. It's the biggest venue in the world, the most prestigious. Harry gets it, Mischa loses. It won't bring our parents back, but he thinks it's something." Ash rubs a hand over his jaw. "Most people want to be near my brother for his money or his reputation. You see the man he could be, like I do."

The invitation hangs between us.

It's impossible to forget that amidst Harrison's compulsive desire to empire-build is a genuine protectiveness for his family, a desire to do right by the people he loves.

Because he does love, in his way.

He put his brother first in a time when he himself was grieving and broken. He buys cars for Toro that the old man adores. Hired Leni as his right-hand woman and allows her to be her quirky self.

Judging by the champagne bucket of waters that arrives when I start to lose myself in a set, he even intervenes on my behalf.

"And if he succeeds in growing his business and buying La Mer, you think he'll be that man?" I ask.

"I think he can let go of his grief and have a chance at it."

I stare at the coffee machine, the encouragement implied by it. "Eleven hundred thirteen isn't enough."

"Enough for what?" Ash demands.

"It's nowhere near," I say, ignoring the question as I grab the note and crumpling it up before tossing it in the trash.

I pull up my social and message the reporter back to say I'll meet her.

Harrison

"This is everything." It's a question, but it comes out like a statement as I stare at the manager of BLUE, my LA club.

"Every incident report filed against the club in the past three years," he says.

The stack must be fifty pages thick.

I flip through and skim dates, names, looking for patterns. The only pattern is that there is none, except perhaps for the bare-bones information.

These aren't "reports." They're bookmarks with handwriting on them.

Judging from the paperwork in front of me, the staff here sees their primary job as making things go away.

"I asked for this information a month ago," I say.

"I'm sorry, Mr. King. Staffing is tight." He presses his lips together. "There've been budget cuts the last two years—"

"Fine." I'd told my managers to tighten up on existing properties to allow us to expand new operations.

Don't be sorry. Be better.

Rae's words echo in my head.

Traveling on business has never felt strange or lonely, but this week feels like both. I've gotten used to having her around my house and around me.

The gala was days ago, and I can still feel Rae's presence. I swear I catch her scent on the air when I step out of a car or off a plane.

Which is fucking crazy.

Rae's not here, and there's no reason she should be. She's doing what she's supposed to be doing—making me money.

So, why would I give a wardrobe full of designer suits for a glimpse of her across a lobby?

"Mr. King?"

I glance up at the manager's voice, realizing I was staring off into space. "Hire more people. Whatever you need to ensure this issue is properly addressed."

"Yes, sir. Thank you. Would you like me to send you any new reports?"

I consider it. "Only if you can't manage them yourself. But if I have to make another request for information like this one, they had better be robust fucking accounts. If a patron so much as gets a drink spilled on them—"

"We'll take care of it." He nods as I shift out of the seat and start for the door. "Your car is waiting outside. It's too bad you're leaving LA so soon and can't stay for this evening's show."

I cut a look over my shoulder. "I'll be in Miami tonight."

"Enjoying your venue?"

I smile tightly.

"Doing the same damn thing we did here," I mutter under my breath on my way out.

CHAPTER 12
Rae

I'd never believed that a house could feel different without its occupants, but since Harrison King left almost a week ago for work, nothing feels the same.

Leni texted me a bunch of links to posts from excited tourists touting their recent visits to Debajo, plus an article listing it as one of their top hidden gems for the summer.

The next show brought in over twelve hundred partiers.

To celebrate, I took the next day to explore the island, Toro more than happy to show me both tourist places and local haunts.

Natalia, having caught me working at odd hours one too many times, decided I needed a hobby. When I told her about the little crocheted dolls I made during my art school undergrad and sold on Etsy for extra cash, she surprised me the next day with yarn and materials.

If I expected to hear from Harrison about the increase in sales, there's been nothing since the night he came after me like a tuxedo-clad god on the steps of Christian's villa.

"I'm fucking sorry."

As if he expected that to undo everything he'd done.

But the sick thing is part of me wanted to accept his apology. Not only for that night but for all of it.

I start typing out a text to him.

> **Rae: Toro's started showing me the island by driving me around, but I'm pretty sure it's so he can tell stories. Ash broke this blue vase shaped like a mermaid while playing soccer inside yesterday. Barney whines every morning when he sees you're not there.**

I pocket the phone without hitting Send.
But later, the thing vibrates in my pocket.

> **Harrison: Tell Toro to take a goddamned day off. Ash needs to fuck around outside. And you can let my dog know I'm catching a flight back today.**

Shit.

I must have accidentally hit Send.

There's no dwelling on the humiliation, though, because he's coming back. And I'm looking forward to seeing him.

Instead of my fucked-up feelings over one mysterious billionaire, I focus on this evening's set.

I choose a black jumpsuit, plus the wedge sandals that were returned to me by one of Christian's staff the day after the gala. Once I got over the embarrassment of being tracked down to return the footwear I left in the hall, I decided to break them in.

I like how feminine I feel. Not as much beautiful as powerful.

A goddess, in Harrison's words.

I line my eyes extra dark and take care with my shiny, neutral lip gloss.

"Are you coming tonight?" I ask Ash on my way out.

"I have a date. But it's a secret." He winks.

"Damn secrets. Between you and Harry—"

"Harry?" He cocks a brow. "Have you called him that to his face?"

I glare. "Are you ten years old?"

"Nope, and neither are you." His gaze runs down my body. "Which is why it'll be interesting when he finds out."

Unreal.

"You get why he's more of a prick than usual around you. He's not used to wanting what he can't have. Between you and La Mer... it's a rough summer for him."

As I get into the front seat of the car with Toro, I'm still thinking of Harrison.

I miss his suits. His smooth voice, his icy-blue stare, the firm lips that make my stomach tighten imagining how they'd feel on mine.

How they'd feel other places.

When I get to the club, I drop off coffee and pastries I purchased on the way with security, wave to everyone as I get ready for my set. I even accept a drink to take the edge off.

The crowd goes crazy when I'm introduced and I take over the booth.

Energy flows through me, hot and electric. A power surge of my own creation reflected back at me.

I take it all.

Without thinking, I look up at his private booth. There's a crowd in suits and cocktail dresses. A dozen men and women are spilling out of the booth and onto the catwalk.

The hairs on my neck lift before I catch sight of his golden head, angular jaw, and square shoulders through the crowd.

Harrison's back.

A surge of emotion rockets through me.

Anticipation, nerves, longing.

I watch as a bartender serves drinks, and they toast.

One woman leans over to whisper in his ear. When her hand lingers on the shoulder of his jacket, I almost fuck up my transition.

But someone nudges my shoulder with a champagne bucket of ice and waters. Plus a bottle of champagne nestled in the middle, a number on a Post-it stuck to the glass.

The door, I realize. Fourteen hundred sixty-three.

It's thrilling. I did this, but it feels like a shared victory. Shared with Leni, the team here, and the man I never thought I'd want to share anything with.

I make a change, dropping in a new song I've been working on. As the chorus comes on, the man I'm totally not watching out of the corner of my eye leans over the railing upstairs.

When I lift my chin and catch him staring, I'm knocked off balance by the expression on his face.

Each beat I feel his eyes on me is a thrill.

A dirty promise that feels less dangerous with the distance between us.

I lift both hands in the air and flip off the catwalk.

A few of the well-dressed people above gasp, but most ignore me.

Harrison King, a decade older than me and probably a dozen tax brackets above, leans elegantly over the railing separating the upstairs VIP booth from the crowd with a glass in one hand.

Then he lifts the other hand and offers me the same finger I gave him.

Good God.

I'm dead. Slain.

If a billionaire flipping me off makes my ovaries flutter, I'm a fucked-up woman.

But it does, and I am, and the smirk on his face is so sexy it makes me throb.

When my set concludes, I drink a gallon of water and take selfies with every fan before I head to the private VIP lounge. Security offers grins and fist bumps along the way.

Leni descends on me the moment I set foot through the door. "You were fucking rad tonight. Keep doing this, I'll take you on a surfing trip the next time I'm home."

"Deal."

Inside, the room is bustling with twice the usual dozen or so VIPs. Harrison's seated in a booth with a handful of the people from upstairs, perfectly collected in a dark suit that sets off his clear, blue eyes. His legs are stretched out in front of him, women on each side looking as if they'd like to crawl into his lap.

I catch his eye and jerk my head toward the bar.

With a cocked brow, he shifts out of the booth.

"More spoiled princesses?" I ask as he falls into step next to me.

"Business associates."

I feel every inch of him in my space. We're not touching, but having him near is oh so good.

Once we get to the bar, I lean an elbow on it and hold up the sheet of paper from Leni. "Guess what this number is?"

He's close enough I can smell his ocean scent.

"Your SAT score."

I smack his shoulder. "It's the door, dumbass."

Harrison lifts his cool, blue gaze to mine, but the triumph behind it matches the way I feel.

I grin as two drinks are set in front of us. We clink glasses, our arguments set aside for a moment as we share in a victory we've both wanted for different reasons.

"How do you like the espresso machine?" he asks.

"It's very shiny."

His mouth twitches. "I meant, are you pleased with how it functions? It's a new model and the best available."

"I haven't used it."

Harrison frowns, and I take a sip of my drink, feeling his attention linger on me.

Finally, I say, "The French press is good enough. Besides, I don't want to get attached. It's not as if I can take it with me."

"Of course you can. I bought it for you."

"No, I mean... thank you." Processing his confusion is hard. He seems offended his gift didn't rock my world. "But I'm always on the road, so I pack light. The only things that come with me are my computer and gear and clothes."

He leans in, as if genuinely willing himself to understand. "Is it so difficult to see yourself staying somewhere?"

"I've tried that. It didn't work out. People have a habit of disappointing me."

"Perhaps you simply expected too much."

I turn that over as I glance past his shoulder to see his business associates talking and laughing.

"Where were you all week?" I ask.

"Visiting venues in LA and Miami. Putting in place new policies to address a few lingering issues." He hesitates, regret flickering behind his eyes. "In building an empire, it's easy to be lured by the facade and miss the cracks. The past year, I was distracted. I allowed the cracks to extend further than they should."

He was trying to fix the mistakes he made. The ones I called him out for.

I blink.

"I thought your next move was buying La Mer."

"I can do both. You'd be surprised what I can accomplish when I set out to."

It's not the first time he's looked at me as if I have what he wants. But it's the first time I can't resist looking back at him the same way.

The feeling deep in my stomach, expanding in my chest, isn't only attraction. It's not only about how irresistible he looks in his dark suit, how his dirty-blond hair and electric-blue eyes lull me into thinking he could have been the boy next door...

If the boy next door kept a safe full of secrets capable of slicing you clean in two.

"You're an asshole," I whisper, but the warmth in my voice betrays me. "And a prick. And a liar—"

"And you missed me." The gleam in his eye is so sexy it derails my brain.

"I did not."

"Then why did you text?"

"It was an accident." A flush crawls up my face, and his grin widens.

"Ah. But you were thinking of me."

"I'm thinking of how much money I'm going to make in my final two weeks here. But if it helps your ego, *they're* thinking of you." I nod to the fan club across the room.

The women are both pouting their full lips and adjusting their skirts to show even more insanely toned thigh. From the way they're staring, they miss his company.

"My attention is occupied."

I can't stop the surge of adrenaline that pulses through me or the breathless smile that tugs at my lips.

I ask something I know I shouldn't.

"Where do you… you know?"

"What?"

"Hook up. You don't do it at the house. I would've heard you if it was in your room, and I explored every inch of the villa while you were gone. There's no secret sex room or anything."

"Ah. Because I'm such a prolific adorer of women, I must be bedding them indiscriminately? Including since you arrived?"

The flash of his eyes should be a warning.

"Pretty much. I mean, you are the chairman of the British Billionaire Club."

"Excuse me?"

"It's a thing," I go on, deadpan. "You have elections, and meetings, and a dress code. Plus closed door events where you whip out your cash and measure how tall the stacks are."

He leans in and tugs on my hair, his expression solemn. "You're not supposed to know about that."

I toss back my head and laugh. It feels so damn good, and when he grins too, I wonder if it's contagious.

"Besides," he goes on, "I'm keeping busy with the DJ in residence at 'one of Ibiza's hidden gems.'"

He holds out his phone.

I scan the social media post from an influencer who happened to be at one of last week's shows.

His hand covers mine. The contact has my pulse thudding harder as I finish scanning the raving post. "That's fucking awesome," I say.

"It'd be more awesome if she'd clean my pool with her thong."

We made that bargain weeks ago. Something has shifted between us since, though I never gave permission. Now, the alcohol and high from the show and the way he's looking at me have me feeling invincible.

This place might not be my home, but I can't argue with the feeling pulsing through me, the familiarity of the staff and the setup and the bar, the hope that I could belong here—not only Little Queen, but Rae too.

And the man who owns it, the one I spent months hating, is one I would have run from once but now I want to lean into.

Every time he pushes me, I push back.

I don't break, only bend.

The newfound confidence makes me bold.

"Are you asking?" I taunt.

I'm close enough to see the tiny dots in his shirt print. His body blocks most of the room, and I can only see one of the envious women eyeing us from the corner.

"Come on, Harry, don't be shy. You can admit that what you want most after coming home from a long, hard work trip is a pair of my underwear to jerk off with."

His nostrils flare.

The hit of triumph twines with attraction surging through my veins, a cocktail more potent than the one I'm drinking.

I take the cherry from the bottom of my glass and suck on it.

If I didn't already know I'd raised the stakes, it's evident in the pulse in his neck. The way his gaze darkens with intent as he leans in, resting a hand lightly on my hip.

"Then give them to me."

His rough whisper in my ear, his firm lips tickling my skin, makes me forget basic functions.

Like how to chew.

The cherry gets stuck in my throat, and a second later, he's hitting me on the back. I spit the thing out on the woman crossing the floor to interrupt us. She squeals, flicking the fruit off her dress.

The other occupants of the VIP room fall silent as they stare at us.

Whoops.

Harrison turns to block me from the rest of the room as if I need protection.

Maybe I do.

"Fuck, you're savage." But his mouth twitches.

That's what I get for trying to out-cool this man.

"I can raid my drawer when I get back tonight if you still want a pair of my panties," I say, my voice hoarse.

"No."

"That's what I fig—"

"They don't taste like you. I want the ones you're wearing. The ones you wore when you lifted those middle fingers at my booth."

Desire slams into me, leaving behind a throb of longing that echoes from the tips of my breasts to between my thighs.

Harrison's jaw flexes as if he knows exactly how his words affect me.

"You can flirt with me, Raegan," he drawls. "I'll even enjoy it. But if you want me to treat you like my equal, you'd better be ready for all that comes with it."

A throat clearing has Harrison wrenching back to look over his shoulder at Leni. "Boss. We need to talk."

He shifts out of his stool, but I swear it's reluctantly. Before he walks away, he says to me, "We're going out tomorrow night."

"Calling in another favor?"

"No. A do-over of the first one. And trust me, you'll want to be there."

CHAPTER 13
Rae

I t started with a picture.

One I posted of the beach when I was out walking Barney one morning.

Since then, I've posted on social nearly every day.

Sometimes with Barney, sometimes the scenery. One day I snapped a photo of Toro, his weathered profile smiling, when he came to work on the house, and we ended up talking for an hour about his daughter and the argument they had about her leaving Spain for a job in Australia with a boy she was dating at the time.

In between, I've reposted pictures from fans. For the first time, my following is growing, and it's people saying they love my shows or my music or want to check out Debajo.

It doesn't hurt that I've been scanning the feeds of some hashtags of local partiers to see what's popular and, more importantly, what people are into but aren't getting in the bright lights and theatrics of the biggest clubs.

It's not Harrison's pressure. It's that I want to make Debajo great. It's less about me, or even getting the money for Callie, and more about believing in a place and the people in it.

This morning, when I check my DMs, the name on top grabs my eye.

Beck, one of my classmates from arts school, who is in LA.

You keep making that party look so good I'm gonna crash it.

I grin. *Don't write checks you can't cash.*

My phone rings as I'm out for a run with Barney. Adrenaline is pumping through my veins as I slow to a walk and answer. After a moment for the video call connection to establish, a handsome grinning face appears.

"I read about you this week," Beck informs me.

"Wow. I didn't know you could read."

His bark of laughter is warm and welcome. Beck's outside too, his hair blowing in the breeze. "Just because I'm an actor doesn't mean I'm stupid."

He's not. My friend took an arts-school vlog and leveraged it into a TV deal after graduation. He stars as a psychic cop in one of the top shows on television.

"How's the club gig?"

"I'm going to fill the place if it kills me."

"Badass. I heard someone's birthday's coming up from Tyler and Annie. Which day is the party?"

I frown. I haven't talked to Annie in a couple weeks except for the odd text. "There's no party, Beck. My birthday's not a day to remember."

He cocks his head, surprised. "Clearly you need to replace it with better memories."

"I'm trying. Tonight, I'm going to the biggest club on the island."

When I woke up an hour ago, there was a note on my dresser

in Harrison's scrawl saying we were going to La Mer to scope it out.

Excitement bubbled through me when I stared at it, then the bottle of pills I had demoted to the dresser from my bedside table earlier in the week and replaced with a tiny vase of fresh flowers from Natalia's garden.

"Sounds like fun."

"It's recon," I say.

"Even better."

Tonight, I dress for the occasion. A cropped white top. A skirt that shows off my legs. The platform wedges Harrison got me. I try my hair a few different ways before twisting it up into buns on my head.

I look like a warrior, and maybe I am one.

It doesn't feel as if Harrison and I are on opposite sides since he went on the trip to clean up his clubs in person.

Tonight, we both want the same thing.

La Mer.

"Come on, Rae," Ash hollers from the other side of my door.

"Bossy, considering I invited you," I call back.

Harrison had frowned over his coffee when I informed him I'd called his brother, but he'll get over it.

If I'm being honest, it feels safer to have Ash there.

The door opens without my permission, and Ash surveys me.

"Jesus," the younger King says before I can protest.

I plant a hand on my hip. "Good Jesus or bad Jesus?"

"There's one Jesus," Ash says solemnly. "And he's always good."

I laugh as I follow him downstairs. "Wait. Where's your brother?"

"He said he'd meet us there. And it's a good thing because if he walked in on you looking like this, I'd be going to La Mer alone."

I glance down at my outfit. It's more skin than I'd normally show but nothing compared to some of the outfits that grace Ibiza's clubs every night, including Debajo.

"It's just me, Ash."

"You don't understand. When Harry sees something he wants, it's game over. He's trying to stay away, but the fact that he can't have you is killing him."

As thrilling as it feels to be the object of Harrison's interest, we can't pursue it. Giving in to him feels like giving in to something bigger. A man like that casts a long shadow, and it's only beginning to feel as if I'm getting myself back after the hellish year I've had.

I won't risk losing myself in him.

Even for a night I've found myself fantasizing about more than once.

"Do you think he'll ever trust someone again?" I hear myself ask. "After Eva, I mean."

"I hope so."

Toro drives us to the club, checking on us from the front with eyes crinkling at the corners. When we pull up, the door opens from the outside, and a hand extends to take mine.

I shift out of the car and look up.

My heart stops.

Harrison King is breathtaking in chino shorts and a midnight-blue linen shirt, and I press my lips together as he surveys me.

"You dressed down," I say.

"A necessary evil to be inconspicuous. You, on the other hand, barely dressed at all."

"I thought you'd like it."

"You wore this for me?" His eyes warm with hunger.

"That's a big leap from 'I thought you'd like it'."

"It's a logical inference. And I do like it. Very much."

His attention pins me in place for a heartbeat, two, before the passing crowd makes me notice the doors of the club are around the corner.

"I asked Toro to drop you beyond where we might be spotted," Harrison supplies, refocusing on our surroundings.

"And I told the guys from the club I'd meet them inside," Ash adds.

"Why do you want this club so badly?" I ask Harrison as I take careful steps along the sidewalk, sneaking another look at him. I've seen him in a tux, a suit, and almost naked. The casual clothes might be my favorite.

"La Mer would be the crown jewel in my collection."

I groan. "What is it with you Brits and your crown jewels?"

He ignores me. "Mischa wants it. I want to take it away from him."

"All because of what happened with your parents?"

"Yes."

"No," Ash says at the same time, glancing over his shoulder. "Don't pretend it didn't start sooner." His gaze drops to Harrison's chest so fast I almost miss it.

"Mischa has a reputation," Harrison says. "People who disagree with him get silenced."

"So, you're the good guy."

He frowns. "Let's say it's good you called me out on my club's security and not Mischa's, or we wouldn't be here talking."

The idea of a person more fucked up than Harrison, someone who'd stop at nothing to get what he wants, is enough to make me shiver.

We approach the end of the huge line, and I reach for my wallet. "I have Christian's card."

Harrison tucks it back in my bag, tugging me by the elbow toward a back door. "We're not letting Christian know we're here."

At the door, Harrison shakes hands with a security guy who lets us inside. Ash leading the way, Harrison at my side with his hand on my back, we head through a dark tunnel, only the music at the other end guiding us.

"So did you fuck your hand to my new song after Debajo last night?" I ask conversationally.

His arm flexes around my waist. "Did you lie awake all night thinking about it?"

I catch a toe on the ground and nearly trip.

The idea of Harrison King thinking of me while he unfastens his dress pants and shoves down the zipper is insanely sexy. His heavy breathing, roughened with pleasure and anticipation as he stroked the hard length of his cock. The flex of his muscles, the way he'd seek out his own brutal pulls as he cursed me.

I wonder how it would feel to wrap my hand around him and watch his eyes narrow to slits. To reduce him to curses, then no words at all.

Too soon, we're in the open-air club, and the impossible tension slips a few notches.

I'm awestruck by my surroundings. It's an ode to the stars. A spectacular amphitheater built for revellers.

The crowd is young and beautiful and ready for the release this place promises.

"If you buy it, you'll need the best DJs," I comment, breathless.

"I'm not concerned. It's not only the crowd that lines up for this place."

"I've wanted to play here forever," I admit, soaking it all in. "To hear my songs, to feel them through the ground, like they're moving the earth." I cut him a teasing look. "If you buy it, you'll let me play, right?"

"La Mer is the biggest stage in the world." His brows lift, and I feel my smile fade.

Hurt slices at me, cutting deeper than I thought this man could cut me.

"And you don't think I'm good enough."

He was by my side as I breathed new life into his club, and despite his sparse praise, it felt as if he was cheering me on. That we were in this journey together.

Harrison shakes his head as if I'm being unreasonable. "I didn't say that."

"Yeah, you did." I twist away from his grip and slip into the throng of people.

Watching the booth, envy settles into my gut like a throbbing mass. The man spinning tonight is Maxx, a DJ I met at Coachella. He has a reputation for being a dick to new talent, especially women.

The thing is he's not alone. Of Billboard's top one hundred DJs in the world, only a handful are women. None of the top ten.

I want to make that list, not only because that list determines who gets booked and who makes bank.

Women have always been involved in music, but when it comes to recognition and compensation, it's still a man's world.

I try to forget the hurt and dance with Ash and his friends while Harrison's off doing whatever he has planned.

A guy from Ash's crew brushes up behind me. He's fit and attractive, but when he moves closer, reaching out to draw me against him, I pull back. "I can't."

He shrugs and returns to dancing.

I'm in the middle of the biggest club in the world, crushed because a rich, entitled man I have no reason to care for doesn't believe in me.

It's not possible to hate someone and like them at the same time.

Is it?

The next time the song transitions, everything changes.

The first chords are familiar.

I feel them in my body before I hear them.

I spin and latch onto Ash, who's dancing with a few other guys, by the front of his shirt.

"Was this you?" I demand, but Ash shakes his head.

I stumble back, searching for Harrison. Pushing through the crowd, I scan the sea of faces and bodies. It's an impossible throng, but I wade through anyway, tripping over my shoes until strong arms grab me at the edge of the dance floor.

I look up to find Harrison King looming over me, cool and breathtakingly beautiful.

"It's my song," I shout, my heart thudding against my ribs.

I squeeze my eyes closed, imagining me playing this song from the stage.

As much as I've grown to care about Debajo, mixing at La Mer would make my career. Hearing my song in the place cements the possibility that it can happen.

That it *will*.

When I blink my eyes open again, he's closer than before. He smells like man and the ocean.

His hands find my waist when I threaten to tip over from the giddiness.

I straighten with his help, his face inches from mine.

Those eyes are hot, his mouth parted.

I'm at the world's biggest party, and all I see is Harrison, filling my vision.

"This was you," I accuse. My fingertips dig into his corded biceps, the tense muscles holding me up.

"You fucking—"

He shuts me up with his mouth.

His lips claim mine, rough and impatient and a little bit desperate.

He's warm and hard, delicious and sharp. His heat and scent wrap around me.

It's less like kissing than an attack, but an unplanned one by a skilled fighter.

The feel of him has me tingling, every nerve ending alive and throbbing. His hard body is pressed to mine, his heart hammering faster than the beat surrounding us—the one I made myself.

The hardness grinding against my stomach would steal my breath if his kiss hadn't already.

The music pulses around us, the crowd throbbing.

I'm throbbing.

What he says about power is true—I feel his, and it's pure temptation even before his touch strokes up my thighs, his hand gripping my ass to fit me against him.

My spinning head can't tell if it's seconds or minutes later when he pulls back an inch, eyes dark as the sky.

"You're welcome," he whispers against my mouth.

CHAPTER 14
Harrison

I'll never admit it to anyone, but sometimes I'm a fucking idiot.

Still, I'm never a fucking idiot two days in a row.

I rise early and punish my body with a hard workout before showering and selecting a suit. It's nearly ten when I meet Toro at the front of the villa for the drive to Christian's house.

"Pleasant evening?" he asks, meeting my gaze in the mirror.

"Interesting."

Getting Rae's song played last night at La Mer wasn't planned.

I believe in her, but I'm practical too. The business part of my brain reminded me La Mer has its pick of the world's top DJs regardless of who owns it.

And she will be one of the best.

The possibility that she needed to hear that had never occurred to me because she's so damn independent.

I'm supposed to want to put things right in my business, and my life. It matters more than anything. Except...

All I could think about last night was proving myself to Rae.

So, I grabbed her and did what I've been thinking about for fucking weeks.

Kissing her on the dance floor wasn't planned, but when I saw her cutting through the crowd, searching me out, a beast unfurled inside me. One that wanted to protect her. To make sure nothing ever hurt her the way I had.

My reward was the single hottest kiss of my life.

She's infiltrated my life, and I have no one to blame but myself. I brought her here, was hellbent on punishing her and reclaiming what she'd cost me.

Instead, she's turned me inside out.

She's a siren with a sound system and the power to move everyone she can reach. And even though she hasn't spilled her problems at my feet, I see her pain as plainly as if she had.

The woman lives out of a single suitcase, has a love-hate relationship with the bottle of pills she hasn't touched since I replaced them, and creates extraordinary music.

But I have to keep the part of me that's obsessed with Raegan Madani in check this morning because we're back to business and Brioni.

"Well, if you have more interesting evenings planned, I hope you will celebrate her birthday," Toro says.

"Her birthday?" I echo.

"This weekend."

I bite my tongue before saying what comes to mind. What the fuck do you get the woman you can't get out of your head when you have no business thinking about her?

We're not dating. At worst, she's my hostage. At best, my employee.

Except neither of those labels feels adequate to describe what's happening between us.

I want her in my bed. But more than that, I want to do something for her, something she can't do for herself.

When we pull up to the villa, I shift out of the car and fasten my jacket, thanking Toro before I take the steps two at a time.

My intention is to conclude this deal today. Of course, the signing will come later, but Christian is a man of his word. He won't reverse once we shake on it.

The door is opened by a young woman with light-brown hair and a familiar bone structure. "Mr. King. Please come in." Her light French accent matches Christian's.

She shows me to a study where the man in question is watching a baseball game.

"Americans. I will never understand them and their sports," he muses.

"But you want to enough to watch a twelve-hour-old Yankees game."

"Don't tell me the winner." He grins. "Perhaps I will need a house there when I retire."

He could buy a dozen. More, if he wanted.

He adds, "My daughter has taken a liking to you."

I glance toward the now-closed doors, remembering the woman who let me in. "That's very flattering."

Christian makes an espresso from the machine in the corner and holds it out. I take the coffee as he makes another.

"As uncivilized as it is, let's be direct," I say. "My interest in the club remains unchanged."

"I'm sure it does." He smirks.

"Your club is unquestionably one of the best. But it is not without weaknesses." I rhyme off a list of things I observed last night, things he must know about.

His smile evaporates, leaving a deep frown.

"All of these things would lower its market value. But I'm prepared to pay full price."

"How gracious of you." His tone drips frost. "Just because you have an idea of what the club needs to be does not mean others share it. You bring it under your empire, it will become a commodity like the others."

"I will not commoditize your venue, Christian. It's a cathedral."

I think of Rae's comments about me being unreasonable and try a new approach. "You knew my parents. You trusted one another, even worked together on a few deals. I'm my father's son, and you can trust me to take care of your legacy."

Christian nods toward two armchairs framing a window, and we each claim one. "On the last point, I agree."

My hands tighten on the overstuffed chair. "So, you'll sell me La Mer."

He takes a sip of his drink—the slowest fucking sip I've ever seen. "Why don't you show my daughter the city first? After, we can talk."

A dawning sense of horror starts at my toes, creeps up my spine, and finishes on a long inhale. *He wants me to take his daughter out?*

"…finishing her third year of university," he's saying. "Sylvie hasn't spent time here since she was a child."

She still is one.

There are two reasons a woman would want me, and only one of which her father would approve of—my money.

I'm not looking to saddle myself with a charge—even if it means landing the property I've coveted for as long as I can remember.

My refusal has nothing to do with the face of another woman occupying altogether too much space in my brain. One who's also too young for me but who elicits an entirely different reaction at the thought of being saddled with her.

I choose my next words carefully. "I'm a terrible tour guide. And I'm quite sure I have nothing else to offer your daughter."

"Are you seeing someone?"

"Perhaps the woman you brought to my party?" Christian presses. "She was charming."

I gesture toward the television. "An American on holiday."

"Ahh. She'll go back to her world, and you'll be in yours."

The truth in his words makes me want to break the espresso cup.

She's back with a vengeance. The way she looks playing the booth at my club. How she flips both fingers in the air.

How I want her not to sheathe her claws but bare them, to rake them over every inch of me.

I hate the idea of her leaving. Once I arrange the purchase of La Mer, I'll finish the season in Ibiza and return to... what exactly? Shuttling between properties in London and Tokyo? Eating expensive meals with socialites and models, doing deals on airplanes?

Even if I wanted to get closer to Rae, her contract is almost up. She'll be gone with the money she so shrewdly bargained for, and I'll have a resurrected club in the form of Debajo.

It seems a fair trade.

But it doesn't feel like it.

"Harrison, I would like to finalize this deal as much as you would. I'm an old man with many things occupying my time until I can divest myself of them. However, I can't focus on them when the most important one is beyond those doors." He gestures toward the hallway, his eyes crinkling. "I'm asking you, as a friend, to take my daughter around town. She hasn't told me she wants this, but I sense it in her. She would not ask for it. And alas, she does not want to be shown by her father."

I set the espresso on the table, untouched.

"As long as you and she understand this is nothing more."

He lifts his hands. "I would not presume to meddle in matters of the heart. I am more interested in matters of finance." Christian drains the last of his coffee before rising, indicating we're done. "And soon, I will no longer be interested in those either."

"Does Toro know you're waxing his car?"

Rae's voice from a few feet behind me later that afternoon makes me straighten from the fender of the Rolls-Royce.

"You wouldn't dare," I say, tossing the rag over my shoulder and wiping an arm across my brow as I turn. "He'll have my head."

In the middle of my driveway, she's a mirage. Her black shorts are trendy, her white top with wide straps that leave her shoulders bare clings to every curve, and her hair is down around her shoulders.

She could pass for a local, and she's stunning.

Rae sidles closer, folding her arms and squinting into the sun to meet my gaze. "He told me he was the first staff you hired back after your parents died once you could afford to."

"A man needs a driver and a housekeeper."

"Did you have a house to keep?"

"A rental at first," I concede, returning to my task.

"I didn't know you owned a T-shirt."

"Only this one." If I'd known a T-shirt would have this effect on her, maybe I would wear them more often. "When I need to clear my head, I try to do something… simple."

I'm still bothered by my meeting with Christian and not comfortable with where we landed. Part of my discomfort has to do with the woman next to me.

Rae surveys the car and me. "Well, your head doesn't seem clear, and the car's shinier than the day it came out of the factory."

I arch a brow. "Meaning?"

"Meaning let's go."

Twenty minutes later, we're at the docks in town, walking amongst the tourists and those who've docked their yachts.

She told me to wear the T-shirt and shorts, but I changed into a short-sleeved button-down.

I might be grumpy, but I'm not a heathen.

Rae frowns at the yachts. "These boats are ridiculous."

Her surprise makes me grin. "It's Ibiza. The owners come here to play and to show off."

I nod toward the nearest vessel. "The *Ariadne*. She's here every summer."

"What about that one? *Dolce Vita*."

"Usually not until later in the year."

My phone buzzes, and I frown, holding it away to read the screen.

"You do need glasses," Rae murmurs, and I scoff.

"A sign of weakness."

"A sign you're smart enough to know you can't fucking see." Her plain tone makes me press my lips together. "And I think they'd look good on you."

I pocket the phone, conflicted. A single word of praise from this woman turns me into a damn teenager.

"You've never been on one?" I nod at the yachts. "They have all manner of toys. Saunas, pool, theaters, private chefs."

"Because there's nothing like a meal from your private chef on a boat like that." Her voice is dry, but there's a hint of curiosity under the surface, as if she wants to know for sure.

"There's nothing like fucking on a boat like that. Conquering the ocean, feeling as if nature herself can't help but tremble along with the person beneath you."

She turns toward me, and the expression on her face has my body heating in arousal as I think of the kiss last night.

Unplanned.

Disturbingly provocative.

Like her.

"You will play that club someday, Raegan."

She didn't need my belief in her last night, but she wanted it. I've told myself the past few weeks have been about repairing my business, that she was a tool to build Debajo back up to its prior profitability.

The fact that I've immensely enjoyed watching her do it is natural. It is my club, after all.

But perhaps it's more than that.

Perhaps it's about *her.*

My words have the opposite effect than the one I intend, making her frown rather than smile.

A group of tourists shoves past us, and I reach out and tug her to my side.

Her curves fit to my body, the ripeness of her breasts, the soft give between her thighs.

We could be any couple on vacation taking a break from devouring one another to enjoy the sights.

Her lips part as she feels how her closeness affects me.

"Ash said something to me—"

"Fuck my brother." I thread my fingers in the hair at the base of her neck, caressing her skin. "It's not my brother you get off to. It's not Ash you lay in bed thinking of."

Rae's eyes darken. "Sex doesn't solve problems, Harrison. It creates them."

"Then you haven't had the right partner," I contend.

But when the group has passed, she pulls away.

"You don't have to like me to want me," I say as I fall into step next to her, pretending the rejection doesn't sting.

"I don't sleep with rich, entitled assholes."

I shove both hands in my pockets, hard, and squint into the sun. "Then you'll have to continue to get yourself off."

"Or I'll have to decide you're a good man."

Surprise has me jerking my head to look at her.

"You can be," she goes on. "I've seen it. When you stop being so consumed with conquering the world and you take a moment to appreciate what's in it."

She sweeps her hair off her shoulders, revealing a faint sheen of sweat glistening on her neck.

My next step falters. I'm glad we're not still touching, because she'd feel my heart kick beneath my ribs.

Because I want her body.

But Christ, I might want her approval even more.

CHAPTER 15
Rae

"Well, well. What is all this?" Ash calls from the front door.

I jump up from where I'm working on a track on the couch, headphones around my ears.

Ash already has the case open on the dining table, lifting one of the two dozen items inside.

He fumbles it, nearly dropping it on the floor. "Ah, bollocks."

"I thought you were an athlete. What happened to hand-eye coordination?"

"Footballer. Foot-eye coordination. This a new part of your costume?" he asks as I trail a finger over the pairs of glasses.

"They're not for me."

"Ahh." His eyes soften, and I hate how transparent I feel. "You know, the moment you flipped him off at Debajo the first night, I told him if he wasn't going to make a move, I would."

"But you haven't," I point out, pushing the attention back onto him. "It's never been like that with us, even at the start."

He frowns at the lenses in his hands, but I press.

"What is your type, Ash?"

Before he can answer, the door opens and Harrison walks in.

The room gets smaller the instant he steps inside, and it's not because of his size or the tailored suit clinging to every inch of his hard body. It's the way his attention finds me in a heartbeat.

"It's not Ash you lay in bed thinking of while you make yourself come."

The only thing hotter than imagining his filthy mouth on me while I touch myself, the tight-woven sheets smooth on my damp back, is imagining him down the hall *knowing* I'm imagining it.

It's making it harder to remember I'm here to work for him for less than two more weeks.

Three shows, to be exact.

"Hi," he says.

"Hi."

There's a beat of awkward silence before he continues.

"I spoke to Leni about moving your last show. You'll still play Thursday and next Monday, but instead of closing Thursday next week, you'll finish Saturday. I trust that's acceptable to you."

Surprise works through me. He's offering to have me finish on the biggest night of the week. More exposure, and per our deal, more money. I should be irritated he didn't ask me, but there's another aspect of this proposal I'm focused on.

"You want me to stay here two more nights?"

He cocks his head, parsing my response. "Echo will cover any fees to change your travel plans. But you deserve to close on a weekend."

I feel myself nod.

"Well?" Ash slides a pair of glasses onto his nose and turns to face his brother.

Harrison's attention slides to his brother. "You look like a banker."

"Fortunately, I don't need glasses. You do." Ash pulls them off and tosses them at Harrison.

"See? Hand-eye coordination," I mutter as he catches them.

Ash snorts as he heads for the kitchen.

Harrison crosses to me and scans the table. He looks taken aback, as if the designer case sprouted legs and began scuttling over the floor.

"A mix of designers," I say, pressing my fingers together behind my back as self-consciousness kicks in. "I figured you were a 'don't fuck with the classics' kind of guy. Since you won't see an optometrist, they sent options. You can keep the ones you want, send the rest back."

With a moment's hesitation, he slides a pair up his nose and lifts a brow at me.

I'm thoroughly unprepared for how hot he is. Like a barely tamed beast of a man.

"Um, yeah. Those ones."

"I thought he's supposed to be able to read with them," Ash comments helpfully from the kitchen.

I grab my phone and pull up my social media feed, handing it over so Harrison can test the strength of the glasses.

"These seem very effective." But he's no longer looking at the phone as he backs me into the table with slow, deliberate steps.

I'm aware of him and the fact that his brother is a dozen steps away.

"You failed to disclose something important about this weekend," he says softly. I wait for a beat, then two. "It's your birthday."

Dammit. I press both hands to my eyes. "Who do I have to kill?"

"Toro."

"It had to be the old guy with kids." I curse and blink my eyes open as he smirks.

"Don't make plans."

To buy myself an inch of breathing room, I shift up so I'm sitting on the table.

"I'll have to prepare for my final two shows. Especially since one is next Saturday. Besides, I thought you were spending every second convincing Christian to sell you La Mer."

His gaze flickers. "I decided to leave him time to sleep, and eat, and fuck his wife."

"How charitable," I tease.

I realize my mistake immediately as he steps between my knees, forcing my legs apart.

"A man needs a release, Raegan. It's not healthy to work all day without satisfaction at night."

There are mere inches between us, and my heart is racing.

Keeping my voice level is an impossible task. "I don't celebrate my birthday." I lift the glasses from his face, folding them and tucking them into the breast pocket of his jacket. "It's cursed."

He snorts. "How do you figure?"

"It's a long story. And you should be warned… everyone has a birthday. I might get you back on yours."

Blue eyes darken to a flinty gray. "You'd have to stick around."

Surprise has me straightening even as footsteps from upstairs interrupt. Natalia.

Harrison leans across me to close the case of glasses, near enough his scent invades my senses.

"Two extra days is one thing, but I can't imagine staying longer," I murmur, though suddenly I'm wondering what it would be like. "For one, there's the small issue of you hating me."

"I never hated you. I wanted you to fix the damage your words caused."

"You wanted to punish me," I challenge. "I got up in your business and dared to ask questions, and you didn't like it."

His gaze roams my face, then lower. Harrison moves my hair behind my shoulder before wrapping it around his hand like a rope. He tugs on it, forcing my head back, and leans in, his mouth grazing my ear. "I still want to punish you."

His hips press closer, near enough that I feel his hard length between my thighs.

With one jerk of his hands, he could have me on my back.

I want him to.

But when his phone goes off, he shifts away. I resist the urge to wipe my forehead and see if it's damp as the rest of me.

"Don't bother arguing about the birthday," he says when he pockets the device again. "You'll need to pack a couple of bags for our outing."

"I only have one. What kinds of activities are we doing?"

He turns for the door.

"Drinking? Walking? Swimming?" I demand.

"Yes."

I exhale, irritated by the lack of specificity. "Are there sharks?"

He turns back, his heated gaze sweeping my body. "Count on it."

I think about those words.

As I try to work on my set for the night, then as I meet up with Leni to talk through new ideas for next weekend.

We hit a high of more than sixteen hundred people, and the bar staff makes me do shots until I trip out of the VIP room high-fiving everyone along the way.

The next day, I head down to a café I like, wearing my wig and sunglasses to meet the interviewer I agreed to see from social media.

The costume helps me feel protected, like this is part of my onstage persona and not edging into my personal life. It reminds me I'm still Little Queen here, not Rae Madani.

"How did you get into producing? You're notoriously tight-lipped about that," she asks when we're seated at a table.

"Just caught the bug as a teenager. Helped when I got a computer and a synth."

"Did your parents buy them for you?"

I flex my hands under the table. "My first one, yeah."

She laughs. "Guess that gave you something to channel your angst. What do they think of your career now?"

Tension climbs up my spine, settles into my shoulders. "We don't talk about it a lot."

"You're one of the only women playing the White Isle this summer. You've stood up for women's rights even when it cost you."

This is why I hate live interviews. It's impossible to filter out these kinds of things. "It's important to speak up for the people who can't protect themselves."

Despite the fact that she's recording, she makes a note. I force myself not to lean over the table to see what she's writing.

"Harrison King is lying low thanks to you," she comments, and the right turn has me straightening. "Have you heard from him?"

It's not common knowledge that Harrison owns Debajo. He doesn't advertise the fact, and she clearly hasn't put it together. I'm not going to do it for her.

"I'd rather focus on the future."

I manage to steer the conversation away from me and toward my music.

As she rises to head to the door, I ask, "When are you expecting to finalize the article?"

"Soon. I'm pulling in more sources, and I'll come by Debajo to take some photos."

"Sure thing. I'm actually closing next Saturday."

There's a wave of nerves as I watch her leave. Playing a show is high stakes, but you get immediate feedback. With the media, you never know what they'll come up with until it's served up to the public on a platter.

I shake myself before dropping back into my seat to review some logistics for the upcoming shows.

Press is good. It'll help Debajo, and my career.

My phone rings immediately after.

"Greetings, cousin. You're unreal," Callie declares.

"Um. Thanks?"

"Truly. With the money you sent, I've been able to cover payroll for another two weeks."

"More will come after the last show," I promise.

"I'll pay you back every cent. I swear."

"You don't need to."

I can almost hear her roll her eyes.

"How's your mysterious, infuriating hottie?"

I turn it over. "Still hot. Still infuriating."

"So, why do you sound as if you've softened?"

"He's planning something for my birthday."

I haven't been able to get details out of Harrison about the birthday outing, though God knows I've been trying.

We've been in tense, flirtatious limbo for the past few days.

I spent extra time on my appearance before my set, hoping he'd be there. He was, and even though he was taking meetings, he spared me a hungry look from upstairs and texted me a song request.

Then we crossed paths when he came downstairs in shorts last night while on the phone. I was grabbing a snack.

"Who're you talking to?" I mouthed.

"China," he mouthed back.

I threw a napkin at him, which he dodged.

Yesterday, he texted me a picture of Barney with a toy in his mouth.

Harrison: ??

The toy was a crocheted doll a little longer than my hand, with blond yarn hair and a stitched-on frown. It wore a dark-blue costume with a tie.

Thanks to Barney, one of its arms was ripped off.

**Rae: Natalia got me some craft supplies the
week you were gone.**

**Harrison: And you were trying to send me a
message?**

I laughed out loud.

"He sounds romantic." Callie's voice brings me back.

"I guess so," I admit.

Harrison's not the kind of guy looking for an excuse to do
something sweet.

If anything, he's the opposite. Determined, single-minded.

The fact that he found out it was my birthday and is making
something special from it despite my protests has my stomach
flipping like a girl with a crush.

I'm not doodling "Mrs. Harrison King" in my notebook or
anything. I've never pictured myself as the other half of any guy,
and he may not even go there again given what happened with his
ex.

But the little flutter in my chest feels entirely foreign.

After we finish talking, I respond to some emails and social
messages before heading for the door of the café.

The sight through the glass makes me still.

Harrison's strolling down the street as if I conjured him with
my mind, looking like elegant sin.

When did I become the girl who has fantasies about a guy in
a suit?

But he's not alone. The woman next to him is pretty, with big sunglasses and pale skin under a wide-brimmed hat. She smiles at him as he talks animatedly, gesturing with his hands.

My stomach knots, twisting into a heavy mass.

We're not dating. I'm not looking for a partner, someone to settle down and create one life with, to argue with and compromise with and lie awake at night next to.

No matter what Callie says, I need to keep my feelings for this man in check.

Starting with whatever he has planned for my birthday.

CHAPTER 16
Rae

"**I** feel like a mole," I say.

Blackness surrounds me, but the sun warms the bare skin of my face and shoulders.

"The spy sort? As in *Mission Impossible*?" Ash calls from somewhere ahead.

"No, the underground animal sort. As in I can't see shit."

The wind tugs at my hair, but the cloth around my eyes holds it firm as I walk. It doesn't help that the firm hand on my back is warm and distractingly low.

"Being blindfolded is not my thing," I mutter.

"Then you've never been blindfolded by the right person." Harrison's mouth at my ear sends shivers down my spine.

I'd glare if I could see him. Lucky for him, I can't. "I got up early on my birthday—"

"Eleven," Ash corrects cheerily, sounding farther away.

"To be kidnapped and forced to trek through God knows where." All my attention goes to my other senses—the scent of the sea and the sound of shorebirds. The next step I take, the surface changes, giving and creaking beneath my feet.

"I could carry you," Harrison suggests.

"I'd rather be thrown into the ocean."

"Don't tempt me."

Then the blindfold is gone and light floods my eyes, leaving me blinking in the brightness.

Blocking part of the sun is a huge white boat.

I'm riveted by the monstrosity tethered at the dock.

"You got me a yacht?" My voice rises an octave as I turn to take in Harrison, who's watching intently.

"It's a charter."

"It's a behemoth. A leviathan. This thing blocks out the sun."

Yet it's not the boat but the faces appearing over the edge that take my shock to the next level.

"Hey, birthday girl!" Annie calls. My roommate from performing arts school waves. A big, straw hat protects her pale complexion.

Her husband, Tyler, is next to her, a possessive arm around her shoulders.

Elle, another friend from school, who's now a comedian, holds a bottle of champagne over her head. "Get your ass up here before I drink this all myself."

Ash heads for the boarding ramp, but I turn to stare up at the man by my side.

He's wearing chinos and a dress shirt, his hair ruffling in the barely-there breeze as if even nature can't resist the chance to touch him.

His handsome face is drawn, eyes shielded from the sun with a hand.

I've been to some of the biggest parties in the world, but

here, at a private dock with a handful of friends and this man, I'm overwhelmed.

"This is… obscene," I say, struggling to form words.

"You haven't even seen the inside."

I make to grab my bag from him, but he holds it over the water. "You already lost it once," he warns.

"Don't even think about it." I wrench his arm back toward the dock while he smirks.

Even out here, there's an undeniable pull between us.

He sets the bag on the dock and steps closer as if he's thinking the same thing. But when he reaches up to touch my face, I duck away.

"What is it?" he demands.

"Nothing."

He frowns, unconvinced.

I have a dangerous fascination with a billionaire who buys and sells properties like secondhand synths on Craigslist, and I can't shake the memory of seeing him with another woman as if they were friendly.

More than.

He's around beautiful women all the time for work, but not usually alone, and not looking as relaxed as he did strolling through the streets.

It's not as if I have a right to him. I can't blame him for spending time with another woman.

But what does throw me is how it felt.

Like the fluttering in my stomach was quashed with a baseball bat.

I turn away from his scrutiny, and as soon as I step onto the deck, Annie wraps me in both arms and squeezes hard.

I shove any other thoughts from my mind as I pull back to stare at her stomach.

"You're huge." I glare accusingly at Tyler, who only lifts a shoulder.

It makes sense the rock star gets along with Harrison. They have the same serious, distant vibe.

Annie, by contrast, is warm and genuine as she leans in. "You want a play-by-play on how the pregnancy thing went down?"

"Not as long as you guys are good. Hey, E, thanks for coming. You guys know Harry. Harrison," I amend, flicking him a look as he responds only with a raised eyebrow. "This is his brother, Ash."

They exchange greetings.

"Welcome aboard." The captain introduces himself with a smile, gesturing to two waitstaff. "We're here to provide for your every need. We'll be heading to Formentera shortly, which is only a short trip away. I expect you'll want to take a look around. But first, would you like something to drink?"

"Yes to the drinks," Elle decides. "Aren't we short a person?"

Annie holds up her phone. "Beck called. He's running late."

Ash checks his watch in irritation. "We'll miss our chance to go snorkelling. You don't want to spend your birthday at the docks, do you?"

"Let's wait for him and take a look around," I decide.

The sundeck has sun loungers at one end, plus its own dip pool. There's a huge dining area with a table set for six that could easily seat double. We head belowdecks next, and it's even more insane.

"There's a sauna and steam room. Plus, a screening room," Harrison says.

He shows us the theater, and Elle sucks in a breath in admiration.

"Six cabins. Choose whichever you like." He gestures to the doors along a small hallway. "Except the master suite."

My friends chatter about the space, but Harrison's loaded stare locks with mine.

Does he think we'll room together? Is he planning to seduce me this weekend with the boat and the big gesture?

As conflicted as I am by what I saw yesterday, the idea of him and me, nothing between us but a giant bed to muffle our sounds, makes my body ache.

I'm empty in a way I wish was only physical.

He's older. Experienced. He's probably had a ton of sexual partners, and it shouldn't matter if he has.

But there's nothing casual about the way I feel. I want him, but not if I'm wondering whether he's comparing me to someone else he's sleeping with… or planning to once I leave.

"There're two jet skis, plus a small fishing boat. A million other toys also," Ash is saying as we finally head back upstairs.

"How big is this?" Annie asks as the staff bring our drinks.

"Forty-five meters," Harrison says.

"Ridiculous."

"It's just big enough," comes a voice from behind me.

I turn to see a handsome man step onto the sundeck. His dark hair is swept up by the breeze, his eyes shielded by designer glasses. The only other thing he's wearing is swim trunks, his shirt hanging from the back, revealing a torso and arms even more toned than the last time I saw him.

"Beck." The grin that tugs across my face is genuine.

"Good thing you got the big boat. My ego has grown." He crosses to me and sweeps me up.

"Impossible." I wheeze around his thick forearms digging into my ribs.

Beck finally sets me down. "Happy birthday, Little Queen. You look good."

"You look like a Hollywood douche." My gaze drops to his toned stomach. "Shit. Did you buy an ab roller?"

Beck chuckles, nodding to the waitstaff for a drink. "Yeah right. I have a trainer who makes more an hour than I used to pay in rent."

I catch Harrison staring.

"Why are we mov—oh!" I suck in a breath as the engines kick in and the yacht pulls away from its mooring.

Beck hands me a towel, and I lay it on one of the lounger-style seats facing my friends. Harrison takes my bag toward the doorway that goes belowdecks.

"Where are you going?" I call.

"Taking your bag to your cabin. Given how protective you are of it, I wouldn't leave it to the staff."

I trot over to him. "I need to get something," I murmur, bending to unzip my bag.

He waits while I open it and riffle through for sunscreen.

A scrap of black lace falls out onto the deck, and he picks up the panties with one finger. "Care to explain?"

My heart stops. I grab the panties out of his hand and stuff them back into the bag. "They're called underwear."

"Lace," he corrects.

"A woman can wear lingerie for herself."

"But you don't. You wear T-shirts and cotton knickers."

My jaw drops, and he cocks his head.

"No, I think this means you've decided you respect me. Or you did, before today."

I shield my eyes, staring up into his gorgeous face.

I want his hard mouth on mine, those strong hands touching me. But if we do that, I want to know I'm what *he* wants.

Even it's only for a night.

"You can't buy me with a boat," I murmur.

"Wasn't trying to." Harrison leans closer, smooth and determined.

He stops when our lips are an inch apart, not meeting. I suck in a breath that's salt air and him.

"I know you're young," he says. "I'm giving you space because it's your birthday. But whatever shit thoughts have been going through your head? I promise they don't change what's between you and me."

The next second, he's belowdecks, my bag in hand, and I stare after him until my friends call my name.

CHAPTER 17
Harrison

When the yacht docks at Formentera, I'm still in the master cabin taking steadying breaths and willing my gut to unknot.

This day hasn't gone the way I planned. Rae was supposed to see the yacht and her friends and fall at my feet.

I've never met a woman who wasn't swayed by a gift either expensive or heartfelt. This one was fucking both. Yet before getting on this ship, she looked at me as if she would rather spend this weekend with anyone else.

Even though the chemistry between us scorches hot enough to burn through the shiny white hull of this boat.

The vibration of my phone on the bed next to me does nothing to calm my restlessness.

"What?" I bark into the speaker.

"How's your weekend away?" Leni asks.

I inhale, straightening to stare in the mirror across from the bed. "Not as advertised."

"Christian wants to invite you for a private dinner. Apparently, he lost your cell number, so he called me at the club."

The time I spent with Christian's daughter yesterday, playing attentive host to her flirtations, only reinforced that I'm not interested in a pretty young face. Once, I would've entertained such a flirtation. A few dates, some lingering looks, and she would've been telling her father to give me the club for free.

Now, I have no appetite to play the game. It feels not only tired and pointless but wrong. Since when did I start caring about people I barely know?

"He told me to tell you he's inviting Mischa too."

Leni's words cut through the haze in my brain.

No. I'm not playing games, but the old man is.

"There's something else," she presses. "The LA club you went to visit? There was a hiccup early this morning. An incident."

The face looking back at me in the mirror grows still. "What kind of incident?"

"A woman claims she was assaulted."

I switch to speakerphone so I can pull up my email. There are dozens of messages, which is to be expected, but there's nothing from my LA club.

"Where was security?" I snap.

"Not by another client. By a staff member."

Christ.

The room is too small. I yank open the door and take the stairs to the top and step into the bright daylight. I feel in my pocket for my sunglasses and find only the reading glasses Rae got me.

I stare at them a moment before setting them carefully on a nearby table. "I was just in LA last week dealing with this. We cleaned house. Agreed on new policies."

"With the number of clubs you have, there are bound to be problems. But this is shitty timing. She hasn't spoken to the media yet. But there's a possible lawsuit and obviously the PR issue if this gets out."

My mind races. "Is the woman hurt?"

"She's fine. But it would really help all of your venues to have the good press right now."

"What are you suggesting?"

"You're spending a lot of time with the same DJ who accused you this spring. If she went on the record saying she's seen what you're doing and supports you, that could go a long way."

The sounds of laughter from below us draw me to the railing around the anchored boat. I squint into the shadows to see Rae, Ash, and the others playing in the water twenty feet away. Her black bathing suit shows off every curve of her body. Curves I could be touching, or at least experiencing up close, if I wasn't up here.

Rae had something on her mind this morning when we arrived. I wish I could get her alone and force the truth out of her.

I drag my attention back to the call and grip the phone tighter. "She's already playing my club."

"And no one has made the link publicly. Yet."

"It's not happening, Leni."

"Because you have feelings for her?"

I exhale heavily.

"DJs would kill to play a club in Ibiza for a month," she points out. "You've given her an opportunity—one she can use to not only get back to where she was but take her career to the next level. If she has feelings for you too, maybe you could help each other."

"Is this guy for real?" Ash demands from the row ahead of us in the theater room, nodding toward Beck.

Tyler and Annie are huddled together at the front. Elle's in the second row, along with my brother and Beck. We're here to watch Beck's screening copy of the pilot for his new reality show.

I waited for Rae to head into the back row, then I gave her zero outs as I shifted in after her.

From the moment we started watching, half my attention was on the antics of the guy on screen and the rest was on the woman beside me.

"How was Formentera?" I ask under my breath.

"Fun. But you missed it."

I extend my legs in front of us. "Business came up."

I feel her turn toward me. "Why do all this if you weren't going to participate?"

"Because you deserve it."

She turns that over. Her black shorts and sleeveless top leave her long, curvy limbs on display. Her hair, swept up in two piles on top of her head, makes my fingers itch.

"No one deserves to rent a forty-five-meter boat," she decides.

My lips twitch. "*Charter.*"

I think about Leni's suggestion that we could use Rae to get good press. To show the world Echo Entertainment is moving in the right direction. A month ago, she wouldn't have considered it. But now...

"Look!" Beck calls, leaning over the front row of seats.

"Remember the releases you signed for this clip from your wedding party in LA? We used the footage."

Annie and Rae are in the background, and as the video captures Beck's speech, Rae stiffens next to me.

"What is it?" I ask, instantly on alert.

"At the party, I had bruises on my wrists. A fan got past security the night I played your club and grabbed me."

Every muscle in my body goes tight, anger simmering up from somewhere deep and dark.

"You told me another woman was hurt," I grind out. "You didn't tell me *you* were hurt."

She returns to watching the screen, but I can't.

Annie laughs in the front row, and Tyler ducks his head to kiss her, making her laugh more.

"I can't promise to have every woman's back," I hear myself say. "But I will do my utmost to ensure that never happens in my clubs again. And I will damned well have yours."

Rae stiffens for a moment, then relaxes.

I rest my thumb and forefinger at the back of her neck, pressing lightly through the rest of the show.

CHAPTER 18

Rae

Dinner is chef-prepared and exquisite, and I wish I could enjoy it fully.

From the head of the table, barefoot in chinos and a white shirt, Harrison watches me with a protectiveness that's unsettling. But somewhere between the cool evening breeze, the laughter on the air, and his grin when he brings out the cake, I can't hate it.

Beck insists on feeding me cake, and I don't realize until I'm laughing through a delicious bite that Harrison has gone still.

Annie groans, bracing an arm on the railing as we sit on the lounging deck after dessert. "That was better than sex."

"I came at least twice just from the cake." Elle rubs her stomach.

"Where's the testosterone?" Ash appears from belowdecks, his hair blowing in the night breeze.

"Drinking at the other end of the boat."

Ash's smile vanishes as he cranes his neck that way. "Hollywood too?"

I shift forward. "You don't like Beck."

"The guy made us watch his home movie," he gripes.

"Come on. It was a screener of his TV show. That's a little different."

Ash waves it off. "He's the self-indulgent type who does anything for attention. Trust me, I've met lots of them over the years at private school and in sports."

"Well, you're missing out," Annie says. "They're drinking a new line of bourbon I brought from my dad's company."

"Jax Jamieson's personal collection?" Ash rubs a hand over his jaw. Annie's dad is an even bigger rock star than her husband, though he's semi-retired from the stage to raise two kids with Annie's stepmom in Dallas while working on his own label. "Fuck, I can't pass that up."

Ash walks in the direction of the other guys, and a moment later, the deck is quiet.

"Just us girls," Annie murmurs.

I cut her a look. "Time to paint each other's toenails?"

"Let's play 'Never Have I Ever,'" Elle decides as the waitstaff comes to top up our champagne.

"Annie's not drinking."

"That means I'll win." Annie winks.

Elle starts. "Never have I ever... fucked a musician."

Annie and I both drink.

"Careful of all those bubbles," Elle drawls, and Annie kicks her.

"Really? Not even at Vanier?" Annie asks when she's done.

Our blond friend cackles. "Just because you go to arts school doesn't mean you need to make the rounds of majors. Rae, who was yours?"

"Evan," I recall. "In second year."

"How was it?" Annie leans in.

"He was a yeller. Like, projecting-from-the-diaphragm loud. You'd think the man had conquered a large fishing village instead of my vagina."

The other two crack up.

"Okay, my turn," Annie decides.

"Hey"—I lift my glass—"it's *my* birthday."

"So shut your mouth and enjoy it."

"I am enjoying it," I admit, looking down the boat to where the guys are barely visible at the other end, as decent as they are handsome. We spent the afternoon on the beach, had an incredible dinner and dessert. I'm so happy it hurts. "I can't believe you came all this way to see me."

"Yeah, the scenery's crap," Elle supplies, and Annie slaps her arm.

"Mostly we love you," Annie says.

"Your billionaire boy toy made it easy. The plane tickets were delivered to my door," Elle adds.

"Yes. About that." Annie straightens. "Tyler and I were a little surprised to get an invitation from Harrison for your birthday. You want to catch us up?"

I turn the glass in my hands, wondering whether its contents or Elle's words are responsible for the sudden tingling in my stomach. "We started out as enemies. Now I don't know what we are. I think he's genuinely trying to improve his clubs, in LA and everywhere else. He had a pretty rough breakup last year, and his ex was part of the reason he lost focus."

"They weren't right for each other?" Annie asks, curious.

"That, plus he doesn't trust easily. He's not the kind of guy to put a relationship ahead of everything else he is."

Elle says, "He's doing a hell of a good impression of caring about you."

Her pointed words have that hopeful tingling starting up in my chest again.

Or maybe it's the alcohol. I catch the eye of one of the attendants who tops me up without so much as a word.

Annie takes advantage of my distraction to continue the game. "Never have I ever… slept with someone ten years older."

Elle drinks.

I freeze with my drink halfway to my lips, then lower it again.

"Seriously?" Elle screeches, loud enough to wake whatever bones have settled at the bottom of the ocean beneath us. "He's smart, he's rich, he's the kind of gorgeous that only gets better with age… though I read men reach their sexual peak in their twenties."

She looks to Annie for corroboration, and our friend lifts her hands, surrendering.

"If Tyler gets any better, I might not survive."

I roll my eyes as Elle laughs and says, "Wait. How old is Harrison?"

They both pull out their phones before I can answer.

"He's thirty-five," Elle declares loudly.

"Thirty-five what?" a familiar British voice demands from behind me.

I swallow, shifting on my lounger to stare up at the man in shorts and a linen shirt, the top two buttons open.

"Nothing." It's the most innocent voice I can manage, and it's terrible.

"How old you are," Elle, the traitor, supplies. "Have you read that men's sexual performance declines after their twenties?"

We're joined by Tyler, who sinks onto Annie's lounger and pulls her against him. Beck drops onto Elle's, while Ash's athletic gait carries him to the edge of the boat, where he leans against the railing.

"Patently false," Harrison replies. "Men in their twenties have physical stamina but no subtlety. Women are intellectual creatures. You need mental stamina to please one."

God, his mouth is beautiful. I want to trace it with my finger.

Then shove it between my thighs.

I take another sip of my drink, and the pleasant buzzing feeling intensifies.

We keep drinking and talking. Tyler shares stories from his tour while Beck presses Ash on his workout routine. Annie talks about pregnancy surprises and their plans to settle in LA once the baby arrives. Even Elle weighs in with cringe-worthy moments from a comedy competition she just finished.

It's fun, until eventually everyone heads to bed.

"I think I'm drunk," I mumble as strong arms carry me down the stairs.

"Indeed," the person carrying me agrees, the word vibrating through his body and mine.

I scrunch up my nose. "What language are you even speaking?"

"That would be English."

"That wood bee ingleesh," I parrot.

I'm deposited on a soft surface, and I sigh as I force my eyes open.

Harrison's over me, his shirt unbuttoned enough I can see the edge of his scars. His hair is sticking up, his expression amused and more relaxed than I've ever seen it.

I'm so enchanted that it takes a moment for me to notice Harrison pull away.

I grab for his arms. "Where are you going?"

"To bed. You're drunk."

I scramble forward onto my knees, a posture I'm sure looks as sexy as it feels. "And if I wasn't? What happened to the big, bad billionaire? The legendary ladies' man?"

He studies me for a moment before his lips brush across my cheek. "Happy birthday."

Anger rises up, along with panic. Maybe I sabotaged this night on purpose, let myself be confused by the big gesture. But I want him. I want this. Tonight.

I shift up onto my knees, grabbing his bare forearms before he can leave.

"No," I protest, knowing in my bleary brain that I'll regret this. "Don't pretend you didn't rent me a boat—"

"Charter."

"—to fuck me on it. There's no other possible reason a man like you would do this for a woman like me."

It's quiet here. No soft lapping of the ocean against the boat. No hum of equipment.

Harrison's gaze lowers to my shoulder, where my bra strap is exposed. "I won't pretend to know what you think a man like me does. But as for a woman like you? There are no women like you. At least as far as I've seen. You arrive at a place with an exit strategy. You look out for people you don't even know, and you demand that others do the same even though God forbid someone look out for you in return. You put yourself on the line every night on that stage, but when you look in the mirror, you don't recognize the girl looking back. It should be too painful to watch, but I can't look away. You are an exquisite train wreck. So, if there's a way a man like me is supposed to treat a woman like you, forgive me. I've never met a woman like you."

Before I can react, the door shuts in my face.

I stare at the ceiling and try to sleep for an hour before stumbling to the bathroom to throw up, brush my teeth, and drink a gallon of water.

Then I stare at the ceiling some more.

We're so damn different. He's older, experienced, at the height of his career while mine is still growing. He's comfortable in his skin while I'm learning how to wear mine. He's a billionaire with a vendetta and enough baggage to sink this yacht, and me…

I have baggage too.

Despite it all, I want him.

The alcohol burns off before my insomnia, so I pull out my computer and headphones and grab a light blanket, carrying all three up the stairs as quietly as I can.

Above deck, night hangs like an indigo blanket. Distant sounds from shore and the soft swish of waves are the only interruption to the silence. In one of the loungers, I open my computer and put on my headphones, opening Ableton Live.

I'm a few minutes into working on a track when movement by the stairs has me stiffening.

An intruder.

Yachts don't have intruders.

Unless there are pirates?

But I recognize the way this pirate moves.

He grips the railing, grimacing.

"Are you sick?" I demand, sitting straight up. "How much did you drink?"

Harrison spins, looking caught out. "Not enough."

I'm barely buzzed now, and my brain is functioning far better since I rid myself of most of the alcohol earlier. "You're seasick. So, why are we on a yacht?"

"Because you wanted it! And I wanted to give it to you."

Oh.

Oh, no.

This larger-than-life, rich, untouchable prick. He wasn't supposed to get me a birthday yacht. Or the cake I like. Or host my friends. Still, he did it all knowing full well he couldn't relax and enjoy himself. That makes my stomach flip in a way that has nothing to do with the slight swaying of the boat.

He braces himself on the railing, a warrior guarding his wound.

But the vulnerability was one he endured on purpose. For me.

I don't know how to respond to that.

But I try.

"My parents split up on my birthday. That's why I hate it." *Part of it, anyway.*

"How old were you?"

"Sixteen." The muscles in my chest and stomach knot. "But high school was pretty shit even before that."

I lean over the railing a few paces down from him.

"You want to tell me about it?"

The lights of the harbor are visible from where we're anchored. Ibiza looks like a fairy island.

But I only half see it, remembering how many birthdays passed without the friendship and love I felt on this one. How many other days, too.

I shake my head. "Today was good. I don't want to mess with it."

He's silent a long time. "I'm not trying to diminish what you experienced. But if you ever think you're damaged, or broken, or less of yourself because of what happened in those years… you're not."

The backs of my eyes burn.

I don't talk about my life with men. Not my life before or now. Hell, I don't talk about it with my friends.

Letting him in makes the distance between us feel smaller. I shouldn't want that, but sometimes I think I'm drifting.

A boat without an anchor.

"You asked me why things were weird between us earlier," I start. "I saw you in the city with a woman yesterday."

He shifts off the railing, crossing to me. "You were jealous."

"It threw me," I correct when he stops close enough that when I breathe in, I can't tell him from the ocean.

His eyes dance, his hair lifting in the breeze as his tight lips curve. "You were jealous."

I exhale an exasperated breath. How is he amused by this?

"Stop—"

"You were jealous. Say it."

"Why? So you can tell me I can't have you? Trust me, I've already told myself enough times."

His eyes flare with heat before he banks it again. "She's Christian's daughter. He asked me to take her around town as a favor."

He lets that sink in before continuing.

"The only woman on my mind is a brat who plays in my club. Lives in my house. Is altogether too distracting."

His confession cuts my protests off at the knees.

My gaze drags down to his shirt hanging open to reveal his firm pecs and abs.

I trace the shape of the scars on his chest with a finger, brushing his shirt back so I can.

"Tell me what happened?"

It's a request, not a command. And when I meet his gaze, I have the feeling he'd tell me anything I wanted.

"Mischa."

My stomach twists, and it's not from the alcohol. "He did this to you? You told me it was at boarding school."

Everyone's teenage years are fucked up.

He nods. "There's a tradition when you win head boy, you get marked by the boy who lost to you. It's a sign of mutual respect. Teachers don't condone it, but they tolerate it. There was only one time in our school's history it got bad and a kid almost bled out."

My eyes widen.

He says, "Usually it's a letter. A few shallow scores with a pocketknife."

"Yours is a crown."

"Thirteen cuts. Prick fancied himself an artist. Took four days for him to complete it," he says, grimacing.

"You didn't complain?"

"No. Nearly passed out once, but I didn't say a fucking word."

"You've hated him since you were a boy."

"He's hated me," Harrison corrects. "Since my parents left

his parents' business. They told Mischa to convince me to work for them, to be groomed for the same position my parents held. I turned him down in no uncertain terms. They weren't happy with him, and he's hated me since. It's why he was so intent on taking Eva from me. Now, I want to finish him. Put it behind us once and for all. La Mer is the nail in the coffin."

The world of buying and selling businesses like they're moves on a chessboard feels so far beyond me. But at the same time, it's not.

Because what they're chasing isn't the money.

It's the feeling.

The feeling of being right. Justified.

Of laying your head on the pillow at night and being satisfied you did the best you could.

"She's missing out," I murmur.

He laughs. "Trust me, if Eva wants a yacht, he'll get her one."

"Wasn't talking about the yacht."

I press my hand over his heart.

His lashes tremble as his gaze searches mine in the dark.

I can't deny how I feel anymore. It's not only attraction. I care about him, whether I have any business caring or not.

I want to distract him from his sadness, the effects of the sea beneath us. "Come on. Let me show you what I'm working on for my final show."

He shifts onto the lounger and sits behind me. I move between his legs and tug the blanket over both of us. His hard thighs wrap around me, making it impossible to focus entirely on my computer.

"I've had this melody I can't get out of my head." I shift a few clips around, frowning. "There's an easy kick for now—I'll figure out the rest of the drum structure later—but I'm working on the frequency. I want to drop the frequency down on this part"—I point at the screen—"probably eighty hertz, close to sub. You don't really hear it anymore, but you feel it."

After making the adjustment, I hit a keystroke to play the phrase again.

Harry tugs me back against him. "How do you know what to change?"

"Experience. Intuition. Fucking it up enough times." I tilt my head up to grin at him, and the expression on his face hits me square in the chest.

His scent is like the ocean surrounding us—mysterious, undeniable, overwhelming.

"Sounds like running a business." His voice is full of humor as he strokes my arm lightly.

"I can change frequencies to change the feel of something too."

When I lift my arm, his touch lands on my side.

I suck in a breath. It's more intimate now.

Instead of hesitating, he strokes down farther.

"Every amateur with a computer thinks he can make music," I quip, but when his fingers slip down my stomach, I have to swallow my groan.

His breath is warm on my temple. "I could."

"Oh really? You're a prodigy?" It's a joke, but when the loop starts again on my computer, his fingers move with it.

I bite my lip as I try to focus, but his touch is lighting fires between my thighs. He nudges the waistband of my shorts, revealing the edge of dark lace beneath.

His exhale is hunger and satisfaction at once as he strokes a finger where my panties meet my skin.

"Did I mention I like these?" The low pitch of his voice is pure seduction.

"You might've hinted at it."

My heart thuds harder, all from the slow touch of his fingers. From knowing he's looking at the lace I put on. Knowing I put it on for him.

"I've watched you give in when you play, but I never see you give in anywhere else. I want to see it." Harrison's chest vibrates under me. "I want to feel it."

His touch slips lower, where I'm already wet.

I arch up off the lounger, but his other arm bands around me to hold me to his chest, the impressive hardness probing my lower back.

I'm a knot of pure need, every part of me reduced to the spot where his fingers touch me. The connection feeds the part of me starved for attention, affection.

"Oh my God," I mumble.

It's the most exquisite feeling. He knows what he's doing to me. It's deliberate and every bit as sexy as his shallow hiss of breath at my ear.

I want to turn over and look in those cool, blue eyes, see if they're shattered with heat. I want to kiss him, to press every inch of me against him, to feel as if we're coming together and I'm not at a disadvantage anymore. But I'm trapped between his hands and body, and when I move an inch, the computer slips.

I grab for it.

This was supposed to be a demonstration.

I try to refocus on what I was saying, but his finger moves

lower, sliding through my wetness, and I inhale sharply.

"I've never understood why a producer invests so much time getting the parameters just right," he murmurs. "Humans can handle limited sensory input. Like right now, you can feel my breath on the side of your face. But when I do this…" Harrison adds the heel of his hand to the mix, rubbing against my swollen clit. It's dissonant and raw and euphoric at once.

"You lose track of everything except where I'm touching you." His rasp in my ear makes me clench, aching to have him fill me.

It's not the kind of safe pleasure I give myself. It's strange and overpowering.

My nails dig into his thigh, and when he slips a finger lower still, teasing my entrance, I shiver.

"Tell me how it feels."

"Big," I confess.

I meant the feelings, not his finger, though that is too, but he chuckles softly.

"Beautiful girl. If this is big, you have no idea what you're in for."

The insistent outline pressing me from behind is a reminder he's right.

"You'll have to pace yourself. You're not in your twenties anymore," I chide, reminding him of the conversation earlier.

His groan is full of promise. "You're fucking right I'm not. The things I'll show you."

My blood heats more, and even the ocean breeze isn't enough to cool my damp forehead. "You think you can teach me about sex?"

"No. I think I can teach you about yourself."

He adds another finger to the first, pressing so deep my mouth falls open, my thighs squeezing and my heels scrambling for leverage beneath the blanket on the chaise.

But before I can respond, a light goes on farther down the boat.

And it's moving toward us.

My throat closes.

"Someone's coming." I grab Harrison's arm in warning.

"Yes. You."

The one thing crazier than letting Harrison King finger-fuck me on his rented yacht is having someone catch us.

The crew member pauses a dozen feet away. "Mr. King. Ms. Madani. Would you like anything to eat or drink before we retire?"

I shift, trying to straighten both of us, but my companion doesn't budge. Including the parts of him inside me. I feel every inch of his fingers as he holds me in place like a butterfly pinned to cloth.

"We're fine." Harrison's even reply suggests he does this all the time.

His front presses against my back. I can feel the impossibly thick outline of his erection, his heart thudding through our clothes and skin.

She smiles. "All right. Have a wonderful evening."

His mouth is at my ear the second she departs, his voice heated. "You think men like me rent forty-five-meter yachts to not fuck on them?"

I reach back with one hand to grab his hair. "*Charter.*"

His exhale is half laugh and half groan as his thumb drags a slow circle over my clit and he works my entrance with both fingers.

Oh my God.

I've seen Harrison playful before, and it's fascinating. But now, he's playing with *me*. My body is a game, and only he knows the rules. He's teaching them to me one skilled move at a time.

It feels way too damn good.

The orgasm sneaks up on me, a wave I'm thoroughly unprepared for. My toes squeeze under the blanket as I clench around him, my back arching. He growls his satisfaction against my cheek, his other hand cupping my breast, his thumb absently rubbing my nipple. I gasp as he draws out my pleasure almost painfully.

Each wave grips me in turn.

I'm so consumed with sensation I don't notice the computer slide off my lap.

"Motherfucker!" I jerk upright at the sickening sound of it hitting the deck. Horror slices through the bliss as I tumble off the lounger onto my knees to retrieve it before looking at him with accusing eyes. "This better not be broken." At least it's backed up.

Harrison's voice is languid. "I'll buy you a new one."

"You can't fix my problems with money, King."

"Watch me, Queen."

The expression on his handsome face makes my heart skip. Lust, satisfaction, and an emotion more than both. He's cocky, but beneath the surface is a genuine will to please me, a simple gratitude for this moment.

"That was... unexpected."

His slow grin is wicked in the dark. "Really? Because I've been picturing nothing else for weeks."

Harrison takes the computer from me and sets it gently on the end of the lounger. "Time for your real gift."

I turn to stare at him. "You're shitting me."

He rises and disappears belowdecks, returning a minute later with a box a little smaller than my computer, wrapped in velvet and a gold ribbon.

"Open it."

He draws me between his thighs again and tucks the blanket in around us as I tug at the ribbon until it gives way. The velvet wrapping is a bag, and I unfold it and slide out the box inside.

He waits patiently while I open it.

In the low lighting, the black Sennheiser logo is just visible against the impossibly shiny silver of the headphones, but it's the sparkling letters across the earpieces that grab my attention.

"I called the CEO and had him make them for you," Harrison says under his breath.

"Little Queen," I murmur, tracing the word on each side with a fingertip. Each letter is spelled out in a dozen tiny gems. "In crystals?"

"No."

Harrison's abs clench under me, and I lift my gaze to his, disbelieving.

"Tell me you didn't get me diamond headphones."

His eyes aren't cold tonight. They're warm like the sea, teeming with life and possibility.

"You're the real thing. Don't fucking forget it."

My chest aches.

I'm on a yacht celebrating with friends who flew halfway around the world to be with me, and it's all thanks to a billionaire I should hate. Except he's not the man he lets the public believe he is, and he just gave me the most incredible headphones and the most incredible orgasm.

But it's his words that affect me more than anything we've done.

"Did you make a wish on your birthday candle?" he prompts when I'm silent.

I hook the headphones around my neck because I can't stand to put them down. "I haven't believed in that since I was a kid."

He pulls my back to his front, and I relax into him, lifting my chin to stare at the stars overhead.

"Then it's time to start again," he decides, tucking a piece of hair behind my ear.

Maybe he's right.

Before I fall asleep, I send up a wish.

CHAPTER 19
Harrison

"**Y**ou were a difficult man to contact this weekend," Christian says from the end of the dinner table.

"I spent a few days on a yacht."

There are hints a man is mortal if you know where to look.

Tonight, the *sirvia* is overcooked.

When I bite into the fish, I know there's a crack in Christian Geroux's facade.

This weekend, I felt the cracks in myself with Rae. Spending time with her and her friends, I found myself caring less about my need to conquer and claim every property Mischa has so much as glanced at and more about her.

"I didn't realize you were a seaman." Mischa, opposite me, digs into his fish as if it's still alive and he wishes it was.

Like me, he's in a suit, his a gray so dark it's nearly black. His pocket square is red. A signature. I heard a tailor once tried to influence his style. The man died of a heart attack the next week.

"He hates being on the water," my ex weighs in from next to Mischa.

It's the world's most fucked-up dinner. Mischa, my ex, Christian, his wife, and their youngest daughter Sylvie.

We're here to talk business, ostensibly to finalize plans for La Mer. But Christian's not ready to divest or divulge anything until after dinner and drinks.

"So, what made you do it?" Christian muses. "I thought Harrison King did only what he wished."

I reach for my *vino blanco*, but someone else answers first.

"A woman."

We turn toward Sylvie.

"It's the only reason other than business that a man does what he does not want to do," she goes on. "Even business is in service of his ultimate pleasure."

Perhaps she's not as naïve as I figured.

"Pursuing a woman is in service of a man's ultimate pleasure too." Mischa grins at my ex, who allows it, but she cuts a look at me the moment he drops her eyes.

I couldn't care less about them tonight. For the past two days, I've let myself live in an alternate world. Seasickness aside, it was enthralling. Spending time with Rae's group—most of them successful, all of them hardworking and earnest.

Rae was at the heart of it all.

Those dark eyes loaded with willfulness. Her soft curves making my hands burn to touch her.

That night on the deck, her jealousy over Sylvie was laughable.

It also made me hard as steel.

When Rae settled between my thighs, I couldn't help myself.

My hands trailed down between her legs, needing to know if she felt the scorching intensity I did.

The damp heaven I found there was the sweetest fucking temptation. The way she let me touch her, then rubbed against me for more.

It's not only the promise of sex that captures me. It's the way she challenges me. I can show her things, but she's no wallflower. Every time I push her, she shoves back harder.

Most women want what I can give them—the trappings of my world.

Rae doesn't want them.

I can't buy her affection. Instead, I'm toiling for every inch of trust she parcels out in a muttered admission or an allowed touch.

I don't know who hurt her in her life before she took my stage.

When I find out, I will bury them.

My parents were good people who provided everything for me and Ash. I'll never be a saint, but thanks to their influence, I look after my own. A small group that expanded to include Rae while I wasn't looking.

Her final show is coming up, and I'm not ready for it.

I don't want her to go.

"At the risk of sounding patriarchal," Christian says, his voice dragging me back, "the men will now talk business in the library."

Our plates are cleared, my ex murmuring her appreciation. "The sirvia was excellent."

Fucking liar.

Mischa and I follow Christian to the library, where we take seats.

Christian doesn't waste time with more small talk. "La Mer is the jewel in my collection. Forty years ago, I would have dreamed about having two businessmen such as yourselves vying for it. Alas, men become greedy, and I am but a man. So, with two such suitors, I must weigh the relative offers."

He shifts back in his leather chair. Despite the words, he enjoys holding court.

"There are day-to-day concerns with a club of this size. For instance, millions in revenues. I have a request of you both first. Consider it a practical test."

I shift forward.

"We lost a performer due to unforeseen circumstances and must find someone suitable to put in his place. The long weekend."

"The big producers have been booked for months. Years." But my mind is already scanning through possibilities. Between Leni and me, we could probably call in a favor.

"I'll find the perfect act." Mischa's teeth are bared in my direction, but not in a grin. He'd like to hurt me right now, but we're not boys in school anymore. Even if he wanted to make this physical, he wouldn't dare. It's an unspoken rule that we fight our war with money and strategy, not with blades or blood.

Christian strokes his chin. "I would like to speak to each of you in turn about your vision for my venue. Mischa first. Harrison," he goes on before I can argue, "allow my daughter to refresh your drink while you wait."

I rise, fastening my jacket with one hand. Each stride toward the door is tight with frustration.

Sylvie greets me in the hallway with a tentative smile. "I'll get you a drink from the kitchen."

I follow her there and help by retrieving the bottle she wants from a shelf. The moment I set it on the counter, her mouth is on mine.

She's innocent and determined, and I hold her arms gently as I push her away. "I can't."

Her expression caves. "You don't find me attractive."

"It's not that. There's someone else."

The light in her eyes dies.

I pour a drink and hand it to her. "Perhaps you could use this more than me."

She accepts it with a tiny nod.

I was going to pump her for information, but the sadness on her face makes me reconsider.

When did I go soft? I wonder as she heads toward the patio.

"Lovers' quarrel?" A familiar voice interrupts my thoughts. "What a shame. You'd be perfect together."

I turn to see my ex hovering in the hall.

Her blue cocktail dress compliments curves I once memorized. Now, Eva is a piece of art that doesn't resonate—the objective quality is irrefutable, yet she leaves me cold and unmoved.

"I'd run right over her."

"Precisely. You need a woman who lets you be the man you are."

"Like you did?" I'm surprised to hear there's no bitterness in my voice.

She frowns. "A woman who wants all of you will never have you. You are on this earth with a purpose, and you will die to fulfill it. You would never die for me."

I smirk. "Who would've bought you jewelry if I had?"

"A woman who demands more from you... you'd wear one

another down."

I turn that over. "Perhaps that's the point. Sanding one another's roughest edges doesn't make you weaker—it makes you better."

The door of the study cracks down the hall, and I turn my back on Eva's stunned expression.

"Mr. King?" Christian beckons, and I trade places with a smug-looking Mischa.

I ignore the seat my host offers, instead resting an elbow on the back of the armchair. "I have a DJ for La Mer. She's young, but she's talented. Capable. Charismatic."

I tell him about Rae's success filling the club while he listens thoughtfully.

"You are quite taken with her."

"I'm confident she'll be an asset to the stage." I pause, unable to read him. "You want to hear my vision for the club? Here it is—"

"Marry Sylvie and the club is yours."

I'm stunned silent. Of the things I expected he'd ask in exchange for his club, this isn't one of them.

Christian continues. "Not immediately, of course. Court her. Take what time you need. What time you both need. I worked hard on my business and my family. This club is like another of my children. I want to see it in the right hands."

Sylvie's attempts at seduction in the kitchen were sweet, if wholly misguided. But the man before me is serious.

I don't point out the archaic nature of what he's proposing—his child for his club. Clearly whatever her father said to her made her think I would be an attractive partner. And she's not alone in that.

Women take a look at me and decide who and what I am,

whether it's money, an attractive package, a ticket to the right social circles.

I never had a problem with it.

I spent months engaged to a woman more caustic than Sylvie could ever be, one with ambitions that clashed with mine, though she hid them well. Christian's daughter would be more loyal, and amenable.

But it's none of those thoughts that has my body clenching in denial.

It's the thought of another woman entirely.

One who sees what I am on the surface and insists I could be more.

One who wants me *in spite of* my money and power.

One I may never be with… but ruling that out entirely feels like a rip in my soul.

"I can't be with your daughter, Christian," I say at last. "She's lovely and intelligent, and she'll find someone well suited to her." *Without your help*, I don't add. "But that man isn't me."

He sighs. "That is indeed a disappointment. I was looking forward to the idea our empires might one day become one."

He's withdrawing. I feel it.

This can't be over. I won't lose La Mer this way.

Adrenaline pours through my veins.

"My parents were married in Ibiza," I hear myself say. "A small ceremony."

"I remember."

"After, they danced on the beach in the place La Mer now stands. When it opened, they thought it the ideal place—not a club, but an altar. A slice of heaven where the sea meets the sky."

Christian chuckles. "One you wish to possess."

"One Mischa doesn't deserve to." There's an edge of desperation to my voice. "He's playing to your vanity."

"And you to my morality? Surely there are better men for that."

I circle the chair, shift onto the edge, and look the man dead in the eyes. "My father was your colleague. Your friend. You were business partners occasionally. Friends always."

His gaze sharpens. "Friendship is easy to portray. A smile here. A handshake there. I'm sure there are moments you and Mischa could be mistaken for friends, in a polite room."

The hairs on my neck rise. Was there bad blood between him and my father? If so, that's news to me.

I regroup, vowing to get to the bottom of that later.

"Think about my recommendation. I stand behind her unreservedly."

He rubs his chin, eyes altogether too knowing. "If you are certain she's available, I will consider it."

I nod. "I'll make sure of it."

Despite the unresolved nature of the La Mer deal, conviction surges through me.

Now, I have a reason to ask her to stay.

On my way out of the study, I nearly run into Mischa, who's waiting in the hallway.

I don't know how much he heard, but as I start down the hall, his dead eyes leave holes in my back.

CHAPTER 20

Rae

"**I**mpossible." Leni drops onto a stool at the VIP room bar, putting a shot of tequila in front of me.

"What is?"

"We broke sixteen hundred on Monday," she reminds me. "Tonight, we're at eighteen hundred and you haven't even taken the stage yet. There's a line around the hotel."

We clink glasses and toss them back.

"At least I can go out on a high note," I say after I swallow, the alcohol burning down my throat. "Thank you for this."

I'm a few minutes from my final performance at Debajo, and it's bittersweet.

In a month, this place has become familiar in a way I never asked for. The leather seats of the VIP stools creak predictably. I know the names of all the security guards and most of the bartenders. Even Leni and I have become more acquainted through working on concepts for my nights here.

"You know that having you close on a Saturday was Harrison's idea," Leni says. Under my stare, she finally rolls her eyes. "Fine, I didn't argue much. You're going to be big. It's clear to anyone who watches you. You're not so Little, Little Queen."

She nods to my outfit, a fitted, sleeveless gold dress with a raven black wig, plus eyeliner that makes my eyes look even darker than usual. It's a subtle channeling of another queen.

"It wasn't a snake bite," Leni says. "Cleopatra, I mean. The artists tell whatever stories they want," she waves a hand in the air, "but she poisoned herself. A tragic end."

"A realistic one," I correct. "The most powerful people spend their lives fighting external battles. It's the internal ones that get them."

Leni clunks the empty glass back on the bar. "You should stick around for the rest of the summer. We could find a couple nights a week for you here."

Surprise sets me back. "I have some other gigs lined up in July and August, but nothing for a few weeks. I guess I'd have to talk with Harrison. I haven't seen much of him in the last couple of days."

He said he's been working on persuading Christian to sell him La Mer.

"Since your birthday." She rises with a wink, nodding toward the headphones around my neck.

I've barely taken them off because they're precious in a way that has nothing to do with the diamonds I can't begin to value.

But as she goes, I stare after her, wondering exactly how much Harrison told her.

I know he and Leni go back, that she's the right hand of his business, but what happened on that yacht is personal. At least it was for me.

The birthday party was spectacular, but the part that left the biggest impression was the time I spent with him on the top deck that night.

I'm supposed to leave in two more days, and maybe that's the last moment we're meant to have together.

If it was, I should be grateful. When I arrived here and learned who I'd be playing for, I thought there was no way I'd make it through the month.

Now, I've turned around this club that deserves to be full, earned enough money to help my cousin keep the doors of her charity open, and met a man who makes me question everything.

That's why I don't want to think my birthday was our last night together. I'm not ready to let him go.

I shove it from my mind and put the finishing touches on my set.

When I get to the stage, I'm home. The crowd erupts, delight on the faces of hundreds of men and women.

The music is in me, around me, consuming me.

The countless hours I put in were worth it.

Tonight, in this club that's as close to mine as anything ever was, pieces of that persona fall away.

I love this club.

The patrons love me.

It's not enough.

When I look up toward the VIP section, Harrison's leaning over the railing.

My heart kicks in my chest at the fact that he's here.

I wanted to believe he wouldn't miss this but couldn't be sure.

He's alone tonight, dressed in another impeccable suit. The bespoke armor clings to every inch of his hard body. Those shadowed eyes bore into mine as if he knows me.

I want to be known.

"Eighteen hundred!" I holler, my voice lost in the pulsing beat and driving bass and throbbing melody of the club.

There's no way he can hear me, but he lifts a glass in my direction.

I never thought it would feel so damn good to have this moment and, more than that, to share it with someone.

When I flip both middle fingers in the air, his smirk fades.

He's too far away to read what's in his eyes, but he holds my gaze.

What passes between us is more than reciprocity. Connection, understanding, a tacit agreement that we built this together.

I want to celebrate with him. To tell him how fucking good it feels.

"You think you can teach me about sex?"

"No. I think I can teach you about yourself."

Each song bleeds into the next, and I bleed with them. When the set wraps, I don't know if it's been an hour or a year.

I'm energized and exhausted, sweaty and exhilarated.

I need to take selfies with fans, but as I trip out of the booth, someone beats me there.

The man looms over me in a designer suit, a shock of red silk in his breast pocket resembling a wound. "You are a rare talent."

He's all muscle, his head buzzed, his eyes cold. As if there's nothing behind them but emptiness.

I look over his shoulder at my waiting fans that security is holding at bay.

"I'm a friend of the owner," he says, answering my unasked

question of how he got back here.

"Which friend?" I don't want to cause a scene, but I also don't want this prick in my face.

"I'm sure you don't know all Harrison King's friends."

"Try me."

His grip tightens on my wrist, and I twist away. He grabs my other wrist too, and I bite down on a cry of pain.

"I've been asking myself a question all day. Why would he give this up for you?"

He must be talking about Harrison, but I have no idea what he means.

My breathing is off the rhythm of the afterparty song, but all I feel is my ribs expanding and contracting against the gold dress I chose at a boutique yesterday with Ash's help.

He pins me in the curtains backstage, his cloying cologne drowning me.

Sweat rolls down my neck, my body already straining to run. I reach for the only weapon I have—the defiance I've clung to for weeks, months.

"If you have a thing for Harrison," I manage, "you're out of luck. I don't think you're his type."

Fireworks explode behind my eye socket, impossible heat blossoming across my cheek. The physical impact stuns me.

On the other side of the stage, security is dealing with the crowd and giving me a minute to get ready.

I wish they weren't.

"You think I don't know what to do with bitches?" my attacker spits.

This isn't happening.

Do something.

No one answers my silent plea.

The man hulks closer, his body looming large and threatening.

Do something!

This time, I'm screaming at myself.

When he comes at me, I dig my fingernails into his neck. He bellows, his hand flying to the wounds.

They're not deep enough to keep him occupied long, and he's about to land another blow when there's motion at the curtains.

The next second, my attacker is gone.

Harrison drags the man out of the curtains, tossing him against the front row of the crowd. The patrons stare as the owner of the club pulls back a fist and looses it on the man before him.

The man lurches, listing as if he's been drinking before straightening with a cruel grin. "Is that it?"

It's his opponent's turn to land a punch, leaving a streak of blood across Harrison's cheek. My heart hammers until I realize it's the other man's. From where he was covering his neck.

Harrison barely stumbles before straightening. Even without the tic in his jaw, the heavy breathing, the icy fire in Harrison's eyes would be terrifying.

He grabs the other man by the collar, dragging him close to whisper something I can't make out. Then Harrison hits him again, hard enough the man topples.

Harrison shakes out his hand, his grim expression cast in the semidarkness of the club.

"Get him the fuck out of here, or you'll never work again," he bites out to security.

Across the crowd, Leni runs interference, trying to get things back to normal despite the fight that broke out.

My back hits a speaker, and I shift up onto it, my hands curling into my stomach. The sight of blood under my fingernails makes my stomach lurch.

I didn't feel the full effects of fear when everything was happening so fast, but now I do.

I haven't felt that fear in a decade, but it's fresh. A forgotten record pulled out of a box and set beneath a needle to play as fully and crisply as the day it was inscribed.

There's a bucket of waters in ice next to the speaker, and I force myself to reach for one as my cheek throbs.

Before I can press it to my face, the curtains move.

My head snaps up.

Harrison's usual elegance is rumpled. His shirt has lost two buttons, his jacket hanging haphazardly from his shoulders as if it refuses to let go. His hair is sticking up as he rubs a hand across his jaw, each knuckle dark with blood.

He closes the distance between us, stopping when my shins brush the tailored fabric of his dress pants. He inspects my face, lingering on my cheekbone that feels as if it might explode.

He's a king tonight, and for the first time, I see its weight on his face, his bones.

"You're hurt." The words are forceful, but strained. His eyes narrow on the unopened water bottle in my hands. "Where did he touch you?"

When I don't answer, his hands go to work searching for damage.

I stiffen as his touch roams my bare arms first, then my torso, finding a rip in my dress I hadn't noticed.

He shrugs out of his jacket and loops it around my shoulders, warming me before I realize I was shivering.

Then he presses between my thighs, lifts my skirt.

My mouth falls open as he runs his hands up my thighs. It's confident, competent, not meant to arouse but to assess.

"Stop," I whisper.

The backs of my eyes burn. Outside, I'm as frozen as the moment the man came at me. Not in fear, but in shock.

"Harrison, don't touch me." I want to scream the words but when they come out, they're barely audible.

It takes everything in me to grab his face and force his attention up even as his hands linger under my skirt.

His jaw clenches as he leans his forehead against mine. "I need to know you're all right."

I'm not.

I don't say it, but I might as well have.

The shaking starts somewhere in my chest and radiating out to reach my fingers, my toes, my lips.

Without warning, his arms are around me.

He lifts me, carrying me through the crowd before I can protest.

Leni grabs him on our way past. "Harrison, the police need to talk to you!"

"Tomorrow."

Then we're through the door and outside.

He settles me into the Ferrari, and I yank at the pins securing my wig with shaking hands.

Then I throw all of it on the floor and stare at the pile the entire way back.

"I can walk," I murmur when Harrison opens my car door at the villa.

He loops an arm around my waist, unwilling to let me support myself.

We step inside and Barney trots sleepily to the door, whining when neither of us reaches down to pet him.

Harrison helps me out of my shoes and up the stairs, but when I try to turn toward my room, he pulls me gently the other way.

"I have first aid equipment in my bathroom."

Of the ways I imagined seeing his space for the first time, this never entered my mind.

There's dark wood furniture, a dresser and night tables without photos or adornment. A tufted area rug that's soft beneath my bare feet.

My brainpower is limited, a highway reduced from four lanes to two for some unauthorized repair.

Harrison seats me on an enormous bed with navy covers. "Don't move."

He disappears, returning a moment later with ice from the kitchen. I shift over to let him on the bed, but instead he kneels on the floor, lifting the ice to my cheek.

The cold burns my bruised flesh.

I take the ice from him, and he gently slides the jacket off my shoulders, then reaches around me for the zipper on my dress. I suck in a breath but don't argue as he drags it down.

Tonight was supposed to be my crowning achievement. A

victory lap.

Now, it's tainted.

He shifts my hips so he can lift the hem, work it up my body and over my head.

Another inspection begins, more thorough than the one he did at the club.

"So that was Mischa," I guess, mostly to make sure I can still speak.

Harrison's attention lingers on my side as he nods. I didn't think I could take his touch, but being here, safe in his home, every stroke of his hands helps to steady my breathing.

"No offense, but I hope he's not the only friend you kept from school."

Harrison huffs out a breath at my attempt at humor.

He takes my hand with the ice and lowers it, brushing his thumb over my half-stinging, half-numb cheek. "Did he speak to you?"

A memory scratches at my brain. "He said you gave something up for me. What did he mean?"

Harrison doesn't answer. But when he lifts his clear, blue gaze, the anger's gone. "I never should have brought you here, Raegan."

He's inches away, but it feels like he's putting more distance between us with every breath.

The sudden ache in my chest eclipses the pain in my face.

Moments ago, I wanted to erase tonight. But he wants to erase the past month.

All of my time in Ibiza, my time with him.

His jacket in the pool. Our kiss at La Mer. My birthday on the yacht.

The tragedy of that hits me harder than anything else.

I don't want to forget.

That thought has me straightening, lends me the strength I've been seeking for the last hour.

"You're an asshole," I decide. The words land between us, raw and loaded. "You think you decide everything? That you have all the answers? You don't get to decide what this month meant. You don't sure as hell don't get to take this away from me."

I shove myself off the bed, ice burning my hand, and head for the door.

He beats me there, filling the doorway. "Take what away?"

I don't want to talk, and I can't stand the distance he's putting between us as he tries to reason out what happened tonight.

There's no reason to be found in violence.

I grab his neck and drag him down to me.

He stiffens when our lips collide, surprise evident in every inch of his taut body.

His breath mingles with mine. He's fighting his need, every bit as determinedly as he fought the man at the club.

Whatever we've become in these short weeks is real.

The moment of danger, of remembering that all I am could be gone in a moment…

I won't lose it without experiencing this.

I rub my shuddering body against his.

The words I can't say are clutched in my grasping hands, clinging to my desperate lips.

I've never begged Harrison for anything, but now, I am. I'm demanding and pleading in the same breath.

"Fuck, Raegan."

The moment he takes control, my heart skips in warning, in anticipation.

His tongue thrusts inside my mouth. His groan reverberates through my body, his need colliding with mine.

I want him in me everywhere with the same driving possession.

I grab his hair to change the angle between us, seeking relief even as he chases more friction.

When his hands slide up my legs, no longer inspecting but *memorizing*, the hunger inside me grows into something alive and throbbing.

The ice falls from my fingers to the floor. My hands run down his untucked shirt before sneaking beneath to caress the hard lines of his abs. Harrison groans, pressing his hips closer.

"So many buttons," I mutter as I work off his shirt.

He shoves my hands away and rips the garment down the front.

This isn't sweet—it's a race to the bottom. The only relief we'll find tonight is the kind we can give each other.

He backs me into the wall, his hands racing over my breasts, my pebbled nipples.

His fingers settle between my thighs, rubbing through the wet panel of lace.

My face hurts, my body shivers, but his capable fingers make me ache—for more, for him.

He drags my panties down, the lace digging into my hips.

"Fucking beautiful," he murmurs once they're gone.

Appreciation isn't what I need from him.

He's a storm I can't control—but he's one I can choose.

I reach for his belt, fumbling until it falls loose. I drag the zipper down over his straining length.

When my hand closes around him, my throat dries.

He's strong and male and undeniable. The arousal beading at his tip is for me. The tension in every inch of his glorious body and the fierce possession in his eyes is mine alone.

For the first time outside of a DJ booth, I feel powerful.

Harrison reaches for the bedside table on a hiss, returning to rip at a package and toss the wrapper to the floor.

He rolls the condom down his length, then lifts me against the wall, encouraging me to hook my legs around him.

My head hits the edge of a picture frame. Harrison bats at the frame until it slides down the wall and hits the floor with a thud.

He grabs my hip, positioning himself between my thighs. "Need you now."

It's a warning or a declaration, because the next second, he thrusts.

He's big and thick. My body has to stretch to take him the way he's demanding.

Every inch he buries inside me is one more reminder he's unlike any man I've experienced.

My back arches, my nails digging into his arms hard enough to leave marks.

"God, you're slick." His voice is thick with arousal.

Pleasure and pain blur, the throbbing core of need deep inside me the only thing I feel.

He withdraws, a slow drag, then shifts back in on a groan.

His jaw works, and I don't know if it's from the effort of what we're doing or the effort of holding back.

It's decadent and brutal, his muscled body pinning mine. Giving and taking. Daring and fulfilling.

He bends his head to bite the curve of my breast, and my body clenches around him.

My legs ache.

Wallpaper scratches my back.

Sweat has my fingers slipping on his.

The more I writhe, the tighter he holds me. His lips skim my neck, my jaw, my ear.

I was already close to shattering tonight, and I thought this was what I needed.

But it's not. It's more.

He's over me, inside me, around me, part of me. This man I thought was the last person I'd ever trust.

Every punishing stroke of his hips chases away my fear, his regret.

It's another few strokes before I arch, my climax starting at my core and rippling outward.

He moves through it, hips thrusting faster, deeper. I shudder with every movement of his gorgeous body.

The pace is relentless until the moment he freezes over me, going still. His jaw clenches in anguish as his release rips through him.

I'm in awe. It's as if I'm seeing him for the first time.

When he shifts forward, his lips brushing my ear as he groans, "Fuck, Raegan," I wrap my limbs around him to hold him there.

After, he pulls down the covers and tucks me into bed before heading for the bathroom. I hear the sound of the sink, water running, then nothing.

I stare at the ceiling, my heart echoing in the darkness.

I feel...alive.

Instead of healing me, what we did made a new edge, bright and gleaming and raw.

The difference is this edge is exhilarating. Full of possibility.

But most of all…

I'm not alone.

It feels like an epiphany.

When he returns, reaching for his discarded clothes, the feeling deflates.

"You're leaving?" I ask quietly.

"I have to talk to the police. Leni texted to say it can't wait until morning." He dresses quickly and competently, knotting his tie and adjusting it. Every motion is as smooth and natural as how he moved inside me moments ago. "I'll be back before you wake."

The wave of anxiety sneaks up on me, settles into a vicious knot in my chest. I press a fist to my ribs under the sheets and silently count each shallow breath. "Promise?"

His gaze flicks to mine.

I'm not the woman who needs anyone's assurance. But now, in the dark, after what happened tonight… I'm not ready to be alone.

Whatever he sees on my face has him crossing to me, pressing a soft kiss to my lips.

"I promise."

Then he's gone.

CHAPTER 21

Rae

I 've had a lot of sleepless nights. I was prepared for this to be among the worst.

But when I roll from my back onto my side, the first thing I notice is warm, golden light.

The soreness creeping into my awareness is the second. The spot between my thighs aches, but so does my face.

I blink my eyes open to see pale curtains waving in the breeze from the half-opened window, beckoning me into the world.

The scent of Harrison King lingering on the pillows makes me want to press my face into the covers.

But he's not here.

I sit up. There's no clock, but judging by the light, it's late. I reach for my phone on the bedside table to see if he's texted.

He hasn't.

But there's another slate of messages.

Callie: WTF is going on?

Followed by a link.

Confusion crowds into the worry as I click the link she sent, waiting for the article to load.

Feminist DJ Caught with Businessman She Trolled: Was It All a PR Stunt?

It's by the reporter I met in person here in Ibiza. I barely have time to process that before the photos load.

The first is of me in the booth at the club last night. It's my wig, along with my gold dress, and I look powerful. It's the kind of shot clubs want for their promotions, that makes people groan they missed out on the hottest party and line up for next week's tickets.

The second photo is darker and harder to make out.

A woman, seated on something dark and out of frame, her dress high enough to expose her legs. Legs wrapped around a man in an untucked dress shirt, his dirty-blond hair and sharp bone structure visible in profile.

His hand is fisted in her hair, the other on her hip beneath the edge of the gold dress, just visible beneath the jacket wrapped around her shoulders.

They could be fucking. He could be deep inside her the moment this image was taken, his grip on her helping him chase his release.

Except they're not, because they're us. Harrison and me in a moment I never imagined being captured by another person. But the photo was taken last night at the club.

As I read the article, my breath comes so shallowly I might as well not be breathing at all.

The text cites an incident at his LA club this week. Plus, a list of issues at his other properties.

My lips tremble.

He said it was getting better.

And I trusted him.

Every line of the article guts me more than the last. It doesn't outright call me a slut—which would've pissed me off but not hurt. Instead, I'm a hypocrite. I called out the man running the show only to cave to him, let him control me, at the first opportunity.

That's not what this was.

Unable to stomach any more, my face throbbing in earnest now, I click out of the story.

The final text message rips my heart in half.

Callie: Tell me you're not with that man. Did he hurt you? Pressure you?

I shut off the phone and head to the closet and grab one of Harrison's dress shirts, slipping it on.

I slowly turn the door handle and step silently into the hallway.

There are noises downstairs, and suck in a breath. "Harrison?"

Natalia appears at the doorway of the kitchen, looking worried. "Señorita. Toro went to take him from the police station hours ago."

"Take him where?"

She dries her hands on a towel. "I don't know."

"But he's all right?"

"I believe so."

He's fine.

The knot in my chest eases, only to retighten.

He's fine, and he didn't return.

I head for my room, where I stare at the article again.

My throat aches. The stinging spots on my cheeks are tears.

I reach for the untouched bottle of pills on my dresser, fumbling with the lid. I take one dry.

The article wasn't entirely correct… but it wasn't all wrong either. Last night might not have been a PR stunt, but I did get caught up in something I was too naïve to handle.

I believed what I wanted to believe. I trusted a man I had no business trusting. Got comfortable in a place I never should have stayed.

I call him again.

He picks up on the third ring.

"Hello—"

"Harrison, I need you." I choke out the words, but his voice continues.

It's voicemail.

"You've reached Harrison King. I recommend you don't leave a message. If I need you, I will find you."

If I need you, I will find you.

He clearly doesn't, because he's not here.

CHAPTER 22
Harrison

By the time I'm finished with the police, I want nothing more than my home and the woman waiting for me there.

Rae and I have things to discuss, things we didn't get to last night.

Still, I have to make one stop on the way. There's something I haven't been able to shake, something made more real by Mischa's appearance last night—an act not of calculation but of desperation.

"If you're following up about your suggestion of a DJ, I've considered it. She's not ready."

Christian's voice comes from the doorway of his study.

I snap shut the book I was pretending to read.

"She is. She filled Debajo for the first time in years."

"Debajo is not La Mer."

"No. It's harder. It was empty. Desolate." And it came with me. "Give her the chance. I promise she won't disappoint you."

"You would risk your reputation in this?"

"Yes."

"Then have her meet me this afternoon. We can discuss it."

Grim satisfaction grips me. I have no doubt Rae will convince him.

"I'm surprised you're not with her now."

Seeing Mischa looming over her at Debajo set a cold fury loose in me I haven't felt since my parents died.

I wanted to kill him.

But I wanted to save her more.

The irony didn't escape me, because it was my fault she was hurt. Mischa heard me admit to Christian that… what? I care for her?

He overestimated what I meant and went after her.

Or he didn't overestimate it.

All I knew was I needed to get her home, to make sure she was safe and comfortable.

But when I took her upstairs, the girl from the club slowly melted away, replaced with the woman I've come to admire and appreciate and fucking hunger for.

I had no right to ask her for anything, but her raw response ripped away what was left of my control.

"I'll be with her soon," I promise Christian, picturing her asleep in my bed now.

I'll make it up to her—last night, and everything else I've done.

Including how I claimed her against the wall in a furious, graceless rush.

There are countless ways I've imagined being with her, a thousand temptations to explore together that would take more than a single night, not to mention a single hour, to enjoy.

Her term at Debajo is concluded. On paper, we might be finished.

In reality…

We're far from it. And now I have a reason to keep her here while we figure that out.

I start for the door, but Christian's voice interrupts me. "Is that what you came to say?"

I pause. "If things escalate with Mischa," I say, "know that I wasn't the one who initiated. Since school, we've kept things civilized. But I want La Mer. And if he won't play by the rules, I can't promise to."

"Breaking the rules. You come by it honestly."

I frown, ripples of discontent making me turn back. "Tell me what you meant about my father yesterday."

The older man crosses to the windows, peering out into the bright morning. "He's not the paragon of virtue you seem to think."

"My parents were above reproach. The second they learned about the drugs and other activities the Ivanov family was running behind the scenes, they wanted out. They would've died rather than supporting that kind of evil."

In the end, they did.

But Christian's silence is unsettling.

"You idolized them," he says at last. "It's dangerous to paint anyone as more than human. Particularly those we love."

I don't have the time to argue with him now, or to play games.

"If I promise to prove you wrong about my parents, promise me you won't sell the club to anyone else in the interim," I say. "You're a patient man. Give me the benefit of the same."

This deal is everything. I will him to agree.

"You have three months," he says, sighing.

I stride out of his house and out to the waiting limo.

The ride back feels interminable. I glance at my phone, seeing the barrage of missed calls as a result of turning alerts off for the morning to deal with more important things than business.

They don't matter.

I picture Rae's face when I tell her about Christian's offer to meet. This could be the single most important show of her career. It won't make up for last night, but it's a start.

The second we pull up to my villa, Natalia is out front, wringing her hands.

"Señor King." She crosses to the car, her expression a mask of distress.

"What is it?" I think the worst. Rae. She's hurt, or sick, or…

I shove past her and stomp inside, looking all around.

Nothing is out of the ordinary.

There's not a single item of Rae's clothing on a table or chair.

My chest twinges. A warning.

I take the stairs two at a time to my room. The bed is empty, the sheets rumpled.

I pace down the hall to the room at the other end, bypassing every other door as if they don't exist.

Hers is ajar, and that small crack of light fills me with trepidation.

I open the door, and my heart stops. There're no messes, no clothes. No computer. No bottle of pills.

The closet is empty, save the dress and shoes I bought her to attend Christian's party.

Impossible.

The woman I slept with last night. The one I sacrificed for, the one I denied the man who owns the club I want more than anything else in the world for…

She's fucking gone.

PART 2

BEAUTIFUL SINS

CHAPTER 1
Rae

T he cable is loose. It's fucking irritating. What kind of club doesn't have the right gear?

The kind I used to play when I was hustling to get where I am.

Where I was until last month.

This is the best of the three gigs I've played since returning to LA. The caliber of clubs I've booked has gone down since the article released featuring the photo of Harrison and me backstage at Debajo.

My renewed infamy has created a new roadblock. Now I'm not just the woman who might publicly call out a club on their bullshit.

I'm also a hypocrite.

Still, we're in LA, and this venue is full of beautiful people in various stages of intoxication.

A small film crew occupies one side. Beck's in the center, security watching him and the crew surrounding him.

The entire set, the loose cable bugs me. Every minute, I expect the music to cut out and a bunch of partiers to throw their designer vodka drinks in my face.

But hey, at least I get to do what I love.

A month after what happened with Mischa, I still get tense during the changeover, doing a scan of the crowd before I unplug and give up the stage to descend into the throng of partiers.

Tonight, there's a college-aged kid who leans too close, trying to look down the loose black shirt that's sticking to me with sweat.

A duo of guys flanks me, making God knows what symbol over my head while they snap a pic.

A young, platinum-blond woman drags her friends over. They shift from one deadly high heel to the other while she squeals.

"Girl, I'm a huge fan! Will you be at Wild Fest next year?"

I fix on a "we're all having fun here" smile I learned from Beck. "You'll have to wait and see."

"Ohmigod. It's going to be the biggest thing." She makes a duck face next to me as she wraps an arm around my shoulders. "I want life lessons from anyone who can land Harrison King. He's loaded and gorgeous and that accent... I bet he fucks like an animal."

As the flash goes off, I'm not seeing the camera or the woman.

All I can remember are the memories I've tried to shove down. Harrison King, body straining and damp with sweat, me clinging to him and gasping as he drove into me until we both collapsed.

But it was all a lie. It meant nothing.

"Dammit, one more?" the girl asks, but I'm already pushing away.

"Hey!" A whistle cuts through the noise, and I wait for Beck to catch up. "Heading out early?"

My friend is Hollywood-leading-man handsome, with dark hair and darker eyes that see more than they let on. His looks might've helped land him his primetime show, but his shrewdness got him the reality series he's filming now.

"Yeah. Thanks for bringing the crew here," I say.

The club made a few extra bucks, plus free publicity, for allowing Beck's crew to film an episode of the reality show here. If they didn't already want me back on the strength of my set, they will now.

"How many selfies did you take before someone brought your boy up?"

I shake my head. "It's been a month. He's living his life. I'm living mine." I eye his crew. "You should get back to the girl you were sucking face with. She's already bailed on her friends."

He glances back that way, where a beautiful, fresh-faced woman stands next to his security.

He goes to speak with her, then two minutes later, he's back, ushering me into the rear seat of a limo.

"Shouldn't have done that," I tell him as I drop my bag on the floor and he reaches for a bottle of champagne in the fridge.

"You're my friend." He pops the cork and pours a glass, passing it to me. "So, I heard that chick ask about Wild Fest. *Are* you mixing there?"

I stare into the champagne flute, its tiny bubbles at odds with the leaden feeling inside me. "I got on their radar this spring before everything, but they've been dodging me since Ibiza."

"That's why you're pissy? It has nothing to do with Harrison King?"

"Nothing." I take a long drink, the bubbles tickling my throat, then burning after I swallow.

I pull off the headphones still around my neck and tuck them carefully into the bag at my feet.

Beck leans over, his handsome face suddenly close.

I frown. "What are you doing?"

"Testing your claim."

He covers my mouth with his.

His lips are determined and playful at once as he kisses me.

My hands freeze in midair, too stunned to do anything else. He dares me to pull back.

I let the feeling wash over me. He's warm, masculine, compelling in a totally unselfconscious, totally Beck way.

But it's not dangerous or breathtaking. My heart rate is up from surprise, not arousal.

When his tongue parts my lips, I shove at his chest.

Beck drops back against the seat with a laugh. "See? You're still hung up on the guy."

"Just because I don't want to fuck you doesn't mean I'm hung up on someone else."

"You're kidding, right? Have you seen me?"

His words eat at the wall around my heart. "Thanks for trying to make me feel better. Even if it was a fucked-up way to do it."

"I can't fix your heart, but I can say you have no reason to feel ashamed of what you did in Ibiza. Whatever makes you so critical started a long time ago with shit you don't think about in the light of the day, not to mention talk about."

"You get all that from me not letting you stick your tongue in my mouth?"

He shakes his head. "Been watching you a while, Little Queen. You haven't made peace with who you are. You want to play the Wild Fests of this world, you gotta do that sooner or later." His phone rings, and he mouths, "My producer," as he answers.

I drag out my own phone and pull up my social accounts.

Harrison King watch has resumed. He has left Ibiza. Since the photos of us surfaced, he's been seen in London. Paris. At his clubs, but also with women.

What surprises me most is how the pictures make my chest ache. An unrelenting ache that lingers through days of trying to work, dinners with friends, nights alone.

How I feel has nothing to do with his hard, beautiful body or strong hands or firm lips or piercing blue eyes, and everything to do with the fact that I felt as if he showed me parts of himself he'd never shown anyone else.

Admitting what happened to his parents, that he's on a mission to redeem them. He'd do anything to win La Mer and rebuild the empire that fell when they died, the same empire I threatened when I exposed him on social media.

Anything—including using me.

I don't believe he set up the pictures of us at Debajo, but he must have seen them, and he hasn't reached out once.

Not a damn word. No defending what happened in his clubs or how it looked as if he used me.

I need to move on.

I haven't been up to New York because I know Annie will want to talk—the kind of talk with way too many feelings—and I'm avoiding getting into that.

Which is why I'm in a limo with Beck, who has not only given me a place to stay the past few weeks when I didn't want to be alone, but who should be fucking a perfectly nice girl instead of looking after me.

There's an email with a subject and sender that leap off the page.

"What's wrong?" Beck asks, and I realize he's hung up his call.

"My brother Kian's getting married in a month. He's inviting me."

"Short notice. Where's the wedding?"

"Napa." I fold my arms at his raised brow. "I grew up in Orange County."

His low rumble of laughter has me sighing. "You've been back a month, and I bet you haven't told any of them."

Shadows flick across his face from the streetlights, but it's the darkness inside me that makes me shiver.

"We haven't been close since high school."

Beck pulls my head down on his shoulder and lays his on top of mine. "Here's the thing. You could be a superstar. Have the Wild Fests of the world begging you to show. But you won't get there until you make peace with where you've been. No matter where you're going, you can't run from you."

"Have you made peace?" I ask him pointedly.

He's had trouble with his parents—they're flush and part of New York society, and from what I understand, having their son turn his back on the career his father wanted for him to pursue acting and come out publicly as bi pushed their self-righteous buttons.

He sighs. "Work in progress."

I grab the champagne and chug the rest, then turn off my phone and shove it in my bag, leaving the top open. The glint of diamond headphones follows me home.

CHAPTER 2
Harrison

It's not the first time I've tried to open a new door in my life—metaphorically or literally.

Nor is it the first time the way has been thoroughly barricaded.

"How long will this take?" I bark into my Bluetooth headphones, kicking at the stack of cinderblocks barring the entrance to the warehouse.

"Depends. The documents you shared about your parents weren't much to go on." The other man's Northern Irish accent abrades my ears.

"So go to other sources. You're the investigator." Cobwebs cover my hands as I lift a brick and set it a dozen feet away.

"You can't just go around asking whether dead people were involved in illicit activities."

I toss my tie over my shoulder as I bend to grab two more.

"Should be easier than when they were alive."

My top priority is convincing Christian my parents were innocent so he'll sell me La Mer. Hence the investigator.

My father helped build the legitimate side of Mischa's family's business, acquiring and managing real estate and venues. I didn't think much of it until the summer after my fist year of uni in Connecticut. I arrived home to find them looking so drained even a self-indulgent nineteen-year-old would notice something was wrong.

They looked over their shoulders when we were out. Stayed in the living room, speaking in hushed tones late at night. While I had been at school, they'd become unhappy ghosts of the people who raised me.

Which was why I told them to leave the Ivanov family's business.

They were in the process of doing that when they were killed, their deaths made to look like drug overdoses.

"Someone is alleging my parents not only knew the full nature of what transpired in that business but enabled it."

If anyone but Christian needed the kind of proof I hired the investigator to find, I'd have dismissed it as ugly conjecture. However, what Christian thinks matters because I need to buy his club in order to bury Mischa once and for all.

"You have thirty days to definitively return evidence they were innocent."

I click off more forcefully than necessary and toss the earpieces in my pocket as footsteps approach me from behind.

"Sounds juicy, boss." Leni pops a hand on a hip as I grab the last of the blocks blocking the door.

"Christian's holding out on La Mer. I thought he and my father were good friends. Turns out there was something between them. A misunderstanding, no doubt. My father was a decent man."

"And if he wasn't?"

I frown at the sun over the top of the warehouse, sweat making my shirt stick to my back. "Everything I'm doing to rebuild what they started is for them. I can't believe he would have knowingly helped build an empire on people's suffering." I grab my pocket square and wipe the dirt off my hands, the sweat at the base of my neck. "Digging up the truth is my investigator's business. In the meantime, this is ours."

She turns to survey the property. "Looks like shit."

"Most diamonds do before they're polished." I unlock the door and gesture inside. "After you."

The space is massive, a single open rectangle with concrete floors and industrial lighting suspended thirty feet up.

The floor plans I reviewed say there are offices at one end, which we can use. The dozen loading docks are overkill. We might use one, but the rest need to be closed off or redesigned.

"How long to renovate it into a nightclub?" I ask.

"Assuming the permits and zoning are lined up... a year."

"They're not, and I want it in six months."

Her laughter dies. "You're serious?"

"I'm not waiting around while Christian passes judgment. Echo will continue to expand. We've been making acquisitions, but we can't ignore development opportunities. This will be our next nightclub."

Rumors of the nightclub industry's downfall are overblown. The clubs that are closing are ones where the owners don't understand the business they're in and don't evolve to deliver their function in new ways.

A club isn't a venue that serves drinks.

It's a theme park.

A secret rendezvous.

Hell, even a runway.

It's a vehicle for thrills. The thrill made by being swept up in the darkness, the music, of watching and putting on a show.

Leni sighs. "I'll see what I can do about the timeline. Work our contractor contacts, assuming we can pay twice regular rates."

"One and a half," I correct. "I'll take care of the zoning and permits."

LA is a city built for that twisted intersection of the elegant and the hedonistic, the cultured and the primal.

This area includes some studio buildings and storage. It's close enough to Hollywood and most LA neighborhoods to get people in, and transit is established, though I expect most people will arrive by car.

Still, I've heard it's tough to get through the zoning committees. We need to show them that putting a mixed-use entertainment venue here will be an asset to the local community rather than a liability.

"Why are you even here, converting some warehouse instead of running La Mer?" Leni prods. "I thought you and Christian were working it out."

"I told him I'd prove to him I could run it and suggested an artist who could step in for the long weekend."

"And?"

"And the day after I promised that, she left."

My feet echo on the concrete as I cross the space, heading for the doors at the far side.

Leni cocks her head. "Let me guess—she doesn't know about La Mer. Because your pride stopped you from telling her or from asking her to stay."

"It's not pride. She made it clear she wants nothing more to do with me."

I grimace as I reach the door labeled OFFICE, try the handle. It gives. I peer into the darkness, feeling for a light switch. When I find it, the overhead light clicks on, showing a surprisingly decent space with furniture still in place.

This summer with Raegan was unexpected. I might've been the one to trick her into playing Debajo, but the joke was on me.

I felt way too fucking much around her. Not only was she beautiful and talented and stubborn. I wanted to fix the damned world for her, to make myself and everything around me worthy.

None of it mattered because she left at the first opportunity.

It's unreasonable to blame her after what happened with Mischa. But I do.

I blame her.

Because whatever I felt, she didn't feel the same, or she would've stayed.

Leni passes me and drags a finger across the dusty desk. "Rae's playing in LA, you know."

My abs clench at the sound of her name.

When Rae left, I needed to get my head out of my ass and move on with my business. Part of that was being seen at events, which I squared my shoulders for and undertook. I needed to play the game and be seen playing it.

Still… Every suggestive look, every overt invitation from women in my social circle, I've turned down.

It's a strange combination, being available and being utterly uninterested in anyone but the one person I can't have.

"You've been a bear since she left. What're you going to do about it?"

I glare. "I liked you better when you weren't up in my business."

"You're the one who hired me. Still can't quite figure out why you picked up a bunch of misfits. Me, Natalia, Toro, half the people in your business."

"My father always said to put the right people around you. I need a team that doesn't require coddling to do what has to be done."

Leni cocks a brow. "And she fits right in. Rae's tougher than I thought. I like her. And you do too, or you wouldn't have taken a sudden interest in a Burbank warehouse that's sat vacant since you bought it a year ago."

"I'm not here for her. This is business." I survey the room, imagining the dusty furniture replaced with more modern trappings.

"Let's pretend that's true. Rae's taken a hit, but her cult following is devoted. If we can get this place ready in six months, we'll need to book talent. You've gotten a lot of bad press this year but still came out on top. Mischa didn't press charges. No patrons were hurt at Debajo the night you two decided to bring your little fight club to town. Not that I'm complaining, but next time? Give me a heads-up so I can sell tickets."

My gaze snaps to Leni's.

I knew Rae was here when I decided to move this launch up the priority list for Echo, but she wasn't the reason. I was done hiding out in Ibiza, licking my wounds, and needed to get back to running a growing corporation—one ready and able to bury Mischa's once and for all.

"Not everything comes back to her," I say.

My friend crosses to me and brushes off my suit. "So, why did you have a check printed instead of having her final payment wired to her like the others?" She taps my breast pocket. "Don't worry, Harry. If I didn't know you so well, I'd have no idea you were still obsessed with her."

The check burns a hole in my breast pocket.

Through my suit, my shirt.

Possibly my skin.

When a member of Echo's team reached out to see where we could deliver the check this morning, Rae responded with the address of a studio lot. They purposely didn't say I would be the one coming.

The sun bakes my neck, my face damp under my sunglasses as I approach the trailer. The door opens, and two figures emerge—a young, athletic man with a woman slung over one shoulder and a stack of papers in his other hand.

The woman's curvy legs are encased in faded skinny jeans. One flip-flop falls off her foot, landing next to the steps of the trailer.

"You owe me a shoe," she huffs.

"Call my people," Beck replies cheerfully.

"Fuck your people. I'll stage an uprising in your closet while you're sleeping. Throw one of your five-hundred-dollar loafers out the bedroom window and see how much you like that."

The familiarity of Rae's low mutter is a kick in my gut. The feelings I've been shoving down rise up at once, colliding and combusting in a way that feels uncannily like heartburn.

"Excuse me, do you have ID?" A woman shifts out of a golf cart in front of me.

"I'm Harrison King."

Before she can stop me, I round the golf cart, leaving her behind.

"Well, this I didn't expect." Beck's amused, and his insolent drawl when he spots me has my nostrils flaring.

Rae shifts on his shoulder. "What's going on?"

"We've got company." He releases her, bending to set her on the ground with a thud.

It's an easy movement, as if they do this all the time.

I fucking hate it.

Rae straightens her top as she squares to face me.

She's the same as I remember... and different. Slow curves even understated clothes can't hide. Dark hair tumbling over her shoulders, eyes framed with thick lashes narrowed in my direction so I can't read the emotion beneath even if I want to.

And I want to. I'd give every dollar in my damn wallet to know what's going through her head when we look at each other for the first time in a month.

It's been thirty-two days, actually, since I left her in my room in Ibiza.

That night, I wanted to stay with her but forced myself to carry out my duties as owner of Debajo and as a King. I went to see the police, then Christian.

Beck holds up the sheaf of papers. "I'm gonna go read. You need anything, I'm on lunch for another thirty."

She nods as he walks away.

Of the things I've pictured her doing since she left me, Beck wasn't one of them. Jealousy is a living thing in my chest as I consider what they were doing in that trailer together.

The possibility that he gets to touch her, gets to see her smile, gets to fucking *make* her smile…

It's agony.

Rae closes the distance, grabbing my jacket and tugging me to the side of the trailer as a golf cart flies by.

"What are you doing here?" she asks.

I drag my sunglasses off, tucking them into the pocket of my suit. What am I doing here? If I had a reason, it's lost in her eyes.

That's when I remember the envelope. "I was in LA for business and wanted to drop this off."

Rae's brows pull together as she accepts the envelope, opens it, and sucks in a breath. "This is more than my cut."

"We filled Debajo, which exceeded even my expectations. You deserve it."

Dark, troubled eyes search mine.

"Besides," I go on, impulsive, "I wasn't sure where to send the espresso machine, and you wouldn't use it anyway."

Rae shoves a hand through her hair, looking as if she can't decide whether to laugh or scream.

I want her to say she made a mistake by leaving. That she still thinks of me late at night after her shows.

Instead, Rae lifts the edge of my suit and tucks the envelope back in my pocket over my heart, her gaze lingering on my shirt as if she can see the scar beneath. "You don't owe me anything."

But it's the look she gives me before turning and starting back toward the trailer door—not angry but sad, overwhelmed—that steels me.

"You owe me something." She stops, and I press on. "You left my bed without saying goodbye."

Rae turns slowly. "You didn't see the article?"

"I saw it. That's what happens when you're in the public eye. You grow a thick skin because the arrows only get sharper."

Her voice rises, her hands fisting at her sides. "I woke up to that news story, to the world calling me a hypocrite and someone I cared about shoving it in my face."

"Are you a hypocrite?"

"I don't know!" she retorts. "You didn't come back all night. I tried calling you. Waited for hours."

Each word is a knife in my gut.

I figured she'd decided I wasn't worth sticking around for, like everything else in her life. I wasn't going to reach out to her and beg her to reconsider.

The possibility she'd taken the article to heart never occurred to me.

She's so fucking young right now. It should be a warning, another brick in a fortress of reasons I can't have her, but all I want to do is drag her against me.

"You tried to reach me when I was at the police station," I say, clenching my hands into fists so I don't touch her. "I stopped to see

Christian on the way home. When I got back, you'd left."

Raegan doesn't blink. "What about the issues with the clubs?"

"I swear I cleaned house. I told you I would make them better, and I did. There've been no issues since. Not a single claim."

She wants to believe me. I want her to, though I have no right to ask.

"The article made me question a lot of things," she says at last. "Things I'd stopped questioning while I was in Ibiza, playing for a man who was my enemy. One I swore I'd never support again."

"He's grateful."

Her eyes cloud, either at the expression on my face or the humility in my voice.

I won't beg. But seeing her like this, knowing where she's coming from, I need to make her understand.

I can live with being a villain, but I won't let her be one.

"I have somewhere to be," she says.

"I'll walk you out."

She reaches into the trailer, coming back with the same backpack she toted around Ibiza. The top is open, and I catch a glimpse of the contents before she flips the top closed.

"He can't do what I can do, " I say as we fall into step next to each other and head down the road between studios, runners and golf carts passing every minute.

"I'll be the judge of that."

The clawing in my chest has my hands clenching into fists.

Hello, jealousy. It's been a while.

"Tell me you're not fucking him." I laugh, but underneath, I'm livid.

"That is every shade of not your business."

"It is because you still have feelings for me."

Rae pulls up, looking indignant.

"You kept the headphones I gave you."

She follows my gaze to the now-closed bag on her back, where I'd caught a glimpse of them in the sunlight. "They're diamond."

"And you live out of a single bag. You wouldn't want the reminder staring at you every day. So, if you were over what happened between us, you would've pawned them without blinking, love."

The endearment slips out, but I hide my surprise. She can't mask hers, though, and it's worth the mistake for the way she swallows hard.

When I talked with Leni, I was still telling myself I could move past Rae. Now, I realize...

I don't want to.

I resume my ambling toward the road until she catches up to me, her fingers digging into my skin through the jacket. This might be the first time I've wished I was wearing a polo shirt instead of a suit, if only to feel her touch without asking for it.

"What are you doing here, Harrison?" she demands. "You think you can keep an eye on me?"

"I purchased a lot in Burbank. It's an industrial warehouse I've been planning to convert to an entertainment venue."

"You're opening a new club."

"I need an act opening night. And whether you get off on my cock or just thinking about it"—her dark eyes flash—"you still owe me two favors."

"Not legally enforceable." Her voice is full of disbelief.

"But you're not a woman who goes back on your commitments. It's why you don't make them lightly. When you're done arguing with yourself, you know where to reach me."

I savor her stunned expression as I press the envelope into her palm.

It's hardly enough to tide me over until she comes back, but it'll have to do.

CHAPTER 3
Rae

"**N**o way that's going to happen. We need staff on those hours," says Callie as she rounds the corner to her cubicle and pulls up when she spots me.

"We'll catch up later," she says to the phone, clicking off. Her outfit is tidy business casual, a threadbare blue skirt and knit white T-shirt with nude sandals.

"Greetings." I lift a hand.

Since returning from Ibiza, I've only had a couple of texts from my cousin in response to mine, and I'm done with it.

That's why I'm showing up in person at the small office in a strip mall that houses the charity where she works.

"You can't stay. I have a meeting in ten minutes." She glances around the room as if she's looking for a door to eject me from.

"We've both been there for one another over the years. On some serious shit," I emphasize. "So don't go hating on me all of a sudden."

Her expression clouds, and I know she's thinking of our shared past.

"Come on, Callie. You don't actually think I was having some affair with a man I thought was bad news?"

She tucks her dark hair behind her ear and sighs. "I think you might've gotten caught up in what he was selling. You did lie to me about who you were with. I don't want to see you get hurt again."

It's true that I lied. But Harrison showed up yesterday and rocked me—not with the check, but with his words.

He's not in LA for me, but fuck… it felt like it.

"I got carried away," I admit.

Callie cocks her head, lowers her voice so no one outside can hear. "On some level, I get it. He's pretty extra, Rae. An actual billionaire? He's nothing like the guys we went to high school with."

"Because they were such princes," I remind her.

Her shoulders slump. "Fair enough. They were all assholes back then. The guys and the girls."

My chest tightens at the unwanted memories that rise up. The rejection from the people who claimed to have my back. The isolation of feeling as if no one else I knew was going through the same thing.

It wasn't Harrison's money or status that seduced me. It was the way he wanted me, the way he made me feel more than myself. In Ibiza, at Debajo, I started to believe I was part of something again.

The shock of Mischa's appearance and the article the next morning about me and Harrison reminded me I'd slipped into that dependence without noticing.

A woman sticks her head in the doorway with an apologetic look. "Callie, you need to be out of here in half an hour. Even if you'd work all the hours for free, Ramona needs the office."

"Who's Ramona?" I demand as the woman leaves again.

"The money you sent helped—it helped a lot, and we'll pay you back. In the meantime, we gave up a couple of offices to another organization to save money."

I look out into the hall to see women filling a waiting room, some reading, some staring at the floor. Another is pacing the floor, her dark hair swinging in a long ponytail that reaches her belt.

"I can get you more money," I tell Callie.

She folds her arms. "No. You've already given us more than enough."

I think of the check from Harrison.

What affected me more than the gesture was his words. The fact that he thinks I'm still into him.

It's crap, of course.

But with his blue eyes staring into me, it was hard not to feel something...

Still, even if he's here, I can't just forget everything that went down. Callie's right that I got caught up in his world. We're back on my turf, and it won't happen again.

"I RSVPed for Kian's wedding."

My cousin's words jar me out of my head.

"He invited me too. I'm thinking of going."

Her brows shoot up. "Really? That would be...big."

My stomach knots and I shove my hands in my pockets, thinking of Beck's comments the other night. "Do you think we have to make peace with the past to move forward with our lives?"

"Peace seems ambitious. But I do know that arguing with things that have already happened only brings us more pain." Callie's gaze flicks toward the hall. "A lot of the women who come through these doors think they're broken in some way. They're looking for justice, or vindication, or absolution. But often what they really need is to know that they get to choose how to act, how to feel, who they want to be today. That's all any of us can control."

BLUE is darker than its namesake color. A black club with fish tanks around the perimeter.

I haven't been here since the week before Tyler and Annie's wedding when I played and saw a woman assaulted.

Harrison promised he fixed the problems at this club, and the others.

I need to know if he's telling the truth.

I put on high heels and a short, black dress and plum lipstick. There's mace in my bag, though it's more of a security blanket than anything.

Inside, I head to the bar alone.

This place is a shark tank, but I'm not the bait. Instead I scan the crowd, looking for men doing the same kind of looking I am. Searching for a particular kind of partner.

The DJ is good, a guy I've heard locally and in New York. But I'm not here for the music tonight.

"Can I buy you a drink?"

A tall guy with dark hair and a leering grin cuts off my view of the dance floor.

"I'm a big girl, I can get my own."

"Baby, you shouldn't have to."

Ignoring my rejection, he reaches a hand around my waist to grab my ass.

I shove at him. "I said I'm not interested."

"Sure you are. We're getting along great." He tries again, and this time I shove harder, stepping back, bodies bumping mine in the dense crowd.

"Excuse me. Is he bothering you?"

My heart pounds as I look up to see security at my shoulder.

"No," the guy snorts, annoyed.

"Yes," I say at the same time.

The security guy moves between us. "We have a zero-tolerance policy for harrassment. That means you have to leave."

The guy puts up a protest, but security escorts him to the door.

A breath trembles out of me. This time when I scan the room, I spot security at several points around the perimeter. They're attentive. Focused. On the crowd *and* the DJ booth.

Tonight could be an anomaly. But judging by the robust staff, this isn't the same club it was.

"Yes?" the bartender shouts over the music, and I reluctantly turn to face her.

"Whisky. Neat." She reaches for a bottle, and I lean over the counter. "Wait."

I see Harrison's fingerprints all over this place, and I want to believe he meant it when he said he changed things here.

"Glen Scotia. Thirty-year-old."

She stares at me long enough I think I spoke Greek. But finally, she bends under the bar and retrieves a bottle.

"It's two hundred," she says as she pours.

"I'm celebrating."

"Anything in particular?"

"Faith in mankind."

I click into my messages and fire off a text.

Harrison King might not be finished with me, but we're in my territory now.

I can handle myself. For a moment in Ibiza, I questioned it, and that was my mistake. Not trusting him, but failing to trust myself.

Rae: I have a DJ who might work for your opening. But she's expensive.

My phone rings, and I answer, straining to hear over the music. "Expensive is my favorite price."

God, he's arrogant. The British accent only makes him sound more elitist. But damn if I don't love the sound of his voice over the line.

"You want me working for you again?"

"I enjoy you under me. I think of little else."

Heat blazes down my spine, settling into an ache knowing he replays our too-short night together as much as I do.

"Meet me tomorrow," he says. "I'll send you directions."

CHAPTER 4

Rae

My GPS announces I've arrived, but the single nondescript rectangular building on my right makes me frown. It's not a club—it's a warehouse, and I'm already regretting agreeing to meet.

The building is massive, and I park in the lot next to a row of construction vehicles and turn to the mutt in the passenger seat. "Let's go, Ernie."

I round to the passenger side and lift Beck's pet out of the car, careful of the stitches from his surgery.

"For a dog, you've got the princess act down," I comment as I set him on the pavement, fastening his leash as he cocks his head up at me.

We head for the door nearest the parking lot, which is propped open with a two by four. The moment I enter, I'm astounded by the sheer size of the place.

"What do you think?" Leni calls from the other end.

"It looks like an empty Target," I point out as she approaches.

Two dozen workers are bustling, alone and in groups, many on ladders and scaffolding.

"Try telling *him* that. We're insulating the walls," Leni supplies. "Floors are next. Anything we can upgrade as a 'warehouse'"—she makes air quotes—"until we get the rezoning approved."

I stop halfway across the huge room, and she bends to scratch the dog on the head.

"New man. You traded up."

"I can hear you," comes an irritated British voice.

I straighten as Harrison makes his way across the floor, his dark suit fitting his form to perfection.

The little tremor starts in my stomach, spreads lower into a tingling between my thighs and up to my breasts. I'm a teenager thinking dirty thoughts about the bad boy in school. The older one who's the kind of trouble you'd risk everything for.

Since Ibiza, the memories faded a little every week, until I could get through almost a day without remembering his scent, his presence, the way he looked at me as if I were a piece of fine art.

Now, it's roaring back.

"Oh good. I thought I might have to speak louder," Leni responds as he stops in front of us.

"Don't you have a job to do?" Harrison gripes.

"Sure, boss." She winks before offering me a fist bump. "Good to see you. We need to go surfing sometime. Girls' day."

The next moment, she's gone and it's Harrison and me. We might be surrounded by construction workers, but the pull between us is electric.

My attention drags over every perfectly tailored inch of him. "What would it take for you to ditch the suit? Global wool shortage? Zombie apocalypse? Male menopause?"

"I'm pleased to hear your interest in getting me out of my

clothes hasn't waned." Warmth dances in his eyes, and I feel it everywhere. It's impossible not to respond to this man.

"I said I'd talk about opening a club. Which, by the way, this is far from."

"Good thing I have a talent for seeing what things could be."

Is he still talking about the club?

"There need to be lines." I nod toward the tape on the floor.

"Some boundaries are legitimate. Others are notional, have zero grounding in reality, and are simply erected to protect things not worth protecting." He crosses the line of tape without a second look. "I won't play by made-up rules. Yours or anyone else's."

Those lashes are a mile long, and I'm caught between staring at them and his firm mouth.

"What's with the dog?"

I jerk back, realizing he was looking at my feet.

"Ernie's Beck's. He had surgery, and I didn't want to put a cone on him. Beck has a busy day at the studio, and E doesn't like hanging out in the trailer, plus the PAs don't have time."

"You're living with Beck." His gaze sharpens.

"Careful. I'll put a cone on you."

Harrison leans in. "I'd like to see you try."

If I told myself I'd exaggerate the power of what was between us in Ibiza, I was wrong. He might not be the happy-ever-after kind, but Harrison King and I have a boatload of chemistry.

A forty-five-meter yacht's worth and then some.

"So, according to Leni, you're praying this behemoth will be a club?"

He folds his arms. "In six months," he confirms. "And there's no prayer involved."

"Really? Because when my brother, Kian, built his medical practice from scratch, there was a shit ton of zoning and permitting and paperwork, none of which is easy here, where 'not-in-my-backyard syndrome' is elevated from a pastime to a full-on passion."

His eyes darken dangerously, and I raise a brow.

"I never knew you were acquainted with real estate development. It's distractingly sexy."

"Then stay focused. This is going to be the dance floor?" I motion to the center of the space. "What about bars?"

"On either side. Come to my office. I'll show you the drawings."

"It's better out here."

Harrison's slow grin is devastating. "You don't trust yourself alone with me."

"I don't trust you."

But I need more than his word that this place will be performance-ready in six months. So, I follow him.

"You think I'm sufficiently base," he murmurs as I fall into step beside him, "that while you're looking at floor plans, I'll reach over and unfasten the button on those jeans. Peel them down your legs but leave them on your ankles when I lift you onto the desk because the idea of you being trapped turns me on."

His words might as well be stroking up my inseam, rubbing against my clit at the top, for the way they affect me.

He pauses outside the door, angling his aristocratic profile toward me. "Or do you think I'll find out if you're wearing the lingerie you bought to wear for me on your birthday?"

He's smug, but the way he grips the door handle, as if all of this matters more than he's letting on, makes me ache.

"I didn't buy it for you."

"You bought it to see if you could bring me to my knees," he corrects. "Be careful what you wish for. You might enjoy the view."

He holds the door, and when I finally brush past him, I'm still thinking of him that night after Debajo, how breathtaking it was to have him over me and inside me, dragging us both over a cliff to a fate neither of us wanted to escape.

How much more devastating could he be from his knees?

His control is one thing. His reverence would be another.

I understand he had reasons for not being available the morning after he left me, but that doesn't mean I'll fall into bed with him now. Neither will I give up who I am or what I want to get caught up in his world.

The office is spacious, a large L-shaped desk facing the door and a coffee table with a low gray sofa and two plush-looking chairs in one corner. Behind the door sits a row of filing cabinets. It's a mashup of used minimalist pieces and opulence.

He doesn't seem uncomfortable with the contrast.

"I'm surprised at your persistence," I comment.

He leaves the door ajar, possibly to make me more comfortable.

Or to prove that whatever's going to happen between us won't be derailed by a dozen contractors.

"At recruiting a DJ?"

"At recruiting me." I select the chair nearest the door and sink into it, lifting Ernie into my lap—possibly to use as a canine shield. "There are plenty of people you could hire with less baggage."

"You've repeatedly told me you only have one bag. And still you manage to lose it."

I ignore the tug in my chest at his familiar teasing. "Is this about sex? Because if you think what happened between us the last night in Ibiza is enough to make me fall back into bed with you, you're wrong."

"If it was only about sex, I'd have you on your back right now."

He's utterly confident he's right. But if it's not about sex for him, what's left?

"You were engaged once," I say. "It ended badly. I have a hard time believing you're here to sweep me off my feet."

Harrison rummages through a stack of papers on his desk, tugging at the knot on his tie. When he crosses to me, laying blueprints out on the coffee table and claiming the next chair, I can't help inhaling his scent.

"There's a fascinating mile between you screaming my name and me on my knee with a box, love."

Those soul-stealing blue eyes bore into me.

What would it take for Harrison King to put his scars and suspicions behind him and open his heart, his life, to a woman?

I reach across Ernie to tug the papers toward me, but Harrison doesn't release the blueprints, and our fingers brush, heat zinging through me.

His thighs clench under the expensive fabric of his pants, and his exhale is half groan.

All I hear is the hammering of my pulse. Harrison's smoldering gaze burns me up from the inside.

Our faces are inches apart, his firm lips parted. "La Mer isn't yet mine, but with this in my collection of venues, I'll surpass Mischa in growth. With or without La Mer."

I turn my attention back to the blueprints, scanning the scale drawings that include the bars, the lighting, the stage.

They're impressive.

"So, I'm supposed to believe you'll get everything done on schedule because Harrison King wills it so?"

"Because you know what I'm capable of."

It's what makes him a powerful ally, and a dangerous one.

"If you can get your approvals lined up and show me this place is coming together, I'll sign on. For this amount." I reach for the pen in his jacket pocket, pull his hand toward me, and scrawl a number on his palm as he watches, bemused.

"You're joking."

"My rate's gone up since Ibiza."

My rate for him has, anyway.

Harrison stares at me incredulously. Every inch of his perfect body is tense, and he's not bothering to hide the impatience on his face. "Are you forgetting I *made* you in Ibiza?"

"Actually, I made *you*. The Debajo door doubled under me."

"And you trembled under me."

Before I can respond, he jerks me toward him.

His lips claim mine, hot and possessive.

There's no questioning in this kiss. It's punishment and regret, a dark cocktail crafted by his hard mouth and demanding tongue.

I try not to respond. His grip on my hair is demanding, but I can't bring myself to pull away.

I've been fantasizing about kissing him for an entire month, afraid it would never happen again. Now that it's happening, that low throb in my body starting up like it never stopped, I remember why.

Ernie whines in my lap, but Harrison doesn't relent until he's tasted me to his satisfaction, until I'm panting and my heart is racing against my ribs.

When he pulls back, his arrogant face is clouded with desire.

"You don't have the right to do that," I manage.

"I never had the right. Wasn't a problem before." He rubs a hand across his hard jaw, eyes dancing. "And don't pretend you didn't enjoy it."

I want to slap him.

I want him to press me down on this coffee table and see if it'll hold both our weights.

Before I can decide, his phone buzzes and he glances at it. "I have a meeting tomorrow with the man in charge of zoning. We've gotten permits to upgrade the walls, flooring, anything that wouldn't raise suspicions for warehouse use. The rest will have to wait until the zoning is completed. In the interim, I've had my marketing team mock-up some options for promoting opening night. I want to go over plans with you. Tomorrow night, over dinner."

"We could meet for a drink after dinner. I have dinner plans."

He frowns. "With?"

"None of your business. Drinks after," I repeat. His eyes flash as I rise to stand.

He walks me to the door of the building, Ernie trotting at our heels.

"It's a date," Harrison calls.

"It's drinks, asshole."

His slow grin is smug, as if our banter gives him divine pleasure he's been denied for too long. With a look that steals my breath, he turns and heads back inside

My fingers tighten on Ernie's leash, and as I head across the parking lot, I call Harrison King every filthy name I know.

CHAPTER 5
Rae

"Come on, baby. Give it to me," I mutter.

"All you had to do was ask."

I glance over my shoulder as Beck enters the kitchen in shorts and nothing else.

"Your coffee maker's acting up." The gleaming silver machine is the same brand Harrison bought in Ibiza.

"When sweet talk fails…" He bangs a hand on the side. "Try now."

I do, and it runs. "Huh."

He winks. "That's what I'm here for."

"I decided to go to Kian's wedding. Maybe I can put the past behind me."

"Need a plus one?"

"Nope. I'm not inviting anyone into that cesspool."

"Rae, there's a lot of ugly in this world. You can't handle your own family, maybe you're not ready for it."

I fold my arms. "Nothing ever happened to you in your past that you wouldn't want to revisit, or have dragged out, or have connected to who you are now?"

He frowns. "I'm not hiding anything. Are you?"

Steam erupts from the coffee machine, and I attend to it. My stomach knots, and I force myself to keep breathing. "I'd rather think about my future."

"Wouldn't we all." Beck barks out a laugh as he grabs a mug from the cabinet.

The huge silver fridge is stocked with healthy prepped foods. Beck won't let me contribute to the mortgage, but I hacked his grocery delivery account and switched it to my credit card.

When I first met Beck through Annie in college, I never could've predicted I'd be staying with him now, sharing coffee, not to mention a roof.

Beck's good at making friends and keeping them. I'm suspicious of everyone's motives, waiting for them to bail, but he's the opposite—he expects the best and often finds it. He has a knack for seeing through someone's defenses to what's underneath. But unlike many, he doesn't use it against people.

That's probably why I find myself letting him in a bit at a time and why he's often my go-to hang-out partner.

Beck's phone buzzes, and he grabs it, reading the notification with a grin.

"Who's making you smile like that?"

"Emily. Chick from the club the other night."

"You can bail on our dinner plans if you want to take her out," I offer.

He slaps a hand on the counter hard enough Ernie jumps. "No way. I'm taking you for dinner tonight. A nice one. As a thanks for sitting Ernie yesterday."

The dog perks up from his designer doghouse across the

kitchen.

I lean a hip against the counter. "He only tried to eat his stitches twice. I took him to see Harrison's new project."

"How is the chairman of the British Billionaire Club?" Beck asks, mischief glinting in his dark eyes as he flips his hair out of his face. "It was delightful seeing him on set. Too bad I couldn't stick around and pick ice slivers out of my chest. You know, from all those daggers shooting from his eyes."

"It wasn't that bad."

He crosses to a brown paper back next to the fridge and pulls out a pre-cut bagel before popping it into the toaster. "Dude was ready to whip it out and piss a circle around you. What'd he want?"

"To give me a bonus for Ibiza," I say as I grab the cream.

"For your legitimate, fully clothed work there," he drawls as he presses the toaster lever down.

"What are you saying?"

He turns back to me, folding his arms. "Just that he's pussy whipped. You left the boy wanting more."

I set the cream on the counter harder than necessary. "I'm not the woman who leaves guys wanting more, Beck. I'm the one who flies under the radar—unless she's on stage in a costume—and I like it that way."

"Some people are so blinded by the sun they miss the stars. Someone gets a good look at you, they're gonna find something to like."

"Wow. I was going to offer you cheese with that bagel, but you brought your own." But my chest twinges anyway.

"So, are you gonna give him another chance?"

"To what. Irritate me? I'm already playing shitty clubs from the last time I let him in.”

“Maybe he wants to make it right.” The bagel pops up, and Beck reaches for a plate.

“He’s turning a warehouse into a club. It’s bold,” I admit.

“Mmm. Bold new venture for the hotter, more insolent James Bond who wants nothing more than my girl at his exquisitely tailored side.”

I roll my eyes. The man is a business titan. He has money to burn, and he didn’t get that way by taking detours chasing skirts.

It’s possible there’s something to be learned from that.

“I’m not giving in to him. But I’m a little envious,” I realize. “I think I want a warehouse.”

“A warehouse,” he echoes.

“Not an actual warehouse. A project I can go after no matter what. Something that’s mine, that no one can say Harrison had a hand in.”

My phone buzzes with a notification from Wild Fest announcing a new DJ.

“This is it.” I hold up the phone, excitement surging through me. “Wild Fest. My warehouse.”

“How’re you going to get it? You said they’re not returning your calls.”

I square my shoulders. “I’ll figure it out.”

CHAPTER 6
Harrison

"**H**ope the construction outside didn't give you too much trouble. They've been working on that intersection forever. I'm Zack."

"Harrison."

The kid who heads up the zoning department for this part of LA shakes my hand. He's probably thirty, clean-cut, smells like ambition and family money. I don't need to look inside his head to know for him this is a stop on the way to something bigger.

Mayor. Governor. Maybe senator.

"I understand you're looking to develop a property in Burbank."

"It should've been zoned commercial. Everything around it is. I trust it will be straightforward after the hearing to approve the request so we can move forward with construction."

"Unfortunately, our hearing process has been delayed. We need to move yours back six weeks."

Unacceptable.

The delay will put me behind Mischa's expansion and cost me money. Every damn day this building sits empty costs money.

"This is a priority. I have significant stakes riding on finishing this on time."

He jams his hands in his pockets, eyes crinkling at the corners.

It's not a smile—it's a warning.

"I don't know how fast things move in the UK, but there can be hang-ups in California and the planning office has limited resources. We advise developers to anticipate sufficient time for approvals."

Fucker.

He's one of those types. The ones who hear I'm coming and want to make my life hell.

"If it's resources you're short, I'm sure we can expedite things."

"Just because you have money doesn't make it fast."

The rest of the meeting goes about the same, and by the time I leave, I'm in a bad mood. I slam a fist into the brick outside before heading to my car.

This new venue is my best investment to grow my company until I can clear my parents' names and convince Christian to sell me La Mer.

The entire drive back to my penthouse condo in one of LA's best hotels, I'm clenching the steering wheel.

I toss the keys to the valet and head up to my condo.

I bought the suite three years ago. Its stunning skyline and modern décor are lost on me as I toss my tie on a chair and strip down, heading for the shower.

The water makes my agitation worse.

Is it possible I was off my game?

More than once today, I've caught myself thinking of Raegan's mouth.

How I'd like to taste her everywhere else.

Whom she's going to dinner with.

When I get out and towel off, there's a buzzing in the back of my brain I can't ignore. I grab my phone and check Beck's social media.

Good food, better company.

The image shows Beck grinning, his arm around a woman with her hand in front of her face. But her amused smile is visible and, for me, recognizable.

My abs clench.

When she said she had a dinner she couldn't change, I assumed she meant it was something important.

Unless he's more important to her than me.

The napkins on the table, deep plum, edge into the frame. I stalk to the kitchen and yank open the top drawer to find the same napkins.

But I can't get over the way she's smiling in the picture. I can't remember making her smile like that.

On impulse, I veer away from the closet full of designer suits.

Instead, I choose trousers and a gray shirt, fasten the cuffs.

Top button?

I undo it.

Better.

I take the elevator downstairs and head for the restaurant.

It's full of stunning couples and small groups. It's one couple I'm looking for. I don't see her, but I spot his dark head.

I catch sight of myself in the mirror. The casual shirt can't hide the agitation beneath the surface.

Cutting the maître d' a look that brooks no argument, I head back to the table.

"We're good on wine, thank… you." Beck's brows lift as I sink into the chair across from him.

"You're the dinner date."

He spreads his hands. "Guilty as charged."

My gaze runs over the tablecloth. They've eaten their entrees, and a single dessert menu rests between the two place settings.

"We're sharing," he drawls at my look.

I came down to see her, but I want to hit him. "You're not going to keep her."

Beck cuts a look behind him before leaning an elbow along the back of his chair. "She's not a tea set. You might be a king in London, but this is LA, my friend."

I take him in, dragging my gaze slowly from his white sneakers to his designer jeans to his button-down and too-long dark hair. "We're not friends. But you don't want to be my enemy."

He leans closer. "Rae's my girl, and I don't need to fuck her to prove it. I will, however, ask the waiter to hold my phone while I use a butter knife to cut your limbs off and stuff them in any available orifice if you hurt her."

I'm still reappraising the man when Rae's startled voice cuts the tension.

"What the hell is going on?"

She's beautiful. Even the dark shadows around her eyes that I want to erase. The dress is orange, the color of the one she wore to Christian's gala, only shorter. It's as casual as the other was formal, with a scooped neck and a hem that ends halfway down her thighs.

"I decided to pick you up rather than meeting you at the club. Simple, seeing as you're eating at my hotel."

Wariness edges into her expression. "You're staying here?"

"I own the penthouse."

Rae's attention doesn't budge from me, but Beck chuckles behind his napkin. "There's an easy way to settle this." Now we both look at him. "Join us for dessert."

The waitress is at my side in an instant, eyes widening in recognition. "Mr. King. I'll bring you a whisky."

"And a chocolate mousse. Three spoons," Beck drawls.

She disappears.

"Rae and I were just discussing her next move," our smug host says.

She shoots him a warning look.

"She's opening my new club," I say.

"This is bigger. Wild Fest."

"Red Rocks amphitheater in Colorado," Rae says, shifting in her seat. "Massive outdoor event, record-breaking despite being in its third season."

"Fourth season," I correct.

"You've heard of it?"

"Of course I've heard of it."

"We're still figuring out her audition tape," Beck says.

My brows lift. "They want an actual tape?"

"Beck's talking metaphorically. It's competitive."

It's rational she would focus on a prize like that, but I'm still irritated she's spending her evening brainstorming with Beck while I was off my game because I couldn't clear my head of her.

The waitress returns with my whisky, plus dessert. Beck reaches for a spoon and dives in with an appreciative wink for the waitress, which has her flushing as she leaves.

Is this what Rae is into? Some Hollywood wannabe who's my brother's age?

She's not the woman I thought she was.

"How was your day, Harry?" Beck asks.

I ignore the nickname and swirl my drink before taking a sip. "I was preoccupied by a problem I need to resolve."

The problem being the woman in front of me.

I shift in my chair, and my knee brushes Rae's.

She jerks in her seat and her spoon clatters off her plate, falling to the carpet.

"Beck, would you excuse us?" Rae says tightly when she straightens from picking up her utensil.

Beck looks between us in amusement.

"You know, this has been fun." He rises and rounds to hug Raegan, who tries to glare at him.

"Let me get you another spoon," I say when he's gone.

I shift out of my seat to seek out new cutlery, heading toward the kitchen. I overhear our waitress talking with another whose voice I recognize. She's served me before, and I try to recall her name.

"I wasn't planning on the double shift, but when someone calls in sick, you have to," she says quietly to the other waitress. "Now I'm not sure I have time to walk home before my kid gets back from his dad's, but I can't afford to take a car."

Melanie. Madison. Mary…

"Maria," I say.

"Mr. King." She straightens, flushing. "I'm so sorry if we were too loud."

"Not at all." I order a town car while she watches, slack-jawed. "It'll be here in five minutes," I say when I hang up. "Take it wherever you need. The charges are on my account. Could I get a spoon?"

She runs to grab one, murmuring thanks as she passes it to me.

I shift back into my seat and hold out the spoon to Rae. She takes it, her gaze holding mine long enough that I wonder if she overheard the exchange.

"We have unfinished business."

"And it couldn't wait."

"No."

Rae shifts back in her seat, scanning the room behind me.

I see her shut down, feel it in her body language. It pisses me off that she can pull away emotionally while she's still within reach.

I like to come across as in control because I've had to, which only highlights how painfully ill-equipped I am to deal with *her*.

There's no reason for me to feel out of place in this restaurant full of attractive Angelenos in their West Coast business casual. But I do. It took everything in me to walk out the door without a jacket.

And I did it for Raegan.

"I'm trying to help both of us, but you're making it exceedingly difficult," I state.

Now I have her attention. She leans in, eyes flashing as if she can burn me from the inside out. "Really? Because so far, every time I'm near you, I get holes shot in my reputation and my career. You don't get to show up here and demand I follow your rules. There's no contract this time. Who do you think you are?"

I pick up my drink and drain it. "A man who keeps asking why the fuck he bothers."

She rises from her seat and she stares at me with eyes full of fire. "Then stop."

Before Raegan reaches the door, I'm on my feet.

CHAPTER 7
Rae

I'm over the games.

Harrison King might get any woman he wants, but he's not getting me.

I shouldn't have opened the door enough to give him a chance, but I wanted to talk about the gig. And maybe to see him. But he behaved like an utter prick, crashing my dinner with Beck like a jealous boyfriend, then acting as though I'd fucked up.

Just because he helped one of the waitstaff when he thought I couldn't hear doesn't mean he's not the devil.

I'm nearly at the front doors of the hotel when someone grabs me and tugs me behind a huge potted plant. My shoulder hits the wall. "What the fuck?"

Then he's pinning me in place with his fierce expression, filled with anger and desperation.

"You want *me* to stop?" he demands, his voice dripping with incredulity. "You came into my club, my house, my island, and turned them upside down." Harrison angles his body to box mine in, and his fingers find the nape of my neck, squeezing hard enough it steals my breath. "You fucked me like you needed it, and the next morning, you were gone. So at least be honest about your reasons. It wasn't because of some paparazzi shot. It was because you didn't believe in me enough to stay."

He's breathing as if he's been running. His corded throat is bobbing, that firm mouth parted, those piercing blue eyes full of shock and desire.

The accusation in his tone doesn't affect me, but the hurt beneath does. The rawness of his words is a reminder he was left before by a woman he trusted. I didn't leave him for another man, but his betrayed expression makes it seem as if I might as well have.

I lift my chin to meet his gaze. "What did we have? What *could* we have had, Harrison?" I swallow hard. "You were this arrogant, untouchable god, and I was this angry girl who wanted no part of your world. At least... I didn't at first."

His nostrils flare as he searches my face.

I'm playing a dangerous game, showing vulnerability to a man who crushes his, who succeeds by exploiting weakness in others. Except the throbbing low in my gut wants to believe he's not unaffected either.

"If I look like a god right now, you need reading glasses more than I do."

His self-deprecating comment makes me suck in a breath.

My attention drifts down to his open collar, the rolled-up sleeves revealing muscled forearms. I pop his collar, trailing a finger along the edge. "You're missing your suit."

He's a warrior without his armor, and I'm aching to know what convinced him to lay it down tonight.

Before I can ask, his mouth crashes down on mine.

His tongue presses at the seam of my lips, demanding

entrance. I grant it to him, my body responding before my brain gives permission.

He tastes like whisky and man and I'm drowning in him.

My palms flatten against his chest to steady myself.

The rational part of me screams to get away.

Instead, I press up on my toes to kiss him back.

His arms band around me like steel.

"Too public." His muttered words cut through my haze of arousal.

Harrison doesn't take my hand but steers me across the foyer and toward a private elevator using only the force of his presence.

We step inside, and the doors shut.

His gaze is loaded with hunger, and I revel in it before he drags me up to him. Those wicked lips land on mine before sliding lower to my jaw, my neck, tracing down to my cleavage. I fist a hand in his shirt.

"Fuck." My fingers tighten in his hair as his mouth moves to cover my breast through the fabric, licking its hardened peak.

He's a storm intent on killing me and making me grateful for the mercy.

The elevator dings, and he guides me out, a firm hand on my back as we step into the huge living room of a suite.

"You never do anything halfway, do you?" I pant.

"What I want, I get." Harrison pulls back to study me, his eyes nearly black with desire. "I want you to repeat every smartass thing you've ever said to me while you're laying over my knee. I want to ride you bare before your show. To come inside you and watch you go out and play in front of a thousand people and know I'm still there. Where they all want to be. I want to tie you to my bed and make you come until you're begging me to stop."

His words seduce me. "Too many orgasms doesn't sound like a thing."

"Sweet, naïve girl."

He grips my face, his expression turning serious as he stops either of us from taking things further.

"There was one thing I wanted in my life. But since you crashed into it, I want you. Seeing you with Beck makes me crazy."

Thrilling. It's thrilling to hear him talk like this.

"How crazy?"

My lips curve, because what's crazy is the fact that this billionaire wants me, a girl with no permanent address and a closet full of damage. Harrison's shoulders pull tight under the shirt. He's gorgeous and a little reckless, his hair sticking up as if he's been running his fingers through it.

"Crazy enough I only wore a damn shirt to dinner."

I slide a hand under the edge of that shirt and rest my palm over the scars on his chest. My thumb traces the edge, and I get off on the way his pulse skips beneath my touch. "It's a good shirt," I whisper.

Riding a wave of arousal, I reach back for the knot on my dress and unfasten it. It falls to the floor.

Harrison's gaze roams my body, from my bare legs to the curve of my hips to my simple, nude lace bra, before landing on my face. "Beautiful. Everywhere."

My skin hums at his praise.

He inches closer, threads his fingers into my hair. "Feel how hard you make me." He takes my hand from his chest and places it over the bulge in his pants. "You have no idea how long I've wanted you."

"Pshh. The tiniest fraction of your life," I breathe. "You *are* ten years older."

"Means I know how to make you mine."

My hand wraps around his length through his pants. His grin fades, his gaze flaring with heat.

I unfasten his shirt one button at a time, pushing it off his shoulders. He tosses it to the floor without looking.

What's between us might not end well, but I've never felt the rush I feel around him—outside of the booth.

I'm willing to take this chance…

As long as he'll let me drive.

I sink to my knees and take him out of his dress pants. He's huge and hard, and I've never salivated for a dick before, but apparently there's a first time for everything.

"I prefer it when—"

"I know how to give a blow job," I retort, earning myself a chastising look.

"I'll enjoy it more if you do it the way I like."

I flip him off, for old times' sake. He grabs my hand and sucks my middle finger into his mouth.

A jolt of pleasure grips my spine as heat wraps around me, settling into a dull ache of pleasure between my thighs.

"Is that a request?" I manage, but his wicked tongue is messing with my head.

"I prefer those hands engaged in more productive pursuits," he rasps when he releases me.

For once, I'm not arguing.

I turn my attention back to his hard cock. I wrap my fingers around him, using the wetness from his mouth to slide up and down.

His exhale is half-groan and entirely sexy.

I take him in one long ambitious stroke until he hits the back of my throat.

"Fuck, Raegan. Your dirty mouth is so fucking sweet."

He wants to take control. His hand fists in my hair, pushing me down, and I shove him away. Eventually his touch comes back, cupping my face, fingers threading into my hair, thumb brushing my hollowed cheek as I suck him.

Having this kind of power is like the feeling of playing to a huge crowd, only this is better.

"You're preening," he rasps when I pull off him to catch my breath.

"I deserve it."

He drags me to the carpet.

He's filthy rich, but right now, he's just filthy.

His hands stroke down my body as if he's memorizing every inch before his mouth comes back to claim mine. It's brutal, punishing me for every day we've been apart.

His grip finds my throat, and a ribbon of fear snakes through me. But it's overtaken by pleasure as he works a finger inside me. I can't do anything but arch my back and take him deeper.

"So wet."

It's a curse and praise at once.

He drags his cock over my mound, a cruel tease.

I feel as if I've never had him inside me. But before he can make good on his implied promise, he parts my legs and shifts down my body.

"First, you'll beg."

That dirty mouth settles between my legs. If you can call it settling, because he's restless, his tongue and lips moving together to drive me wild with need.

A slow, leisurely lick.

A hard suck.

A rhythm more compelling and brutal than anything I've ever laid down on a track.

My fingers grasp at the carpet, his hair, whatever I can find. "Oh shit."

I could tell him how I usually get myself off, but I can't even think. There's no way to tell him what to change because I wouldn't know how to ask for this if I tried.

He plays my body as though he was born to. Not because the first time he touches me is perfect, but because he takes every shiver of my body, every hitch of my breath, every incoherent murmur from my lips, and uses it against me.

The man is a fucking doomsday machine set out to destroy me, to teach my body to ruin itself.

"Tell me you missed me." His lips vibrate against my skin.

"Your smug elitist mouth? Not likely."

His fingers twist inside me and I gasp, yanking on his hair. He holds me in place.

"My smug elitist mouth is going to make you scream."

When I come, it's a record-setting explosion, even for LA. The aftershocks rack me for seconds, minutes, hard enough my toes ache.

He appears over me, hair mussed, and suddenly he looks ten years younger by virtue of the cocky expression.

I manage to prop myself up on my elbows. "That all you've got?"

His low chuckle is sexy as hell. "On the contrary. Just getting started."

He grabs something from his pants pocket, then graces me with those intense blue eyes while he rolls on the condom.

How I ever thought those eyes were cold I don't know. They're white-hot.

He positions himself at my slit, the head of him bumping where I'm wet and making me ache. He sinks into me, an impossibly thick inch at a time.

So full.

I'm full of him, everywhere. My body, my head, my senses. There's no denying it.

Every instinct to struggle against the invasion ends with my fingers clenching, my body clenching, as he slides deeper.

When his cock hits resistance, I gasp in relief.

The last time we did this, we were swept up by the emotion of the night and needing escape and comfort.

This is intentional.

I told him we had no contract now, but it's not true. We signed on an implicit line tonight, possibly from the moment he sat down at that table.

A promise we'd play this out tonight with clear eyes and clear heads. And this time, neither of us is running.

His groan ends on a hiss, and I realize he's struggling with control as much as I am.

"Feel how deep I am," he rasps in my ear. "Memorize it. Every second I'm not inside you, you'll wish I was."

Those words send blood pounding through my veins.

"I'm going to cover every damn inch of this body before we're through. But first…" The flash of cockiness in his eyes is the hottest thing I've ever seen. "You'll come for me."

I wrap my legs around his hips, squeezing hard enough to make me gasp and his jaw tighten.

"Don't make promises you can't keep," I pant. "I understand endurance is harder at your age—"

"Just for that, you'll count. Every fucking stroke." He shoves me back, his chest brushing mine so there's no question I'm staying down.

I'd laugh if I wasn't so caught up. I count the first stroke in my head, almost losing track at the firm thrust of him stretching me, the sight of him, a powerful and determined flex of muscle and man over me.

The next second, my butt is on fire, and I yelp. "The fuck?"

His eyes flash with satisfaction. "Count. Out loud."

"Two," I pant, my voice wavering at the edges. The angle is different this time, hitting me where I'm aching, and the knowing look on his face says he knows.

Still, there's no way I'll…

"Fuck… three…"

My back arches up off the carpet, unbidden.

Harrison's lazy mouth is in direct contrast with the rest of him, descending to leave a trail of heat up my throat.

Unreal.

"Five…"

More, overtaking me.

I'm at twelve when he presses on my clit and I clench around him.

"That's cheating," I mumble as the orgasm crashes through me.

He moves through my climax, harder and faster and relentless. Until his body stills inside me and his muscles seize.

The heavy exhale is torn from deep inside him, his shoulders flexing and eyes squeezing shut.

It's a thing of beauty, watching this tightly laced man fall apart. I can't help tightening around him as he spills himself inside me.

When Harrison collapses over me, he's still in me.

"No fucking clue why people would want to come at the same time." His dry accent is so close to my ear he might be in my head. "I prefer to watch you."

When his head lifts, he's grinning. My heart skips. He's breathtaking like this. Happy and gorgeous and relaxed, and it reminds me of the strange closeness I felt while we were in Ibiza.

An alarm goes off, and I lift my head in confusion.

My phone.

"I have a show," I state.

"You have a show," he agrees.

When he says it, the meaning sinks in. "Fuck, Harrison, I have a show."

I shift out from under him, shoving both hands through my hair. I start to stand, but there's a hand in my face.

He's already up, helping me.

My phone buzzes, and I find it lying on the floor next to my clothes.

Beck: Heads up that I have a girl staying over tonight. In case you two run into each other naked in the kitchen.

I'm barely done reading when I notice Harrison reading over my shoulder.

"You never slept with him."

"Is privacy dead?" I complain, lowering the phone to my side.

But he stares me down.

"Beck's really into this girl," I admit as I grab my dress and tug it on.

"Stay over. Come back after your show."

That feels like too much of him—a dangerous amount.

"No."

"You're punishing me for leaving you that night."

Surprise has me jerking toward him. He's only wearing black boxer briefs, his gorgeous body moving easily as he slips on his shirt and fastens the handful of buttons from the bottom.

"You were with me long enough to make me come," I say.

Where is my damn underwear?

Harrison holds up my panties, and I cross to grab them out of his hand.

He holds on. "Just not long enough to make you stay."

I pull harder, and this time, he lets go.

CHAPTER 8
Harrison

Texts are meant to be responded to promptly.

They're not an email or a goddamned letter.

But when I text Raegan the next day at noon to say, "I trust you slept well…"

There's no answer.

I wanted her to come back after her set last night. We would've made it two steps in the door before I pressed her up against the wall and her hands were under my shirt. We would have fucked in the living room—again—before she crashed.

But I got out of bed alone this morning, except for memories that made my cock twitch against my leg. I headed for the shower, jerked off for momentary relief.

I'm not finished with her, not by a long shot.

I've never wanted a woman who challenged me on every level. Normally I date beautiful women interested in enjoying life and being enjoyed. Raegan's anything but that.

In the kitchen, I take a moment to miss my housekeeper's

cooking before reaching for the fridge door handle. Since I arrived, I haven't opened it once. The hotel chef brings my food himself, and I eat most of it around work—in my office here or at the warehouse with Leni.

Now, I scan the fully stocked shelves.

Juice. Milk. Fresh vegetables, precut. Even chicken.

The pantry contains everything from nut butter to protein powder.

Who knew?

I settle on coffee with the French press I had delivered since I was last here.

If only my problems could vanish as easily as the woman whose scent still lingers in my condo.

The new club, for one.

Leni and the team are full-on into a major renovation, and I need to get the zoning approval so we can open on schedule. The more research I do, the more convinced I am that this is the right time for this operation. It could add significantly to Echo Entertainment's bottom line and its reputation.

I take my coffee and phone out to the wraparound patio overlooking LA and the ocean beyond, hitting voicemail.

"Boss, it's Leni. I've managed to broker deals for most of the materials we need on short order. But some of the sound equipment is backordered and might push the club opening. Unless we can figure out another solution—"

I hit End, cursing.

And this isn't the only venue in my empire.

I've heard almost nothing from Mischa since he invaded Debajo and I slammed a fist into his face. With anyone else, that would be comforting. With him, it's concerning because it means he's working under the radar.

I have to win La Mer, and the stakes have never been higher. If I don't succeed, I will have disappointed my parents, failed before the man responsible for their downfall.

Which is why I take the offensive position when I dial a contact. "Christian."

"Good morning, Harrison. I understand you've left us."

"For America, not for the dead," I say dryly. The old man does like his drama. "Acquiring La Mer is still my number one priority. To that end, I've committed to a robust investigation to alleviate any concerns about the legitimacy of my parents' activities."

"You're in Los Angeles. It doesn't seem like a priority."

"On the contrary. I'm sparing no expense." I shift, scanning the horizon. I haven't heard anything conclusive from my investigator yet, but he emailed me a status update with some of the areas he's chasing down. "What I don't know is why it's so important to you."

Christian sighs. "There was a deal that went wrong. A property I was going into along with Mischa Ivanov's company—only your father pulled out. The reason was obvious—it would've interfered with the drug trade. But it lost me millions, cost me an entire month with my family. I missed my eldest daughter's graduation picking up the pieces, and that left a bad taste in my mouth. I need to know who made the call, your father or Mischa's."

"And you think learning whether my father was aware of the drug activity will give you that answer."

"Yes."

I frown, pacing the patio. "You've granted me two months. I will get to the bottom of this."

"The terms are changing. Mischa raised his offer yesterday by a million."

The blood in my veins heats. "My offer was more than fair, and it's untainted. Do you want Ivanov's way of doing business as a stain on your soul? A father, a grandfather, has no reason to carry that burden."

"You have thirty days. Provide me the assurances we discussed and the club is yours."

"What does Ivanov think of this?" I challenge. "He doesn't know, does he?"

Christian clicks off without answering.

CHAPTER 9
Rae

When your requests don't get a response, it's a good idea to escalate.

Sure, doing that with Echo Entertainment, and Harrison King landed me an unplanned gig with an unwanted billionaire that sent my world spinning, but that was an anomaly.

Once I saw a social post announcing two new headliners at Wild Fest when I got out of bed at noon after last night's show, I knew I was running out of time.

Despite my verbal jousting matches with Harrison to date, I'm not good with confrontation. But I tracked down one of the Wild Fest organizers and am following her down Santa Monica.

I catch up to Victoria Ames at a stoplight where she's riffling through her handbag, cursing. She knocks it to the ground, and I bend to help pick up the contents.

"Thanks. I have a meeting in an hour, and this wasn't on my schedule."

"Victoria? Don't freak out," I go on when she stiffens. "I'm Little Queen. I was talking with the cofounders about playing Wild Fest but haven't heard from them in awhile."

She relaxes a degree. "I know who you are."

I hold out a lipstick, the two pieces of which have come apart. She frowns.

"Five-second rule?" I suggest.

Her mouth twitches, but she takes the tube from me and recaps it. "Everyone wants to play this festival. We have the best acts in the world lined up. Why are you the right fit?"

"Come to a gig I'm playing in town next weekend and I'll show you."

"Post the details on your social and I'll take a look," she counters.

"I'll send them to you." I pull up the graphic and DM it to her account that I found earlier. I call after her, "You notice anything about the headliners you've announced so far?"

She slows her steps but keeps walking. "They're all top-100 DJs?"

"They all have dicks!"

I shout it loud enough the entire block looks over.

"A donut break was a good idea," Callie says as we head out the door of the place a few blocks from the charity, our small paper bags in hand, later that afternoon.

"I was in the neighborhood."

"This is LA. No one's ever in the neighborhood."

"I had a meeting about this huge festival, Wild Fest, at Santa Monica and Sepulveda."

"What's there?"

"Nothing, I mean actually on the street corner. I chased down one of the organizers and made her talk to me."

She laughs. "And how did it go?"

"I think she's going to come to my gig in Long Beach next weekend. Which reminds me, I need to confirm specs with them." I frown and make a mental note because I haven't heard from them since returning from Ibiza.

"Well, if Wild Fest doesn't want you, they're nuts. Do you remember when we were in high school? The first gig you played?"

"You held my hand."

"Literally." Callie's lips twitch. "You were shaking."

I'd been mixing my own music for a year when I got the chance to play a party. A friend of a friend—at least a friend of one of the girls who had been my friend at the time.

It had been dark, and I was alone in the back.

Until I took over the booth.

There I could be anyone. I didn't need to justify myself or defend my feelings. All I had to do was play.

"I'm surprised you chased that woman down. You must be desperate. Lurking is more your style than full-on attack."

"Maybe my style is changing." *I'm changing*, I realize as I cut her a look. "I'm opening a club for Harrison King."

My cousin's smile falls away. "What?"

"It's in Burbank. He's not a bad guy, Callie."

"He's a billionaire who lives in the tabloids. Yes, LA is full of people like that. But not ones we hang out with. At least, not who we hung out with growing up," she amends.

"Harrison's intense. He pushes, and with anyone else, I'd tell them to fuck right off. The reason it works is I don't have to live in the past with him."

"Because he doesn't know your past?" she counters.

"Because I don't have to get into that shit. We can have fun."

"Fun?" She arches a brow as I grab her arm.

"Yes. He's fun."

She rolls her eyes, and I laugh.

"You mean the sex is fun."

I pull my donut from the bag, swipe a finger through the icing, and lick it off. "The sex doesn't suck."

Last night at his place was beyond hot. The first time we were together in Ibiza, the sex was desperate and hurried. This time, I got a taste for how he'd be in bed if we were together.

Not that we made it to the bed.

He demanded I fall in line the way he does when we're clothed. The difference is when we're naked, I'm tempted to give that power up to him. Probably because I know I'll benefit from it in the form of orgasms I could never give myself.

I've never wanted to trust a man with my body or my heart.

That's why when he texted me a few hours ago, I didn't rush to reply. It's not about pretending I'm unavailable. It's about reminding *myself* I'm not available, in the sense that I'm not going to start jumping every time my phone goes off thinking it's him like a teenager with a crush. I want more, but there's a big difference between wanting to christen every surface of his penthouse condo and letting him into my deep, dark secrets.

"I guess I'm protective," my cousin goes on. "This guy dates models and buys clubs and owns yachts—"

"He charters yachts."

"—and you're my cousin. We used to watch South Park and

make fun of the preppy snobs and talk about how much better life would be when we didn't have to deal with those people."

"We're having fun," I insist, although my heart beats faster. "I'm not marrying him."

Even if he intended to go there again with a woman, it would probably take the rest of her life just to read the prenup.

Callie nods after a moment. "Speaking of weddings...I'm still surprised you didn't open up to Kian back then."

My fingers tighten, and I drop my donut. "Motherfucker."

"Sorry."

I pick it up and toss it in a nearby trash can. "Kian wouldn't have wanted me to tell him what happened. He'd only feel like shit about it."

The past dredges up feelings of weakness, of powerlessness, and the people who never noticed.

"Maybe he should feel like shit about it." I shake my head. "I know I was giving you a hard time about Harrison, because I can't see you with a guy like that. But if you don't let *anyone* in, you forget how. It's a different kind of pain. A slow one, a subtle one."

I squint into the sun. "You know what'll be a slow, subtle pain? Watching Kian deliver a romantic speech at the wedding."

Callie's laugh almost makes me forget her words.

Harrison: Need your take on some new equipment.

His text is imperious, but since I agreed to play opening night in exchange for an exorbitant fee, it makes sense I'd do it.

So, it's before noon the next day when I head to Burbank.

Despite the dozen trucks in the lot, when I head in the side doors, only a handful of tradespeople are working. There's no sign of Harrison or Leni—until a roar goes up from the office, the door half open. I head that way and see nearly twenty people gathered around a television screen.

"Wrong time of year for an Oscar party," I comment.

Harrison crosses to me, doing a slow, thorough sweep of my figure. "It's Ash's first match of the year. They refused to keep working once I put it on, and I don't have the heart to kick them out. You're out of bed before noon. Are you unwell?"

His firm mouth tips up at the corner, and I shake my head at his mocking expression.

"I'm fine."

It's not entirely true. Since talking with Callie about the wedding, I've been spinning over the idea of confronting my past there and what she said about letting people in.

A roar goes up again, and I snap my gaze to the screen. "Who scored?"

"No one," Leni comments. "It was close though."

"That's the noise you make when someone *almost* scores?"

Harrison chuckles, and Leni offers a wry smile. Though I'm not a sports fan, I can tell Ash is really fucking good. He moves the ball easily up the field, passing effortlessly.

"Where's this equipment?"

Harrison brushes a thumb down my cheek before I can stop him. "I'll show you tonight over dinner."

I look around the room. "I thought you wanted me to come

look at gear on-site."

"The equipment will be custom order, Raegan," he says as if I'm being deliberately slow. "You inferred I meant here."

"You say jump and I say how high?" I return his stare because, dammit, he could've sent me a link rather than waiting for me to drag my ass down here.

Harrison tugs me to the back of the room. "Let me be clear. I enjoy you. Naked and under me, but all the other ways too. I won't apologize for wanting to see you."

"Being seen together in LA is serious, Harrison."

"Then maybe I'm serious."

His smoldering blue eyes pin me in place, but it's his earnest tone that leaves me speechless.

Images of *TMZ* and *ET* articles splash through my mind. People speculating exactly why we're together. The career I'm trying to build being subordinated to an online dialogue about whether it's a hot affair or whether we're in love. Who I am reduced to a ranking on the "Most Unexpected Couples" list.

I turn away, shoving a hand through my hair before stepping out of the office. He follows, pulling the door after him.

"Whatever you think you want," I say, "it isn't that. Maybe it's companionship. Someone to share your bed who also has your back—"

"Just go the fuck out with me, Raegan."

My chest tightens. There's a question I've been needing to ask, but one that exposes me more that I can stand. "Why me?"

If I expect him to hesitate, he doesn't. "Because under the layers of doubt and questions, you're a woman who knows what she wants and how to get it. The day you see it, I want to be there."

Would it be so bad to fall for Harrison King?

Would he even be there to catch me if I did?

A roar goes up from the other side of the door, and Harrison leans in.

"Now someone scored," Leni calls.

I poke my head in too, and my gaze finds Ash on the screen, a huge grin on his face as teammates carry him up the field.

Something nudges my foot, and I glance down to see Harrison's dress shoe leaning against my sandal.

"What's with the heels?" he murmurs.

"I'm breaking them in to wear for my brother's wedding next month."

His gaze sharpens. "I'm partial to weddings. We met at one, if you recall."

"I chewed you out."

"I loved every second of it."

Part of me blooms, a tiny flower in my chest that's never dared look for the light.

"Wear those tonight when I take you for dinner. I want to fuck you in them." He brushes his lips over mine, and heat streaks straight to my core, settling into a low ache between my thighs.

"Dinner doesn't lead to sex," I say when he pulls back.

"I would never make such a basic assumption about two people as complicated as we are, Raegan."

"Good."

His gaze traces my lips, the same path his mouth just did. "But dinner will lead to fighting. And fighting will lead to sex."

CHAPTER 10
Harrison

I've never found a deal as challenging as the woman sitting in the passenger seat of my car.

"Leni sent me specs, but I must be reading them wrong. All the industry standards are sold out?"

"Correct."

"But if you don't get the best, you'll lose talent," she finishes. "DJs won't want to play."

"It'll take another three months to get the standard installed. The cost in lost revenues is too high. Do you know how much a club like that will make every night it's open?"

"It'll hold two thousand people. Cover, drinks…" She runs through multiple facets of my business and drops a number at the end that's startlingly accurate.

I nearly groan.

Listening to her talk business is sexy.

Which is fucked up because we're talking about how screwed my club is.

"I need to make this work," I mutter. "I will force my way up the supplier list. Find a pressure point and press on it. Whatever Leni did, I'll double down."

"Come on, you didn't ask me to weigh in because you wanted an audience to how you'll go all 'tough guy.' We need to get creative."

I glance at her as we stop at a light. "This isn't MacGyver. I can't use a roll of duct tape and some toilet paper rolls to make a sound system for a high-end venue."

"But venues used other setups before this one was available," she argues. "Hell, you have others in your clubs."

She runs through them while I listen.

Rae is making it difficult to focus. Tonight, she's dressed in the heels from earlier, plus ripped jeans that hug every curve of her legs and hips, a black T-shirt, and oversized sunglasses. She could be a student going to class at UCLA, her hair pulled back in a high ponytail that tickles the headrest of the car when she turns to look at me.

I stare out the windshield as I navigate traffic, but all I'm picturing is twisting that hair around my hand while she comes on my cock.

"What about Blaze?"

I blink. "What's Blaze?"

"The club in Venice Beach. It closed not too long ago, and I heard it's getting sold off and converted into stores."

"You think there's a chance of getting their audio equipment."

"Has to go somewhere." She shrugs. "I could ask."

"Thank you." I read far too much into the fact that she's offering. She's smart and beautiful. My own damn kryptonite.

It'll be easier when we get to the exclusive beachfront restaurant.

A white linen tablecloth between us will keep me civilized.

When we arrive, there's no sign of the valet. I curse, and we park half a dozen blocks away.

"It's fine," Rae says. "Let's walk on the beach."

Most women I've dated would have pouted at having to walk, but she sounds as if she prefers it.

"Coming around to the idea of being seen with me?" I murmur as I hold her door.

"There are worse things."

"When was the last time a man you fucked, or wanted to, took you out for dinner?"

Rae considers as she starts down the sidewalk next to me. I get the feeling she's weighing something bigger than an offhand comment.

"Never."

It's my turn to be stunned.

"That would require someone to ask me," she goes on, "and for me to say yes."

"Endless complexity," I say dryly, but I'm fascinated. "Let's start simple. You tell me what's bothering you. I fix it, or use noncommittal male vocalizations to empathize."

She laughs, and the sound pleases me long after her smile fades once more. "I approached Wild Fest about a spot next spring. One of the recruiters is coming to my show next weekend in Long Beach. It would be a huge deal. They've never had a DJ headline who wasn't in the top twenty of Billboard's Top 100 DJ list."

We start down the concrete steps to the beach.

"I've met the cofounders. I could—"

"Don't you dare intervene for me," she says. "I need to do this on my own."

"Even if it was partly my fault your career was hindered? For the record, I don't feel an ounce of guilt," I go on. "The media will watch you and judge you as if it's their job. Your job is to live your life."

I take the last three steps to the beach as Raegan pauses to pull off her heels. When she straightens, I take advantage of her busy hands to lift her by the waist and set her on the sand in front of me. She's close enough her body brushes mine through our clothes.

"Just because you can do something yourself doesn't mean you should." I skim my hand around to her ass and squeeze lightly. She sways closer, and I bend my lips to her ear. "Goes for all manner of things, love."

When I step back, her eyes are nearly black.

We're surrounded by people, but I wish we were alone.

I want to run my fingers down between her legs, see if she's wet.

"I'll keep that in mind," she murmurs.

With every taste of her, I only want more.

It's startling and unnerving.

Rae's attention drifts past me, and I turn to see a food stand, half a dozen patrons clad in swimming trunks and casual wear waiting to order. I want to recoil on instinct, but she doesn't look away.

Fuck me.

"You want tacos." The three words land heavy in my gut.

"No." Rae turns back, pasting on a quick, false smile I never want to see again. "The restaurant is fine."

I've never been with a woman who didn't want the most

elegant things I could give her. Rae's differences are challenging to understand, but I want to try.

That's why I pull out my phone.

"What are you doing?" she demands.

"Texting the concierge to cancel." When I'm done, I hold out a hand for her shoes. "If we're going to eat at a restaurant with a queue, at least I can carry these for you like a gentleman."

"You don't have to."

"Too damn bad."

She hands them over, but the wry shake of her head has me frowning as we take our spot at the end of the queue.

What is she saying—no one's ever been a gentleman with her? Fuck.

"No more shop talk tonight," I decide, and she arches a brow.

"That a rule?"

"Yes. Besides, you might have already solved the equipment problem."

She grins, and I can't help but return it.

I want to show her something different.

We order tacos and find a spot to sit on the beach. Before Rae can sit, I spot a beach hut where I can purchase a towel embroidered with crabs so we can eat without getting sand in our food. Ash would piss himself laughing if he could see me now. We talk about all kinds of things.

"Most embarrassing moment?" I ask.

"A show in New York during arts school. I was mixing from my notebook, and it tried to run an update installation midcycle."

I laugh silently.

"What about you? I have a hard time picturing you

embarrassed."

"Fuck, there are loads," I insist, scanning my memories. "Oh. Initiation the first year of boarding school, we were at the beach, and some other boys stole my swimsuit. I had to walk back to the dorms with a piece of food wrap"—I hold up the paper from my taco—"to cover myself and explain to the headmaster why I was out without a uniform."

Her shoulders rock with laughter. The humiliation was worth it for this one moment.

"Favorite TV show?" she asks once she's recovered.

"*Great British Bake Off.*"

"You're lying."

"Am not," I insist. "And if you so much as think of telling another human, you won't live long enough to do it. What's yours?"

"*South Park.*"

I shake my head. "Unbelievable."

"That I like a cartoon?"

"Mhmm."

No. That I'm falling for a woman who likes a cartoon. I finish my taco, mostly managing to avoid dropping coleslaw on the sand.

"Proudest moment?" she asks me.

I don't have to think about it. "I've bought my share of venues, but I was twenty-five when I opened the first one I built from scratch. The moment we turned on the sign and those lights lit up the night, I swear I could feel my parents watching me. It was the first time I felt as if I was doing the right thing."

Rae studies me without blinking. "Well, that's intense. What was it called?"

"Brillante."

"I'm surprised you didn't name it something more personal."

"It never occurred to me," I say honestly. "Would you have? You never stay in one place long enough for anything to become personal."

"If it was a building, brick and mortar... I think I would."

I turn that over before asking my next question. "Most awkward sexual encounter?"

Rae knocks over her drink with a knee, cursing as she rights it. "I don't want to talk about it."

So, I change the subject, but I'm still wondering why that simple question threw off our conversation.

"I've never been to the beach in LA," I admit as I reach for the mineral water I bought.

"Seriously? How many times have you come here?"

"Dozens."

"Huh. I'm glad I can give you a first."

I reach a hand out to lift her chin. Then I lean in and brush my lips across hers.

She tastes like her soda, and I want to drink her dry. I want to lay her back on this towel and strip off her clothes and show her how fucking exquisite she is.

Instead, I allow her to finish her dinner before I walk her back to the car.

"Aren't we going back to your place?" she asks when I drive us away from my side of the city.

"No."

She looks over in surprise. "Why not?"

I'm torn between a laugh and a groan. "You've never had a gentleman. I wanted to give you a first too."

Her eyes soften in the twilight, and I grab onto that as my hands clench the steering wheel. She flicks on the radio, humming to the music as we drive.

I've never had someone I can coexist with. But her, right here… it feels surprisingly right.

Except for the blood diverted below my belt at the sound of her voice or any time I glance at her.

When I pull up to Beck's gates and put the car in park, she turns to face me.

"You can come in. But you can't stay ov—"

"No."

She blinks at me in surprise.

Her palm slides down my chest, rubbing across my erection through my pants. My body leaps under her touch. "You still want to be a gentleman?"

She's teasing me. I like seeing her empowered.

No.

"Yes."

Her hand threads through mine as she tugs me toward her.

I follow her lead, mostly because I have no idea what she's planning.

When she works open the button and fly of her jeans and slides my hand inside, I swallow my tongue.

She's slick and ready for anything I might wish to do to her. Knowing she was getting turned on by our conversation, by simply spending time together, blows my mind.

I rub a slow circle over her clit beneath her underwear, and her eyelids fall to half-mast as she arches against my touch.

"I want to see you tomorrow," I mutter.

Rae squirms, a noise of tortured pleasure escaping her lips before she answers, "No."

The fuck?

My fingers slip inside her heat.

First one, then a second.

My cock chafes against the zipper of my trousers. "The next day."

I could be free of these trousers in a minute. Inside her in two. Making her scream my name loudly enough her smug roommate can hear.

But I want to show her she means more to me than sex. I want her to trust me, to know that I want more of her. I want all of her.

"I'm busy this week," she pants, gripping my wrist as I slowly pump her with my fingers. "Working on this set."

She's letting me in physically but pushing me away emotionally.

I can't use my normal approach of pinning her down. Brute force does nothing with this woman. She turns to vapor.

It takes everything in me to withdraw my hand, leaving behind her sweet, tight heat. "I'm going to add you to my calendar. You look at it and let me know when you're available."

If it takes her more than three damn days, I'll be back over here. But I don't say that.

Raegan blinks in surprise, shoving at a chunk of hair that's fallen out of her ponytail. "You don't know what you're missing."

"I know exactly what I'm missing." I suck her off my fingers, and her jaw drops. "And what I got tonight is worth even more."

My balls ache the entire way home.

CHAPTER 11

Rae

"I Can't Feel My Face" streams out of my headphones, but it's my feet that've gone numb. Ernie's been lying on them for an hour while I sit on Beck's patio and work on my set for Long Beach.

I drum my fingers on the arm of the chaise, reviewing the set list.

When I approached them with the midsummer "zombie beach" theme a couple months ago, they were down with it. Though I'm still waiting on a final equipment confirmation, it's going to be great.

It has to be because Victoria said she'd come, and this is my chance to prove I deserve a spot at Wild Fest.

I gently move Ernie onto the patio despite his whine of protest. The track changes, and I shut my eyes to listen.

The dog licks my bare calves, and I hold out the headphones. "It's really fucking good, right?"

He sniffs them gingerly, his wet nose flaring.

"Don't tell Beck I was swearing around you. He thinks you're too impressionable."

Light glints off the diamonds set into each earpiece, the band connecting them. They're always with me now.

And so, it seems, is the man who gave them to me.

Harrison took me for dinner on the beach two nights ago. We ate tacos and talked about stupid bullshit that somehow felt important because of the man I shared it with. Seeing the billionaire relax enough to sit on the sand and laugh affected me. It made me think about how things could be, if I let them.

He's the one pushing us forward, pushing us closer. He peels back parts of me, even without words.

It's disconcerting.

By the time we were done with our food, I was having a really good time. Plus, I was looking forward to seeing him put his beautiful body to better use. When he drove me back to Beck's and told me good night, I nearly died.

I don't know if the way he fingered me in the car made it better or worse.

After cursing him in the foyer, I finally gave in, went upstairs, and made myself come twice, imagining his dirty mouth on me, his fingers inside me.

No matter what I felt while we were eating tacos and talking about his childhood antics, I'm not handing my heart to a man whose primary directive is to claim and conquer.

I grab a snack and return to the chaise as an email pops up. I read it twice.

Re: Next Weekend's Show

We apologize for the delay in responding to your request. It is no longer in our mutual interest to retain you for the engagement. Of course, we don't expect the deposit to be returned to us.

We look forward to collaborating in the future.

The club where I was booked to do my Zombeach just bailed on me.

This is not a small problem. It's a huge one.

I check their feed, and they've already swapped out my name for someone else's on the poster. Disbelief rises up. *What the actual fuck?*

I put all that effort into getting Victoria to this show, and I've been working on the set for two days straight.

I could curl up in a corner and squeeze my eyes shut and wait for the waves of emotion to rack me.

I could see Beck at the lot. He'd cheer me up, tell me not to sweat it.

Or I could call Annie in New York, who'd no doubt encourage me to make them see my side of things with some impassioned plea.

I don't want either.

This is Harrison's fault.

He insisted on giving me access to his calendar, which I haven't enabled on my phone. Now, I click into my calendar on my phone and check the box that syncs Harrison's calendar.

Events start to populate, dozens this week alone. There are meetings and calls and dinners and invitations at all hours of the day and night. Some of them even overlap.

I had no idea how busy running his empire really is. But it looks like he has a break in thirty minutes.

All I need is to see him. I want to chew him out. To say this is all his damn fault and my life was better before he entered it.

So, I drive to his penthouse, and the concierge lets me up.

"Harrison?" I call into the condo when I step inside.

There's no answer, and I stalk toward the office. "I'm not here for sex," I warn.

When I round the door, I pull up as I see two other men in suits inside, in addition to the man I'm here to see.

Three startled gazes fly to me, including one that's amused as it is surprised.

Shit.

"I didn't mean…" I hold up my phone. "I thought you had a break between meetings."

"Raegan. Wait." Harrison comes after me, catching up to me before I reach the elevator in the hall. "What's wrong?"

His gray suit is perfectly pressed, his jaw freshly shaved. He's as composed as I am wrecked, and the contrast has never felt so obvious as it does in this moment.

"The show I was supposed to play in Long Beach next weekend. They canceled it. Someone from Wild Fest was coming and…"

His probing gaze is compassionate. Genuinely caring. "Don't move."

He goes back into the penthouse before retuning with a sheaf of papers he hands to me.

"What are these?" I ask, flipping through the pages.

"A list of clubs with contact information. These are my competition. They're not all as shortsighted as the one you spoke with today."

I didn't come here for him to fix it. I came here to yell at him, but I can't. Now that I'm here, that's not what I want at all.

My chest tightens, and I step closer, folding the list in half and tucking it into my bag. The backs of my eyes burn.

"It's not fair." I sound like a kid but can't bring myself to care.

"No. It's fucking not."

He threads his fingers into my hair at the nape of my neck—to comfort, not to arouse. When he pulls me to his chest, I don't resist.

His arms go around me, and I can't deny how good it feels to be held by him.

Maybe I didn't come to yell at him. Maybe what I wanted even more was to look him in the eye and have him tell me I matter and all the reasons we shouldn't be together don't matter.

"Come inside," he murmurs against the top of my head. "My meeting ran late. I'll end it now."

"You don't have to. Your calendar is full, and—"

"It's only business." His mouth brushes over mine. Soft, not clinging.

"Never be ashamed to ask for what you want. If I can give it to you, it's yours."

"She's not answering," Harrison mutters from where his head's stuck in the cabinet. Phone glued to his ear, he searches out the perfect pan.

"Let me look online. There's got to be a good paella recipe."

"It's not the same. Natalia used to make it for us as boys. Ash loved it as much as I did, even helped make it." Harrison rises from his crouched position, bumping his head on the counter on the way. "Fuck."

I head to the freezer and pull out some ice, wrapping it in a towel.

He accepts it with a grimace. "I'm a dangerous man."

"It's occasionally sexy. Why don't you wear casual clothes?"

"I used to, but my father told me before I went to boarding school as a teenager, 'If they're going to catch you with your pants down, at least ensure your cufflinks are fastened.'"

I turn that over. "Well, no one is going to see you here. At least lose the dress shirt."

He peels it off, leaving an undershirt beneath. "Better?"

Now I'm staring. "You could put something else on."

"No. No, I think you're right. You should take something off too."

"Strip cooking isn't a thing."

"Just because it hasn't made it to America…"

"Oh. It's all over *GBBO*?" I roll my eyes and tug off my jeans. My underwear is a pair of plain black bikinis since I didn't plan on being here, so I'm basically still covered everywhere that counts. "There."

Harrison's gaze tracks unapologetically south, skimming the curves of my legs before lingering at the apex of my thighs.

"Where were we?" he murmurs.

"Tracking down Natalia's paella recipe."

I snap my fingers in front of his face, and his amused gaze flicks up to meet mine.

"Ah. It may be a lost cause. We could move to another of my

preferred activities when I've had a terrible day."

"Jerking off?"

"An excellent idea. But not where I was going. Sometimes I take Barney out. He reminds me things are simpler in his world."

"He's in Ibiza?" A nod. "He must miss you."

"Toro and Natalia take good care of him when I travel."

"We could borrow Beck's dog. But let's not give up on comfort food yet." I pull out my phone, then hit a FaceTime contact I haven't used in months.

I'm not seriously expecting an answer, so when Sebastian appears on the screen, the movement of a city street behind him, I'm delighted.

"Hey, Ash," I say.

"Raegan. To what do I owe the pleasure?"

Harrison's brows shoot up. "Why do you have my brother's number?" he mouths. He looks like a jealous teen, and I wave him off.

I say, "This a good time?"

"Sure, I'm heading home from practice."

"We're trying to make Natalia's paella."

He grins. "You with Harry? Or is this an attempt to impress some new boyfriend?"

Harrison grabs the phone from my hand. "I'm here, you prick. Now talk chorizo."

"Thought you'd never ask." His handsome face scrunches up, then he comes out with the ingredients.

I make notes on a piece of paper. We're going to have to go out and get these or have them delivered. There's tension between the two men, which I want to know more about.

"We watched your game the other day," I say.

"Match," they correct in unison.

"Right. It looked good. Does that mean things are going better?"

He freezes as if caught out. "Work in progress. I should let you get back to your activities."

After we hang up, I probe Harrison. "What's with the tension?"

"Since our parents died, he doesn't see me the same way he used to. He knows it's my fault they're not around."

"He got you a dog after you broke up with your fiancée. That means he cares."

"Or he wanted to punish me. He doesn't think I have a soul," Harrison says darkly. "He figured a dog would out me."

"And you proved him wrong."

His slow smile has my heart skipping.

"You don't talk about your family," he comments.

"A lot of people I trusted let me down when I needed them."

He brushes a hand through my hair. "Tell me what happened."

"Hard pass. You're not my therapist."

I try to make it sound light, but he doesn't smile.

"Listen," I go on, turning to pace the room, "despite the whole 'crashing your workday' thing, I'm not spending time with you because I need a well-tailored shoulder to cry on."

When I turn back to him, he's already closed the distance between us.

"There are moments in our lives that defy description.

Sometimes we cause them and sometimes we don't. But they are painful and incomprehensible, and pretending they're not doesn't make us more human. I need people around me. Leni, and Toro, and Natalia, and even Ash. You need to let someone in."

The openness in his voice and his face is undeniable. He's lived through his share of shit, but even if I wanted to invite him into mine, he can't possibly understand.

"Well, this army of one thing has been working out for me so far." I force my attention to the shopping list. "Should we go out and get these?"

It's an obvious subject change, and I think he's going to argue.

"Let's have them delivered."

He places the order with the concierge, who promises to have all we need delivered in an hour. When Harrison tugs me toward the doors to the deck, I follow.

On a chaise, he tucks me between his legs. "What are you going to do about Wild Fest?"

"Well, I have to tell Victoria the gig's off. But I saw on their page they have a dark horse spot. Basically, fan votes," I go on at his questioning look.

"Are you in the running?"

I pull it up on my phone and make a face. "Twenty-fifth. There's one spot." I frown. "I'm playing in Miami on Thursday. If I can get enough fans to share the show, it'll be a boost."

"I'm visiting my club there Friday, plus I could use the change of scenery. Give Leni a few days to work on this warehouse without me. Suppose I could head over early."

"You'd come to my show? At someone else's club?" I ask, surprised. Every part of me hums with anticipation. The idea of him watching me is thrilling.

"You going to ask me?"

My lips twitch, and I fight the impulse to smile, squaring my shoulders. "Come to my show, asshole."

"Fuck, you're irresistible."

But when he drags me against him, I can't help laughing.

CHAPTER 12
Rae

avana Nights looms on Collins Avenue in Miami, an art deco monument. I'm at the bar early to set up.

I need this gig in order to make my case for Wild Fest. Most of all, I need the line of partiers to vote for me. Normally, I wouldn't ask for that kind of help, but I'm desperate. So, I hired someone to make graphics encouraging my fans to vote.

The club is full, Harrison talking to the owner and some patrons in one of the VIP booths. Of course he made himself at home.

The crowd is mostly people who want to escape for the night. I give them every ounce of my focus, sweat and attention.

I catch Harrison's eye once, and I'm rewarded with a long, smoldering look of appreciation that adds to the high of being onstage.

When he finally turns away to speak with someone, I notice another man in the adjacent VIP booth watching me over the rim of his drink. Unlike his buddies, he hasn't averted his eyes once in the last two songs.

I play my mind out. At the end of my set, I sneak a look at the voting for Wild Fest on my phone as I duck offstage.

Twenty-third. It's a minor blip. But people can vote more than once. Ten times in a twenty-four-hour period, technically. Which means every person in line for selfies is that much more important.

"Two minutes," I shout to security before ducking out back.

I need to catch my breath before heading back in.

The alley is a reprieve—no cooler than inside, but I inhale deeply anyway.

I'm going over what went down in my mind, reliving it with a breathless smile in this moment of privacy until movement at the mouth of the alley draws my attention.

A large, dark form.

Harrison.

I start to call out, but as he comes closer, I realize it's not Harrison.

This man's coarse where Harrison is sleek, jerky where he's smooth.

"I was watching you in there. Making everyone want you."

He wedges up against me, and I can't breathe. My heart explodes.

"I thought you were someone else," I manage.

"Come on. You want this."

Really fucking don't.

There's a chance to lunge under his arm and run for the street, but I'm a second late and his hand goes around my throat and cuts off my air.

I grab for his wrist, fingernails digging into his skin. He flinches but doesn't let go.

An icy sheet of fear slices me in two.

It's not like what happened with Mischa. I was freaked but knew someone was only a breath away.

This is dark. No one is here.

The sounds of the party are distant, and no matter how strong I am on the inside, all that matters is this man's grip.

"Miss?" security calls into the alley from way too far away.

I can't speak, can't breathe. I wave my hands, trying to signal.

"Hey!"

The man pulls back, and I shove at him and duck away, staggering down the alley toward the club entrance.

My surroundings are a blur. I trip inside, looking both ways, and find my way back to the green room.

I press my head between my knees and gulp air.

I need space.

"Raegan. Are you all right?"

Harrison's voice comes from above me, but I don't look up.

"What the hell happened?" he barks but not at me.

"A man approached her outside. Seems it triggered… this."

Security radios the manager, whose voice I hear a moment later.

"I'll take it from here," Harrison says.

I'm swept into the back of a car, the leather seats worn yet too formal for the rawness eating me from the inside out.

I want to scream.

I want to die.

I wrap my arms around my knees and do neither.

Harrison

She's gone.

Raegan is gone, and the woman curled in the back of the limo is someone I don't know. Her cheeks shine with tears, her dark lashes blinking rapidly as she stares at the floor.

"Did he hurt you?" I ask, trying to keep my voice low and calm for her benefit. Inside, I'm enraged and worried.

She shakes her head once.

He might not have hurt her, but he scared the hell out of her.

Management said they'd captured the man and that he didn't have a weapon. Which means he terrified her with his body or his words.

She's swaying with the motion of the car, and I lean forward to tell the driver to keep driving. It seems to be helping, or at least not hurting.

"Raegan," I say when I return to her, kneeling on the floor so I'm beneath her. "This happened before."

She doesn't answer.

"At my club?" I barely force out the words.

A slow headshake.

But my negligence did this—worse than this—to other women. Regret is heavy in my gut, a roiling grief that won't relent.

"A long time ago," she says at last.

She's so fucking young now. That someone met her years before, wanted her, hurt her—it makes me murderous.

"I don't talk about it." Her grip on her knees tightens.

My fingers dig into the seat upholstery to keep from ripping the roof off the car. "If you tell me now, I won't ask you to again."

I need to know what happened. I can't stand her keeping secrets, not only because I'm used to having full information, but because they're eating her alive.

Her glassy eyes scan the street beyond the window. "I don't want you to look at me differently."

What the fuck?

"There's nothing you could say that would change how I look at you."

Her gaze finds mine, and it's full of fear. "Are you sure?"

"Yes."

She takes a slow breath. "It was sophomore year, and my brother was having a party with some friends from campus. My parents were gone for the weekend. There was a guy from his class—older, preppy, good looking. Like my brother, he'd gone to our high school, and a lot of the girls had a thing for him. I thought I did too. Until I didn't.

"We were under the deck outside, drinking. He kept saying I wanted it, and I kept telling myself maybe I did, but it wasn't true."

The streetlights fly past the window, but I don't bother to look out. I'm numb to everything but the woman in front of me.

"Did he rape you?"

The voice sounds like mine, but I don't remember forming the question.

"Yes."

I die.

A piece of my soul shrivels up, but my heart keeps beating because she keeps talking, and I need to be here for her. With her.

"There are parts of the night I remember, and others I don't. I woke up in my bed. I was…" She swallows. "I was sore."

Fuck. "He slipped something in your drink."

A nod. "I went over it a hundred times. That's the only thing I can come up with. I remember not wanting to be part of it. But the party was thirty feet away, and I didn't scream. I didn't do anything."

"Did you report him?" My voice is even, as if listening to what she's saying doesn't make me feel as if I'm being burned alive.

None of it matters. I'm focused on her.

"I went to the police station but couldn't go through with it. I didn't tell my parents, not at first. But the burden got to be too much to keep it inside. I struggled in school. Couldn't sleep. Stopped eating. When I admitted to my parents what happened, they fought over what to do about it. My mother wanted to have him charged and expelled from school. My father disagreed."

If my teeth clench any harder, they might break. "How is that possible?"

"It's not the way it sounds. The guy was from a connected family. My dad didn't like seeing me hurt, and he thought reporting it would hurt me more. He tried to fix it in his own way. Got me a new computer. A synth. I wasn't able to do anything productive, so I threw myself into making music.

"It was something I could do when I couldn't do anything else. I'd spend hours working on tracks. Mixing and mastering. I didn't need to act a certain way. I didn't need to feel a certain way. I could put my headphones on and drown out the world. Hell, sometimes I could even drown out my thoughts."

My chest is raw, scraped down to my ribs.

I wanted to know her.

I didn't expect *this*.

"When I stopped going out to parties, my supposed friends decided I wasn't interesting anymore. The one person who believed me and didn't leave me or make me feel like an outcast was my cousin, Callie."

I hate that Rae suffered that kind of torture, and I hate that she kept this to herself. No wonder she doesn't trust anyone to take care of her.

"I have one more question." My voice is surprisingly even considering I'm a second from burning down the world. "Who was he?"

Before she can answer, her phone buzzes. She glances at the notifications.

"Fans are pissed I didn't stay for selfies." She curses. "I needed those extra Wild Fest votes. Did you know you can vote ten times in a twenty-four-hour period?"

It's totally irrelevant given what went down. But it's not irrelevant to her. She's focusing on something she feels she can control to block out the grief. I know what that feels like. I did it after my parents died, channeling every part of me into building an empire.

I grab my phone and navigate to the Wild Fest page. "Here?"

She presses her lips together, nodding. "But you have to create an… account."

Her voice trails off as I complete the signup. Then I vote for Little Queen, one time after another.

When I'm done, I tuck the phone away and look up to find her watching me. In her dark eyes and pressed-together lips, I see a semblance of Raegan returning.

"I'd like to stay with you tonight," I say. "I'll sleep on the couch. The floor. Whatever makes you feel safest."

"I don't need that." Rae exhales heavily, and her feet descend toward the floor on either side of me.

My chest contracts as I take her in, a long sweep. "I do."

Rae

When we get out at the mid-rise boutique hotel, Harrison lets me go first. Not because he's being a gentleman. Because he's concerned. It's written on every inch of his handsome face, every tense line of his body.

I told him a secret I never meant so share. One I buried so far down it hasn't seen the light of day in years.

And we can't go back.

Tonight was my chance to make a statement that I'm worthy of Wild Fest. But by this time tomorrow, there'll be a ton of comments about how I left without saying goodbye and no more votes.

Nothing was gained, and it feels like something huge was lost.

The elevator gets to my floor and the doors slide open, but he doesn't move.

I brush past him. "You should go." He planned to stay in Miami for longer, so he booked a penthouse on the ocean a few miles north of the one my gig secured for me. "I'm going to take a bath and go to bed."

"I'm not leaving."

My hands clench into fists. "I mean it. Fucking leave."

"You were right," he says from behind me, and I pause near my door. "Tonight changed something between us."

My eyes squeeze shut. This is what I was afraid of. Our relationship has been filling a void I'd told myself didn't need filling.

And now it's over.

I reach for the key and slip it into the lock.

"I understand why you don't let people in. I can't promise to make up for all of them, Raegan. But I'll fucking die trying."

The raw confession as he steps toward me has my heart thudding against my ribs.

I let go of the key and turn slowly, the carpet soundless under my feet.

He fills the hallway in his dark suit. Somewhere along the way, he lost the tie. The blue of his eyes is like a stormy sea. His throat works, his scent washing over me as he closes the distance between us.

I trust him more than I ever thought I would. But he's asking for more. To be let in when I'm vulnerable, when all I want to do is shut out the world.

I reach for the key once more, pushing in the door before pausing.

"You can sleep on the couch."

CHAPTER 13
Harrison

I can't remember the last time I slept on a sofa.

But I am now, springs digging into my sides and my feet hanging off the end. I've never humbled myself like this for a woman. If tonight's events weren't enough to keep me awake, the discomfort would be. Somehow, though, I manage to fall asleep, because the next time I blink my eyes open, there's movement by the door to the bedroom.

I shift onto my elbow, ignoring the pain in my neck from sleeping on a throw pillow. "Raegan?"

She approaches without a word and stops next to the sofa. Her hair is braided over one shoulder after her bath, an oversized T-shirt covering her body.

"How much is sleeping on that couch killing you?" she murmurs.

"Never better," I lie.

In the dark, I can't see her face, but she holds out a hand. I lace my fingers through hers, running my thumb across her skin.

"C'mon." Rae tugs me to standing.

I'm awake in an instant, following her toward the bedroom. I fell asleep in shorts, my suit draped across a chair. The hairs on my chest lift in the cool air as we cross to the bed.

My eyes adjusting to the dark, I stare at the dent on the right side of the king bed and chuckle.

"We sleep on the same side, don't we?" she asks.

"It would be too easy if we didn't." I stroke her hand with my thumb. "I'll wrestle you for it."

This time it's definitely a laugh.

She turns toward me, our hands still linked.

"Tell me how to help you," I murmur.

She's quiet a moment, as if no one's ever asked her that. "After a show, I can lie awake for hours. Sometimes, in my head, I wind up back at that party as a teenager. No matter how many years or gigs or miles I put between myself and that night, I can't forget it. I don't want to be there. I want to be here, with you."

I've always needed purpose, and the trust on her face gives me a new one.

I inch closer until she's a breath away. She doesn't move.

My lips caress hers. Gentle, simple, without the intent to tease or arouse. She sighs against me, her palm flattening against my bare abs, making me tighten under her touch.

I kiss her like I've never kissed a woman, but then everything is a challenge with her. Even taking things slow with her is torture. Her tongue brushes mine, and my cock hardens.

I meant what I said. Something did change tonight.

Just not what she thought.

I back her toward the bed until her knees hit the sheets.

She breaks our kiss. "You still want me."

There's no inflection at the end, but it's a question. Every inch of her body, the trembling of her lips, tells me it is.

"I wake up wanting you." I drag the shirt over her head. "I go to sleep wanting you."

Her soft curves have me aching, and I slide my hands to touch her breasts with nothing between us.

"I breathe, I fucking want you."

Her eyes are wide, cheeks flushed, and lips already bruised from mine. "Show me."

I don't know how to fix her, but there's nothing to be fixed. She's made the way she is. Like me, she's a combination of everything that's happened to her.

She's not broken. She's beautiful.

A piece of art as exquisite for its flaws as its perfections.

"I'm not going to let you out of this bed."

"All night?" she asks.

"Ever."

I spread her knees so I can stand between them, her eyes darkening. I want to leave every part of her swollen and humming. Use every part of myself to worship her and every trick I've ever learned.

My body is tight everywhere, already anticipating my release, but it's a long time away. I'll make her lose her mind first, to see only me when she closes those beautiful eyes.

Her nipples are hard in the cool air, and I bend to suck one. Rae's head falls back, her hair splayed out like dark silk on the duvet.

"Every time I make you come, you say my name."

She snorts. "Seems redundant. Unless you're worried I'm picturing Daniel Kaluuya when I close my eyes. He is handsome and British…"

I bite her and am rewarded by a yelp and her hand tightening in my hair. I want her to trust me to make her feel things. To not run away from me.

I start with her breasts, licking and sucking until she's breathing roughly. Then I skim down her body, kneeling between her legs to press my mouth to where she's hot and wet.

The lace is rough, and her flesh is slick and smooth. I would tear it off except that it's frustrating her every bit as much as me, and that's my goal.

I grab the side of her thong and draw it up, pulling so it tightens everywhere, leaving lines in her skin and making her slit puff against the lace.

My other hand slides up to rub her breast, tracing a thumb around her nipple before pinching. I suck on her until she breaks, shaking and shivering.

"Say it." I trace a finger up the inside of her thigh, and she trembles from the climax.

"I'm not even naked—"

I press my tongue against her once more where she's sensitive, and she squirms, but I don't let her inch away.

"Harrison. Okay?"

I shift over her, the dazed expression on her face and the fact that her eyes are glazed with pleasure instead of haunted telling me I'm on the right track. She traces her nails down my chest and stomach. I love it enough that I hate what I need to do next.

"Flip."

With a suspicious look, she does.

The sight of her arse in the air has me biting my tongue. I run both hands over her, squeezing and admiring how good she feels as much as the little sound of pleasure that escapes her.

I brush the hair back from her ear. "I'm going to fuck you now."

"You didn't last long."

"Not with my cock. Need to leave something to look forward to."

The underwear stays on, and the next time she comes, it's around two of my fingers, my thumb pressing hard against her clit.

"Harrison," she pants against the duvet, her hands fisting in the fabric.

She shifts to look over her shoulder, eyes full of hazy pleasure and accusation as I lick her off my fingers.

"How many more times can you come?"

Her sigh is tortured. "None."

I press my lips to the base of her spine. "So much to learn."

I rip the lingerie off her hips, ignoring her gasps as I plunge two fingers back inside her, adding a third when she's rocking toward me even as her legs shake.

My mouth finishes her off, and she cries out against the sheets, her sounds muffled.

"Can't hear you," I rasp.

"Harrison."

I shift her up the bed and onto her back, lifting her knees and instructing her to hold them there. "Again."

The next time, her toes tighten around my neck as I suck on her, my hands squeezing her ass.

"Stop," Rae pants, one hand fisted in my hair to hold me away as she scrambles back toward the headboard.

I firmly pry her fingers away, pinning them at her side.

"Why?" I ask.

"It hurts."

"Physically or because you're not used to someone putting you first?"

"Both."

It's devastating she's never had anyone take care of her, even though the woman she's become through that independence is admirable.

I want to be that man.

I bend down to press my lips to hers.

When I pull back, I reach for my trousers to grab a condom, but her cool touch on my arm stops me.

"We don't have to."

"You want to stop?"

Not being inside her after what we've done might kill me. My cock aches, leaking more every time she moans and writhes through a climax I dragged her to.

"No, I mean you don't have to use protection. I'm on the pill. Have you...?"

I don't answer because I'm stunned silent.

My muscles are tight, as if I've been worked over rather than her.

"Yes. I've been tested."

Relief washes over her, and she moves first, her lower lip caught between her teeth as she tugs down my shorts.

I rise and kick them off before shifting back over her, leveraging myself over her body with my elbows. Lowering until we're skin to skin, heat to heat.

I move between her thighs, nudging them wider and grazing her wetness to feel her tremble. The head of my cock slides against her soaked flesh, and the feel of her makes me groan.

Man on his knees.

That's what this would be called.

Because as I grab her hip and sink inside her, one inch at a time, I am fucking *fallen.*

She trusted me tonight, and that tells me we're going to be okay. Everything else, the club, I can handle. The greatest gift I've ever gotten is the one she's given me.

Not sharing her body with me, but her life. Her hopes. Her fears.

I'll guard her with every shred of my being.

I let us both adjust, her to the stretch, me to the exquisite tightness.

I draw back, all the way to the tip, on an inhale. And on my exhale, I sink back in.

The curves of her body are addictive, demanding my attention. But I can't look away from her eyes as my thrusts grow deeper.

"You're a goddess."

I'm on the edge, ready to explode.

"I'm a queen," she corrects with a breathless smile.

We come at the same time.

I've never wanted it, never understood why it would matter for our bodies to agree even when our lips couldn't.

With her, it's everything.

After, she lets me hold her in the dark.

"You're my queen," I murmur as I brush the hair from her face.

But she's already asleep.

CHAPTER 14
Rae

"We can't let it go for that amount."

The manager at Blaze turns away from me and Leni, marking something off on his clipboard.

When I told Leni I'd made a call about buying the former club's audio equipment after returning from Miami, she agreed to come for a meeting. I decided to tag along in case I could help and because I needed a few hours away from my own thoughts.

I chase the manager, Leni hot on my heels. "It's a good offer for used gear, Tony. Wouldn't you rather it go to another club?"

"I'm not the owner. But if I were him, he'd say fuck no. Why should someone else succeed at this game when Blaze got squeezed out?"

It's petty, and I'm still turning that over as Leni sidles up.

"Listen, friend." She flashes teeth, but I'm not sure it's a smile. "This place is being demolished. It's being taken apart around you."

And it is—as we speak, tradespeople are passing through, taking measurements to convert this into whatever it will be.

"In a few months, it'll be like this was never here. Your owner might not give a shit because he's onto the next investment. But you do. If some of your crew need jobs?" She holds out a card. "You can send them my way. Sick days. Flexible shifts. I'll treat them right."

He takes the card from her, considering.

But I'm watching Leni. Dressed in shorts and a floral-printed tank top, she doesn't look like the right-hand man to a billionaire. But the intensity on her face sets her apart.

"If you can add a few thousand to your offer and promise you'll interview my staff," Tony says slowly, "I'll go to work on the owner."

This time, Leni's smile is genuine. "You do that."

As we head out into the sunshine, rounding the back parking lot to Leni's beat-up Jetta, I'm still turning over what happened.

She shifts into the driver's side, and I get in opposite her.

"How did you end up working for Harrison?"

Leni laughs as we pull out of the parking lot and slip into the glut of traffic. "That is a long-ass story."

"Will you tell me?"

My visit to Miami had started on a high before taking a rough turn. That man in the alley reminded me of things I've tried to leave behind.

But Harrison wouldn't let me run from myself or the memories.

He wrapped strong arms around me and refused to budge.

From the moment I woke up in that bed alone, I knew I wanted him with me. I hadn't planned on sex and sure as hell didn't plan on skipping the condom.

The fact that we did was one more wall coming down between us.

What happened physically was beyond anything I've experienced, though I'm not about to tell him.

It's always felt like two steps forward and one step back with us, but lately, it's only forward. I keep waiting for him to pull away, but every vulnerability, every moment, he moves into it. Occupies it as naturally as if he's always been in my life and my heart.

I'm consumed by him, when he's with me and when he's not.

Leni reaches for the radio and turns it on. "You know, while we're in Venice Beach, there's this thrift store I love."

I don't feel much like shopping, but there's nowhere I need to be.

Jagged Lovely, the thrift store, is large enough to hold maybe ten people. The woman inside greets us with a warm wave before returning to stock merchandise.

Leni makes a beeline for the dresses, and I tag along.

"You must need something," she prompts without looking up.

"I have my brother's wedding to go to in a couple of weeks."

"And you don't have a dress?" She grins. "You sure aren't like the usual ones."

"The usual what? Women Harrison hangs out with?"

She doesn't answer, but her hand flips through the hangers with reverence. She stops on a soft aqua cocktail dress with a white lace overlay. It's vintage and beautiful.

"What about this?"

"Um. Yeah, it might be long on you—"

"I meant for you."

I hold it up, surprised. It is beautiful. More delicate than something I'd normally choose.

"We have someone in house that does alterations," the woman working calls over.

"Thanks." I shove a hand through my hair. "I could try it on."

"You do that."

When I head toward the single changeroom stall in the back, I'm regretting the move. So much for Leni telling me about Harrison.

But as I strip out of my street clothes and start to tug the dress over my head, her voice drifts into the stall.

"There was this amazing thrift store back in college. I still have clothes from it today." She laughs. "Not sure how it stayed in business when everyone in that town was flush. Me, on the other hand? I was there on a mashup of scholarships and student loans."

My hands still after I tug the fabric down around my hips, facing away from the mirror. "That's when you met Harrison."

"Yep. He was the Richie Rich type. Add in that accent… whew. You can bet all the Park Avenue princesses wanted a piece of him."

I grin as I reach for the zipper.

"He indulged them. But no one caught his attention long enough to stick. He was smart, serious about his studies as a matter of pride even though he didn't have to be. That's how we got to be friends. I had this crappy basement apartment in town, so I practically lived at the library. He spent his share of time there too—I think because people didn't bother him."

I snort, enjoying the idea of a twenty-year-old Harrison King having to hide out to avoid unwanted attention.

"We were teamed up for a project for business school. Once he realized I was legit and I got over the idea that he was just like the others, we got to be friends. After graduation, I started working in PR in New York. It was my dream job, and I was going to pay off the massive student loans. But the man in charge of the agency—

the same one who hired me six months before on the strength of my portfolio—fired me and took my ideas. I had no money and no options."

My chest tightens at the thought. "You called Harrison."

"No, he called me. He'd been keeping tabs and somehow heard what happened. He offered me a job running his first club. At first, I was too proud to take it. But when he assured me it wasn't just running a club, that he wanted to build an empire and he needed someone he trusted to help, I said yes."

"You're saying Harrison doesn't care where you come from."

"No. I'm saying he does."

I turn toward the mirror, and my breath sticks in my throat.

"Well?" Leni demands. "Is it on?"

She yanks on the curtain without waiting for me to respond.

"Damn, Rae," she whistles, inspecting me from head to toe. "I'm two for two today."

"It's a little loose here…" I pinch the back.

"You heard the woman. You can get it taken in. Problem solved."

After I change out of the dress and make arrangements for purchasing and alterations, Leni says, "I assume you're taking the boss to this wedding?"

"We haven't talked about it."

Miami was a big step for us, and I want to bask in the enjoyment of that before taking another crazy leap.

"Which is Raegan for 'I haven't given him a chance,'" she calls as we head back outside.

"Are you pissed or something?" I demand as I follow her up the sidewalk.

"I'm protective," she tosses. "I won't let anything bad happen on my watch."

I pull up a few feet from where the car is parked. "You're worried I'm going to hurt Harrison?"

Her sigh makes me feel as if I've missed something entirely.

She turns, leaning a tanned arm on the roof of the Jetta. She surveys me as if she's a teacher trying to decide if I'm worth the effort of educating.

"Before you left Ibiza, he did something big for you. I shouldn't even talk about it."

"Well, now you have to tell me."

Her expression says she doesn't have to tell me shit. But I stare her down, and finally she relents.

"Christian made him an offer that would let him get La Mer. But he'd have to give you up to do it."

Shock rises up, twisting my stomach.

Harrison had a chance at winning the club he's always dreamed of, and he gave it up for me.

"He said no," Leni says, interrupting my thoughts.

The wind whips at my hair, and I brush it out of my face with unsteady fingers.

It doesn't make sense. None of it does.

I shake my head. "What kind of deal would even require—"

"It doesn't matter. There's nothing else to say," she says, her voice rising, "except that he said no."

Harrison

"Bank. Wasteland. Knot. But with a K," I add, disgusted.

Leni laughs from across the office in the future club. "That's all marketing sent over for names?"

"The others are worse."

"If it doesn't sound like a place people want to go, no one will come."

It's been a week and a half since Miami, and we're making progress on the venue. The floors are coming together, and the walls are nearly complete.

With Rae and Leni's help, we've gotten most of the equipment sorted from the other club.

Of course, there's still the major problem of having this place rezoned.

My phone rings with a familiar number, and I hit Accept. "Leni's here too," I say by way of an answer.

"We should talk privately," comes my finance lead's voice over the speakerphone.

"You can say whatever you have to in front of her." But I rise and cross to the door, shutting it to keep out any ears from the other side.

He still hesitates. "Mischa's escalating. Buying more aggressively, a new club in Tokyo and one in Milan. Our intel doesn't show any major upgrades or changes to his venues, so we don't know where he's getting the capital—"

"From scaling his drug operations."

The words hang in the air.

If he has enough free cash to finance that, it's a bad sign for my planned acquisition of La Mer. My investigators are working around the clock on finding the evidence Christian wants, but I need it fast.

"How much can we afford to offer Geroux for La Mer?"

He names a number.

"I need more." I can't have Mischa blinding Christian with money, possibly making the old man succumb to greed when I need him to remember his honor.

He pauses, seeming to consider. "I could see about refinancing a couple of lease agreements. Find another five million. But's a short-term option at best."

"Do it. And stop Mischa from buying anything else in the interim."

"Stop him?" he echoes.

"Red tape," I reply, thinking of my own situation. "Miles deep. I want him focused on his problems, not on La Mer."

"If you're using short-term financing," Leni comments after I hang up, "making this new club a success is more important than ever."

And we're still waiting on a bloody hearing.

"It sucks that you have to play fair and Mischa doesn't…" She makes a face. "If it were Mischa waiting on an approval, Zachary would be hanging by his toes in a basement somewhere."

"On the contrary. Much can be achieved through reasonableness. What success requires is knowing when each is called for."

She watches as I place a call to the man who's causing my

headaches—my stateside ones, at least.

"Zachary. Harrison King."

"To what do I owe the pleasure?" His tone is guarded.

"I have box seats to… a Lakers game," I decide on impulse.

But Leni waves her hands, shaking her head, and I frown.

"Ah, opening night. In—"

She mouths a word.

"—October. I understand you enjoy sports."

The quick investigation done by one of my staff says so.

"I couldn't accept them. I avoid all possibility of impropriety."

"I see. And the courtside seats to the Masters tennis tournament in Palm Desert this spring. Those are public sector seats?"

Leni throws up her hands. Evidently, she's not impressed with my idea of reasonableness.

"Family friend," he says at last, his voice perceptibly cooler after my veiled threat. "Now, I don't know what you're implying, but if you'll excuse me—"

"I'm implying that we understand one another."

Some people can be bought. Others are persuaded by shows of strength, and by threats.

Neither will work with Whelan. Or at least, he's unwilling to be seen as being bought.

I'm not surprised given my research also suggested he comes from a moneyed family, but it's irritating nonetheless.

So, I change approaches.

"We're both men with significant influence."

My influence is far greater than his, but this is a negotiation, not a pissing contest. The reality is, he can make my life difficult. Which I don't want.

"You have a city to run and decisions to make as to its future. I respect a man who can't be distracted from his core mandate. I respect that more than you know. I'm committed to this investment, Zachary. The sooner we can get this queued up, the sooner we can make a toast to our respective futures and continue with our important work."

He's silent a long time. "I'll have our scheduler get it on the books. She'll follow up in the next day or two."

I hang up, grimly triumphant as a delivery arrives. Leni watches, obviously curious, as I open the garment bag and laugh.

"Jeans. Is this a joke?" she asks.

I grab the note from around the hanger.

Don't say I never bought you anything. Rae.

"No. It appears she's quite serious." My lips twitch.

We've been spending more time together. Since she and Leni went to negotiate the deal on our equipment with Blaze, she's stayed over at my condo twice, though she contended it was only because I let her have her preferred side of the bed.

The past few days, she's been traveling, busting her ass to make up more ground on the Wild Fest fan vote list. She's a powerhouse, and I dare anyone to try to keep her from something when she's made up her mind.

I've been aching without her.

So, when she proposed our plans for this evening, it felt like a step forward.

"We're going to a concert tonight," I tell Leni as I shuffle through the papers on the desk, tossing the list of potential names in the recycling bin where it belongs. "Tyler Adams's final show in Denver."

Leni sighs. "Well, fuck. You are in love with her."

I can't stop the way my chest tightens at the word. "Because I'm taking a beautiful woman to a concert?"

"No, because you're planning to wear those to do it." Her smile fades. "Your final year of college, before your parents died, you were ready to walk away from the family business."

"I was going to take my trust fund, move to some island, start a small tourist business to keep me busy, and never come back."

It sounds foolish now. Not only because that life wouldn't have sustained me, but because I was a naïve child who had no idea what the future held.

When my parents died, it hit me. The guilt. The emptiness. My responsibilities.

Now, I'm at the helm of a massive company. One that will expand until I crush the man who took this business and made it the kind of personal he can never take back.

"I'm still glad to see you doing something like this," Leni goes on, nodding toward me. "Even if those clothes will melt off your skin."

I shift out of my seat and cross to the door, lifting the garment bag off the hook on the back. "I'm not the devil, just a man who likes suits," I gripe.

But Leni's right. This matters even more than I figured. To Raegan and me, but also because the world will see us.

After our date on the beach with tacos, my PR firm emailed a number of photographs paparazzi took of the two of us.

I told them to buy the images. I didn't want anything scaring Reagan off when I was trying to convince her to spend time with me.

Now, I feel my pocket for the outline beneath. The box burns a hole in my clothing.

Soon enough, everyone will know what she means to me.

"Leni." I pause halfway out the door. "Have security lined up for Raegan. Starting tomorrow."

CHAPTER 15

Rae

Rae: Sorry, traffic's a bitch. Be there in 15. Save me some whisky.

I'm late to meet Harrison at LAX to fly to Denver for Tyler's concert.

Harrison's going to be pissed. I get that it's a private plane and he won't be leaving without me, but still. He's used to things running a certain way, and he was the one who insisted on providing the transportation when I asked him about tonight.

So, when he texts me a picture of a drink, I nearly drop my phone.

Harrison: No promises. :)

Rae: Did you just smiley-face me? Who the fuck are you?

The limo pulls right up to the runway when I arrive, and I shift out with a single bag in tow. My boots click on the metal steps, echoing off the body of the plane. In the distance, others land and take off, but this section of LAX is quiet.

"Traffic was murder…" I say as I step into the private plane.

Harrison looks up from his phone. His mouth is pursed, brows pulled together on his handsome face. He's wearing the reading glasses I got him, but it's the way he's dressed that has me pulling up.

His windowpane button-down shirt is a blue that matches his eyes. The dark denim underneath clings to his strong thighs.

"Damn," I breathe. "I didn't think you'd actually wear it."

"In that case, I have a suit to change into." But he motions me over, and I drop my bag on the floor before sinking onto his lap.

"Quick, tell me you want me." My murmur is barely audible as the plane engine starts.

Harrison's pale lashes jerk as he looks between my eyes and my mouth. "I'm wearing denim. There's no greater evidence."

I grin and press my lips to his. One arm bands around my hips, pulling me closer, while his other hand angles my mouth against his so he can invade me with his tongue.

I used to chafe at the possessiveness, but it's growing on me.

Since Miami, we've been getting closer. We haven't revisited the conversation after my show, but knowing he knows what happened to me means one less thing between us.

Our time together is addictive. I don't need an excuse to see him. All I have to do is text him and we make plans. This man, the ruthless billionaire I used to hate, is a phone call away to share a joke, run an idea by. He makes me coffee before I'm awake, and even watched South Park with me for an entire evening when I didn't feel like going out.

The sex hasn't slowed down either. I take back my comments

about age doing things to a man's endurance. He's relentless.

In bed, he takes me apart with his skilled hands and mouth. His body is a finely tuned machine, hard planes and smooth muscles that know exactly how to make me split open.

And though I'm no porn star and don't play one on TV, you'd never know it by the way he looks at me, the sounds he makes when I'm touching him.

We haven't defined it, but it's so much more than casual. Not that anything with him has ever felt casual, but if there was any doubt, I'm pretty sure we blew past it the second I walked in on his stubborn ass sleeping on my couch in Miami, his rangy form contorted to fit the furniture because he refused to leave me.

Now, Harrison's lips slant deliciously across mine, sending waves of desire down my spine that settle into a sweet ache between my thighs, and I ignore that part of me.

He pulls back an inch. "As much as I'd like to continue this, we have to go. And to do it, you need to sit there."

I look at the leather seat over my shoulder. "Unfortunate."

But I comply, fastening my seatbelt as the plane prepares to take off.

"I can't believe you've never been to Red Rocks," I say after settling in. "One of the world's greatest outdoor venues."

"I'm glad you can show it to me," he says. "Thank you. For inviting me."

Warmth floods me, has me looking away. "In fairness, we are taking your ride." I gesture to the plane.

"I'm serious. When was the last time you invited someone to join you and your friends?"

My instinct is to say it's not a big deal or deny the fact that

I think about him all the time, that I naturally look to include him, and when I'm deciding what to do, I automatically check his schedule.

"Never," I admit.

The vulnerability creeps up. Since Miami, I've felt it more than once. Normally, it makes me shut down, but I'm learning to live with it.

There've been no games except the kind we're both on board for. I've never dated a man who's so direct about what he wants.

Although he still has an irritating habit of expecting he'll get it.

The plane takes off, and we stick to safe subjects for the majority of the two-and-a-half-hour flight.

"Your hard work this week is paying off." He holds out his phone, and I glance at the screen.

My brows lift. "Lucky number seven. Moving up in the world."

"You have two more weeks before they announce the fan vote. Any plans during that time?"

"It's a secret."

"Come on."

"It involves leather and a bullwhip and a video shoot on top of the Wynn hotel in Vegas."

"One, I don't believe you. And two"—his eyes darken—"if you ever do that, I swear to god I'll be the only one to see it."

I grin, because I've never dressed solely to provoke a man's reaction, but now I'm tempted. "How was your day?"

"You wouldn't believe what marketing is coming up with for the club's name."

"You should name it yourself. It's your crown jewel, after all."

"This club is regular business. The goal is still La Mer," he corrects. "Did I tell you my parents met there? In the early eighties. They fell in love in a single summer."

My chest aches at the longing in his voice. "You miss them."

"All the fucking time," he admits.

I still haven't figured out what Leni meant about Harrison giving up a chance at La Mer to be with me. Now, I wet my lips. "Back in Ibiza, it seemed you were close to a deal with Christian. Why couldn't you get it done then?"

He rests his head in one hand, studying me. "The price was too steep."

He's not telling me everything. I still don't know why he was willing to take that chance on me.

"No more talk of that," he says, picking up on my mood shift. "Let's discuss something pleasant. Like this wedding you're going to."

"My brother and I haven't spoken much in years. Things were tense around the time of…you know." I wave a hand in the air.

"But you've decided to go to his wedding."

I blow out a breath. "Seems that way. I ordered a dress."

"Show me."

I pull up a selfie on my phone that I snapped at the store.

"You'll be stunning in it."

"It cost forty-three dollars," I say proudly.

He flinches, as if personally wounded by the bargain I scored. "I'd like to go with you."

I shift in my seat. "Harrison, I like the dates we've been on. But this is different. It's family."

"Are you ashamed of me or of you?"

He holds out my phone and I struggle for words.

"It's not shame. It's more like… blame," I decide, rolling the word over on my tongue. "I blame them."

I've never said it out loud, but it's true.

I blame them for not having my back when they should have.

"May I give you some advice?" he murmurs, and I sigh.

"Is it something I don't want to hear?"

"Probably. Get even or get over it. If you don't, it will rot you."

I take the phone back and glance at the dress before clicking it off.

"Isn't that what's happening between you and Mischa?"

Harrison steeples his hands, surveying me with sudden intensity. "It's not the same. Did I tell you Ivanov tried to recruit me when we were still in school?"

"Recruit you to what?" The metallic taste in my throat makes me swallow.

"His family business. Drugs, not clubs. I'd spent time with his parents over the years, and they knew I had the skills to take their business to the next level. I said no. Mischa tried to convince me."

My stomach tightens, and I feel my gaze drag down to where the scars sit on his chest under the shirt. "What did he do?"

"Everything he could. But in the end, I sent him back to his parents with his tail between their legs. What they did to him for failing?" He shakes his head. "That I don't know."

"He wants to beat you as much as you want to beat him," I realize.

"More," he says quietly. "I ruined his relationship with his parents. He killed mine. Neither of us will stop until one of us wins."

"You mean La Mer," I say, needing him to confirm it because this shit is taking on a scarier dimension than I expected.

He hesitates a beat. "Yes."

Damned men with their egos and war games.

"No matter who buys it, it'll still be Christian's baby," I point out. "This club in Burbank is yours. It will have your fingerprints all over it. Isn't it more of an accomplishment to create something from scratch than just to conquer what someone else built?"

His eyes glint with appreciation. "I suppose we'll find out."

When we arrive, a limo takes us from the tarmac straight to Red Rocks. Security gets us IDs and helps us meet up with Annie, Elle, Beck, and another woman in a VIP section. In addition, there's Annie's dad, Jax, and his wife, Haley.

Beck nods when he spots me. "Can't believe you're not passed out after the way we worked you over today."

"I'm going to sleep well tonight," I toss back.

Harrison's hand is on my hip. "Care to tell me what's going on?"

I hook a finger in the front pocket of his jeans, enjoying his irritated expression. "Nope."

On my way back from the bathroom, security is holding back a young woman.

"Little Queen, right? I'm a huge fan."

Normally, I would tense up at someone recognizing me out of costume, but I nod at security to let her through. "What's your name?"

"Amber. And I want to be a DJ. You're seriously my hero. I've been working on music for a few years, but it's nowhere near as good as yours. I wish I knew how to make it better." She flushes, looking embarrassed. "School's hard, and the music helps me stay focused. I shouldn't be telling you all this, but I'm nervous."

"It's cool. Music helped me get through shit too. Tell you what—send me something. We can talk about it."

I give her my email, and she clutches her phone to her chest. "Thank you."

When I get back to our booth, Harrison tugs me against his side. "Friend of yours?"

"A fan who wanted some advice about producing. I told her we'd talk."

The look in his eyes contains so many emotions—admiration, respect, something more than both.

"I recorded a set poolside at Beck's today," I blurt. I've busted my ass playing five shows in the last six nights, but I need to do more. "That's why I was late. His crew filmed it for his show, and it's going to drop in a couple of weeks. But we arranged for me to preview it on my feed and push the fan vote. Hopefully, it'll be enough to put me over the top."

His eyes shine. "You're brilliant."

The concert is spectacular, an orgy of music and lights and the energy of the crowd building and diffusing in that magical way only an outdoor venue seems to make possible.

For his part, Tyler's incredible. Annie watches with so much emotion and adoration it makes my chest hurt. I glance over at Harrison, his strong profile, and wonder if he watches me the same way.

After the show, we head backstage to hang with Tyler, celebrating with our friends.

By the end of the evening, we head back to our hotel. I'm thinking about Harrison's words from earlier about blame and revenge.

"Do you ever wonder how your life would be different if your parents hadn't died?" I ask in the back seat of the limo.

"Yes. I would be avoiding all responsibility. I would be the man the tabloids make me out to be, careless and unfeeling. Except the irony is the tabloids would no longer care because I wouldn't matter."

"It's funny how the worst things in our life give us a reason to do better."

His gaze locks on mine. "Sometimes I'm not sure. I've never much thought about what I'll do after claiming La Mer and burying Mischa."

I cock my head. "Well. You'll have more time to watch *GBBO*."

He snorts. "And after that?"

"You can catch up on *South Park*. There are a lot of seasons. Hundreds of episodes of social commentary and crass jokes that will make you do this."

I reach over and press one of his brows up his forehead.

He's laughing, and the idea of him sitting through my favorite episodes has me grinning too.

"I know what it is to want justice for your past," I say once we've recovered. "But if the price is your future? It's not worth it. You can start over."

He tugs me toward him.

"You're too young to be this wise," he murmurs, capturing me with his eyes as much as his hold.

I've never felt the way I feel under the intensity of his study. The strong, commanding man is still there in his handsome face, sharp brows, and nose and jaw.

"This thing between us, Raegan. I didn't plan on it."

My brows shoot up. "Oh, and you think I did? You think I tracked you down at Tyler and Annie's wedding, tanked my career, followed you to Ibiza to have a shot with you?"

He frowns but doesn't answer. Only reaches into his pocket and produces a square red box with gold writing on top. *Cartier.*

Nerves grip me. It's clearly not a ring, and I can't picture him proposing since he said he never would again, but it's jewelry.

As outrageous as the diamond headphones were, I justified that they were related to my work, what I was doing with him.

Whatever's in that box is about us.

There's nothing to hide behind.

"Open it."

"I don't want to."

He taps a foot, impatient. "It won't bite."

My hands shake a little as I open the case, and I'm accosted with the sheen of gold. The bracelet is a dazzling circle, wide as three of my fingers.

"A cuff?"

"Figured it was more your style than a tennis bracelet."

The bracelet is simple and elegant. Edgy too. It would take on the style of anything you wore with it while maintaining its own classic perfection.

When I lift it from the case, it's heavier than I expect.

"Does it come with a lock and key? I assume this is to keep me from running away again."

He doesn't laugh. "It's to tell you *I'm* not leaving."

I shift in my seat, fidgeting as I look away. "The most expensive gift I've ever gotten was from my parents after…" I trail off, shaking my head. "Are you asking me to be your girlfriend?"

Harrison's eyes grow flinty, and the words hang between us long enough I feel like a fool.

Maybe I misread this. He's been spending a lot of time with me, but now a lump rises up my throat at the idea that he's not in this the way I thought. Jealousy. Insecurity. One ugly emotion after the other, and I can't shove them away fast enough.

I'm the girl who didn't want commitment. And now, suddenly, I do?

I turn away, but he plants his hands on either side of my hips.

"Labels like 'boyfriend' and 'girlfriend' aren't for people like us." My chest tightens, twists, but he plows on. "We live at the edge of success and failure. Where falling down causes more than a scratch. I see you. You might be young, but I know you. When I fuck up, it impacts thousands of people. When you fall, they feel it. I will be with you when you do.

"There's a name for that. It's not 'girlfriend.'"

I turn the bracelet in my fingers, and my gaze lands on the inscription.

My Queen.

My heart stops.

It's not about me or about him. It's about us. The magic that happens when we're together.

The way I feel when I'm around him.

I was afraid the feeling was fragile or that I'd be fragile if I leaned on it. But I realize it's not. And I'm not.

"I hoped you'd like it." There's uncertainty in his voice. "If not, I—"

I press a finger against his lips. "Put it on me."

CHAPTER 16

Rae

The slippery feeling on my skin won't go away.

My eyes blink open. There's a hint of the sun coming through the curtains in our hotel room, but the clock says it's nine.

Harrison is asleep next to me—unusual for him. I steal the chance to watch him, his aristocratic nose, firm mouth, thick lashes. Golden hair falls over his forehead, his firm chest rising and falling with his breath. The scar he'll never erase, the one that seems carved into his brain as much as it's carved into his body.

I'm starting to see the power of forgiving your past while it feels he's going deeper into his. The worry he carries worries me, for him and for us.

I play with the bracelet still on my wrist, glinting defiantly even in the dull light. It's nothing I would ever buy myself, but the more I look at it, the more I see me in it—the inscription, which makes my stomach quiver with an emotion I can't name out loud, but also the cuff. It's not classic jewelry, and it's even more special for it.

He asked me to keep it on after we got back.

Since we returned to the hotel, it's the only thing I've kept on.

Now, my body is heavy and languid in the best way, as it always is after a long night with him.

My phone vibrates on the nightstand, and I pick it up.

Beck: Can you check on the house? I need to fuck off for a couple of days.

I'm not the kind of person to overthink other peoples' internal worlds, but when I set down the phone, I can't kick the feeling of concern.

The carpet is soft under my bare feet as I shift out of bed and pad naked into the living room, pulling the door closed behind me.

"Yeah," Beck answers raggedly on the second ring.

"What's wrong?" I ask under my breath, hoping I don't wake Harrison in the other room.

"We're done. I overheard my supposed girlfriend last night saying she was dating me to get on the show and help her own career."

My ribs ache. "No. I thought you guys were good."

"Guess you can't change someone's heart, you know? She wanted me, but she wanted fame more. The fucked-up thing is I would've given it to her if she'd asked."

I squeeze my eyes shut against the hurt in his voice. "Where are you now?"

"The airport. About to get on a plane for a change of scenery. Shooting's done for the drama, but I can't even think about *Being Beck* right now. If I go on camera trying to live my life, I'm gonna break down. My producer would say the fans'll be down with it, but he'll want to vilify the girl."

"It sounds like she deserves it."

"I'm not the guy to decide what people deserve."

Beck might be hurting now, but forgiving her will let him move on. I wish the rest of us could learn the same.

"Don't leave LA," I say as I hear Harrison stirring in the other room. "We're flying back in a couple of hours. I'll meet you at your place this afternoon."

The bedroom door opens as I hang up.

"Good morning," I tell Harrison, who looks rumpled and sexy as fuck. His hair is a mess, his blue eyes at half-mast. He's naked except for black boxer briefs, the fabric stretched thanks to a very discernable erection, and every muscle and plane of his gorgeous body is on display. My throat dries.

"It is. But we could take a shower and make it better." His eyes darken as he takes me in, and I'm already wet from his indecently slow inspection.

He wraps both arms around me, the heat of his skin feeling like home.

I hold up my wrist. "Is gold shower-proof?"

"Let's find out."

"I want to. You have no idea how much." He rubs his erection between my thighs, which only makes me groan. "But I need to get back for Beck."

"I have an eight-figure investment burning cash until it's rezoned, and you don't see me sprinting onto the plane. Though perhaps I should bring you with me to the hearing. No doubt you could charm that prick Whelan and his zoning committee."

I stiffen. "Who?"

"Zachary Whelan. The head of the zoning commission."

There's not enough air in the room, and I pull out of his arms to get a glass of water from the bathroom.

Once I've drained it, I turn back to him.

"Harrison… I know Zach Whelan."

"From what?"

"He was a friend of Kian's growing up."

He crosses to me, folding me in his arms once more. My skin prickles with awareness even though my head is a million miles away.

"Then you *can* charm him." He curses. "Dammit, we should've figured this out sooner—"

"It's better I don't see him. And don't mention me to him."

"Tell me you didn't break his heart." Harrison smirks. "If I learn you slept with him, I'm going to have to kill the poor asshole, and then I'll never get my permit."

"I'm serious." My fingers dig into his muscled arms, and he frowns.

I don't think he's going to let it go, but finally he relents. "Well, we both have reasons to get back, but surely they can wait long enough for me to take you in the shower." Harrison's mouth descends to my neck. His teeth and lips send sparks along my nerve endings, making my body pull tight in arousal and distract from the dark thoughts in my head.

"Surely."

"What's in the bag? Weed?" Beck asks when I arrive that

afternoon, a paper bag in my arms.

He peers in the top, eyebrows lifting. "Ice cream. Solid."

We take it to the living room, Beck grabbing two spoons from the kitchen on the way.

"You gonna paint my fingernails too?" he quips, sinking onto the couch.

"Don't hold your breath."

He peels off the top of the carton of fudge marshmallow and takes a bite. His low groan is half satisfaction, half longing. "That's good."

I turn on the TV and navigate to the channel I've memorized since spending more time with Harrison.

"You want to watch soccer?" he scoffs. "You're a terrible wingwoman."

I say nothing, wait for play to end, and the cameras to zoom in on one of the players at the end of a sequence.

Beck shifts forward, frowning. "Yeah. Okay, sure." He reaches for another bite of ice cream. "Half a pint of this, I'll be nonverbal."

I take the carton from him and scoop a bite of my own. The rich flavors hit my tongue, and I groan.

Beck cuts a look at the screen, a low rumble of laughter escaping his chest. "Shit. That the kid from the boat?"

Ash brings the ball up the field, his expression tight with intensity.

"You have two years on him. Stop pretending it's a generation."

The camera zooms out as Ash passes the ball off, gets it back. Then with a lightning-fast move, he redirects it toward the goal.

There's no chance. He's too fast, the ball slicing through the air.

The goaltender dives…

And suddenly, a defenseman comes out of nowhere to deflect the ball.

Ash's handsome face is anguished, the camera showing him tug on his hair before running back up the field the other way.

The commentators speak overtop of the broadcast, stats I don't fully understand appearing on a digital graphic on one side of the screen. Apparently, it's been an up-and-down season for one of the sport's most promising talents.

"Looks like he's having a rougher year than I thought."

Beck's gaze narrows on the TV. "He doesn't know what the fuck to do with himself. He doesn't know who he is."

"You got all that from meeting him once and seeing him on TV?"

"How could anyone not get that?" Beck chuckles. "Things must be going well if you're DVR'ing the little bro's games." The look on his face tells me he won't put up with me holding back on account of his broken heart or for any other reason.

"He gave me this bracelet."

I hold out my wrist, and Beck grins. "I'm glad he's taken his head out of his ass long enough to know you're the real deal. That'll go with the dress you ordered."

He points at a garment bag in the living room that I somehow missed. I shift off the couch and unzip the bag.

"All you need is a billionaire on the other arm to match," Beck says.

"Harrison's not coming."

"Why the fuck not?"

"I didn't invite him. Him being there would complicate things."

"Seems to me if you trust him, you should give him a shot with the family," Beck goes on. "The guy's heavy handed, sure, but he cares about you. I saw it when he crashed our dinner. If you're worried he'll go AWOL and interrogate Grandma over spinach puffs, tell him to stay in his lane or he won't get invited back."

"It's not my life I'm worried about him fucking up. If he talks to the wrong people…he's not going to like what he finds."

I thought Harrison knew my secrets, but this morning I learned there's one thing tying my past to the future he wants. The one he needs.

I won't put that future at risk, even if I have to hurt him to do it.

Before I can respond, there's a knock on the door. A huge guy with a buzzed head is on the step, dressed in a black suit and sunglasses. There's a handheld radio on his belt.

"Who are you?" I ask.

Those glasses slide down his face as he addresses me. "Security, ma'am."

"Whose security?"

"Yours."

CHAPTER 17
Harrison

"**Y**ou're still angry about the security," I say, surveying my girlfriend from the four-poster bed where I'm lying fully clothed. "That's why you won't let me come to this wedding."

"You arranged it without my knowledge or consent. Sent an armed meathead to Beck's door—"

"I would've thought he'd enjoy that."

Rae's quiet, even for her, industriously gathering her bag, lipstick, fussing with her hair in the mirror of our boutique hotel in Napa.

"That's beside the point. It's not why you're not coming to the wedding."

"Then what's the problem?"

She straightens, turning to look at me. She's beautiful, her blue dress hugging curves I dream about every second I'm not touching them. Her eyes are dark, lined to make them darker, her lips full and parted. Her hair falls in soft waves around her shoulders thanks to a curling iron she burnt herself on while she was finishing.

"You can't come because it's family and in public and a cesspool of emotions and damage, and I didn't ask for a plus one. Especially a plus one who's recognizable and infamous and going to draw attention like a magnet."

Frustration rises up. "So, I'm good enough to drive you up here but not to attend the ceremony."

"That's bullshit."

"Is it?" I cross to her and box her in against the dresser.

The wedding is at a vineyard. I drove with her and stayed over, thinking a night away would be refreshing.

I get that she RSVPed for one person weeks ago, but it feels as if she doesn't want me to know where she comes from.

"You knew who I was when we started this," I murmur. "Don't invite me in one moment and shut me out the next."

She steps into her heeled platforms, tossing her hair over one shoulder as she bends to fasten the straps.

"Inviting you in feels like inviting a circus," she says, still bent double. "I want you, but I can't take the monkeys today, Harrison."

Perhaps I should have anticipated her reaction. But I've rarely encountered a woman who didn't want to be with me, who didn't welcome all that came with it. Even my ex acted like she wanted it—until she didn't.

But there's a larger issue.

Rae's my girlfriend, as trite as the label is. That means I get to claim her as mine—in public when we're walking down the street and in private when she's panting beneath me. It also means I get to tease her. That she's the person I think of first when I run into a problem.

From the way she's been carrying tension since Colorado, the way she burnt herself with the styling tool she could use in her sleep, today is a problem.

But she's not fucking confiding in me, and that eats me alive. She's using this event as an excuse not to let me in. She can't shut me out whenever it's convenient, whenever something triggers her to raise the walls she's spent years carefully building.

"There's a brave woman I can't stop thinking about," I bite out. "You're not acting like her."

She straightens, eyes wide with shock. It's the first sign I've landed a blow. "You should drive back to LA. I'll get my own ride back."

We go downstairs in silence and wait while the valet brings the car around.

When she drops into the passenger seat, her handbag falls on the floor. As she fishes under the seat to retrieve it, I put the car in gear, not bothering to help.

The moment we pull up the long driveway of the vineyard and I park in front, she shifts out and shuts the door.

The car is too quiet as I head back to the highway, so I crank the satellite radio. My knuckles are white on the wheel.

I came to LA for business. To put Mischa in the ground, professionally speaking. Instead, all I can think of is the woman I left twenty miles back.

Being this consumed by another person isn't healthy, but I don't know how to change it or even if I want to. I've never had someone this tightly linked to my work and life.

A ringing sounds from the passenger seat.

What the…?

As the ringing cuts out, I pull over and reach under the seat.

Her phone.

She must have dropped it when she dropped her bag. She'll almost certainly need it.

I turn the car around.

Rae

There's a rule that weddings should be happy. A day to reminisce about times past, dream of the future.

But with Callie at my side, my small talk with relatives and family friends is loaded.

"I haven't seen you in forever. What are you doing?" is the inevitable question.

"I work in the music industry."

In most crowds, that would inspire more questions, but with my family, that's usually enough to shut people down. It's better to be in law or medicine or politics.

We claim seats in the back, and I open my clutch to text Harrison and say I'm sorry for what happened earlier. He was being unreasonable, but his intuition wasn't wrong.

I've been dreading this day, and I have been keeping him at a distance.

Still, I wish Harrison was with me now—not as protection but because I enjoy his company. The vineyard makes me wonder whether he'd like it or scoff at the natural flowers, which Callie told me cost thousands. If, when pressed, he'd say something like, "If you're going to spend on flowers, make it look like you did."

"What's wrong?" my cousin asks when I curse.

"My phone is missing. Maybe I dropped it." I stand and dash up the aisle to the main building but run smack into a tuxedo-clad form on the way. I look up to see my brother's equally surprised face. "Kian!"

"Rae. Shit, it's good to see you."

"You look great. I haven't seen you in anything other than scrubs in years."

"I haven't seen you in anything in years," he points out. "You haven't come home."

"I know." Loaded tension settles between us, and I swallow hard.

"It's okay," he says before I can find words. "I forgive you."

I lift a brow. "*You* forgive *me*?"

"Yeah. I mean, when you left for arts school and never came back to visit, even when you worked in LA, I took it personally. But I'm your big brother, and I know I was caught up in my own shit with med school. So, I forgive you. It's that easy."

Suddenly, the music starts. As I look around, I'm thinking of all the good times we had as kids, and the heavy stuff falls away.

"This is a big day," I murmur.

"Start of forever," he agrees, looking nervous for the first time I can remember. "I keep thinking she'll come to her senses and say no. Like the officiant will say, 'Do you?' and she'll respond, 'Fuck this noise. I'm out.' I never thought I'd be getting married. But life changes you, right?"

My throat tightens as I nod. "You have your something old, new, borrowed, and blue?"

"Think that's a bride thing, sis."

I tear a tiny piece of lace off the overlay hem of my dress. "Here. It's repurposed vintage and borrowed. Just in case."

His eyes soften, and he pulls me in for a hug.

When Kian heads to the altar to take his place, I remember my missing phone.

It's too late to go look for it before the start of the ceremony.

I huff out a breath as I slump back in my seat.

"Did you see Kian?" Callie asks when I sink back into my chair.

"He looks good. Happy."

She squeezes my hand. "Are you happy?"

"I will be," I say.

There's a man I care about, and the second I get back to LA, I'll tell him how badly I wished he'd been by my side today.

The procession music begins, and the first couple comes down the aisle. My attention lingers on the bridesmaid's dress. The hem kisses the ground as she walks.

"Pretty sure I heard them fucking in the cellar when I got here," Callie comments, and I swallow a laugh.

The second couple starts, but this time, all I can see is the back of the groomsman's suit. Every muscle in me stiffens.

"What's wrong—oh, shit." Callie grabs for my hand.

I can't look away.

"I didn't think he and Kian were still friends. I didn't know he'd be here..." Callie's furious whisper echoes in my ears, and I feel her turn toward me. "Did you?"

There's no way I can answer.

Because when the couple reaches the front and the groomsman turns, I feel as if I've been shot in the stomach.

CHAPTER 18
Harrison

I park at the end of the row, not bothering with the valet.

The ceremony is over—the bride and groom are outside, taking pictures. Guests mill about, cocktails in hand. I cross the green expanse toward the vines and the bar, Rae's phone in my grip.

None of the faces are hers.

A pair of women glances toward me, and their attention lingers as they freeze. Then one of the women grabs another passing by, drawing her in and whispering.

But I press forward toward the bar, where my gaze catches on a familiar profile. "Whelan."

Zachary turns, and the man who holds my club's future in his hands straightens his tailored suit. "Harrison." His mouth curves. "And here I thought putting you on the calendar for this week would get you off my back."

I extend a hand, and he takes it.

"What are you doing here?" I ask.

"Friend of the groom."

"Right. I recall my girlfriend saying she knew you. Raegan Madani," I go on as I look past him, searching for her amidst the crowd.

When I turn back to the man in front of me, he's transformed.

"This some kind of joke?" His voice is low, his lips thinning into a line.

I don't answer. I'm too busy trying to figure out what could've happened to set him off in the space of a single breath.

Not even a breath. A *name*.

Rae's name.

My body tenses. There's something I'm missing, a piece just out of reach.

"Not a joke." I'm bluffing but match his low tone.

I didn't like this man the first time I met him, and that emotion is quickly seeping toward repulsion as he looks around furtively.

"Anything that happened was a long time ago, and it was between us."

What the fuck?

"You've been around," he goes on. "You know how it is. In college, you like to drink, experiment. Girls see an older guy they want..." He wets his lips. "It's how rumors get started."

The vineyard falls away, the world receding down to a point that's Zachary, his reddening face and shifting eyes and expensive tux with the boutonnière.

When I speak, each word is soft. "Ah, yes. Those rumors."

Sweat beads on his face. "It was Kian's party." His throat bobs.

"She shouldn't have even been there."

In Miami, she said started making music in high school after she was raped, that her parents began fighting after something disrupted their family, ended up divorcing.

The way she doesn't rely on anyone to look out for her. The identity she forged, the one that makes it easier for her to be free, to separate herself from someone who doesn't have fears…

That's why she didn't want me here today. She knew he would be, or could be.

Zachary Whelan isn't only the man responsible for the fate of my club.

He's the man who raped my girlfriend.

People are watching us, recognizing me.

I don't care. I step closer, fisting his lapel and leaning in until his awful cologne hits my nostrils.

"Say another word," I mutter, "and I will break one of these wine bottles and castrate you in front of the bride and groom."

His eyes widen in shock.

But before I can rip Whelan to shreds, a woman's voice calls my name.

"Harrison!"

I turn, but it's not my girlfriend. Though she's physically similar and around the same age, this woman is taller, wearing a different dress, and the expression on her face is a warning as she looks between me and Whelan.

"Callie," I guess, and she nods. "I'm in the middle of—"

"I can't find Rae anywhere."

Rae

The cellar's damp but comforting. Quiet and far enough from the rest of the party that no one will find me.

Except footsteps have me tensing, and dress shoes appear on the stairs.

I made it through the ceremony, focusing steadfastly on my brother and his beaming bride.

The moment it was done, before the recessional, I asked Callie to cover for me and snuck out.

I found my way down to a room with wine barrels and sank onto the floor. I don't have a watch, so I can't know how much time has passed.

The dress shoes' owner descends.

I thought I could handle seeing family and old friends. I didn't expect *he* would be here.

Making peace with your past is one thing. Sitting twenty feet from the man who assaulted you is a stretch.

When dark dress pants appear, followed by a belt and a pale blue shirt I personally picked out this morning, my chest eases.

The soft, yellow overhead light shines on Harrison's hair as he emerges into the cellar.

"You came back." My voice is rough.

He crosses the space between us and holds out something. "You left your phone in the car."

My fingers close around it, the case cool and familiar.

"I ran into Whelan upstairs."

Harrison's fists clench at his sides. He shifts onto a barrel near where I'm sitting, easing back to stretch his legs. There's a smudge of dirt on his pants, but if he's uncomfortable, he doesn't let on. "Why is the man who assaulted you at your brother's wedding?"

I swallow hard. "Kian didn't know. I blamed him still, which wasn't fair."

"What happened to you wasn't fair."

"But I can't control that. Forgiving my brother… I can do that."

Each breath is a little easier with him here.

"You didn't tell me it was Whelan because I need him to get the venue approved?"

I nod. "I didn't want you to lose the project over it."

With a heavy sigh, he shifts off the barrel and eases himself onto the dusty floor next to me. He's anything but relaxed, and he's obviously trying to fight whatever dark instincts are inside him.

After a moment's hesitation, I lean my head against his shoulder and breathe him in. "Did you kill him?"

"Not yet. Would you like to watch?"

My exhale is half laugh and half sob. He takes my phone and sets it on the floor, threading his fingers through mine.

We sit like that for minutes. Maybe longer.

Finally, the device buzzes with a message from Callie.

> **Callie: I don't know if you found your phone, but I'm not sure how else to find you. Where are you? Are you okay?**

> **Callie: I lost track of you when the aunts cornered me after the ceremony. Did you bail?**

Callie: Kian was looking for you, and I wasn't
sure what to tell him.

Callie: I ran into Harrison, who's looking for you
too. Keep an eye out for the beautiful blond man
who looks like he's going to rain down hellfire.

My mouth twitches. I reluctantly pull my hand from Harrison's to type back. He caresses my knee as if unwilling to stop touching me.

I don't hate it.

Rae: I'm okay. I needed some space, but I'm
with Harrison. Tell Kian he did great.

"What I said earlier about you not being brave today… I was wrong. You're the bravest woman I know."

Harrison's gaze locks with mine. In it is the compassion I didn't know I needed.

Back when it happened, I didn't have many people to talk to. The ones I did confide in made it seem like I put this problem on them. The ones I tried to hide it from acted as if my withdrawing from the activities I previously did was an act of selfishness.

Now, the man I care about is looking at me like there's nothing wrong with me.

More than that, like there's something admirable about me, in me.

My gaze drifts to one of the wine casks next to me. "Want to get drunk tonight?"

His lips tug up, his handsome face rueful as he rises to standing. He brushes the dirt off his pants before offering a hand. "After I drive us back to LA. I'll have the hotel sommelier bring us a selection."

I consider. "Maybe have him take the night off and we can raid the wine cellar."

"Done."

I grab his hand, and he tugs me up in one easy motion.

"Before you suggest laying charges, I've considered it," I say as I adjust my bag on my shoulder. "Not at first, but later. The statute of limitations is up, though, so I couldn't if I wanted to."

He exhales heavily, then pops the top button on his shirt as if he needs the air. "In that case, let's go home."

I don't argue with his choice of words.

CHAPTER 19
Harrison

Rae didn't protest when I brought her back to my place or when I fumbled with the kettle to make tea. In truth, I felt more shaken than she looked. We spent the evening watching *South Park*, half my brain trying to understand the statistical likelihood of a boy named Kenny being plagued by such obscure, violent threats week after week. The other half of my brain was simply grateful to have Raegan curled against my side.

The next morning, I look at her in my bed. My chest twists like there's a knot of muscle deep in my torso. She's too fucking young to have gone through what she has. Too brave for me to taunt her about being weak.

She will never go through it again and the man who hurt her will beg for a fate like Kenny's.

Leaving her in bed, I close the door before I pad barefoot out to the kitchen and start coffee. The smell might wake her, but I don't want my sounds to.

I ignore the dozens of notifications on my phone as I pull up her social profile, going right back to the post she never deleted, reaming me out this spring. I watch it again, emotions colliding in my chest.

Now I understand why she's so fixated on ensuring women are protected in clubs—mine or anyone else's. It's not only an issue that matters to her—it's one that shaped her.

It's shaped me through her.

I swipe a finger up the screen, and the feed scrolls, dozens of images. From Ibiza and since. Plus the live feed she did from Beck's last week, fresh and grinning.

Thanks to that, she's at number three on the Wild Fest fan vote.

I'm beyond proud of her.

The way she glows on stage. The way she tries. The way she'll fight for other people but hides her heart because she doesn't want it trampled.

The most recent photo is a poster for her gig in New York this week—her last push before the organizers decide. I can't attend thanks to an important meeting in London later this week.

I want to be there for her.

What I want more, though, is to kill the man who hurt her with my bare hands.

The hearing is scheduled for tomorrow. The fate of my club rests in the balance, but suddenly there's something even more important at stake.

I click out of social media and into my contacts list, dialing a number I rarely use.

"You don't need to handle this," Leni insists. "We have lawyers and petitioners who can do the heavy lifting."

Hearings are a place for the general public to trot out their objections and for officials and the committee to ask questions. They're not something I'd deign to participate in if it weren't important. And since the head of zoning is the man who raped my girlfriend, it's fucking important.

When I show up at the meeting, there's a modest crowd. My lawyers handle most of the conversation on my behalf. There are some ridiculous questions and pressures from a local interest group that make me sit up.

"Mr. King has a reputation for taking over clubs only to mismanage them. We don't want a large venue in our community."

"Those claims are unsubstantiated," my lawyer says.

"I have reports dating back years." He holds up a stack of papers, takes them over to the commission.

"Give me a copy," I demand.

The man does.

They're the usual "not in my backyard" allegations, plus some disturbingly short-sighted arguments aimed at dismantling our claims that the club will enhance the surrounding area.

"The committee will take this under consideration," Zachary concludes from the front. "We'll take a short recess before our next agenda item."

He gets up to use the washroom. I follow him in.

The man goes into a stall, and I wait at the sink, meeting his gaze in the mirror when he comes out to wash his hands.

"That was… disappointing," I say.

Another man starts to enter, but I cut him a look and he quickly reverses out the door.

"I told you. Interest groups are very active here."

A few days ago, I was convinced we could work together. He'd be one more bureaucrat I'd manage.

By Saturday afternoon, I realized that would never happen.

"You're from a good family," I start. "Political. Affluent. Elite golf course memberships. Old money. It must be nice to be so connected. To have kids. A wife."

"Ex-wife," he bites out.

"The divorce is before the courts. Do she and her lawyers know you raped a teenage girl?"

"You can't threaten me." He sneers, his confidence bolstered by the lawyer he dialed the second he left the wedding—the one who no doubt reminded him he was in the clear for whatever heinous acts he committed more than ten years ago.

"That's not why I'm here." I jerk on a paper towel, and two sheets tumble out.

"Then why?"

I toss him one sheet. "Because I needed to look in your eyes, but more than that, I needed you to look in mine." The second paper towel crumples into a ball under the pressure of my fist, and I toss it into the trash without taking of my gaze from the man before me. "You hurt someone I love. In the most repugnant, despicable way a man can hurt a woman."

The protectiveness I feel for her is different from anything I've ever experienced.

"God might absolve you of that sin." I lean in, savoring the fear edging into his eyes. "I will not."

CHAPTER 20

Rae

Rae: How was it?

I text Harrison when the plane pulls up to the gate at La Guardia. I'll be in New York for a few days to see Annie and perform my final gig, but the timing meant I had to leave the same day as Harrison's meeting with the zoning commission.

Harrison: No bloodshed.

My chest unknots a degree, but I don't totally buy it.

Rae: I want a picture.

Moments later, the joke's on me because he sends through an image of of his chest, abs, and the trail of hair leading to the band on his boxer briefs.

I nearly drop the phone.

The woman next to me must be pushing seventy, and she makes a sound of appreciation. "Well done."

"Thanks." I swallow a laugh and type back.

**Rae: Just getting off the plane. I'll call you
later. My neighbor thinks you're hot.**

I tuck the phone away to disembark.

I've got it bad. Since Kian's wedding, I'm falling even harder for him.

We're both on the go, and I don't know what getting more serious means, but I miss Harrison when he's not around.

Uncharted territory. That's what this is.

Tomorrow is a huge gig that will decide Wild Fest, but I'm thinking about Harrison.

By the time I get into the hotel and get through some emails for the show tomorrow, it's late.

It's three hours earlier in LA, I remind myself as I hit his contact.

Harrison answers the video call on the second ring. "I was concerned my photo gave you a heart attack."

His gruff voice makes me grin.

"No, but the woman sitting next to me on the plane enjoyed it."

He cocks his head. "She single?"

"And at least seventy."

"Perfect."

"You're not," I remind him. "Single *or* seventy."

He laughs, and I notice his shirt, open at the front to expose a tantalizing glimpse of skin. I swallow.

"Why were you naked earlier?"

"Trying on some new suits." He's in motion the next second, flipping the camera to display half a dozen jackets.

"You're a clothes whore."

"I bought you something too." He flips the screen back,

smirking. I'm curious what he got me, but he continues before I can ask. "I'm flying to London tomorrow for a few days. A few conversations with senior Echo staff."

"Oh." I'd almost forgotten he has work outside of LA because he's been here so much. "Did you get the approval for the club?"

The backboard of his bed appears as he shifts onto the mattress. "Not today. I have more urgent matters to attend to first. Mischa's been causing problems."

It always seems as if his vendetta trumps what he could create in the future.

"Are you ready to decimate the competition and claim the top spot in Wild Fest's fan vote tomorrow?"

I stop pacing and sink onto the couch, staring at my computer on the coffee table that contains the set I've worked and reworked. I make a face to hide the nerves. "I have a set. But nothing feels right." I pull up the track I was planning to open with, then click to another and another. I leave the third one running, turning down the volume so it throbs in the background as we continue talking. "I've done some research on the crowd. The club sent me some demographics, and..."

He groans, and I trail off.

"My beautiful girlfriend is an exceptional producer who still doesn't understand what the people want."

"Which is?"

I frown at my Ableton software, wishing there was an answer that didn't rely on my own intuition.

"What I already have."

His voice lowers, and I flick my gaze back to the phone screen. His firm mouth is parted as he shifts back, eyes darkening.

The music pulses in the background like a dark metronome.

Awareness heats my blood, has my body taking notice.

"Set your phone down. Somewhere I can watch you."

A breath trembles out from between my lips. But I do it, glad to not have to make a decision for once today.

When the phone is propped against my computer, I lift a brow. "Anything else?"

His gaze takes me in, my pajama shorts and tank top, my messy hair around my shoulders.

"Lose the shirt."

I hesitate a beat before stripping it off.

I'm half a dozen feet from the window but on a high floor. It's unlikely anyone can see in, but I feel exposed anyway.

I've been naked in front of Harrison plenty of times, but this feels different. When his breath goes shallow, his gaze lingering on my lips, my shoulders, the curve of my breasts, the hard points of my nipples, I shiver.

"You're stunning, Raegan. If you knew half of what you did to me..."

A wave of light-headedness washes over me at the desire in his voice.

"Touch yourself. Let me see it."

My heart thuds in my chest, skipping at his request. It's a challenge, but more than that, it's a plea.

When I skim a hand up my stomach, over my breast, he exhales tightly.

I like that I have this much power over him.

That high urges me on. I pinch my nipple and squeeze the mound of flesh surrounding it, rewarded once by the sensations flooding through me and again by Harrison's groan.

"Fuck. You do this to them too, you know. You can't see it from the stage, but they want how you make them feel. More than that, they want who you are."

They want Little Queen, I correct in my mind. But it's hard to think with what we're doing. What I'm doing.

His hand slips out of the camera's view, and the visual glitches. I imagine his hand wrapped around his cock. Stroking.

If I asked to see it, would he let me?

But that's not what this is about, I realize as the track changes to another of my songs.

I rise from the couch and tug my shorts off, laying them on the cushion before I sit back down.

My hand goes back to my breast, the other one drifting down.

I slip it between my folds where I'm wet, and my head falls back on a silent moan.

"You like watching me?" I murmur, loving the flare of his nostrils, the rise and fall of his chest with shallow breaths.

"Almost as much as I like fucking you."

My laugh is low. I rub two fingers over my clit, gasping in surprise at how sensitive I am already.

I stroke myself, slow at first, half tempo. Any self-consciousness ebbs little by little as my music swells in the background. My man's ravenous expression and groans turn me on even more.

"The first time I knew you were going to be a problem was in Ibiza. You were rubbing your head because of tension headaches and planning your second set for Debajo. I'd just thrown out your meds and you were spitting venom and I kept wondering what you'd say if I laid you down on the kitchen table and ate you."

"I would've said less lip, more tongue," I tease.

His eyes flash with heat, and an emotion that makes my chest tighten.

Heat floods my skin as I dial up my strokes, my other hand slipping down my stomach to help as I arch, my head dropping back against the couch.

"Raegan, fuck."

He's agonized, but I'm enthralled. It's a spell I'm weaving on myself as much as one he's weaving on me.

It feels so good. Wild. Free.

I come on my own fingers, crying out as the shockwaves start at my core and ripple through every part of me.

Moments later, I hear his hard groan.

I shut my eyes and imagine him coming on me, spilling over my body.

When we finish, my breath coming back to normal, he asks, "How do you feel?"

I crack my eyes open, my attention cutting from his handsome face and dilated pupils to my computer and the new track that started just moment ago.

I shift forward, biting my lip as I scan the screen. "I think I'm going to open with this."

"My ass is burning. You willingly do this?" I demand.

"Four times a week," Annie confirms as we grab our bags and head out of the studio barre class.

"Can't picture Tyler doing that to look good on stage."

"He doesn't have to. He's done four shows a week all summer. His ass is great."

"And you're moving back to LA in a few weeks?"

"Yup. He doesn't have family, and my dad's in Dallas. We always thought we'd come back east when Tyler's contract was up, but LA is growing on me and the winters bug him. I like the idea of raising kids in California."

I nod toward her stomach. "Find out if it's a boy or a girl?"

"I want to be surprised. Tyler would prefer certainty, but I reminded him nothing in life is certain." She grins. "What about you? Are you sticking around in LA?"

"It's as good a home base as any," I say, shrugging. "I have the cash to get my own place and leave Beck alone."

Between Ibiza, royalties, and more recent gigs, actual money is starting to pile up in my accounts.

"Beck says he never sees you."

I cut her a look. "Harrison and I are dating. It's getting serious."

"You think? The man wouldn't switch his breakfast cereal without a motive."

I round on her. "I didn't plan on this. He found out something that happened in my past, and I was so sure it would be the end, but it only made us closer."

"What?"

I haven't told anyone about this in years, but since the wedding, something in my chest has come loose, and I'm processing all these feelings. So, I fill my former roommate in on what happened with Zach, how I tried to bury it.

Her eyes shine with compassion, but she only puts a hand on my arm.

"If Harrison's the reason you're opening up about this, I'm glad."

"He's the reason for a lot of things," I admit, thinking of last night and how it felt to let loose with him.

"Such as?"

"He makes me coffee," I say bluntly.

Annie cocks her head. "And that's bad?"

"He used to drink this terrible fucking coffee. Until I bought a better kind. And a French press. The first night I stayed over, he made it for me. The man has never cooked a day in his life, never so much as made his own tea. But he makes me coffee every day."

"That's really sweet."

"This morning, I woke up, and my first thought wasn't about the gig tonight or even seeing you. It was that I didn't have a cup of coffee to drink knowing that he'd made it with his own damn hands."

My exhale is heavy. "It's like the more real I am, the more he gets me."

"It's awesome?"

"It's fucking terrifying."

"I know what it's like to have someone see you, Rae. And I wish I could tell you that fear goes away, but it just changes. Hell, we're married, but there are still moments I'm terrified to lose Tyler. Not because I don't believe in him, but because I don't believe in me. Or I don't believe we deserve everything we have. There's only one thing I know for sure."

"What's that?"

"You're a performer. Whatever you feel, use it."

When I get ready for my show that night, I pick out a low-cut black top and tight pants with killer boots. Then I flip through my wigs, holding up one after another in the mirror.

None match my mood.

I stare at my reflection. Dark liner, top and bottom, frames my eyes. Thick eyelashes. A tube of plum lipstick waits on the dresser.

I reach for a lip balm instead. My lips are dry from chewing on them.

Little Queen is me, and she isn't. At the time, I thought I created her because I wanted a place to feel free and safe to experiment.

But lately, I've been forced to step outside my comfort zone without that protection. And I've survived.

They want how you make them feel. But more than that, they want who you are.

I ignore the wigs and tug the elastic out of my own hair, scrunching it so it falls around my head.

If tonight is my last chance at getting to Wild Fest, I'm going to give them a show.

I'll give them me.

CHAPTER 21
Harrison

From the second I landed in London, the city that should've felt like home, I've wanted to get back to Rae. The posh flat I've spent hundreds of nights in felt empty without her next to me.

"I did what you asked," my finance lead informed me from across the table in our London offices. "I have the bridge financing so you can increase your bid for La Mer. And we tripped up a new deal of Mischa's to make it harder for him. But there's a problem. He caught one of our men looking around after hours on one of his new projects. Apparently, faced with the prospect of losing something of value to him, the man talked. Which means he knows you're behind it."

I need to finalize the La Mer deal. And quickly.

That wasn't the only bad news.

My investigator informed me he discovered records of a seven-figure payment more than a decade ago—not *to* my parents, but *from* them. His hypothesis was it was an investment in the expansion of the Ivanov empire.

"They must have brokered a deal as part of their exit," I told him.

"Except other stakeholders in the organization made the same payment. People who are working there to this day."

I didn't have an explanation for that, as much as I wanted to.

The words haunted me all the way back to LA.

My parents weren't criminals. It's impossible.

They were decent people. Everything I've done is for them—the business I've built, the Ibiza club I've done everything to claim.

Not everything, a voice says.

I had a chance at it earlier in the summer.

My future in exchange for the club.

In some ways, I've already pledged it. But it felt different pledging myself to Christian's daughter.

At least, it did once Raegan Madani barged into my life.

We haven't talked much in the past forty-eight hours thanks to work and traveling. But when she called me from New York after I finished packing, the night turned into one I won't soon forget.

Her touching herself, letting me watch, fucking *getting off* on me watching...

It was the hottest thing I've ever seen.

I need to touch her. I've been rubbing myself raw since that night.

It's not only her body I miss, it's the snippy comments, the way she goes into a trance when she's working hunched over her computer, the little sigh of contentedness when I pull her against me in the morning and she's still asleep.

She's scheduled to get back to LA today, too, and I have plans for her.

Unknown: Thought you'd be interested in this.

The text that comes in when I land at LAX comes with a photo. It's taken from a distance, but the men in it are clearly visible. One in particular is familiar, and he's the one that counts.

I head to my condo to shower and change—shirt only, no jacket.

On impulse, I grab some of the books I brought to LA as reminders of home, a few from my father's collection and ones I've acquired since, and pack them into a bag I take down to my car.

On the way to the club, I text Rae to remind her I'm picking her up for dinner and she's not leaving my bed for a week.

As I enter the warehouse, the gazes of the workmen flick toward me, then away.

Leni looks up from her phone on the couch of the office. "Your girlfriend is hot. Did you see the posts?"

I grab the phone out of her hands to find a video of Rae mixing. Not Little Queen, either, but *my* Raegan. She's a goddess with straight dark hair, dark clothes, rimmed eyes that blaze with enough intensity to steal a man's soul when she looks up.

She's moving to the music. The crowd is in it with her. The headphones I bought her are around her neck, and I have a brief fantasy of locking them there to hold her in place while I fuck her until we're both sweaty and sore.

I want it, but I also want the moments after, when I'd hold her so tight her breath fans my skin and her heart beats against mine.

"You're in love with her, aren't you?"

The words have my gaze snapping to Leni's. I could argue, but there's as much sense lying to one of my best friends as there is lying to myself.

"Do you wish I wasn't?"

"I like her, Harry, and I'm glad she makes you happy. But I remember what happened last time."

"Raegan is twice the woman Eva was."

"I know. I just don't want it to mess with your head, or your business." Leni grabs the phone back. "No more until we get this figured out," she chastises.

I arch a brow as I set the bag of books on the desk. "This being…?"

"It's been three days and there's nothing on the zoning approval since the hearing." Her frown deepens. "The audio equipment is arriving any moment."

I think back to my confrontation with Whelan, and the consequences of it.

She's not holding any sharp objects—I do a quick scan to make sure.

"There's going to be a delay in the planning department. The head of zoning has been arrested."

I unzip the bag, carefully remove two of the books, and take them to the shelf opposite.

"Arrested? For what?"

Pleased with how they look, I go back for two more.

"There are already steps underway to mitigate the inevitable delay this will cause in zoning approvals," I go on. "So, I need you to pay a visit to the deputy director before this breaks. The committee reports have been filed. Explain that Whelan signed off verbally and promised to rubber-stamp it for us today. If he balks, remind him of the revenue projections and tax implications. If he stalls or says he needs to discuss with Whelan, convince him that would be unwise."

"And it would be unwise because…?"

I retrieve the last of the books, including the plastic-protected second edition Dumas that Rae pulled off my shelf in Ibiza, nearly dropping once she realized its age and value.

"Because Whelan's not returning to work. Today or ever."

I arrange the books on the shelf and step back to admire my work. There's still too much room on the other shelves below. If I'm going to be sticking around awhile, I need to add more books, or perhaps a sculpture.

Leni steps between me and the shelf, her eyes wide with horror. "Harrison, what the fuck have you—"

"Time to celebrate?"

The low, feminine voice from the doorway has me turning, though Leni doesn't release her grip on my arms.

My girlfriend stands in the office doorway, holding a bottle of champagne. She's wearing the dress I bought her and had delivered to Beck's. It's black and strapless, hugging her curves. As she reaches up to pull the sunglasses from her hair and set them and her phone on the desk, her cuff glints gold in the overhead lights. She looks healthy and happy and *mine*.

It's been three days since I've been inside her, and I'm about to die from the injustice of it all.

Leni crosses to Rae and takes the champagne bottle. "That's the good shit. What's the occasion?"

"I booked Wild Fest. Just got the email this afternoon. More than that… the stream from my show racked up a million views in two days. I have offers coming in from everywhere." Her slow smile is dazed and my chest aches with pride.

"Good for you," Leni comments. "I wish we had as much to celebrate, but—"

"Leni, could you find us glasses?" I cut her off smoothly.

I don't want news of Whelan's arrest taking away from Raegan's day, her triumph.

Thankfully, Rae's oblivious. "It's fine. I figured we'd pass it around."

I take the bottle and unwrap it, then open it with a pop.

Leni takes a long swig before passing it back to Rae. "Well, it's not a zoning permit"—my friend gives me side-eye—"but it's something. Excuse me while I get back to work."

As Leni heads out to the warehouse, I round the desk to Rae.

Waves of dark hair fall around her shoulders in a way that should be haphazard but only makes me want to fist it while I fuck her.

When she takes a drink from the bottle, my attention locks on her lips. I want to kiss her mouth.

I want to own it.

Rae offers me the bottle, and every part of me tightens, including my grip on the neck of the champagne.

"Congratulations. Your show was incredible," I murmur. "I watched every clip I could find. Eventually I stopped because there wasn't a newspaper large enough to cover the tent in my trousers when I got off the plane."

She laughs. "Chartered flights, the official sponsor of dirty old men everywhere."

"It wasn't only a great performance, Raegan. It was you."

I'm in love with her. But I can't say it now, not with everything going on.

The expensive fabric of her dress is thin, but it feels too thick under my thumbs where they stroke her sides. I drag her farther into the office and kick the door shut.

"Can't take this," I mutter when I press her back to the door. Her lips are champagne and possibility, and I'm giddy on the taste of her. "You're dressed head to toe in things I got you. It's fucking hot."

My fingers find the zipper at her back.

"So why're you in a hurry to get them off?" Her voice is breathless.

"Because what's underneath is mine too." I unzip the dress and push it off her. If I had the upper hand, it's gone when she straightens from laying the dress over my desk and I take in her lingerie-clad body.

Her golden skin peeks through the black lace of the bra, the triangle at the tops of her thighs.

"I see you did some shopping yourself."

She shrugs. "I was in New York."

I skim the curve of her breast, the lace and her heaviness beneath making my throat dry. "I approve."

"Well thank fuck, because I was waiting for that." Her sassy comeback makes me grin.

"These curves are soft," I murmur. "Inside, you've got edges."

"I'll take that as a compliment."

"Take everything I say as a compliment."

Her eyes shine as she presses up to kiss me. "Even when I'm stubborn?"

"Perfect," I groan when she tugs on my hair.

"A hermit?"

"It's cute."

"Sleep until noon?"

"Means I get to watch you dream."

I drag her harder against me, loving her gasp as the best parts of us collide.

"I used to think you were this beautiful, untouchable asshole," she murmurs. "But you're just a man."

"I wish I was a better one." I search her face, memorizing every line and curve. "I've done things I'm not proud of, for good reasons and bad ones. My sins can't be erased."

"I like you best when you're not perfect. When you can be yourself with me, because it means I can be myself with you."

Fuck.

She wants the unvarnished version of Harrison King.

I've never shown it to anyone. Not the way I have with her.

I reach for the button on my pants, and she lifts her chin, lips parting in anticipation.

She takes a long drink of champagne, for fun or courage, then holds it out. "You don't want any?"

I shake my head. "That's your reward. You're mine."

CHAPTER 22

Rae

When I got the official word that I won the fan vote spot at Wild Fest, I had a mini meltdown. I'm not a girl who's used to getting what she wants. The fact that I had to work my ass off for it only made it sweeter.

Harrison King, on the other hand, knows exactly how to get what he wants.

From the second I walked in and spotted him, his gorgeous face tight and his expression intent, it was clear he wanted me.

He shifts me up onto the desk, stepping between my thighs and squeezing my ass.

My pulse races. There's a fine line between thrill and danger, one made sharper by the look in his eyes.

The man might actually be an animal.

He cups my breast in one large hand, the coarseness through the lace I wore for him feeling so damn good. I'm suddenly aware of tradespeople working outside.

"Is this room soundproof?"

Harrison's grin is wicked as he shrugs out of his jacket and strips off his shirt. "You have a problem with anyone hearing you,

you're going to have to stay quiet."

My attention drags to his beautiful body, all angles and ripples of muscle. If I did have a problem, he'd stop. But I've already faced down one fear. This is a celebration of that, a way to show myself I can take more.

Until he shifts closer, rubbing his impressive erection against me through the lace and the fabric of his pants. He takes my other breast too, his fingers and thumbs rolling my nipples, and my head falls back.

"Oh, shit." The words spilling from my lips only make him twist harder. Heat drags a line from my breasts to my core, where I'm already wet.

"Beautiful girl." It's a praise and a taunt at once, and when his lips claim mine, I moan into his mouth. Most of the time, the difference in our ages and experience falls away when we're together. But once in awhile, he reminds me.

Like the commanding way he says, "Lie down."

Harrison reaches for the champagne, holding it over my reclined body. My stomach tightens as he tips it over and...

I hiss out a breath as it hits my breast, cold on my already peaked nipple. His mouth is there the next second, sucking roughly through the damp lace in a way that makes my thighs shake.

"The desk—"

"Christening it, and you."

"Like a boat?" I taunt. "You hate boats."

He retaliates by dropping fizzing champagne in my belly button and sucking it up. It tickles and thrills at once, and my legs wrap around his hips on instinct.

Next between my legs. The cold makes me jerk, but his hot

mouth is there to lick it up.

When he drags off his pants and black boxer briefs, he steps back. "You trust me?"

"Yes."

He pins my wrists over my head and my body tenses instinctively at the feeling of being restrained and helpless. But the look on his face tells me I'm safe with him, that he'd take on the world for me.

"I don't take that for granted one goddamned second, Raegan."

My heart skips a beat.

He yanks my thong to the side, sinking two fingers inside my wet core.

The grip on my wrist doesn't relent. After a few pumps of his fingers that build the ache inside me, I'm grateful he's holding me down. Otherwise, I might float off into space.

"You're beautiful, and you're mine," he rasps, bending close to run his lips along my neck, my jaw. "Today. Tomorrow. No matter what. Tell me you want that."

His thumb presses down on my clit, fingers still playing with me, and I explode under his hands.

"Yes. *Fuck*, yes."

Harrison soaks up every second of my reaction with blazing eyes and tight body.

"How is it possible that every time we finish, I want more?" I pant.

"You saying you're not satisfied?" We both know he's joking, because I've probably had more orgasms since meeting him than I had in my life before.

"I'm saying you're turning me into a monster."

He strokes down my cheek, eyes softening. "We'll be monsters together, love."

He's dragging my thighs apart to shift between them when my phone goes off on the desk near my head.

"Ignore it," he growls, playing with me as he strokes his hard length, preparing to fuck me.

I do, but it rings again a moment later.

Frustration fills me and I grab for the phone, meaning to switch it to silent, but when I see the name I suck in a breath.

"I have to get this."

"Don't."

There's an edge to his quick response that's more than irritation, but I push on Harrison's bare chest until he lets me up.

"It's my brother."

"What happened to the honeymoon?" I ask Kian when he shows me to a private office at the end of the long hallway of his medical practice.

I haven't been here since he opened it more than five years ago. The standalone building is shiny and new looking, with a cheery yellow waiting room and a perky receptionist.

"I had to wrap up some things here before we left, so I planned a week in between." He reaches into the bar fridge and pulls out a water, holding it up. I shake my head, and he opens it, taking a long drink.

"My wife told me you gave us a very generous gift," he goes on, though the small talk feels awkward. "You're my little sister. You didn't need to do that."

"It was my pleasure." I recall the check I dashed out and stuck in a card. "So, do you want to tell me what you didn't want to talk about over the phone?"

His brows knit together as he shifts a hip against the large desk holding a monitor, notebook computer, and reams of files. "I got a call from Zach. He's been arrested. Technically, it was a call from his lawyer, who wanted to talk to a few of his friends. Sounds like there are multiple charges. Sexual assault. Possession of pornography of underaged women. Girls," he amends.

The blood drains from my head.

The floor tilts under my feet, and I press a hand to my stomach as if it'll stop the sudden lightheadedness.

"I just finished meeting with his lawyer, and your name came up."

He swallows once, again, as if forming words takes an unusual amount of energy. "Did something happen with Zach?"

"I'll take that water."

He listens while I explain what happened ten years ago. I expected it to be impossible, but I've told Harrison and Annie, and the practice seems to have made it easier.

"Raegan, I don't know what to say." He rubs both hands over his face.

"Mom and Dad didn't want to deal with it. I heard them arguing about it. Mom was pissed, but Dad said no one would take it seriously."

"I didn't know what the problem was, but I saw the guilt eat at them whenever I visited," he admits.

"How close are you and Zach?"

Kian straightens, his face a mask of agony and disbelief. "He stood up for me, but now… I don't know how I'll look him in the eye again."

"Dr. Madani?" The receptionist is at the door, looking apologetic. "I'm sorry, but you wanted me to keep you on schedule."

"I'll be right there." He nods, and she looks between us before walking back down the hall. "What do you need from me, Rae?"

"You didn't have my back then. Have it now."

The emotions swirling in me as I leave are less about what happened then and more about processing the news that Zach's been arrested.

There's no way Zachary Whelan went from a career to a future in a jail cell, or that he did something that got him caught in the last few days after a decade. I don't believe in coincidence when Harrison King is concerned.

It was Harrison. It must have been. He's the only thing that's changed in this equation.

Was he waiting for updates while we were fucking in his office? What about in New York, the night before my show? Had he already put this in motion?

When I head over to Harrison's place, I'm remembering how he said we aren't like normal people. The reminder of how easily he can wield that power and for whatever he wants hits me like a bucket of ice.

CHAPTER 23
Harrison

As I pull up to the building, my phone rings with a number from Spain.

"Christian," I say when I answer. "What a pleasant surprise. We're not due to talk for another three days."

I toss my keys to the valet as Christian's cough comes over the line. "I'm afraid it can't wait."

I stride through the door held by the doorman and straight into my elevator.

"I'm selling La Mer to Mischa."

My grip tightens on the phone. "What did he offer? I'll match it," I go on as the elevator reaches the top floor and the bell dings.

"It's not a price you can match." His voice wavers. "It's over, Harrison."

I force myself out into my penthouse condo, standing in the middle of the entryway in front of the mirror.

The luxe backdrop blurs. Nothing matters except the man on the other end of the phone.

"You wanted me to investigate my parents as a way to bide time and run up Mischa's bid."

"No. I wanted to give you the chance to prove your parents weren't duplicitous."

I don't believe him. "From the moment I rejected your offer of La Mer in exchange for marrying your daughter, you weren't intending to sell to me."

I pace the hall, my voice rising.

"This isn't about honor, Christian. It's about money and pride." My laugh is humourless. "You and Ivanov deserve one another."

There's a beat of silence, then a second, before he clicks off.

I stare at the mirror.

Even if I was focused on the club here, it was all in service of winning La Mer. Now, I've lost the thing that mattered most.

I slam my fist into the glass.

Rae

I'm standing in the bathroom freshening up, waiting for Harrison to return and trying to deal with Whelan's arrest.

I need to know if he's behind it. If he is, I'm not sure how to feel. On one hand, I'm grateful Whelan is being forced to account for his crime—crimes, if what Kian says is true.

But having my business handled so neatly by another person leaves me feeling a different kind of exposed.

The sound of the door jerks me out of my thoughts.

Harrison's speaking to someone on the phone.

"…wanted me to investigate my parents as a way to bide time and run up Mischa's bid."

He's speaking with Christian.

I'm about to make my presence known when Harrison's angry voice comes down the hall.

"From the moment I rejected your offer of La Mer in exchange for marrying your daughter, you weren't intending to sell to me."

What the fuck?

His next words are drowned out by the buzzing in my ears.

Christian wanted Harrison to marry his daughter? The woman he showed around town? That's what Leni was talking about him sacrificing for me.

The sound of breaking glass jars me out of my thoughts.

I trip down the hall to the entry and living room.

"Harrison!"

He's not here.

Fear rises up my throat.

A scraping noise from the huge deck has my head snapping around. I run to the glass door and drag it open.

Harrison is the stiffest person ever to grace a lounge chair. He stares out over the skyline, no jacket, sleeves rolled up.

His hands fall to his sides. That's when I see the white kitchen towel wrapped around his knuckles, the rusty stains seeping through.

"Shit, Harrison! What happened?"

I drop to my knees at his side.

"Christian sold La Mer to Mischa." The words are low and brittle. "I've been trying to find evidence to exonerate my parents—

in London and before. But it was all a ruse to run up Mischa's bid. It's over. Everything I've fought for the past decade is gone."

His agony shreds me. I've seen him furious, controlling. I've seen him caring, wanting. I've never seen him broken.

"But why would Christian give you all this time to prove yourself, then go back on his word at the last minute?"

"I offended his pride."

I shift over his lap, straddling him. "Does this have to do with turning down his offer of La Mer in exchange for marrying his daughter?"

Surprise flares in his eyes that I know. "Yes."

"That's fucked up," I breathe.

"His offer or the fact that I declined it?"

"Both." What kind of twisted shit is it that a man would trade his daughter for a property? I think of meeting Christian, how devoted he seemed to his family. "If he made you the offer, he must have thought you'd accept it. So why didn't you?"

Harrison angles his head back against the lounger, looking at me through half-lidded eyes. "You know why."

I run my hands over Harrison's jaw, the unshaven shadow rough against my thumbs.

"Whelan was arrested today," I say. "Tell me you had nothing to do with it."

His eyes go flat. "He raped you."

"I know, I was there," I retort. "Did you know about his arrest when I came to see you at the club earlier?"

His nostrils flare, and I have my answer even without him speaking a word.

"I told you I'm not a perfect man. Sometimes I'm not even a

good one. You said you liked that about me."

"I like that we're both imperfect and we can figure things out together," I argue. "Not that you snap your fingers and make decisions regular people don't get to make."

He shoves out from under me and I nearly fall onto the concrete patio.

"There was no question about turning down Christian's offer last summer, just as there was no question about sending Whelan to prison."

He stalks to the end of the balcony.

"Because you always make the right decisions?" I shout after him.

He turns, the towel falling off his bleeding hand. "Because I fucking love you!" he roars.

Shock reverberates through my body.

He stares down at me, daring me to argue with him.

Harrison King loves me.

This man who buys and sells property, travels the world, pursues vendettas and does it all in a custom suit to hide behind the pain he's endured and the enormous pressure he's put on himself, loves me.

I cross to him and pick up the towel. Reaching for his hand, I wrap the clean side of the fabric around his knuckles again.

"I'm glad you didn't get La Mer from Christian," I say. "Because then I wouldn't have you." My hand slips between the buttons of his shirt, my fingers grazing the scar I know by memory. "People can mark us, but they can't define us. We can move on and live again and trust again." *You taught me that.* "What did Mischa win, really? A pile of concrete built by another man? You've taken a warehouse and dreamed it into a place people can be free and feel alive. It's going to be spectacular. You can make your own legacy as someone who creates, not merely conquers. Tell me you want that."

Because if he does, he'll find a way to get it. This man I fell for without wanting to.

His chest heaves, his beautiful blue eyes clouded with pain of his own. He reaches down with his good hand to brush a tear I never noticed from my face.

"I want to want it."

The cuff on my wrist catches the light, and when he lifts my hand and presses his lips to my wrist right below the bracelet he bought to tell me he wasn't leaving, I feel a glimmer of hope for him.

Hope for us.

CHAPTER 24

Rae

"**S**hit. We're supposed to bring a gift," I call as I fasten my earrings in front of the powder room mirror.

"Only if you want to be invited back."

"It's Tyler and Annie's housewarming. They're not going to unfriend us, right? And he's already been living there for ages."

I duck into the hall to see Harrison stepping into his shoes at the front door. He looks breathtakingly sexy in dark trousers and a button-down shirt. No jacket.

It's a win.

The past two weeks have been a struggle, but we're moving forward. I can tell he's having a difficult time, but he always finds a smile when I'm around. I wish he didn't try so hard for my sake.

One piece of good news is that Zachary Whelan is in jail and was denied bail. But thanks to the delays in the planning department, some of the most important renovations at the new club are on hold. It's eating at Harrison.

"I have a gift for you," I inform him as we step into the elevator and hit the button for the ground floor.

I hold out the notification on my phone.

"The zoning was approved?"

"This morning," I confirm.

Disbelief fills his handsome face. "How the hell did you get that before I did?"

"Leni."

"Fuck."

He crosses to me as the doors open, taking my face between his palms.

He kisses me, long and deep, before coming up for air.

"I need to check on the club on the way. Make sure everyone's on the job working twice as fast."

"No, you don't," I say quickly, and he grimaces.

"I'll pull up the security footage. Just to make sure everything on the exterior is on schedule."

As we exit the elevators at the lobby, he reaches for his phone.

I try to bat it away. "Don't you trust Leni?"

His frown is exasperated. "I did until she booked me to give that presentation yesterday to a group of LA entrepreneurs without telling me. It was out of character."

It's also why I've been working on something special the past few days, something that requires him to be far away from the club in order for it to be a surprise.

In the end, he's too strong and I can't get his phone.

He stops in the middle of the lobby, pulling up the security footage.

Shit. I squeeze my eyes shut…

"The fuck is wrong with the security cameras?" he gripes.

I exhale and peer around his arm at the screen. "It looks like the interior one is fine. Just the street view is shorted out."

Thank you, Leni, I say in my head.

I lay a hand on his cheek, brushing my thumb along his jaw. "We should stop and pick up a gift though."

"No, we shouldn't." He takes my hand, nodding to the doorman as we pass out into the sunshine and approach Harrison's car that the valet has pulled up.

"Yeah, we should. Annie's pregnant, and you're supposed to buy shit for babies, right?"

"Their gift is already being delivered." Harrison rounds to the driver's side.

I pull up, staring at him. Of course he ordered a gift and had it delivered. It's probably something thoughtful and expensive, and he knows I suck at friend-ing and didn't even point it out.

"I love you."

He freezes before turning back. "Say it again."

"I love you."

He comes back to me and kisses me against the side of the car until I'm breathless.

Fuck breathing. It's overrated. Especially when the alternative is having Harrison King's possessive mouth worshipping mine.

"We're going back inside," he murmurs.

"No time," I pant in response.

"Wasn't asking."

Harrison

Eventually we make it to Tyler and Annie's place in the Hills. Apparently, Tyler rented the house last year while he was finishing his album and just bought it. It's stunning, modern and white with a pool facing the view over West Hollywood.

Most of the couple dozen people at the party are familiar. Annie's father, Jax Jamieson, semi-retired yet still fully the most famous rock star in the world, along with his wife and their two young children. Rae's friends Beck and Elle.

"The ice sculpture is beautiful," Annie says, half-serious and half-amused as she surveys the giant form now occupying their table.

Rae snorts and turns to me. "Isn't that what you sent them for their New York housewarming?"

"It is. It's why we also sent something else. Because it'll melt faster here."

Her laugh bubbles up from somewhere deep inside, and fuck if I don't love that sound more every time I hear it.

Annie tugs Rae away to talk with Annie's stepmother, Haley, and I head out to the patio with Tyler and Beck. I can't help admiring at the view—not of the ocean, but back at the house. The family and friends all around.

There's love here. The kind I've missed since my parents died and the kind I hadn't let myself hope for since long before Eva.

"Who's your realtor?" I hear myself asking.

Tyler turns toward me, looking surprised. "I thought your penthouse had three bedrooms."

I shrug as I lift my glass to my lips. "A man always wants more."

He and Beck exchange a look before Tyler shakes his head.

"Does Rae know about this?" he asks.

"I find it's best to work out the details, then start working on her."

They grin.

"Damn," Beck says. "She's got you."

I cut a look over my shoulder to see Rae inside with the other women. I love her, and the way she told me she loved me too today… it was everything.

I've been thinking about what I'd do if besting Mischa wasn't my only goal. Ceding La Mer always felt like a failure, but I've never considered what I'd gain. I could experiment with complementary business lines that interest me. Perhaps smaller venues in new markets. Partnerships with the local community.

Echo Entertainment could slow down and look the fuck around, and so could I.

"Harrison King, family man. Whatever would the tabloids say?" Beck says, smirking.

"He's not a family man yet," Tyler comments. "Did you see the announcement for the new club?"

"*Kings*," Beck chortles. "You've been in the States too long, friend. Whatever British tendency to understatement you had is gone."

Beck pulls up the social post on his phone—the one that went public through dozens of influencers who've committed to opening night, plus my company, scores of media outlets, and, of course,

Little Queen.

"Everyone in the world will be watching you," Beck notes.

I cast a look at Rae talking with the other women. "Fucking let them."

We toast.

CHAPTER 25
Rae

"**Y**ou guys seem good," Annie says over her non-alcoholic cocktail as we sit around the couch. The living room looks out on the patio and pool and West Hollywood beyond.

"We're figuring it out," I admit.

"You sure looked like you had it figured out at Spago last week." She holds out her phone with a gossip column picture of me and Harrison after our meal at the restaurant.

"Since when do you comb the gossip online?"

"Since they started posting pictures of my favorite private couple. What was he saying to you?"

My hand is laced in his, and he's whispering in my ear.

"Don't remember." I blink back at my friend.

"Bullshit."

She's right. I totally remember.

Annie's six-year-old half sister, Sophie, climbs up next to me with a book in hand.

"You want me to read?" I ask her, amused.

"No. I'll read to you."

She starts to, and I tuck back the soft hair that falls over her face.

"Watch out, or you'll have some of your own soon," Elle jokes, dropping onto the chair across from us.

My usual knee-jerk shudder isn't there.

"Not soon," I correct. "Maybe someday."

Annie leans in, hopeful. "Do you love him?"

I sneak a look at Harrison.

"You do," she goes on without my answering.

"It's almost like the harder it gets, the closer we are. If that makes sense."

She nods, enthusiastic.

My phone buzzes with text from Leni, along with a picture.

Excitement jolts through me. "Oh my God. No way."

"What?" Elle demands.

I explain what I've been working on, and Annie sighs.

"Send me a picture of his face when you show him."

Elle nudges her with a toe. "A, His face is going to be eating her once she shows him."

Annie claps hands over Sophie's ears, glaring at us both.

Like it's my fault my boyfriend is a billionaire with a magic fucking tongue.

The rest of the afternoon is fun, and it's almost twilight by the time we leave.

"You're right," I say as Harrison navigates the roads from the Hills. "We should stop at the club."

He cuts me a surprised look. "Since when?"

I lift a shoulder. "Since now."

He reaches over to take my hand in his.

When we turn onto the street, the sun setting behind us and leaving long shadows from trees and buildings, Harrison starts to tense.

High in the air, lights beckon, growing brighter with every second.

"What the…?"

My breath hitches. "We're not even in the parking lot," I prod.

He ignores me and parks the car on the street, shifting out to stare up at the marquee on the side of the building.

Kings.

It's lit up in orange and gold, shaped like a crown. It reminds me of the Ibiza summer or a Phoenix rising.

I round the car and lean against his side. "Everyone who sees this will know it's yours. We wanted to surprise you. Okay, I wanted to surprise you," I amend. "Leni helped."

How we see ourselves is important. How Harrison sees this place is important.

He grabs me and pulls me against his hard chest. His heart hammers through the clothing that separates us, but it's his expression of awe that humbles me.

"You're unbelievable," he murmurs against my hair. "When you said I could put Ivanov in the past, I didn't believe you. But now, seeing this place, it feels possible."

"You don't need to protect your parents' legacy anymore. You can have your own."

His arms are an iron grip around me.

It's three in the morning, and I'm awake.

Not because I'm stressed or anxious. Because I'm *happy*.

We're lying in bed together, Harrison asleep while I replay the moment he saw the sign I ordered over and over, when the phone vibrates on his side of the bed.

He stirs, groaning before he reaches for it to answer.

The moment he does, his gorgeous body tightens, and he shoots to sitting.

"Since when?"

He curses, and alarm bolts through me. I grab for his arm, but he's already halfway out of bed and still on the phone.

"What is it?" I demand.

Harrison hits the lights by the door before moving to the dresser to grab clothing. He drags on sweatpants, still listening.

"What's wrong?" I repeat, shifting out of bed after him.

He hangs up and riffles through his drawer. "Leni got a notification the security cameras are down at Kings."

"We turned off the exterior ones this week so the sign would be a surprise." I grab him a long-sleeved T-shirt and hold it out. He tugs it on with a grateful look.

"There was a problem rebooting them, and now all the cameras are down. We have no video of the premises."

A chill runs through me. "Can't someone else deal with it?" It's late, and this is why he has people who work for him.

"I have a bad feeling."

I follow him to the door. "I'll come with you."

The look he shoots me is quelling. "No. Stay here. I'll call you if something's wrong."

That stalls me enough that I let him go. I stand numbly in the foyer.

I can't reconcile our day with the middle-of-the-night call.

My feet carry me down the hall toward the bedroom.

It occurs to me how different this is from the last time I found myself alone in Harrison King's room in the morning without him nearby. In Ibiza, I was afraid he didn't have feelings, that everything that had gone down between us was a lie or a flirtation.

There's none of that fear now. He loves me.

The bedroom feels disrupted, the covers on the bed thrown back. Hastily opened drawers stare back at me.

I won't wait for him, I decide. I'm going after him.

I pull on jeans and a sweater, not bothering with a bra or brushing my hair. I snap on my gold cuff like a security measure before heading for the elevator.

The concierge looks worried when I demand a car, but he relents, waving over the valet to pull around a Nissan that evidently belongs to the concierge.

I jump in and navigate to the club. Even at three thirty in the morning, the drive is half an hour.

When I get there, the first thing I see are the flames. I hear sirens and see the lights of the approaching fire truck. They cut me off before I can turn off the road. I follow them in, my heart dropping through my stomach as I take in the sight before me.

The club is on fire.

Acrid black smoke pours out of broken windows. The sign isn't lit, or the bulbs have shattered from the heat. The building is concrete, but the inside is wood.

Worse, Harrison's car is in the lot, angled awkwardly with the driver's door open.

There's no sign of Harrison.

The sound of tires screeching in behind me has me whirling to find Leni, who I recall lives twice as far from the club as Harrison.

"Where is he?" she hollers, wide-eyed.

"I don't…" I turn back toward the building in horror.

Firefighters pour out of the fire truck, a couple of them uncoiling the long hose from the vehicle's side.

I start for the building and make it to within a dozen feet of the door before heat blasts open another window, glass flying outward. My hands fly up too late to shield myself, but the next second, Leni's there.

"We need to get you back," she says.

"But Harrison—he must be in there!"

I can't breathe, and it's not only because of the smoke.

I run to the firefighters. "You need to find him."

Before the firefighter can say anything, two others bring Harrison out of the club. He's stumbling between them, breathing through a mask, his arms clutched against his chest.

I'm over there in a heartbeat, and Harrison's pushing something into my hands before they usher him into an ambulance.

"You were with him."

I look up to see an officer blocking the hallway I've been pacing for the last two hours. It's been a long night at the hospital while Harrison has been put through a barrage of tests. I've heard almost nothing about his condition except that he's stable. The doctor told me that as if I should have been relieved—like the fact that the man I love running into his burning building had a happy ending after all.

"Who are you?" I demand.

The officer gives me his name. "I need to ask you a few questions. Let's find chairs and talk."

"I'm not going anywhere."

He sizes me up, his gaze landing on my bracelet. He nods toward the side of the hallway, and I grudgingly step out of the way of traffic.

"You were the first person on the scene."

"Second," I correct. "Harrison got there first."

The last time a police officer surveyed me so intently, I was a teenager at the front desk of the local branch, deciding whether to report what had happened to me. I was nervous, sweating. In the end, fear overtook me, and I turned around and never went back.

Not only fear of the police, but fear of being found out, exposed, judged, ridiculed, hated.

"How did it start?" I demand.

"It's too soon to say."

"Was it…? Tell me it wasn't the marquee." My voice fades to a whisper.

He relents. "I heard the firefighters say there was some kind of accelerant inside. Now, Mr. King was found in the building. The *only* person found in the building."

Hostility slices through the fear in my gut. "You don't think he did this? Kings is set to open in less than three months."

"Why would he be inside?"

"To try and save his damned club!"

He sighs, and I play with the strap on my purse.

"We'll be reviewing security footage. If anyone was staking out the building after dark this week, or arrived tonight, maybe we'll be able to see who."

No, you won't.

Thanks to me, the exterior security cameras have been out for the past two days.

CHAPTER 26
Harrison

"**Y**ou need to lie down."

I look up from where I'm seated on the side of the hospital bed at the nurse's voice.

"I'm fine," I rasp, spreading my hands carefully to avoid jarring the IV in the back of one.

It's been hours since I got here. I have no idea how many as I've been subjected to countless tests and questions. My lungs burn from the smoke. I've been turning over what happened.

How I arrived at my new club to see it engulfed in flames.

I ran inside to see if I could find the root of the damage.

Raegan appears in the doorway, dressed in clothes she must've pulled on in a hurry, her hair tugged up in a messy knot. Her face sags with relief when she sees me, before her brows pull together in concern.

"You're here." My words end on a cough. I grab water from the table, swallowing rapidly.

"I got to the club soon after you did." Rae brushes past the nurse to my side.

I crumple the paper cup in my grip. "I told you to stay at the condo."

The words are harsh, but she doesn't flinch.

"I'm supposed to watch the man I love walk away? I don't think so." Her lips twitch. "Besides, you're not as scary as you think you are."

I glance down to take in the hospital gown. "Christ."

"They were out of Brioni."

My eyes narrow, but her fingers thread with mine, making the IV tug. It's nothing compared to the pain to come.

"They said it wasn't the sign," she whispers, and if it's possible, I feel worse at her expression of guilt.

"It wasn't the sign," I tell her firmly. The beautiful sign she arranged to have put up while I was distracted.

Unfortunately, that distraction had a price.

"But there's no surveillance footage of any vehicles in the area, anyone who could've shown up to set the fire. They said they'll canvass other businesses in the area to look for clues."

"They won't find anything." My words are biting, and she flinches.

"Why not?"

"Because Mischa did this."

Raegan's dark eyes blink. "He has La Mer."

"It's not enough."

Tonight, I realized how serious Mischa is.

This is more than business. It's personal.

He won't rest as long as I'm succeeding. As long as there's a chance for my happiness.

She grabs a visitor's chair and drags it to my bedside, perching on the edge. Reaching into her bag, she pulls out the book in its protective casing and hands it to me.

"They're still going through the building," she murmurs as I turn *The Count of Monte Cristo* in my hands. I managed to get to the office and retrieve it before the fire reached that part of the building. Thanks to its plastic casing, the book is relatively intact. "Leni's figuring out how much can be salvaged, but I've never been so glad it's a concrete brick. The bones are there, and the insurance should pay for the rest."

The businessman in my brain says even if it does, we're now months behind. We'll be burning cash, possibly at unsustainable rates.

"None of that is the problem," I say as I set the book in my lap. "*He* is."

The object of my vendetta, the one I was ready to set aside so I could have a life with the woman in front of me. He won't let me set it aside.

Which means I have no hope of building the future I want, the one Raegan deserves, without stopping him.

"I have to leave LA."

"Is your insurance in London?" She frowns. "I'm sure they can deal with it from here—"

"It's not about insurance."

Her elbow leans on the edge of my bed, and I get a hit of her familiar scent. That, plus her closeness, send a pang of longing through me.

"Okay. I have some shows lined up, but I'll cancel them if I need to." She pulls out her phone. "As long as we need to get this figured out…"

I push the phone away. "I can't take you with me."

The phone slips out of her hands as she realizes my intention. "What do you mean? You said you wanted to move on. There are other good things."

"Things like Kings?" I glance down at the book. "He burned it to the ground tonight."

She grabs my face in her hands, lifts my gaze to hers. "I've spent my life hiding from my past. I'm not hiding from my future." The cuff shines on her wrist. "I know it kills you that you can't control him—"

"This isn't a joke, isn't a game!" I'm shouting now, hoarsely. "This is real life."

"I know it is. That's why I'm not leaving."

I think of the news I got about my parents, that they weren't trying to escape the Ivanov's business but to reinvest in it.

I wanted to deny it, but tonight in the ambulance, I felt the tiniest flint spark deep in my chest. The part of me built for survival woke up for the first time in a long time, possibly since my parents died.

If they were something other than the saints I made them out to be, then part of me is, too.

"But I am," I say finally.

I was never meant to be a man who builds things…

I'm destined to be a man who destroys them.

I'm no better than Mischa Ivanov, only different.

Raegan's lips part in disbelief. Her eyes work over mine, emotion spilling over, but beneath, she's resolute. "In Denver, you gave me this, and you told me it meant you'd never go." She reaches for the bracelet on her wrist, waiting for me to tell her I meant it. That I love her, and that our love matters more than anything else in this world.

"I was wrong."

The words rip from my chest, and saying them is itself an act of destruction.

I see it on her face, in the way her shoulders tighten.

I'm hurting her. The person I love most is sitting in front of me and I'm destroying her.

The pain in my chest is so sharp, so sudden, I wonder if this is what a heart attack feels like.

Fucking stop this, a voice demands. But I close it in an iron fist.

Something lands on the bed next to me. With a last look, Raegan rises from her chair and speaks to the nurse before starting down the hall.

I can't breathe again, but there's nothing the machines can do for me.

My gaze lowers to the shimmering circle next to me on the bed.

The inscription stands in relief against the gold.

My Queen.

This is wrong. All wrong.

One at a time, I pry off the leads attached to my chest, tossing them aside. The machine they belong to emits a single beep of complaint. Next, I shove myself out of bed, the IV tugging itself from my hand.

"Mr. King!" the nurse says from the doorway, sounding alarmed. "You could aggravate your condition."

"You know nothing about my condition." I spit out the words as I stalk past her and down the hall, the tile cold on my bare feet.

I don't care that I'm wearing next to nothing. Don't give a shit what anyone sees. The wrongness in my gut drives me forward, past the burning in my lungs.

At the end of the hall, I'm breathing heavily.

But there's no sight of her.

CHAPTER 27

Rae

As I step off the plane in Ibiza, the wind catches my hair and whips it around my face.

"My bag?" I ask my driver, a kid who subtly checks me out as he holds the door.

"Already in your car, *señorita*. Forgive me. You're Raegan Madani, aren't you? The DJ Little Queen?"

I take off my sunglasses. "Sure am."

He leans in, his handsome face eager and so young. "You were ranked seventh on Billboard's Top 100 DJs list. No woman has ever been that high before."

"There'll be a lot more women that high soon."

I shift inside the car, and moments later, the driver pulls out.

En route, we drive past a familiar venue, my gaze lingering as my stomach heats.

"It's a famous club," the boy in the driver's seat boasts. "The biggest on the island. But you know that." He flushes.

"I've heard," I say, not unkindly.

The car winds up into the mountains before pulling up to the gates of the villa.

In the past eight months, through festivals and gigs from Sydney to Tokyo to Paris, my career has exploded in the best way.

I shift out of the car and start up the steps of the villa. The door opens before I can knock.

I expect to find a doorman, but I'm instantly accosted by a familiar face and body. One that has every muscle in me screaming.

"You're the last person I expected to see at the door of my villa."

If I thought Mischa Ivanov would look the same as I remembered, I was wrong. He's leaner, as if the past year has taken a toll on him.

Like a stray dog, he doesn't look weak. Only hungry.

"Then it's your lucky day."

His surprised eyes flash, cold in the Spanish heat surrounding us. "What would your lover say if he knew you were here?"

"Former," I correct, though I have no doubt he knows that. "And because he's former, I don't give a shit what Harrison would say."

I fold my arms behind my back, my thumb and forefinger lightly encircling the opposite wrist, pressing on the tattoo there.

Habit.

"Now is when you invite me in," I say.

He stares at me in disbelief, stunned the woman he hit wants to be invited into his home.

But I guess I've changed in the last year too.

I hold his gaze, unflinching.

Finally, he opens the door wider and motions with a jerk of his head.

I follow him.

PART 3

BEAUTIFUL RUIN

CHAPTER 1

Rae

How do you know you've reached the end of a journey?

Is it when the pressure eases enough that you can breathe? When you can sleep through a night without waking up sweaty, questioning the choices that got you there?

I keep waiting for that feeling to kick in. The one that says, "I've made it."

I thought it would happen at Debajo. Or one of the half dozen premiere shows since. Maybe when the top one hundred DJs list came out.

It hasn't.

Now, I'm backstage after playing Wild Fest on a cool night in Colorado.

The Red Rocks Amphitheater is a natural wonder, and I rocked my set.

Sweat rolls down my neck and between my shoulders, joins what's already collected at my low back over the past ninety minutes.

My outfit sticks to my body as a circle of guys look over from their booze-filled cups.

"A girl made it to top twenty," one DJ comments as I tug off my wig. "Can't remember that happening."

"You beat Maxx," another says. "Where is that fool?"

"Who the fuck cares?" Eldon, a DJ in his late fifties with wrinkles around his eyes, lifts his cup at me.

I nod in return before going in search of my gear bag backstage. Wig in one hand, I take off my headphones and wind the cord around my hand.

In a dark corner, I bump into someone. "Sorry, I didn't mean to—"

Two guys look up. One has slumped posture and bleached blond hair buzzed short, and the other is Maxx, the DJ I beat out on this year's list.

Maxx tucks something into his pocket and shoves past me, and the other man follows, shooting me side-eye on the way.

I grab my bag, tucking my wig and headphones inside. My attention lingers on the gems flickering stubbornly in the dark. The diamonds soak up every bit of light, as if they refuse to be ignored.

Not unlike the man who gave them to me.

For the past eight months, I've been to every corner of the globe, but I haven't set foot in Ibiza or seen Harrison King. The man who made a stubborn, suspicious girl fall in love.

The one who took it away because love wasn't as important as his vendetta.

For the first time in my life, I felt what love can do. How it changed me, made me feel alive.

Until it didn't.

I'm not that girl anymore. I have a career I work my ass off for every day, music I love, fans who surprise me… even friends who have my back.

I'm not missing anything.

Say it often enough, you'll start to believe it.

I shut the bag, the tattoo on my wrist flashing.

When I look up again, Maxx has rejoined the circle, settling onto a speaker and pulling a tiny, clear bag from his pocket.

"You think you're the shit?" He sneers. "You aren't until you've played La Mer."

"I don't have anything to prove," I reply evenly.

"Come on. Johnny?" He smirks at the stage manager, who looks away from the act on stage and crosses to the stairs. "You made it if you haven't played La Mer?"

"Fuck no." The guy chuckles before returning to his work.

A hand on my arm has me looking over. It's Eldon.

"Don't listen to him," he chides. "He's jealous."

"Of my tits?" I demand, and Eldon laughs silently. "Because it's not of my career. Asshole makes seven figures a gig."

He shrugs. "After a while, the gigs can blur together. It's the curse of humanity. The price we pay for having the best fucking job in the world—after a while, it starts to feel like a job."

The words reverberate through me. I know what he means.

I glance at Maxx, who's cutting a line of the white powder he bought from the blond guy on the speaker in front of him.

"I was glad to land higher up the list," I admit under my breath. "But how do I even know if I'm better? I stay clean and work my ass off while some of these guys spend more on coke than I do on rent, and they still make a killing."

"You have some good gigs lined up this year."

I'll be performing in LA, New York, London… Plus, I just squeezed in a month at new club in Ibiza called Bliss. "I saved some time for producing."

But I can't kick that thought of La Mer, and Eldon sees the look in my eye.

"If you go chasing after the next club high," he warns, "you're no different from him."

I shake my head, turning to face the older DJ. "Easy for you to say. You've played La Mer."

His lips twitch. "Once or twice."

I shove a hand through my hair to shake it out after hours beneath the wig. "When we're even, then we'll talk."

Tonight was good, but the high of a job well done is getting shallow and short-lived. Beneath it, I feel empty.

I turn away, but he calls after me. "You ever even visited this Olympus of yours? How do you know La Mer's all that?"

Because I danced under the stars and fell in love with a man who would never stay mine—a man who smelled like the sea and tasted like desperation—and I wanted them both.

"I just know," I murmur.

The man I hated held me as if I was the only thing he needed.

The only thing better was having the man I loved hold me the same way.

But that's over and it's never happening again.

The phone ringing in my hip pocket jars me out of my head.

When I see who it is, I nearly drop the phone.

"Rae." The familiar voice is flat, the British lilt making my gut tighten. "I didn't know who else to call… I need you."

CHAPTER 2
Rae

The car pulls up to the London townhouse in the rain.

I took a flight from Denver to New York, then New York to London. Now, I knock on the door, cold from the downpour. The wooden panel creaks open, and I hesitate before stepping inside.

The front hall is narrow, the walls a crisp white with a huge mirror. Facing me is a set of steps leading to the top floor.

Sebastian King sits partway up.

"Nice house." I drop my bag on the floor.

"Bought it last year. Came with almost everything." He shifts back onto his elbows. "Curtains are new," he amends, nodding toward the room around the corner.

I step inside, rounding the wall to see rich, green fabric artfully draped from the high ceilings in the living room around the corner. "Why did you ask how quickly I could get here?"

"Because my season was shit and the year went downhill from there. I have a team awards dinner to attend this evening. And you owe me a date for bailing last year."

I stare him down. *An awards dinner? Are you fucking kidding me?*

Before I can chew him out for dragging me across the ocean, he rises and pads down the stairs to the main floor.

He's pale, his mouth slack and shoulders slumped. He looks as if he's lost weight.

I know what self-destruction looks like. Right now, it wears his face.

"It's been a rough season," he repeats.

But there's humor in his face when he eyes my bag, lifting a brow. "You have a dress in there, or do I need to make you a toga from the curtains?"

Central London is a dense orchestra of pedestrians, buses, cars, and buildings that seem elegant and old enough to have been built into the landscape.

The event is at a venue on Northumberland Avenue, just off Trafalgar Square. When we arrive in a private car, we join the short line as Ash reaches for his phone to show his ID.

If I'd thought it would be hard to find a dress on a few hours' notice in London, I was wrong. Ash gave me the names of a few boutiques.

Before heading out, I couldn't miss the takeout boxes and clothing strewn around the beautiful townhouse.

Between trying on dresses, I did a quick online search to try to find hints as to why Ash looks so strung out. There's nothing, except confirmation in numerous sports publications and blogs that Ash's season was subpar. I guess that much criticism would strain anyone, but that doesn't explain the sudden emergency.

Which means it's up to me to find out.

"You look good in a tux," I inform him as we file into the line waiting to enter.

And he does. Showered and dressed, clad in a custom waistcoat and jacket, Ash is every bit the young, gorgeous athlete.

"Better than Harry?" His grin is almost as quick as usual.

I huff out a breath as the line advances toward the door. "No one looks better in a tux than Harry."

Not that it matters. Harrison's not here, and I can't imagine being in the same place as him again.

I came for Ash, a man I consider a friend. Especially given he called me last year, demanding to know what was going on after Harrison returned to the UK. My explanation was the best one my broken heart could give—we wanted different things.

I wanted him.

He wanted to end Mischa.

Harrison's love for me wasn't enough to overcome his desire for retribution.

It hurt like fuck. Still does some nights, when I'm lying awake and close my eyes and reach across the sheets as if I'll feel his body next to me.

Since then, Ash and I have talked a few times. Texted once a month or so. Now, as the door attendant reviews Ash's credentials and lets us inside, I silently curse Harrison for not keeping tabs on his brother.

Evidently Harrison's too busy for me and for Ash.

In a beautiful, wide hallway, round chandeliers dot the cavernous ceiling. My heels slip into the plush red carpet.

Ash told me in the car that it's a club event in recognition of the staff and players.

With the cocktail reception before dinner, we grab drinks and he introduces me around. But when another player from his club approaches, arm in arm with his stunning girlfriend, Ash tenses next to me.

"Gavin," the man introduces himself to me with an easy smile, but when he claps Ash on the back, the hand lingers.

"Another drink," Ash mutters once they leave.

"You haven't finished that one."

He tosses it back in a single gulp.

I drag Ash into a corner. "Who is he?"

My date shrugs, smirking. "Defender. Not the best one either."

"Strange. You're the one playing defense."

His smile fades.

"Was he giving you shit for a bad season?" I ask.

"On the contrary. He was the only one who didn't." Those blue eyes, so much like Harrison's, streak with self-disgust, and his meaning sinks in.

"Oh. Ohhh." That was why I never saw Ash with a woman last summer. And explains why despite his cheeky charisma, he's private about his personal life. "You were together."

"Shut up, Raegan," he breathes. "Not here."

"Did you break up?" Presumably, given the other guy has a girlfriend and Ash invited me.

"We couldn't break up because, according to him, we never dated. We never did anything."

The words are low and bitter, and I connect the dots. "He's not out." I cock my head. "Are you?"

"Not publicly," Ash concedes. "But that man's so deep in the closet it's a fucking wonder he hasn't emerged in Narnia."

Ash shoots me a wry look before grabbing another drink off a passing tray. A warning goes off in my gut as he drains his champagne, then exchanges it for another.

I grab the full flute from his hand. "Think you're good for now." I square to face him. "Though I don't think it was alcohol that had you sweating when I arrived."

His face falls. "Our season ended, and it was my fault. A play I've made a thousand times before. One I should've made again. I knew it, and they did too. I needed something to numb out."

"So you turned to drugs."

"They turned to me." He grimaces.

"How many times?"

"A couple."

Concern has my hand clenching on his glass. "I'm telling you, it's a bad idea."

A beat. "I know. I'm done with it. I need to figure this out and get back to my life."

"You couldn't call Harrison?"

Before the words are out, I know the answer.

I can only imagine what Harrison would say. Given how their parents died, he'd be pissed if he found out what Ash had gotten into. This was the man who tossed my pills before finding out what they were, who insists on running a clean club in the capital of party drugs.

"He's not perfect, Sebastian."

"But he's strong," he bites out, frowning. "When our parents died. When his fucking building burned, he walked out. Harrison deals with his shit, and even when he does it badly, he does it."

I don't know what to say to that. "All right. Lucky for you, I planned a week's vacation after Red Rock. I'll stick around a few days."

Relief has him sagging. "Thank you."

"But after that, I have business to take care of."

"Stateside?"

I scan the room. "Ibiza."

I need to visit a man I never thought I'd see again. Not one I used to love, but one I used to fear.

Ash's eyebrows lift. He's dying to pry more information from me, but before he can, photographers snap pictures, and we smile and pose.

"This your new girlfriend, Sebastian?" one of them asks eagerly.

The man we spoke to is across the room. His girlfriend's turned to talk to someone else.

Ash leans in to wrap an arm around my waist. "Isn't she lovely?"

I kick him in the calf, and he only bends closer to whisper in my ear, "You've got this down."

It probably looks as if he's murmuring promises in my ear, or a filthy joke.

"Not much to figure out," he adds. "Turn the right angle. Smile the right smile. Pretend you're not secretly hoping they'll drop their camera in the street, where it's run over by a double-decker bus."

I've gotten used to the media this past year as I climbed a ladder of my own, making it back up to the status I held before the confrontation with Harrison last spring, then I shot right on past it. Wild Fest was only the capstone of an incredible year by any standard. Somehow, my bank account is full enough the bank is sending my own money manager to my rental in LA.

I could buy a condo in any of the cities I frequent, but I haven't yet. Because I'm still adjusting to the new normal—and maybe a little because nowhere I go feels like home.

Flashbulbs go off, and I try to shift away, but Ash slides a hand around to my ass. I'm about to remove it when his words make me stiffen.

"He'd be proud of you."

Tingles start down my spine. As if the man in question is here, even though it's impossible.

I've been avoiding keeping an eye on the tabloids, but I gave in when I hopped on the flight over here. The publications spotted Harrison in New York this week. Regrettably striking in a dark suit and sunglasses. Thankfully alone.

In the image of him crossing at an intersection, phone pressed to his ear, his hair ruffled lightly in the breeze—an inch longer than before, if I had to judge. But the square jaw was the same, the firm lips I've felt on every inch of me, the ones that have whispered comfort and torment in my ears.

I might not be in love with him anymore, but that doesn't mean I want to see some other woman draped all over him like he hung the sun, and the moon, and the sign at Tiffany's while he was at it.

I look at Ash. "When did you see him last?"

"A few months. While he won't give me details, I suspect he's laying the groundwork to bring Mischa down. As you know, insurance concluded the fire at King's was arson, and there wasn't enough evidence to prove it wasn't Harrison."

My gut twists with guilt. It wasn't my fault, but the fact that the security cameras were off was my doing. All because I wanted to surprise him with the sign.

"Is he happy?" I ask, hating that I want scraps of information about my ex.

Ash sighs. "I've never seen him happy unless he was with you."

Thanks for the gut punch.

Smoothing down my dress, I pretend the words don't affect me. "I'm glad Harrison isn't here now."

Curiosity has him narrowing his eyes at me. "Why's that?"

A knot of tension forms between my shoulders, and I straighten for the cameras. "I need to do something, and he wouldn't want to see me do it."

CHAPTER 3
Harrison

"The robots are suspended from the ceiling to do what—acrobatics?" I demand.

Sawyer leans in, looking impatient. "They serve drinks, you pretentious asshole."

The trendy pub in Brooklyn gave us their prime seating—two low-profile couches and a glass coffee table. Tyler Adams's security is positioned between this section and the rest of the room, dissuading anyone who thinks of coming over or taking a picture.

Mostly, he's watching three grown men have an argument.

"They run on a track"—Sawyer gestures to the space over his head—"along the bar."

"I figured the only club robots were the kind that danced on stage," Tyler comments.

Sawyer shakes his head. "You can use robots for photography, AI for optimizing what's captured. There're clubs in London with interactive walls where you can create your own light displays."

The man across from me is Sawyer Redmond, cofounder of a major tech and industrial company. He's one of a few men I've met who is taller than I am and wearing a Boss jacket and designer jeans like he doesn't give a fuck. His long, unruly hair falls in his face every time he moves, making me itch to grab a fistful and saw it off with a butter knife so I can look him in the damned eyes.

I'm here to see Sawyer about business, but when Tyler said he was in town, I suggested we meet. The only time he had free was now, so I figured I could see two friends at once.

"Sawyer and I went to school together," I inform Tyler. "He was this genius prodigy. Pulling straight As in senior engineering. Hope they kept you warm at night."

"You mean while you used your accent to fuck your way through the female population? You wind up with any souvenirs of that time in your life? I hear chlamydia's a bitch to kick."

"Seems it worked out," Tyler comments, slinging an arm over the back of the velvet couch.

It did, on paper. Sawyer cofounded his company and is on the way to making himself a wealthy man. I have an empire. One my enemy wants to burn to the ground—starting with Kings last year.

I told myself I could move on and have a future untainted by my past, but Ivanov seems determined to make sure that's not true.

The police weren't able to find the man responsible. I know Mischa was behind it, but I can't prove it.

Since then, his reach has only expanded with new acquisitions fueled by drug money.

I've used the time to regroup.

I will get revenge.

That's the only thing that matters.

Doesn't hurt that you've lost everything else.

A woman comes in the door with a stroller, drawing every eye in the room. She's young and pretty, her red hair tucked up into a bun on her head. She could be a student.

Tyler turns to look over his shoulder as if there's an invisible cord between them.

"He's whipped," he comments as her security guard offers to take the stroller and Annie waves him off. But the second her eyes land on her husband, a smile curving her lips, Tyler's off the couch and at her side.

Sawyer and I exchange a look. "Yeah. It's security who's whipped," he comments. "Figured musicians were supposed to play the field."

Tyler bends to check in the stroller before straightening, pulling his wife against him for a hard kiss.

"He doesn't. They're in love." I refocus on my friend who's still here, leaving Tyler to fawn over his wife.

"You envy him," Sawyer scoffs.

"Love is an exquisite diversion from the more brutal parts of life."

Last year, I didn't only let myself fall—I practically held the door for both myself and Raegan. At first, I thought I could handle it. Having her at my side felt natural.

Somehow, when I wasn't looking, it switched from natural to necessary. She claimed me, not the other way around. She brought out emotions I'd never felt before, hopes and ambitions I never expected.

After Mischa burned down my property—the future Raegan and I were building together—I vowed I wouldn't let him get away with it. But the farther away I put that in my rearview mirror, the harder it is to remember why I left the woman I love.

I was the one who ended our relationship.

I knew I'd miss her. I didn't expect to lie awake until morning, wishing I knew what ceiling she was staring at.

If she was alone like I was.

If she was *lonely* like I was.

But there's no place for Raegan in my mission.

In the last eight months, I've doubled down on growing my own business, plus invested in having Mischa and his operations surveilled. There's been some sabotage back and forth, me trying to provoke him, but I want it to be done.

What I never told her was that I hoped it would be over soon. That I could find my way back to her when it was done, that I could force my way back into her heart.

It was harsh of me to leave her.

It would have been cruel to promise to return with no guarantee I could.

I force my attention back to the man sitting opposite me. "I'll take three of the bartender robots."

"They're fucking expensive, Harry."

"And I'm fucking rich, Sawyer."

He grins. "Fine. But technology's not your real problem." He shoves his hair back.

Sawyer has a way of seeing straight to the heart of a situation. It comes from his brutal upbringing—while mine was charmed, at least until I was a teenager, his was the opposite. He scraped by.

He'd say he's thriving, and few would argue with his track record and accomplishments. But every victory has a cost—a personal one, if not a public one.

I shake my head. "The prick who was responsible for my parents' deaths."

They might've been ruled overdoses, but it wasn't their doing. No matter what other ills they were responsible for, they never touched drugs themselves and raised us the same way.

"The police want to nail him for drug trafficking and a raft of other evils, but their timeline feels… infinite," I go on.

Sawyer's eyes darken. "You trust a bunch of paper pushers, you'll be the one bleeding out."

He's speaking from experience. But before I can respond, Tyler and Annie and the stroller approach.

"Congratulations," I say, fixing on a smile.

"Thanks, Harrison." Annie's tight-lipped. "You didn't need to send the stroller, but it's great. It does everything except handle my calendar."

My smirk fades when Tyler says, "Would you like to hold Rose?"

"I don't think—"

Before I can protest, he presses the sleeping bundle into my arms.

Christ. She's all pink and soft, and as her weight settles in my arms, she's not heavy, but precious. She twitches as she wakes, and eyes, dark brown, with little flecks of gold, blink trustingly up at me. Her tiny nose wrinkles, her mouth working. She has a full head of Annie's red hair, and if she has an ounce of her father's talent and her mother's fearlessness, she'll be a force.

She's innocent and loved. I hope it's a long time before she sees the darker sides of the world.

I clear my throat, glancing back up at my friends. "I can see you in her," I tell Tyler.

"Hopefully not for long," he says dryly, tugging his wife against his side as I look back at the baby.

A flash goes off.

"For posterity," Annie says, tucking the phone away as Sawyer and Tyler strike up a conversation.

I'm not sure what she means. "You want a photo of your child with a villain?"

"You're not a villain. Or if you are, she didn't call you one."

Annie holds out her arms. I hand the baby back.

Rae's probably told her I'm a massive prick for how we ended things.

"What did she call me?" I can't help asking.

Annie's gold eyes shine with emotions—a damn rainbow of them. I can see why she's a capable actress. She hitches Rose higher in her arms. "Rae was at an event last night. In London."

It feels like a lifeline. "London? But Wild Fest just happened this past week."

"And you know her schedule."

I'm caught out. "I want to make sure she's safe."

"I was rooting for you guys. Even though it sounds like she's moved on."

With a furtive look toward the stroller, she hands the baby off to Tyler, then retrieves her phone again. She taps the screen a few times before holding it out.

The social media account belongs to my brother's football club, and the date stamp on the post says last night.

The photo on the screen is a kick in the gut.

The woman I love is stunning in a slinky black dress that skims the floor, plunging low between her breasts. She's gorgeous, glamorous, and unlike the Raegan I met a year ago. Her skin glows in the light from the venue and the flashbulbs, her lips full and painted a dark plum. Her dark hair falls in waves around her shoulders, clinging to her perfect breasts.

But it's not her body that makes it impossible to look away.

There's a confidence she wears the fuck out of.

I rip my gaze away from Raegan to take in her companion and get a kick in the gut for my efforts.

Next to her is my brother. His hand rests on her ass and his lips are near her ear, her half smile an afterthought for the cameras given whatever he's telling her.

I clench the phone hard enough my forearm shakes.

This whole time we've been apart, she was still mine from a distance.

Mine when I got off to the memory of her.

Mine when I went to bed questioning whether losing her was worth pursuing the one goal I've had since before I was a man.

She doesn't belong with Ash, not at his side or in his arms.

"Harrison. Are you okay?"

Annie's voice is far away, and I shove the phone back at her.

I'm halfway to the door when Sawyer calls after me, "Where should I send the robots?"

CHAPTER 4
Harrison

"What do you mean he's not in London?" I growl over the phone. "Where is he?"

After the short, tense conversation with one of my staff—whom I'd instructed to drop in on my brother when he wasn't answering his phone—I determine Ash's current location, along with the company he's still keeping four days after the event.

I'm checked out of my Manhattan hotel and on my way to the airport an hour after the close of the business day. The entire chartered flight over, I stew.

When my plane arrives in Ibiza the next morning, I jump in a car, realizing I haven't called Natalia or Toro to let them know I'm coming. An omission that catches me when I barge into my house.

Natalia appears over the upstairs railing. "*Dios mío*! Señor King."

She gets over her surprise and runs down the stairs.

"I'm fine," I assure her.

Her concern turns to scorn. "You didn't call. Toro is out with Barney. I have been working on the gardens."

"I would very much like to see them. Later." My jaw clenches. "I need to find my brother and Raegan. I thought they would be here." I scan my memory for the hotel Ash stayed in last summer. "I'll be back."

Halfway to the door, a voice stops me. "No, señor."

I do a double take because it's the same tone she used to scold me for eating all the salami before my parents' friends could arrive for brunch.

I arch a brow at her glowering face and folded arms. "Toro will be back soon, and he will drive you. In the meantime, I will show you the garden."

"I hope you will be… kind." Toro's gaze meets mine in the rearview mirror.

"I have lots of things to discuss with my brother. None of them are kind."

Like where the hell he got off asking Raegan out, not to mention thinking he could touch her the way he did.

I knew they were friends, but I always figured their common bond was me. I didn't expect them to stay connected without me.

I stare out the window, cracking my knuckles.

"Would you like to hear the news of the island?" Toro asks as he deftly navigates the curving roads.

"Fine."

"Your dog has learned to roll over on command. There is a new hotel in Ibiza Town." He proceeds to regale me, and I half listen until he says, "Ivanov came to the island early for the season."

I straighten. "Why didn't you tell me?"

"You haven't been around."

My teeth grind together. That feels like the damned refrain this week. I'm running a billion-dollar business. I can't be everywhere at once.

"I'm here now," I mutter as the car pulls up outside the hotel. I leap out without waiting for my driver to hold the door.

In the lobby, I tell the concierge, "My brother. Sebastian King."

His eyes widen with fear, and he names the room number. He doesn't want to piss me off.

I jab the button in the elevator, and when the doors open, I stalk down the hallway and bang on the door. Silence greets me.

They're probably out.

Images of them strolling the boardwalks, eating ice cream, and other such nonsense fill my brain.

Or they're inside and the reason they're not answering is that they're otherwise occupied.

I pound on the door again, hard enough it rattles in the frame.

At last, footsteps sound on the other side.

The hairs lift on my neck, and I brace myself for a fight. I'm expecting to see Raegan, but when the door cracks, it's not her.

"Hawhoh, brozuh." Sebastian peers out from the gap in the frame, his mouth full of something, the chain lock still engaged.

"Where is she?" I demand.

"Who?"

I slam a hand against the door, and he jumps.

"Calm down, man."

"Sebastian, if you don't open this door…"

His gaze runs down my form. "You're wrinkled, Harry. You blow in on a tornado?"

I reach through the gap and grab his shirt. "Open. The damn. Door."

Eyes widening, he reaches for the chain and slides it open.

I push the door in and step inside before he can think of getting me back out. My brother looks completely at ease, including the amusement in his expression. He's wearing a T-shirt and boxers, eating…

"What is that?"

"Cinnamon Toast Crunch. Raegan brought it for me from America." The sound of her name on his lips reminds me why I'm here, why my blood pressure feels dangerously high, before he grabs another bite. "This is good, Harry. They've been holding out on us."

I hit him, hard enough the blow or the surprise sends him to the carpet.

The bowl falls from his hands, and cereal flies everywhere—his face, the carpet, the foyer.

"Jesus," he gasps, rubbing his jaw. "Did you have to do that? Waste a perfectly good bowl of the stuff? This was almost the last—"

"What's going on?"

We both freeze as Raegan emerges from the hall in the suite. She's wrapped in a white towel, her hair dark and dripping around her shoulders.

When she spots me, her mouth falls open. She's obviously stunned to see me, emotions chasing one another across her face. Disbelief. Anger.

"What did you do?" she demands.

It's half her sudden appearance that slams into me and half how she looks.

Fresh, wary, beautiful.

The woman I spent months loving and even longer aching for is here, a few feet away.

"Not nearly enough."

Before I can think twice, I step over my brother and cross the room, grab the back of Raegan's neck, and drag her to me.

I crush her lips beneath mine. She tastes like toothpaste and home, and I kiss her with desperation and anger and exhaustion.

Every trip I've taken, every time I've reminded myself my decision to leave was for the best—it all took a toll on me. From the outside, I might look as powerful as ever. On the inside… my soul corrodes.

I need *her.*

My tongue slips between her lips, stroking and claiming as my fingers tighten in her damp hair. Her scent is floral from her shower, but beneath that, it's all Raegan.

A wet hand grabs my forearm and pushes me away.

My heart hammers as I take in her swollen lips, her hazy eyes.

Of all the decisions I've made in my life, I'd regretted exactly one—telling my parents to get out of the business and causing their deaths.

Since I learned they weren't trying to leave, that regret faded away, replaced with rage and confusion. The past year, I've been angry at them, and at Ivanov for killing them and setting me on a path that made me build a business that would redeem and honor them.

But around the anguish, I've found a new regret: losing this woman.

Because I can't regret loving her, not when the feel of her under me is so jarringly exquisite.

Before I can speak, her palm cracks across my face.

Stars explode behind my eyes, a riot of white and black blossoming as pain radiates up my cheekbone and jaw.

When I can see again, my neck is craned awkwardly and I'm staring at Sebastian reclined on the floor and chewing a piece of rescued cereal.

"Fuck," he declares. "I've never seen a woman hit you before."

But when I turn back to Rae, she looks surprised by her own reaction.

"We need to talk," I say. "In private."

"No."

Frustration rises up. "I'll take you for dinner."

"I have a show tonight."

"It wasn't on your schedule."

I catch my mistake at the same time she does.

"A recent addition," she says.

She's changed since I saw her last. Besides the quiet confidence that's more than skin-deep, she has "recent additions" that come up, independent of me apparently.

Her gaze narrows. "I need to get dressed."

"Need help choosing an outfit?" Sebastian offers from the floor. "The two you talked about on the plane sound good, but I'd like to see them in person."

I could hit him again.

"Both of you stay out," she tells my brother before turning that hot gaze on me again. "If someone so much as knocks on the door while I'm getting ready, I will tear them a new one."

She heads back down the hall, her hips swinging under the towel in a way that has me furious and horny at once.

"If we're done with the violence, you could buy *me* dinner," Sebastian says, grimacing at the mushy cereal pieces on the carpet.

When I came here, I thought I knew my intention—reminding my brother he has no business with this woman. But looking at her, sharing space with her, kissing her...

I know it was a lie. I need Raegan Madani in my life again, and it can't wait until my work is done.

CHAPTER 5

Rae

"**N**eed anything?" security half mouths, half yells over the music at my gig.

I shake my head. "No. Why?"

He glances at my setup, and I realize my track's getting stale.

Shit. It happened again. I was staring off into space.

My set at Wild Fest had my full attention, but before that, I caught myself doing this more than usual. Now, thanks to a stop I made earlier today and Harrison showing up at my hotel, my mind is running overtime.

What kind of man barges into your hotel and kisses you?

The same kind who buys and sells clubs like candy.

The kind who drags around a vendetta, who wears a suit as if it's armor, and when he smirks, panties drop in a ten-mile radius.

I thought it wasn't possible to miss Harrison more than I did these past months, burying it under work and my Little Queen costume. But when he appeared in the living room of the hotel suite Ash rented, rumpled and furious, longing hit me so hard I nearly launched myself at him.

I shoved it down, reminding myself we're on different paths.

He's on one he chose over me.

Explicitly.

Remorselessly.

I change the song, segueing into something with a bassline that matches the throbbing in my stomach, and a new wave of energy grips the crowd when they recognize it.

He had no right to kiss me. But from the second his lips crashed down on mine, I was transported to a time and place where I would've done anything for him. For a moment, I forgot everything we aren't, and the friction of his lips and tongue was enough.

If he hadn't pulled back, who knows how long it would've taken for reality to set in?

I shake myself again. I came to Ibiza for work. Both the meeting I secretly took this afternoon, not even letting Ash in on it, and the series of shows I agreed to play at this club for part of the summer.

Harrison King is not part of the plan.

What if he's staying?

A shiver runs through me. I hadn't anticipated that because the reason he wanted to be here—La Mer—is no longer in play. There's no possible explanation for his appearance unless he wants an extended vacation.

As I hit the next transition, a familiar face in back corner of the club has me doing a double take.

Blond hair, buzzed short. A distinctive profile and hunched posture.

It's the guy I saw selling to Maxx at Wild Fest. He's been logging as many air miles as I have.

I watch the club owner approach him, and they argue. The dealer leans in, says something that has the owner pulling back and shaking his head.

Security clearly sees the interaction but doesn't make a move to intervene.

After the show, the owner approaches me. "Thanks for playing. We were lucky to get you at Bliss on short notice."

"Sure. Who needs a vacation?" I flash a smile, but the man only cringes.

"I could use one right about now."

I think about what I saw earlier. "Who was that guy dealing?"

He looks caught out but relents when I raise a brow. "He's one of Mischa's. First showed up six months ago. I should've objected right away, but I didn't until it got worse."

"How bad is 'worse'?" I ask, dreading the answer.

"He's got guys here every night of the week, and rumor has it some of what he was selling was… questionable. I finally put my foot down. Not inside. Not on my property."

"I don't want to look up and see that shit either."

Maybe I'm feeling extra sensitive after seeing Maxx spun out at Wild Fest and after the condition I found Ash in this week.

"Ivanov's started pressuring clubs to sell. Says if they don't, his people will tip off law enforcement that owners like me are allowing this to go down on their watch. I'll lose everything. This way, at least I have money to start over."

"You can't offer to help the police?"

Fear fills his face. "You can't stop this. You'll only be hurt trying."

On my way back to the hotel in the car, I turn it over. Worrying about who controls what drugs in Ibiza is above my pay grade. Except it's in my face every night and it'll only get harder to ignore.

I want a long-ass bath and maybe one of my anxiety pills. But when I open the door to the suite, I know immediately something's wrong.

"Ash?" I step inside, hitting the lights.

Nothing is amiss in the living room. The same stock magazines are on the coffee table.

Except…

I could have sworn I left a sweater on the couch.

There's no way. My stomach knots in disbelief.

I stalk down the hall to Ash's room. His bed is made, his suitcase missing from the stand it occupied since we arrived.

I make my way to my room, my hand shaking as I hit the light.

There's nothing. My belongings are gone.

CHAPTER 6
Rae

The fucking nerve.

He did a reverse me. Vanished my belongings.

I place a call on my cell phone to a number I haven't used in a long time.

"Señorita Madani."

"I'm sorry to call so late, Toro. Is he at the villa?"

"I'll come and get you."

"You don't need—"

"I will come."

I remove my wig and finger-comb my hair. There's no change of clothes, so I stalk back downstairs in my same outfit.

The driver arrives, and I shift into the passenger seat, removing the paperback there. My lips twitch when I see the title. *A Gentleman in Moscow.* "How is it?"

"Surprisingly interesting. Thank you for sending it."

"How's your daughter?" I ask.

"I spoke to her this winter." From the hope in his voice, it's progress. "She called on my birthday. After you did."

"You didn't tell Harrison about that?" I caution.

"No." We drive in silence until Toro adds, "We haven't seen him the entire year. When he arrived earlier today, he was distraught."

"I can imagine. He stormed my hotel room like he was laying siege to a castle."

"His anger hides fear."

I shift in my seat, cutting a look across the car. "There was nothing in that hotel suite he was afraid of."

Toro sighs. "Life takes things we do not wish to give. He lost the people he cared about too soon. When his parents passed, he became angry. But it was when he grew quiet that we worried. He is not naturally reserved. Seeing him like that... It is not stable." He cuts me a look.

I cross my arms. "He didn't lose me. He gave me up. There's a difference."

When we pull up at the villa, I shift out and head up the steps to the door. I push on the handle, and it gives.

Inside, memories of last summer ambush me. Making coffee in the kitchen with Harrison. Taking Barney for his walks. Laughing with Ash on the couch.

There's no sign of any of them, but music comes from somewhere far away.

I head through the villa, the lights on the patio drawing my attention. When I emerge, I see a sight I never thought I'd see.

The brothers are playing soccer barefoot, Ash in a T-shirt and shorts, Harrison shirtless in chinos. Barney is running between them.

What the fuck?

Harrison stops kicking, resting a foot on the ball as he looks between us. Barney attacks the now-still ball, trying to bat it away from Harrison. Until I step onto the patio, my heels clicking on the tile, and the dog lifts his head. His ears perk as he turns toward me.

"Barney…" I hold up a hand of warning, bracing an arm away from my black satin jumpsuit.

With his stunned, deliriously joyful brown eyes on my face, he launches himself at me. I'm knocked on my ass as the creature attacks me with his tongue, seeking any available skin.

"Barney! Dammit!"

It's another ambush, but unlike Harrison's earlier, I can't respond with fists and fury. Instead I wrinkle my nose as I shove at a thick-barreled canine chest and drooling muzzle.

Finally, Ash hooks fingers in the dog's collar and pulls him back.

I shove the hair from my face as I stare up at Harrison. "You kidnapped me," I accuse.

"I kidnapped my brother. Your wardrobe simply came along for the ride." The torch lights play over Harrison's beautiful body, golden hair, and dancing eyes. He's wearing the same smug arrogance as the day I met him, and I'm sorely tempted to tell him where to go as explicitly as I did then.

"Play with us?" Ash calls from where he's dribbling the ball, the dog weaving between his legs in pursuit. "You can even be on Barney's team. He cheats and gets away with it."

I want to hate Harrison. But in this moment, seeing Ash happy and the brothers together and Barney's infectious joy for everything, it's impossible.

Harrison holds out a hand.

"Whatever this is," I warn under my breath, "it stops tonight. I will do more than throw an entire closet of Brioni in the pool. You don't get to fuck with me anymore. We're not together."

An emotion flickers behind his eyes, but it's gone a moment later. He nods.

I brush the dust off my silk pants and take his hand.

CHAPTER 7

Rae

"Time for bed," Ash yawns half an hour later.

I drink the beer I've been nursing at the patio table while the guys kicked the ball around, trading stories and jokes.

"What's Barney chewing on?" I ask, realizing the dog has been quiet since knocking me over, content to lie in the corner and ignore both the ball and me.

"Oh bollocks." Ash cringes.

I cross to the dog and pull a pair of panties out of his mouth. "Seriously? You stole my clothes and fed them to Barney?"

"I stole. He fed." Harrison glares at his brother. "Did you not take her bag up to my room like I told you?"

"I thought she'd like to make up her own mind about you."

"Thanks. I think." I frown as I stare at the mangled fabric.

"I'm going to take a shower before bed. Raegan, I'll put your bag upstairs. You two sleep well." Ash disappears into the house, followed by a whining Barney.

It's just Harrison and me.

I drain the last of my beer and grab the other bottles from the table. "When I left, you were ready to beat the crap out of your brother. What changed?"

Harrison waits for me to go ahead of him into the house, and I try to ignore his physicality. He's as strong as ever, naked to the waist, tan, carved muscles. His beautiful eyes track me, his cut jaw twitching.

"I asked him a question. He answered correctly."

Inside, I turn so fast he bumps into me. "Whether I slept with your brother is none of your damn business."

He takes the bottles from my hands and continues toward the kitchen, chuckling under his breath. "That's not what I asked."

The sound of water comes on upstairs. *Ash.*

"What's so funny?" I call after Harrison, not bothering to keep my voice down now that his brother is occupied.

"It's nothing." He deposits the bottles by the sink before returning. "I'm going to clean up here."

I'm surprised, but instead of commenting, I go upstairs and find my bag in my old room. Unzipping the suitcase, I retrieve my toiletries and some pajamas before realizing Ash is in the second full bathroom.

Harrison's still downstairs, so I head into his bathroom. When I get there, I brush my teeth and wash the makeup off my face. I turn to hang the washcloth on the towel rack, noticing pieces of grass and stuck to the butt of my outfit, plus a smudge that's probably a grass stain from when Barney knocked me over.

This wasn't the plan for tonight. I was supposed to be having a long, hot bath before collapsing into bed at my hotel, twenty feet away from Ash's soft snoring. Instead, I'm in Harrison's bathroom, resisting the impulse to sniff his soap for another hit of familiarity.

I untie the halter neck and strip out of the jumpsuit, tugging it off my bare feet. I'm standing in my underwear, running the fabric under water, when the door opens.

Harrison fills the doorway, a silent, hulking presence. He's stripped down to his shorts, his hard body impossible to ignore.

"Ash was using the other one," I say over the thudding of my heart as I turn back to the sink, continuing to rinse my outfit.

"What is that?" He's at my side the next moment, catching my wrist and turning it over so his thumb presses against the sensitive underside. He traces the shape, and his touch sends my pulse skittering more than the feel of the needle buzzing across my skin.

"A tattoo."

"You copied my scar."

My jaw drops at his audacity. "First, that's not a thing. Second, it looks nothing like your scar. They're crowns. That's the only thing alike. Mine is small. Simple. These parts are curved, and… it's part of my logo. Little Queen is part of me."

I jerk my arm back, balling up the jumpsuit and dropping it on the counter.

Charged blue eyes lift to mine. "Why are you here, Raegan?"

"You're a petulant asshole who stole my clothes."

"In Ibiza."

"You really want to talk about that now?"

"You're standing half-naked in my bathroom," he says softly. "You don't want to know what I want, love."

My eyelids drift down again to the outline of his thick erection against his black shorts.

Distance destroyed my heart, but it fed our chemistry. I've been without him so damn long, and every inch of me is begging to close the space between us. But letting him touch me will mess with my head, make it harder to remember we're not together and we won't be getting back together.

He circles my wrist with his large hand. There's no way he can't feel my thudding pulse.

"Tell me one thing and I'll let you walk out of here. Did you miss me?" he asks.

"No."

His lips caress my wrist, and my knees sag.

"Liar. I can't read your thoughts, but I can read your body. The way your eyes shine. How you breathe through your mouth instead of your nose. The way you sway toward me, daring me to touch you. I know what you want as clearly as I know what I want."

I can't hold in the moan, not when his tongue traces the same path as his lips, sending trails of fire up my arm that have my breasts pulling tight.

His eyes darken with intent. "You have five seconds to leave before I push you against the wall and take what's mine."

"My body doesn't belong to you," I whisper, not moving to leave.

"No. But the way you react to me does. Five."

"You're full of shit."

"You're about to be full of me. Four."

I look past him toward the door. "You'll never have me back, Harrison."

"Three," he rumbles with a wink, and I feel the shiver from that wink all the way through me. "Last chance."

"Go to hell."

"Only if you're coming with me. Two."

I try wiggling out of his grasp, but his grip tightens, pulling my body flush against his. His heat and strength make me gasp.

"Don't play games that I'll win." He swivels around so my back is against the wall. "You knew the second you walked in here where this would end."

Unbelievable.

My heart thuds against my ribs as he waits me out.

I angle up my chin. "Well? Are you ever going to get to one, or is this just—"

He kisses me.

In the quiet moment before his mouth touches mine, I know I could step away, or say no, or even push him away. But I don't. I don't want any of it.

At the first brush of our lips, I open. His tongue slips past mine, and he threads his fingers through my hair, silently begging for more. I give it to him, kissing him back.

His hands drag up my sides, cupping my breasts. The touch feels so damned good, and too soon he's reaching back to unfasten my bra, dragging it down my arms.

He groans against my lips as he grabs my ass. "This get bigger?"

Despite the angst of being apart from him, I've done better at taking care of myself, eating healthy and working out rather than ignoring my body's needs. "This isn't the time to accuse a woman of stress eating—"

"Not what I meant. You're fucking hot, Raegan. Every second that passes, you only get hotter to me."

This is a bad idea. But the arousal pounding through me like a tidal wave won't let me say no.

The apathy I've been dealing with in my gigs, the fatigue, the restlessness, I want him to fix it tonight. And tomorrow can't possibly hurt more than today or yesterday or the hundred days before that.

I brush my fingers across his hard length through the fabric and he twitches against my touch.

I've missed every part of him, including this one. I close my grip around his length, straining to encircle him all the way. A tight exhale forces itself from his lungs, but the look on his face screams approval.

"Yes. Touch me." His hiss turns me to liquid.

I free his cock from his shorts with impatient hands.

He's thick and proud, jutting up toward his clenched abs, his swollen tip already leaking.

My body aches at the sight of him.

"You open that mouth any wider, I'll think you want me to fuck it." Harrison's low rasp strokes along my skin like a dirty caress.

"Keep dreaming."

Far away, I hear the sound of the shower click off.

Harrison boosts me up so I'm braced against the wall. My breath is uneven, my legs wrapped around his hips and my grip on the back of his neck. Our foreheads press together, his fierce blue eyes boring into mine.

My body's resistance is nothing compared to gravity, and he fills me completely on a single stroke. I'm stretched full of him, our angle making him sink farther into me every time I exhale. The feeling of his cock rooting deep leaves me gasping.

As he rocks into me, I grip the back of his neck, holding on for the ride.

"Jesus, Raegan," he mutters against my ear as if I'm the one tearing him apart instead of the other way around.

When I lean in to kiss Harrison, he fuses our mouths. The kiss deepens, his tongue fucking my mouth while I clench harder around his cock. He shudders, releasing the kiss so I can breathe and cry out.

White-hot pleasure burns, makes me rock my hips against his to chase every bit of friction.

Every second is meant to make up for a day, a week, a month. It has to. Because every gig, every smile, every picture was a lie to bury the truth:

That when Harrison King left me, it took an entire persona to hide my anguish.

He swivels his hips, making me whimper. "You're so fucking tight."

Damn, I'm not going to last. I'm too fucking sensitive from missing him, and everything about tonight has me wound tighter than a drum. I'm about to go off.

"Come for me," he murmurs.

The next time he pulls back, my back slips down the wall an inch. I dig my nails into his neck. Instinct.

"Not letting you go."

He means he won't drop me. But as the feel of his body, his closeness, his Harrison-ness, drags me over the edge after all this time, and as my orgasm triggers his, making him clench and spurt inside me…

It would be easy to imagine he means something else.

When he carries me to his bed, tucking me in next to him and locking an unyielding arm around me, I could dig an elbow into his gut and run for the door.

I don't.

Tomorrow, things will go back to the way they were, but I let myself have tonight.

CHAPTER 8
Harrison

I've had a lot of filthy fucking dreams.

This one is the best.

Raegan, the woman who's graced every one of my fantasies since the day she ripped me a new one at a friend's wedding, is on her knees. She licks a line up my cock, and my arse clenches as I tug on her hair.

I want her to get serious.

I want her to tease me for goddamned ever.

It's understandable I'd be hard as a bloody teenager the night after I broke down her door, decided to do whatever it took to bring her back to me, only to have her surprise me in my own bathroom. Practically naked. Startlingly beautiful.

The next time we had sex again—I never let myself believe there wouldn't be another time, though during a couple of dark nights, that thought tried to drag me down—I vowed I would be in control. Show her exactly what she's been missing.

But there was no finesse when I took her against the wall. Only raw need, frustration twined around a shriveled black heart that's only ever beat for her.

Now, I'm thinking of all the things we didn't get a chance to do last night.

When I blink my eyes open, the dream gets better.

"Thank fuck," I groan as Raegan comes into focus, her dark hair in sexy tangles around her flushed face. "I was afraid I'd open my eyes and find it was the dog."

"If Barney gives head this good, I'm going to be concerned." Her eyes flash as she rocks back on her heels. The sheet is wrapped around her decadent body, and I want to rip it away.

"Never. You're far better." I shift up on my elbows. "But something isn't right."

"Because I'm naked in your bed?"

"Because it's"—I check the bedside clock—"eight thirty and you're awake."

"I get up early now, asshole."

Those six words hurt.

Because they remind me I've missed out on her life.

She shifts away, and I grab her wrist, tugging her back over me. I press my lips to the tattoo. I hate that she marked herself without my knowing. Without my even knowing she wanted to.

I lace my fingers in hers, pulling her arms down so I can suck one of her nipples. Her back arches, pressing more of her perfect flesh against my mouth as she adjusts her hips across mine. Her wetness glides across my cock, teasing, and I growl.

"Any man who's touched you? I can fuck him out of your head," I promise. "Because I know you in here." I thread my hand in her hair, brushing it back and stroking her temple with my thumb.

"And here." I press my other hand to her heart, the steady rhythm thudding beneath my palm.

I'm not angry—I'm determined. Committed.

"I didn't come back for you, Harrison."

Her words land like a blow I wasn't prepared for.

I recover. "For Ash, then."

She shakes her head. "I'm playing La Mer. I went to see Mischa."

Every muscle in my body is tight. Hearing that name on her lips in my bed makes me flip her so fast the sheets get caught between us. "You did *what?*"

"He has a house in Ibiza. I took a meeting with him yesterday before you showed up." She starts to slide out from under me.

No.

I pin her hands next to her head, locking her hips under mine. The expression on her face is irritation, not fear, and that makes me angrier.

How the fuck could she think to just walk in and speak to him?

Everything I've been working toward is a path to ending Ivanov—not to avenge my parents, the way I'd always intended, but to preserve my future. And if I accomplish that, I hope it can be Rae's future too.

Raegan won't have a future if she puts herself in harm's way.

"He's dangerous," I say.

"I understand."

"Clearly you don't. How am I just finding this out now?"

"I should've told you before or after we fucked in the bathroom?" She shifts out of bed and grabs one of my shirts from the closet. "You should probably get dressed. Unless you're hoping

Barney will fix that situation for you"—a nod at my cock—"because I'm not going to."

Raegan buttons the shirt and slips out of the room, leaving the door ajar and me speechless.

Rae

"Señorita!" Natalia declares as I come down the stairs, showered and dressed in denim shorts and a flowy black shirt.

"It's so good to see you." I'm not big on gestures, but when the housekeeper hugs me, I can't help returning the squeeze a little.

"Nothing for me?" Ash drawls as he comes down the stairs after me.

Natalia shakes a fist at him. "You made Toro lose money betting on your team."

"You should've bet on the other team," Harrison comments from the kitchen.

"We can't. You're family."

The three of us enter the kitchen, where Harrison is barefoot and drinking an espresso from the machine.

"Lose the French press?" I quip as I get a glass for water.

He stiffens as I brush his hip reaching for the cupboard.

When I mentioned La Mer in bed, he looked at me like a vengeful god ready to rain down fury on hapless mortals. He's clearly not over it.

"On the patio," he bites out before I've had a chance to take a sip. "I don't want Natalia worrying about this."

We head out to the patio overlooking the ocean and take seats on opposite sides of the table.

"Talk."

Though I don't owe him an explanation, Mischa is his nemesis. I understand why he's taken aback.

"I played Wild Fest this year. My career hasn't just recovered. It's exploded," I say. "When the top one hundred list came out, I was swimming in offers. The single I released last fall got new life. I have money."

Sometimes it still feels like a dirty secret.

"I don't own a house, but I could. I could support not only my cousin's charity but half a dozen more."

His jaw works as if he's proud of what I've done but disinclined to deviate from the point he dragged me out here to talk about. "You realize it's not because of the list. It's because of you. You embracing who you are. Playing with joy."

His gaze drops to my wrist, where I'm fingering the tattoo.

It doesn't feel like joy lately. But I don't say that. "I want to play La Mer. That hasn't changed."

The warmth behind his eyes is banked. "Only thing that hasn't."

He rises and crosses to a hedge of bright-yellow flowers, pulls off a dead bloom, and tosses it away.

I want to ask why he left the way he did. If it was worth breaking up what we had.

But I'm afraid of the answers. If he says it was worthwhile, it'll hurt all over again.

If he says it wasn't... then what? We can't go backward. I've started to build a future on my own terms, gigs around the world, even if they don't satisfy the way I thought they would.

There's no way I'd give this man a chance to break my heart again. I've done brave things in my life, and stupid ones. Inviting in a man who makes me feel as if I'll never be as worthy as his vendetta would be the most foolish.

"You must have changed too," I say.

"My parents were liars," he says abruptly. "Building a legacy for them is moot."

The hurt in his voice has my chest tightening. "What are you talking about?"

"After Tyler and Annie's housewarming, I received a call from my investigator confirming my parents' life was a lie. They weren't trying to get out, Raegan. If Mischa or his parents killed them, it was to prove a point. For internal justice. Not because they were leaving."

Horror washes over me. I close my fingers around my mug to avoid reaching for him. "You didn't tell me."

"Mischa burned down the club that night. I didn't have a chance."

I can only imagine what he was going through.

He spent his life trying to do penance for what he thought was his fault—that his parents were getting out of the Ivanov's business on account of him and died trying. It must feel as if he never knew them. The anger he must have, the questions… None of which he'll ever get a satisfying answer to.

Fuck. It's not as if this changes everything, but I wish he'd told me.

"So, why continue trying to bury Ivanov?"

Harrison rubs a hand through his hair, looking the kind of rough-around-the-edges he rarely shows the world but shows me because of what we are. What we *were*.

"He's already shaped my past. Not only through his actions, but indirectly, through who I thought my parents were. He's had even more influence than he realizes. I won't let him have my future."

The edge in his voice makes me wonder if he only means his clubs or if that extends to me too. If he was afraid to commit to a future with me so long as Ivanov had a chance of shattering it.

Even if he was, it can't make up for him leaving. But it lets me understand this complicated man a little more, and it makes me want to help.

"He's running drugs through the clubs. Not just his own," I hear myself say. "He's made himself a nuisance at Bliss. And I saw one of his guys at Wild Fest."

Harrison's expression darkens. "Wild Fest… I didn't realize he had territory in America."

"I've seen his people at parties in London." Ash appears in the doorway, hands in his pockets. From his face, I'm guessing he didn't hear the part about his parents.

"You knew it was Mischa's people?" I ask, shoving my hands in my jeans pockets.

He looks away. "Yeah."

"How can you know?" Harrison presses.

"I just fucking do."

Silence falls over us. I think of the coldness in Mischa's eyes before he hit me that night at Debajo. Then last summer, the unforgiving flames devouring every inch of wood, scarring the metal that would have been Kings.

He's the kind of man who would stop at nothing to prove a point.

Harrison pulls out his phone. "Leni. I know you're on holiday. I need you in Ibiza."

There's a response, agitated but not clear enough that I can make out the words.

"I'll make it up to you. Buy you a damn surf school when this is all over." Pause. "Yes, you can get that in writing."

I exchange a look with Ash.

"You've seen what he does. I have to end this." Harrison says it to both of us when he hangs up, but he's looking at me.

I don't answer. Even if he's right and Mischa's evil—the kind of evil that should be extinguished for the benefit of all—his words remind me that I'll never compete with this burning need to see justice done.

"Law enforcement has been monitoring him for a while, but it could still take years to bring him down," Harrison says. "His parents kept their illegitimate operations under wraps being judicious. Mischa is less discreet. But so far, he hasn't slipped up enough to be caught. He rewards loyalty quickly and punishes betrayal even faster."

A shiver runs through me.

"If he's running drugs through clubs beyond his own, outside of Ibiza, we have a hope of catching him. If the management team at Bliss will cooperate," Harrison adds.

I think of how upset the man was. "They're more afraid of Mischa than the law."

He turns to Ash. "What club were you at in London? And why were you even noticing people dealing?"

Ash shifts on his feet, clearly uncomfortable. He doesn't want to admit to his brother what really went down. "I'll tell the police. But I don't want to tell you."

"For fuck's sake—"

"Harrison." I grab his arm, and he turns incredulous blue eyes on me. "I saw a dealer in both places. The club owner confirmed he was Mischa's."

"The man won't flip. Mischa has a stranglehold on this island."

I lean in. "I'm playing again this week. I'll talk to him. And I need to follow up with Mischa."

Harrison seems to draw himself up even taller. "You will do nothing of the sort."

"We'll move back to the hotel today," I say, ignoring him and turning to Ash.

"I'll make the arrangements." Ash grabs his phone and heads to the far side of the patio.

"I will not watch you put yourself in harm's way," Harrison bites out once his brother's out of earshot. He grabs my arm, and I jump more from surprise than his grip.

The sex we had last night doesn't change anything. Not really.

My chin angles up. "Because you're the only one allowed to hurt me?"

His eyes soften as they search mine, and I see the man I fell for. "It's not the same, and you know it."

"No, it's not." The breeze captures my hair and blows it across my face. "Mischa and Zachary never promised to love me before they hurt me."

I take advantage of Harrison's stunned silence to pull out of his hold and head for the door.

CHAPTER 9
Harrison

Marina Botafoch is a playground for the rich and one of two docking ports for megayachts.

I wasn't thinking of Raegan when I took one of the cars and came down here after sending her back to her hotel. Now, I'm remembering the time we walked around the harbor together. A year ago, we strolled along this same boardwalk, her asking me questions about the boats.

Weeks later, I chartered her one for one of the best weekends of my life. I'd spend the rest of my life on the damned seas, my stomach rolling with the waves, if it made her smile.

She reappeared in my life yesterday, and she's already leaving it again. I barely got her back, and she's gone.

"Mischa and Zachary never promised to love me before they hurt me."

I hoped in time she'd understand why I left. Now, she sees how dangerous Mischa is... and she still blames me.

I hurt her. But Mischa is capable of ending lives. She must

see how much worse that is. How our happiness can't possibly be realized until he's gone.

Regardless, the idea of her being in the same room with the man who's ruined lives and ended others has my gut cold with panic. I can't make decisions from panic.

A young boy playing chase with a friend runs into me, calling out an apology over his shoulder as he continues along his way.

"Harrison." A familiar voice has me turning.

"Christian."

He extends a hand, and I hesitate only a second before taking it.

"Perhaps retirement doesn't agree with you? You look older."

"We all do this year."

"I heard you've been spending most of your time in Paris."

"We are visiting." Christian nods toward a yacht. From this angle, the shiny, white object looks roughly the size of one of Sebastian's football pitches.

"A new prize." I zero in on the name, the *Bijou*. "Your former jewel has made way for a new one. Looks like the disposal of La Mer was profitable." My words are laced with recrimination.

"In some ways," he says cryptically. "Have a drink with me."

We're not friends or business acquaintances anymore, but given what I learned from Rae, things are escalating with Mischa's business in ways I hadn't anticipated. I'm not ready to turn away possible allies, even if I don't trust them, which is why I asked to meet Christian.

My abs clench as I follow him onto the yacht.

Is this how my brother feels about talking with law enforcement? He acted nervous when I put him in touch with my contact, but he promised to share what he knew. Whatever insights he refuses to share with me.

I'm still angry Sebastian wouldn't tell me—there seems to be a lot of that going around—and that I had to act on good faith. But he didn't give me much choice.

I pull up short when I see the young woman sunbathing.

She rolls over and spots me. "Harrison!" She sits up, pulling a towel across her bare chest.

"Sylvie. I hope you're well."

A man—boy?—lies next to her, frowning protectively.

"I finished university," she says. "Papa said my boyfriend could come on holiday with us."

The man-boy's face relaxes a little at this reinforcement. I hide my smile.

"How nice for you both." With a nod, I follow Christian across the deck.

"He's immature and impulsive and dotes far too much," Christian mutters.

"He's perfect for her."

We take seats at a table at the far end of the yacht, and an attendant immediately brings Christian a cold drink, offering me one as well. I wave him off. From here, we have an uninterrupted view of the sea in one direction and the harbor from the other, white and blue and dotted with color.

"What do you have for me?"

Christian sips his drink. "Advice. I want Mischa gone too."

I arch a brow. "You'll forgive me if I don't trust you."

"What happened last summer was unfortunate. Ivanov threatened Sylvie."

My hands fist under the table. Since LA, I've wondered if that might've been why he changed his mind so quickly about selling La Mer to Mischa.

Christian adds, "At one point in my life, I might have gone toe to toe with him. But I'm too old for a war and too old to risk what I've made on one."

Sylvie's laughter carries on the breeze from the other end of the boat. Evidently the man-boy is serving his purpose.

"So, it wasn't because of my parents. Who they were."

My host sighs. "No."

I shift out of my chair and cross to the railing. "Then I found out they were liars and criminals for nothing."

After a moment's hesitation, he follows, leaning both elbows on the railing next to me. "Not for nothing, Harrison. You are strong enough to know the truth. To make your own way."

I turn toward him. "I was making my own way."

"You were making theirs. Doing what you thought they wanted, needed. You reinforced that lesson for me when you turned down Sylvie last year. Young people need to find their own way."

I bark out a laugh. "I'm not young."

"Because you never let yourself be. When they died, you took on a challenge they never asked you to."

My next breath is harder than the last despite the fresh air. "I needed to provide for my brother. To prove that I could be the man they hoped."

"You were. They wanted better for you. By choosing to stay away from Mischa's company when they pursued you, you chose the right path. You didn't owe them a single thing after that."

"I need to fight him."

He shakes his head. "If you're going to fight, don't fight for something ugly. Fight for something beautiful."

I think of Kings, a hollowed-out shell. "I don't have anything beautiful to fight for anymore."

"Don't you? How is your lovely American?"

My head snaps around.

"Sylvie pointed out that you two are no longer together. She reads the papers," he explains. "But then, my wife and I had a period of separation. All it accomplished was proving two things: that she was right and I was lonely." His eyes crinkle at the corners.

My fingers flex on the railing. I still don't trust Christian, and having Rae and I publicly linked is a bad idea for her safety.

"She's playing in Ibiza this summer."

Christian nods. "He understands many things, but not love. Keep it from him."

"Then help me end this fast." I can't keep the urgency out of my voice. "I need information."

He hesitates, glancing toward the laughter of his daughter and her boyfriend. "I still have much at stake."

In that moment, I realize the truth. Christian is an old man who likes to talk, to feel important, but when it comes to doing important things, he's a coward.

I shove myself off the railing.

"Where are you going?" Christian calls after me.

"What I know about war is this—most people don't have the luxury of choosing whether they're involved. They can't sell their stake and disappear with their families." I gesture pointedly at the yacht, and he folds his arms.

"I can't help you the way you would like."

I turn my back on him. "Call me when you can."

CHAPTER 10
Rae

O f the things that have changed since I got big, one hasn't: Working on a song doesn't get any easier.

Back at the hotel, I'm trying to prepare for my set at Bliss tomorrow night and experiment with new material. I keep reworking the melody, but it doesn't have the vibe I want.

Last year, my tracks were moving towards a more joyful sound—stripped down harmonies, major chords.

Now, it's more minors, but when I'm done, it feels thin rather than atmospheric.

Ash has gone out for a few hours, promising he'll stay out of trouble. But now that he's gone, work is harder because I keep thinking of someone else.

Harrison told me that his parents weren't trying to get out of Mischa's family's business after all.

Harrison spent years deifying his parents only to watch the pedestal he'd put them on crumble. Learning that would fuck up a person. Especially when, that same day, Mischa burned down the club Harrison had spent months building.

He needed somewhere to put that anger, and turning it back

on the man who caused all of this probably seemed a reasonable plan.

I wish he'd talked to me instead of leaving.

But it has me thinking that part of why he left was the man who has everything on paper still thinks he doesn't deserve love.

Once, it was because his parents died and he felt responsible somehow. Now, he thinks he's cut from the same cloth as they were.

I wish he could see that they must have loved him. Whatever they did and didn't do, I'm grateful for that.

A text comes through, and I frown at it.

Annie: Has he shown yet?

I hit her contact on my phone, and she answers immediately on FaceTime.

"Hey." Her gold eyes blink, faint circles beneath them hinting at long nights awake.

"Hey. Where's Rose?"

"Uncle Beck's putting her to sleep. He's magic. If I'm lucky, she'll be down for an hour." She moves around her house. "Haley told me to document every moment because Rose will grow up so fast, but I don't know how she found the time."

"Maybe Jax took the pictures."

Annie laughs silently. "Can you picture it? My dad, the paparazzo?"

I shift my notebook computer off my lap and lean forward, thinking back to her text. "How did you know Harrison would be here?"

She tucks a piece of hair behind her head. "Why would you think—"

"Because you're a romantic and you basically outed yourself already," I tell her. "So fess up."

Her nose scrunches. "Fine. Tyler and I saw Harrison in New York a few days ago, and I miiiight've shared that amazing photo of you and his brother in London."

I huff. "That's why he showed up jealous as hell."

"Did he?" Her lips part, her eyes glazing over dreamily. "I want to know it all."

"You don't have enough testosterone-fueled bullshit in your life, you're welcome to some of mine."

"Please. Having a three-month-old isn't great for your sex life. Or any life," she admits.

"I could understand if you don't want to have sex."

"It's not me. It's Tyler," she whispers. "He'll stay up and rock the baby all night. Won't complain once. Then he fell asleep on me last night."

"On you."

"On. Me," she emphasizes.

"Huh." I'm sure it's temporary, because Tyler has seemed one heartbeat away from jumping his wife the entire time I've known them. I fill her in on Harrison's arrival, giving more detail than I normally would.

"He *hit* him and then he *kissed* you?"

"Hit who and kissed who?" A familiar voice comes from out of speaker, and I sigh.

"Hey, Beck."

The screen rotates, and a moment later, they're both in frame.

Beck grins. "Hey, Little Queen."

"Harrison hit his brother and kissed Rae," Annie informs him.

"Damn. Serves that snotty prick right."

"Who?" Annie asks.

"The brother. Pretty boy has no chill." The derision in Beck's voice is laced with something else, maybe from when Ash slammed Beck's reality TV show the weekend we were all on the yacht last year for my birthday.

I think of Ash's issues with drugs—if Beck only knew—but say nothing.

"He's had a tough season. It's a lot of pressure," I hear myself say. "You'd like him if you gave him a chance."

"Fortunately, I'll never have to."

Annie lifts a brow. "Anyway, Harrison's back and you guys have made up."

"Not quite."

"I thought he kissed you," Beck interjects. "Then things escalated from PG and you faded to black for our benefit."

"Please don't fade to black," Annie begs.

I roll my eyes. "There might've been some mature situations. In the bathroom," I go on when Annie makes a "give me more" motion with her hands. "Except things are complicated."

Annie's smile broadens. "Tyler and I did complicated. Your damage can't be any worse."

"He's trying to bring down Mischa Ivanov, this business rival of his. The one who burned down his building. The problem is, I'm also trying to play Ivanov's prize club."

Beck whistles, and Annie's jaw drops. "Rae, I agree with Harrison on this one."

"But La Mer is everything I've dreamed of playing."

"You could have fun playing other gigs, couldn't you?" Annie asks.

"I don't know. It hasn't been fun lately," I hear myself say without thinking. "The last six months, it's felt more like phoning it in. Which is a fucking awful thing to say, but I wonder if I've done everything there is to do. Except La Mer."

"So, once you play it, you can check it off your bucket list and take cover?"

Except when Annie says it, it doesn't feel right.

I shake my head. "I don't believe in revenge, but I agree this guy needs to be off the streets. Ibiza would be better off, his patrons would be better off, the music industry too. I'm playing other clubs. I get up in other peoples' businesses in a way Harrison can't."

"Because you're still hoping you two can ride off into the sunset on a yacht together?"

"He doesn't like boats."

"When he got you the yacht last year…"

"He thought I wanted it."

Annie sighs, and even Beck's brows pull together.

"What are you thinking?" I ask. I don't usually solicit input, but next to my cousin, these two are my closest, most trusted friends. And unlike Callie, they understand the complications of living life in the spotlight.

"Queen's gotta help her King," Beck says wryly.

"It's not about Harrison," I insist. "It's a public service. Anything I find, I'll pass on to the police."

"But if it gets you hurt," Annie adds, "I will kill him."

Your first night playing a club is partly a crapshoot—the crowd, the weather, all of it can conspire to make your set a party to remember or one to forget. The second night is when you find out if you've got it.

Tonight for Bliss, I choose a white dress that resembles leather but isn't. It's fitted, but the fabric has a little give so I can move, and it's not as hot in the booth. White sandals top off the look.

"You're coming with me?" I ask Ash as I put the finishing touches on my makeup.

"Think I'll lay low for the evening." He frowns. "All the talk about drugs… I'd rather keep my distance."

Realization hits me. "Understood." I check the edges of my wig to ensure none of my hair shows beneath. "I get that you didn't want to tell Harrison you were buying, but why didn't you tell him what you saw?"

"I'd rather not say. But it would hurt him if he knew."

"I can keep a secret. I can be loyal to you as much as to him."

"Yeah. But you shouldn't have to be." He comes up behind me, and his gaze meets mine in the mirror.

I fold my arms over my chest. "Just tell me one thing—are you talking with the police?"

He nods. "I told them I'd give them all I know. It's not much, but it's compelling."

The reason he knew he was buying Mischa's drugs in a London club still eludes me, but I trust him.

"Fine. Has Harrison said anything about the investigation into your parents?"

"No. Why?"

Fuck. That means Harrison's been shouldering this alone for the better part of a year. "He was looking into it last year, back when he was still trying to buy La Mer from Christian."

I brush past Ash and grab my phone, cursing as I realize I forgot to recharge it after my call with Annie and Beck. "Hey, did you do something to piss off Beck? You seem to have made an impression on him on the yacht last year."

He shoves his hands in the pockets of his shorts, his mouth twisting. "I seem to make terrible impressions on all men."

"That asshole on your team doesn't deserve you. You'll find someone who does."

Ash smirks. "I want someone I don't deserve. Like Harry found."

My chest tightens as I head to the show.

I snap a picture in the limo and post it to social. New habits, but already ingrained.

My fan base has grown and evolved. I can show up at a venue and find hundreds of people, sometimes thousands, there to see me. It's humbling.

Sometimes it's numbing too.

It's one of the things I wish I could've talked to Harrison about over the past year. My friends understand the fame, but it's not the same as sharing it with the man who sees me, challenges me, like no other.

When I get to the club, there's already a crowd.

I get the owner in a corner. "The drugs sold in your club. You have to speak out about them."

"I don't know what you're talking about."

I blink. "You told me the other day…"

But then I realize the truth. He won't say a word. Harrison's right.

By the time I take the stage, I'm already frustrated.

But I play my set, waiting to be swept up in it as I change from one track to the next. This club is twice the size of Debajo, and it's nearly full. The crowd is loving me.

I should be loving this.

Pressed near the stage is a group in costume. A girl meets my gaze and dissolves into delighted screams. My attention pans to a guy dancing near her, who catches my eye and makes like he's giving oral.

I turn away, needing a breather that's impossible while on stage.

My thumb presses the tattoo on my wrist, the backs of my eyes burning.

Feel alive.

Be alive.

Get it together.

I turn back and motion to security. "Vodka soda."

Then I throw myself into the rest of my set. I'm finishing the drink when movement in the far corner of the club catches my eye.

The same guy from before. Selling.

I look over at the manager at the bar. He knows it's happening, and he doesn't even try to stop it.

The woman from the front of the stage is there, buying.

I want to stop her. To say he's bad news. But from here, I can't. I'm the most powerful woman in the room, and I'm helpless.

I finish my set and do selfies with fans. I half wish the woman would come up since she seemed like a big fan. But there's no sign of her.

Unsettled is the only thing I feel.

I'm headed out through the side door when I trip over something soft and lumpy. When I realize what it is, my stomach drops.

It's a body. A person.

Horror rises up as I recognize the woman who was buying inside.

I drop to my knees, feeling for her pulse.

I should call for the club owner, but he won't do anything to cross Mischa.

There's one person I want to call, and I won't even question my reasons for calling him.

When Harrison arrives, Toro driving, I'm still standing with the woman who was passed out near the side entrance of the club. Harrison stalks out of the car and takes in the scene, his expression grim and unusually blank.

It takes a moment for him to speak, and when he does, his voice is rough. "What the fuck happened? Who is she?"

"I don't know who she is. But she overdosed on something." I hold out what I found in her pockets. "I called for the owner after

I called you. Management wouldn't let me call an ambulance. They didn't want the overdose traced back to Mischa."

"That doesn't make sense. Tourists overdose all the time. Could be the shit they're dealing is cut with something else. Makes it cheaper to produce and more dangerous to consume."

Harrison feels for her pulse, then looks around. Because we could be seen together, I realize. He's risking everything being here.

It's too late to change it.

We pile her into the back seat to take her to the hospital.

The doctors in Ibiza are used to overdoses, and they smoothly take over the second we bring her inside and establish how we found her. She's in a coma, but I make them promise to let us know when her condition changes.

We head back out to the car, Harrison hanging his head.

Inside, Toro flicks a gaze back before pulling out onto the street. Despite his quiet presence, in that car, it's just the two of us and the awful things we've seen tonight.

"Why did you call me?" Harrison asks.

I swallow hard. "Because you're going after Mischa and I figured you would want to know firsthand what was happening."

But that's not true. I'd planned to tell the police, not Harrison.

Calling him was instinct. Something terrible happened, and he was the person I wanted at my side.

"Señor? Are you all right?"

I look between Toro and Harrison, who nods tightly. Then Toro buzzes up the partition.

"What's going on?" I demand.

"Overdoses are hard. Since I found my parents dead."

Shock slams into me, chased by grief.

He found them?

I assumed it had been a neighbor or someone who worked for them.

Now, I picture a college-aged Harrison bursting in the front door, pulling up at the grotesque sight.

"I'm so sorry."

My eyes burn, my cheeks tingling with wetness.

"Don't, Raegan. It's not your fault."

He's stoic, controlled. Maybe this is how he became that way. Put in a position that left him feeling utterly helpless.

I touch his hair, smoothing my fingers through it. "This man is out there hurting people, and we have to stop him."

He pulls me against him, and my face nestles into his suit jacket. The air between us is tight. With grief, with anger. His arms band around me like steel.

We don't live in a safe world, but his resolve reminds me there are people who care about us. That we live in a world worth fighting for.

When we get to my hotel, I don't move for a long time.

"You can't come upstairs," I whisper, his lapel scratching my lips.

His chest rises and falls rhythmically under my face. "Because of what happened tonight or because you don't want me there?"

I pull back to look up at him through damp eyes. "Both."

If we go up to that room together, it won't only be sex.

It'll be therapy.

No, church.

We'll burn one another down to nothing and roll in the ashes before getting up tomorrow and putting clothes on whatever shambles of form remain. And I can't risk that with him. We both have our own priorities, and they're already dangerously intertwined.

"You deserve love, Harrison. No matter what your parents did, no matter what you did. I wish I could convince you of that, but you need to convince yourself. You deserve to be happy."

"Just not with you."

Fuck, that's unfair. But he's trying to push me away. I can see him now. He hides behind his own walls. Mine are high and protective. His are armored with barbs.

"You walked away from me. I loved you. I wanted to spend every day with you. Every damned hour. When you left, it broke me."

My gaze falls to the crown inked on my wrist. "I wanted to remind myself of your confidence, your belief in me. You taught me that loving is worthwhile, even when you don't get it back. That you can be the person you want to be, even when no one's looking. Especially when no one's looking. I will never forget that."

His jaw works, his firm mouth parting in frustration. "I want you, Raegan. If I could tell you how many nights I've lain awake wanting you…But I don't want to see you hurt anymore. I've caused you enough pain. If you ask me to stop, I'll do it."

I stare at him. He doesn't take no for an answer from anyone, merely finds another way to get what he wants. But the expression on his face is earnest.

Mischa needs to be brought down. Tonight, I understand better than ever why this matters to Harrison, why it's so personal he can't let it go.

But letting him break my heart twice would be foolish and might ruin me.

I shift across his lap and grip the door handle. "Yes. Stop."

I'm out of the car before I can take it back.

CHAPTER 11
Harrison

Going through your dead parents' things is an edifying experience. Strange how processing a person's belongings is shaped entirely by your memories of them.

Those memories have changed shape and color since last year.

Growing up, I swore my parents had all the answers. Until they started arguing at night in hushed tones. I challenged them to leave the business they were in and start fresh on their own. When they died, the guilt crippled me. It was my fault they'd left.

Finding them dead only made it worse. The people I loved and admired were gone, and Sebastian would grow up without parents, and every time I closed my eyes for years, I saw their still, slumped forms and blamed myself.

Now, learning they hadn't really been trying to leave, I should feel as if a weight has been lifted. They weren't innocent. Some people might even go so far as to say they deserved their fate.

Except my need for vengeance on the man who killed them has grown—not because they were saints, but because when Mischa burned Kings to the ground. It wasn't only about them anymore.

He attacked *my* business, the one I built from nothing with my own hands.

The Ivanov family molded my past with cruel, greedy hands.

They won't touch my future.

I'm in the third-bedroom closet, surrounded by boxes, unpacking photos and other items that have sat here since I had them shipped from London.

Some items I toss in a pile to get rid of.

I can't sell their things, so I'll donate them.

When I spot a slim, black lacquered box, my chest tightens. Inside the lid, there's a photo of Ash as a baby. Me holding him with a put-upon smile. I would've been fourteen, I think, and home from school on a break.

My mother never kept her things in a safe. She wouldn't let my father convince her, no matter what beautiful trinkets he bought her. She wasn't a suspicious person. Once she said, "If someone cares enough to take them, they need them more than I do."

The exception was her wedding ring.

I lift it from the case, the gold band slim and smooth in my fingers. There's an inscription I never noticed before. *Through everything.*

I'm surprised it's here. When they passed, I had the funeral home dress them in clothes as different as possible from what they were wearing when I found them. Anything to clear that awful image from my mind. I told the funeral home to bury them with their rings. Yet this one's here.

Footsteps in the hall have me glancing up. As they approach the half-open door, I call, "Natalia. Could you—"

"Not Natalia." Sebastian steps inside. His shorts are forest green, his favorite shade as a child, and his polo shirt is a few shades lighter.

I set the ring back in the box and rise, the box still in my hands. "What are you doing here?"

"Rae told me what happened last night at the bar. The woman who overdosed." His eyes search my face.

"Don't do that," I say, irritated.

"What?"

"Try to see if I've lost it. I'm your older brother. I'm supposed to make sure you haven't lost it."

His lips curve, the ghost of a smile.

"Did you talk to the police?" I ask.

He crosses to the bed, the only place to sit, and sinks into the bedspread uninvited. "Yes."

I clench the box harder. He shouldn't be keeping secrets from me. I'm his damned brother.

"When did I let you down, Sebastian?"

"What do you mean?"

"You don't ask me for anything."

"I've asked you for money. You helped put me through school—"

"I mean anything that's going on in your life. You call me when you get drafted, but when your season goes off the rails... I didn't hear from you once."

He flops back on the bed, insolent as a teenager. "You're the infallible older brother with all the answers. If anyone had a different approach, they were wrong. Our parents thought the sun rose out of your arse whether you gave a shit or not."

My chest tightens. "I told them to leave the business, and when they did, it cost them their lives."

He throws his hands wide. "That's not why I'm angry! I'm angry because I didn't lose two pieces of my family that day—I lost three."

His meaning sinks in, prickles lifting the hairs on my neck.

"I took custody of you, Sebastian. Made sure you had what you needed. Not only food and shelter, but the best schools, the top football coaches." I refused to let him grow up with less than I had.

"I didn't need private school or football coaches. I needed my brother. But he was too busy picking up where they left off."

He shoves himself off the bed and stalks toward the window, avoiding my gaze.

I can feel his anger, but it's the hurt in his voice that shakes me. "I had to provide what they couldn't any longer."

"I grew up without a family, Harry. Being a teenager, figuring out what I wanted to do, who I was… it fucking sucked. Not because they were gone, but because I was alone and I didn't need to be."

Fuck. Maybe in trying to protect my brother, I isolated him. I think of Raegan, how her parents made their choices about what was best for her and only hurt her more.

I rub the box between my hands.

I hope to hell I didn't screw up my brother like that. Or if I did, that he ends up a resilient person like she is.

"I'm glad you kept going," I say at last.

He cuts a look over his shoulder at me. "The other option is worse."

Raegan's words about me thinking I don't deserve love echo in my head.

When I tried to protect her last year, convincing myself it was for the best to leave, I destroyed what was left of our relationship.

Perhaps she's not the only one I've done that with.

My next breath is shallow.

"I need to tell you something. Last year, in the course of trying to win La Mer from Christian, I learned something about our parents. Information I wish I could forget."

He's across to me in a heartbeat. "What?"

The sunlight streaming in the window is at odds with how I'm feeling, but I force out the words that have lain heavy on my shoulders for the past year.

"They were liars." My voice is tight, and I swallow. "I thought they wanted to get out of Mischa's family business, and I told you as much. But they had no intention of leaving. Everything I did to build this business was for them. To avenge them, to make them… It's meaningless. Perhaps I should get rid of the villa too."

I grab the pile of things, including the velvet box, and toss them in a bag by the door before pacing the room.

"Don't. You like the villa."

"I wanted it because it was theirs," I grind out, rubbing a hand over my face.

He doesn't answer, and I glance back to see him thumbing through the bag.

"You knew them more than I did. Had more time with them. The thing is, we build people up to be what they're not. I did the same with you." He opens the jewelry box and takes out the photo. He smiles, holding it up. "I remember this."

I snort. "You don't. You were all of six months old."

"Yeah, but I remember being safe. Protected. Most of all, loved. By them and by you."

"You don't care that they weren't who we thought?"

He turns over the picture. "I never saw that. I'd rather remember that they loved us."

My chest tightens unbearably. Holding my brother at a distance has been harder than I thought, but safer.

Sebastian straightens, lifts the ring out of the box like I did. "*'Through everything'*." He arches a brow. "Guess they knew life wasn't perfect either." Sebastian shuts the box and sets it on the bedspread. "You won't save this, I will."

I nod. "Sebastian?"

He glances up.

"When did you become an adult?"

"Legally, on my eighteenth birthday. Sexually… far sooner. Though, honestly, I'd take it back if I could."

My chuckle rumbles through my chest, dislodging some of the pain. "Do you want to go through the rest together?"

"Let's get lunch first."

We head back out to the hall.

"You know," he tosses over his shoulder as we head down the hall to the stairs, "I told Rae you didn't deserve her."

I pull up, incredulous. "What? When?"

"Yesterday." He pauses at the top of the steps. "But I was wrong."

I shove my hands in my pockets. "I asked if she wanted me to stop pursuing her."

"Why the fuck did you ask that?"

"Because I didn't think she would say yes!"

He rubs a hand over his face, and for a second, I feel like the little brother.

"It was a bluff."

"No, it wasn't. You meant it, and that's why you're freaking out, because now you have to honor it."

He's right, damn him.

"She's the only woman I can see in my life. The only one I want by my side. She's infuriating and argumentative and sullen and beautiful. I don't know how not to go after what I want, Sebastian."

I get that she's angry, but I never expected the feelings beneath to erode.

Now, the prospect of life without Rae makes me howl.

My brother's mouth twists. "Take it from someone who's been there. Loving something you can't have is better than not loving at all."

CHAPTER 12

Rae

Last night, I took a sleeping pill.

It's been three days since the night Harrison and I took the woman to the hospital. I haven't heard anything about her condition. Nor have I heard from Mischa since the meeting when I arrived about my La Mer proposal.

Everything seems to be locked into a holding pattern—save my agitation, which seems to grow.

Since the night at Bliss, I replay finding that woman over and over, when I should be working or sleeping. I can't unsee what I've seen, can't help but wonder how many people have been hurt by Mischa Ivanov.

Today, I'm scheduled to do an interview. There's a multicamera setup on this patio in Ibiza Town, and a few fans have clustered around to watch.

The last interview I did in Ibiza was the start of a rough period of my life—the reporter called me out on being with Harrison.

I've done dozens since then. I'm never quite comfortable.

"I'm here with Little Queen, who's playing a residency at Bliss in Ibiza this summer."

Cheers go up from the street, and I turn to grin at the fans gathered, which only makes them cheer more.

"You've built quite the following," the interviewer says.

"I'm grateful to every person who listens."

"Why is it important to you?"

"Because we're all individuals going through our own shit."

Her eyebrows lift, and I wonder belatedly if I can swear on this channel.

"What shit"—she sneaks an apologetic look at the camera guy, and I laugh—"are you going through?"

I uncross and recross my legs on the high stool, glad I wore ripped denim and sandals rather than a dress. "The usual. Working on some new songs. Soaking up the sun."

The man I loved is trying to bring down a drug dealer while I'm trying to get said drug dealer to hire me.

I haven't seen Harrison since the night of my show, and that's eating at me too.

But after our call, Annie sent me a picture of Harrison holding her baby. It hit me hard. Not because I've ever thought of having kids with him. The idea of Harrison as a father seems completely at odds with his mission, his entire ethos.

But is it? Everything he did has been driven by love for the people he cares about. Even if he chose that love over our love.

Before the sleeping pill kicked in last night, I couldn't resist typing out a text that I sent along with the image.

Rae: You better hope this doesn't get leaked publicly. Ovaries will explode.

Harrison replied instantly.

Harrison: Even yours?

I stared at the message for too long. Was he up because he was thinking of me? Thinking of Mischa? Or something entirely unrelated—the direction of interest rates or the last season of the *Great British Bake Off*?

Rae: I'm not maternal.

Harrison: I doubt that very much. But there is a precedent.

Then he sent me a picture of a teenaged Harrison holding a blond baby wrapped in a blanket.

Rae: Wow. Ash looks... innocent. You look as if you'd fight the world for him.

Harrison: I learned early to take no prisoners. Hesitation leads to weakness. Compassion precedes defeat.

I debated before responding.

Rae: That's a good way to make enemies. You'll always be fighting.

Harrison: It's the only way I know how to live.

That was the tragedy.

He taught me how to fight—for myself, for my dreams, for the love I deserve.

But I want him to lay down his weapons.

Another text appeared before I could respond.

Harrison: I never stopped caring.

My heart kicked. Part of me wanted to believe it was true, not only for his sake but for mine.

I fell asleep soon after but woke still thinking of him.

"Something arrived for you before the interview," the reporter says slyly, bringing me back. "Would you like to see it?"

I straighten in my seat, surprised.

One of the crew brings out yellow tiger lilies, and I take them, awkwardly shifting to grab the envelope and slide out the card. I read the single phrase written on the white paper.

Take no prisoners.

My body explodes into tingles as if Harrison himself brushed my hair back and whispered the words against my ear.

"You have an admirer. Well, you have lots of them," the interviewer amends, grinning at the crowd. "This looks like a special one."

Awareness has the hairs on my neck lifting despite the heat.

Harrison's watching.

Flowers could be construed as not backing down, but he'd argue they're just for support.

Too bad him being sweet is as destructive as a full-on assault on my body and my heart.

I tuck the card away. If I say I'm seeing someone, it'll raise suspicion. But when she goes on, my task gets infinitely harder.

"You were linked to Harrison King last year. First in Ibiza, later in LA. Do you think he sent the flowers?"

I turn over my thoughts, knowing he's watching. I shouldn't say anything, but I can't resist. "He's a fighter, not a lover."

"Is that what came between you?"

My smile fades. "A lot of things came between us. But I'm a different person now."

They think I mean a person who wouldn't date Harrison. But that's not it.

I'm a person who can handle the heat. Who can go toe to toe with not only Harrison, but anyone who threatens me and the people I care about.

"What's next for Little Queen?"

"My residency runs another month. And…" An idea clicks into place. "I don't know if I'm allowed to say this." I sweep a coy look over the crowd and see every damn person lean in or bounce on their toes. "I'm working on something special, one night only, at the club everyone comes to Ibiza for."

Screams erupt. Squeals and shouts of "Yes!" and "La Mer!"

"When?" another person hollers when the initial noise dies down.

"I can't talk about it," I say apologetically.

After finishing the show and taking a few selfies with fans, I change in the venue's bathroom before I head out the back door.

A long, black car pulls up in front of the alley.

Rude.

I go to move around the back of the car, but it reverses so I can't.

The front window buzzes down to reveal the driver, a severe-looking man in a suit. "Get in."

Russian accent. My spine stiffens.

"Who the hell are you?" Even though I already know.

He holds out a phone showing La Mer's social media page, where everyone is asking when I'm playing. My heart thuds, hiding the first hint of satisfaction in days.

"You tell me where I'm going and I'll get my own ride," I say.

"You want to work for him, you'll get in."

"Once I work for him, maybe I will. Now what's the address?"

I pull up outside La Mer and shift out. For a moment, I wish Harrison was here. But he wouldn't let me come, and I can handle this myself.

A huge security guard meets me at the door, and I start to go through it. He blocks my way and holds out his arms, motioning for me to do the same.

"You're joking."

A brusque headshake.

The impulse to run is still there, but it's the middle of the day in an outdoor venue.

His venue.

I follow instructions, and the man pats me down before jerking his head toward the hallway. I follow him down it, realizing halfway through that I'm holding my breath.

Excitement starts to outweigh the nerves as we emerge into the main area.

It feels like a circus ring.

Or maybe a coliseum.

Bars line the perimeter. The stage is at the center, an altar for revelers to worship at.

The lights are rigged into the sides, a sophisticated network of technology.

"Don't fuck with me."

The cold voice has me whipping around to see Mischa emerge from another corridor. I haven't seen him since the day I went to see him.

"I don't wait around for things to happen. I thought you didn't either," I comment.

He stops in front of me, inches away. I force myself not to back up.

He grins suddenly. "You need the money? You should've kept King around after all."

"Do I look like I need money?" I glance back toward the sports car I rented. "I've always had a soft spot for this place."

Mischa prowls around me. "Personal memories?"

I think of dancing here with Harrison, him kissing me for the first time. But I say, "This is the biggest gig there is. I fucking want it."

His rasp of laughter scrapes over my skin. "And you will do me a favor by playing here?"

I hold up my phone. "After my interview, you had three hundred comments in an hour asking when I'm playing. By tonight, you'll have a thousand."

"I don't like people forcing my hand."

"Really? I think you do."

"Are you almost finished?" a feminine voice calls from behind me.

I turn to see a familiar blond woman emerge from the same hallway Mischa did.

"We haven't formally met." She wears a smile that's bigger than her companion's but no warmer. A thin veneer of cordiality sheathing a viper's fangs. "I'm Eva."

"Raegan."

"I thought it was Tiny Princess?"

"Little Queen," I correct.

The smile is still in place. "I suppose we have something in common now."

I survey her form in surprise.

"We both survived Harrison King." She holds out a hand. "There's hope for you yet."

Her huge diamond blinks in the light.

"Congratulations. Is this new?"

"Just this week," she confirms. "I trust you haven't seen Harrison in some time?"

I shrug. "Why would I?" It's a bad idea to let on that we've been talking. Or fucking. Mischa might misconstrue that as us getting back together, which would mean my loyalties might have shifted.

"But you've seen his brother. You went to an event together."

I turn to face Eva, new wariness setting up in my gut.

"I saw Sebastian recently in London too. A few months ago. He joined some friends in a VIP room."

The pieces click into place.

This bitch is what Ash wanted to keep from Harrison. She pushed the drugs on Ash.

"Sounds like a party," I say, matching my smile to hers.

"Too bad you missed it."

My pulse is heavy against my ribs, either from the thrill of this place or my hatred of these people. "What would be too bad is you missing out on me playing here."

Mischa's shrewd eyes narrow on me. "Why is that?"

"Because your family has been in this business a long time." I purposely don't allude to the drugs. "Do you know what that means?"

"It means I am powerful."

"It means you're the past. I'm the future."

I sense the surprise in him that I would dare to speak to him this way. It's an opening. One no person in their right mind would use.

Take no prisoners.

Mischa is like Harrison in some ways—egotistical, demanding. But without all of Harrison's graces.

So, I know how to provoke him.

I turn back to the venue, sweeping my gaze over the dance floor. "Men who build theaters like to adorn them with gold and velvet to trick the audience into believing the venue is the spectacle. But no matter how comfortable the chairs, how gilded the balconies, it's still only a blank canvas. A theater is only as good as its performers." I close my eyes, take a deep breath of the sunlight and the fresh air. This place will transform at night, become something else, like I do. "I can't tell you how many people have tried to keep me off stages like this one. But they won't."

Mischa watches me like a predator surveying its prey. "And why is that?"

I step closer, my heart hammering against my ribs.

The man before me is dangerous. As skilled as Harrison at business, more talented at manipulation, without the reservations about hurting people.

But I can be dangerous too.

"Because when I'm up there?" I nod my chin toward the stage. "They can't fucking look away."

Mischa's nostrils flare. Blue eyes glow like cold embers, dragging down my body. The top and jeans cover most of my skin, but under his attention, I feel bare.

Blood pounds in my veins, fear and adrenaline. I'm no longer chasing. I'm being chased.

Eva knows it too. She's at his side in an instant, her arm threading possessively through his.

"Your manager has my rates and terms," I say to Mischa once his gaze returns to mine. "I look forward to hearing from you."

I haven't won, but as I square my shoulders and head for the exit, I know I've done something very brave or very foolish.

CHAPTER 13
Harrison

I've never watched a movie over again in my life, but I'm watching Rae's interview for the third time.

The moment the flowers come in and she reads the card, I see it.

Her lips curve the tiniest bit.

Fuck me.

I'm a fucking teenager sending his date a corsage.

A smile.

The texts yesterday out of the blue, which mean she's thinking of me.

It's like the tiniest interaction with her, the slightest tease of emotion, is my oasis in the desert.

I'm taking a break from entertaining guests at Debajo, which is still packed a year after Raegan took on the challenge of reinventing it. The DJ tonight isn't her, but he has the near-capacity crowd captivated nonetheless.

Spending eight months on opposite sides of the globe was one thing. But now she's here, and I can as easily ignore her as I can ignore my own need for oxygen.

She asked me to back down. I won't force myself on her, but I won't stop protecting her. I won't stop loving her.

Earlier in the week, she called me when she found that woman after her set. I'm glad she did. Even if I can't shake the feeling of seeing that crumpled form, even if it brought up memories of my parents' deaths. I got to hold her in the back of the car, see her eyes damp with the tears she never lets fall.

It made me realize something…

Raegan's strength is my damn weakness.

My phone rings.

"King," I shout over the music as I rise from the leather bench.

The voice on the other line belongs to my investigator in London. "Figured you'd want to hear about the sting police tried to run on Mischa's venue here last night."

I excuse myself from the VIPs in my booth—a handful of investors, plus twin celebrity actresses.

"What happened?" I demand, pressing my other hand to my ear to listen over the music as I cross the catwalk and head for the stairs.

Security holds the door, and the next second, I'm in the quiet hallway leading to the VIP room.

The man on the phone sighs. "A source suggested there was a big deal going down. What they found was a poor cousin of that. And the guy involved… some small-time dealer with no links to Ivanov."

Either the police fucked up, or Mischa knew they were coming.

I pinch the bridge of my nose. "A tourist ODed here the other night and nearly died. Not uncommon, but the drugs were cut with something. Doctors wouldn't disclose, but it was something bad."

He hesitates.

"Our surveillance of Ivanov saw a woman arrive at La Mer earlier today shortly after Mischa did."

I shake my head, impatient. "And?"

"It was Miss Madani."

My hand has a death grip on the phone.

"We couldn't get close enough to hear what they were meeting about, so we can only speculate—"

"I fucking know what they were meeting about."

I hang up and drop into an armchair in the VIP room. It's quiet tonight, just the bartender who left the moment I waved him away.

How the hell could she visit Mischa?

I want to storm her hotel suite again. I'll lock her up in my villa until this is all over. But something tells me she won't be nearly as welcoming as she was last time, and that landed me with a bruised cheek for two days.

Since my brother and I went through our parents' belongings, I've been wondering how much damage I did unnecessarily to people I love.

Maybe if I can destroy Mischa, I'll have another shot with Rae too.

I replay the video of her getting the flowers and watch her try not to smile once more.

"Huh. I knew you were getting old, but napping? For real?"

I straighten and open my eyes to see a welcome sight. My right-hand woman stands in the doorway with her hands on her waist.

"Leni. Christ."

"Evening, boss."

I rise and cross to my friend, clasping her in a hard embrace.

"If I'd known you were this strung-out, I would've come sooner."

"Why didn't you?"

"Told you. Vacation. My cabana boy licked the sand out of my toes and—"

"I'm sorry I asked." I hold up a hand, and she grins.

I cross to the door, shutting it to ensure we have extra privacy. "We need to take Mischa down."

"His goons are selling outside. Pulled a knife on me, but I chased them off."

Alarm works through me. "You're joking."

"Nope. I knew one of 'em from last summer and told him what I'd do with his balls if he tried selling here again. New manager pissed himself when he saw the blade."

I think of the guy Leni put in place once the club was made profitable last year and she accompanied me to LA. I vow to replace him immediately.

"It's not only about Kings, Leni. His reach has broadened. He's in America. In London. He's running drugs through other owners' clubs here, forcing them to turn a blind eye, then blackmailing them after. Interpol has been working to link him to narcotics activities, but they've cocked it up."

She leans in. "So, what do we do?"

"We need to strike him close to home. Everywhere his parents built up, he's well protected. Hundreds of employees without contracts who get fed only the bare minimum info. Whom he can deny having any knowledge of if it comes up. It's the perfect business. But he's not as smart as his parents, which means there's an opening. We need options, and we need to move fast."

"You want to play cop, Harrison? Never figured you for the polyester-and-a-badge sort."

I narrow my gaze. "Raegan came to Ibiza to book La Mer."

Leni's eyes round. "Oh shit."

Her expression says she knows exactly what that means—that the woman I love is working with the most dangerous man I know.

"She's met with Mischa. Twice," I bite out.

"Have you told her not to?"

"Of course."

She grimaces. "Bad idea."

"What?" I demand.

"Let's see. You guys broke up last year—"

"Separated."

"Whatever—because you were an unreasonable prick after Mischa went all pyro on your new project."

"So, a Russian madman responsible for my parents' deaths burns down a ten-million-dollar project and I'm unreasonable?"

"With her, yes. She's more likely to do something if you tell her not to."

I drop my head in my hands and tug on my hair hard enough my scalp aches. "What is it with women?"

"Brains, empathy, and pussies," she fires back. "It's worth taking the time to figure them out. Don't go anywhere." She claps me on the shoulder as she rises and crosses to the bar, where she grabs the good whisky and pours a single glass on ice.

"None for you?" I demand as she brings it back to me.

"I'll come back for mine. First, I'm going to go talk your manager down from the ledge."

CHAPTER 14
Rae

"**Y**ou buy those?"

I look up from my computer as Ash enters the suite, juggling a ball between his knees.

"Buy what?" I ask.

"The flowers."

I look at the lilies from Harrison that I've moved around the hotel room no less than five times. "No. They were a gift."

After doing the interview yesterday and going to La Mer to see the Russian homewrecker and his happily wrecked now-fiancée, I'm trying to enjoy a day to myself.

Instead, I'm questioning whether I made a grave miscalculation by going after Mischa so aggressively.

"We have company," Ash goes on with a grin.

I straighten in my seat at the kitchen table, tugging on the hem of my threadbare tank top. *Is Harrison here?*

Ash holds the door, and the guy from the gala, Gavin, follows him in.

"Hey." The man gives me a wave every bit as casual as his messy-on-purpose brown hair and his easy grin.

If he recognizes me from the event, he doesn't let on. Or maybe Ash told him we're nothing.

"Excuse us." I grab Ash and tug him out to the patio, shutting the door. "This a good idea?"

"Have you seen him?" He tosses an appreciative look at the man, who's perusing the coffee table magazines. "Plus, he came here for me."

I lift my hands. "Last time, the way he acted sent you spinning out. You deserve someone great, Ash, and I don't like how he treated you."

"S'alright," he murmurs. "Gavin is about to make it up to me." He ruffles my hair. "But thanks."

I watch him head inside, grab the man's wrist, and drag him down the hall. Conflicted feelings collide in my chest. I want to see Ash happy, but with someone who deserves him.

Sex is one thing, but if he's trying to hide feelings behind it…

Maybe it's nothing. Maybe this guy won't hurt him again, or maybe Ash can keep physical separated from the emotional.

Before I can decide what to do, my phone rings on the table. I lunge for it, my stomach flipping as I see it's an unknown number.

Possibly Mischa.

"Yeah?" I answer.

"Rae. It's Leni."

My brows shoot up as I close out of the Ableton Live software on my computer. "Oh, hey."

"We've had a little problem at Debajo. I need you."

I'm already visualizing flames like the night Harrison was dragged from his bed to find Kings a pile of smoldering char. "What kind of problem?"

"Our talent for tonight isn't going to make it. He's too stoned to play."

Disbelief rises up. Not because it's the first time in history a DJ has been inebriated on stage, but because Harrison could've had the decency to call me himself.

Just because I told him to back off pursuing me doesn't mean I wouldn't have enjoyed him asking me to come back to Debajo. A little begging would have been nice.

Now that I picture it, him on his knees, looking up at me like I'm his entire damned world, even as he prepares to wreck me...

Focus, dammit.

"Listen, I know Harrison has a problem with people using substances, but you might have to compromise this time—"

"No, Raegan, I mean he's too stoned to play. Like, I'm looking at him, and he's a mumbling pile on the floor." Pause. "Here. I'm waving his hand at the phone. 'Hello, Little Queen. Will you cover my set? I'm a fucking mess.'"

I press a hand to my face, already feeling like crawling back into bed. "It's my day off."

"That's going around. Tag, you're it." She laughs. "I promise it'll be more fun than the place you're playing all summer."

"Bliss has been great," I argue.

"But it's not home."

Home. As I remember the stage, the VIP room, the staff, a familiar longing tugs at me.

"Is there a theme?"

"*The future is you.*"

I make a face. "Sounds like a bad yearbook title."

She laughs. "You got something better? We have time to

change it and let everyone know."

Leni's someone I respect independent of Harrison. Plus, it's not her fault he didn't call me himself, and I'm not going to give another woman shit for asking for help just because her boss should've done it.

I consider the highly produced shows I've been doing at Bliss and my lips twitch. "I have an idea."

I fill her in, sending an image to go with my description.

She's quiet for a long time but finally chuckles. "Let's do it."

After hanging up, I head down the hall.

Groaning and panting drift through Ash's closed door. I don't bother telling him where I'm headed.

I go to my room and pull the closet door wide.

"Thanks for the ride," I say, leaning forward from the back seat.

"My pleasure, señorita. You need to come visit."

"I will," I promise. "Tell Natalia I'm making her a crocheted doll."

I shift out of the car, the trench coat wrapped around me mostly for Toro's benefit.

There's a line around the block, and the marquee reads: "COME AS YOU ARE." As I approach the string of patrons, I get a look at some of the outfits. There's more skin than clothing.

For once, it's not fancy lingerie-inspired outfits. It's simple. Nude bandeau tops and miniskirts for the women. A few even have nipples drawn on. The men are in shorts or speedos, a few painted flesh tones.

I can't help grinning.

Leni, what did you do?

I head in the back, headphones and drive in my bag. Security's stoic faces break as they spot me. I fist-bump one guy.

"You're overdressed," he comments as he holds the door for me.

"Not for long," I toss over my shoulder as I head to the VIP room.

Leni's waiting for me at the VIP bar. She's dressed more like security in head-to-toe black. It's early, and a handful of staff are back here, including the bartender, who nods at me in recognition. I return the gesture.

"Cam, can I get a—"

"Vodka soda coming up."

I grin, turning back to Leni.

"See? Like coming home," she says.

Maybe she's right. It already feels better. As if parts of me are waking up. I remember how hungry I was only a year ago, how every show was shiny and new and a chance to do what I loved.

"How'd you get a thousand people to wear skin with three hours' notice?" I ask.

She shrugs. "Convincing young, beautiful, drunk people to get naked? Not that hard. And I told them Little Queen would be here to show them the way."

I reach for the belt of my trench coat and shrug out of it.

Cam the bartender is at my side with the vodka soda, but he freezes when I toss the coat on a nearby chair. "Jesus."

"Venus," I correct.

"*Birth of Venus*, actually," Leni goes on, scanning me admiringly.

I catch a glimpse of myself in the mirror over the bar. The

custom lace bodysuit matches my skin tone. I bought it to wear under another costume, but I figured tonight called for something simple. The effect is definitely provocative.

On my feet are nude platform sandals. My blond hair is straight, hanging in slow waves to cover my breasts. My eyes are lined dark, and my lips are sheer.

It's more than hot.

And sure, maybe I wanted to push Harrison's buttons, to remind him he can't jerk me around anymore without getting jerked right back.

Sue me.

I reach for my vodka soda and take a congratulatory sip.

"Can I get you anything else, Raegan? Miss Queen? Fuck," Cam mumbles.

Leni pinches his cheek. "Sweetie. You're cute. But if the boss comes down here, you're gonna have to put those eyes back in, or he'll rip them out and keep them."

Cam gulps and heads back to the bar.

Leni laughs silently. "You do look fucking incredible."

"Thanks. I'm missing one thing." I reach into my bag, pulling out my headphones. I loop them around my neck, the cord secured. "There."

She shakes her head.

"What?" I prompt.

"Just deciding if I should call Harrison or wait for him to find out."

My smile dies. "He doesn't know I'm here?"

Her brows shoot up. "Honey, I didn't ask the boss. Think he has a business dinner tonight. Maybe he'll swing by after."

Shit. I assumed Harrison was in on this and had his own reasons for not calling me. But he didn't know…

I catch sight of myself in the mirror once more.

It's too late to worry about what he'll think about it. Two thousand people in the next room need entertainment. And I won't let them, or the staff of the place that made me, down.

CHAPTER 15

Rae

I take the stage to deafening applause.

I play some experimental shit. Some stripped down remixes, even the song I was working on that I can't get quite right.

The crowd is dancing and loving and living, and I'm in it with them. My hands are in the air, and I'm losing myself in the music.

Leni's right. This feels like home.

I might even know how to fix this track now.

I'm hearing the changes in my head, committing them to memory when awareness jerks me back to the present.

The champagne bucket appears at my side, full of waters.

I put off responding for thirty seconds. A minute. Even change the tracks once without giving in to the desire to look up.

When I can't hold back anymore, I lift my gaze to the VIP.

Harrison King is wearing a tuxedo, bracing both hands on the railing. His perfect jaw is set, firm lips pressed into a hard line, his hair mussed as if he caught himself running a hand through it.

His eyes are locked on me.

In a room full of pagans dancing underground…

He's a god.

And he's pissed.

Part of me wishes I could tell him I didn't do this to mess with him. Even though there's nothing he can do. He can't very well drag me from the stage.

Though the idea makes me shiver.

We can't be together in public because I can't have Mischa thinking we're an item again.

And in private, it's too risky to my heart.

But like this, I can touch him without touching him.

We're surrounded. It's the most dangerous place to be, and the safest.

Since he walked into my hotel room, I've been a mass of emotions. Wanting, aching, longing, regretting.

I can wish he didn't leave me, but I can't change that he did. But I wouldn't rewind time and erase what happened between us. I wouldn't even erase the hurried sex in his bathroom last week.

The more I stare at him, the more I realize…

I wouldn't erase a thing.

We never should have been, and that only makes me cling more determinedly to what we were. What we are. Even if we're not a couple and I'm not hoping for a happily ever after with this man, something between us is alive and teeming, now, in this basement.

So, I play for him.

I choose the songs, tracks that will move the crowd and fit the stripped-down theme of "Come As You Are," but that also fit us. I create a new set on the fly, my fingers moving as fast as my mind.

This set is my own personal mixtape for my fuck-hot ex.

He watches like he knows it.

My body is on fire. After a couple of drinks, coupled with the power of this place, I could touch myself right here.

I could come from it.

I could beg for it.

Does he feel the same way?

He's still watching. He hasn't looked away.

Take no prisoners.

I flip him off, then run my tongue along the side of my finger. I swear his eyes darken.

In the VIP booth overhead, he widens his stance, adjusts his pants, then rubs the bulge in the front.

My throat dries.

I change the track to the one I made last summer, the one I told him he could jerk off to and think of me.

His movements stop as if he knows what I'm doing.

It's a filthy dare he can't possibly take me up on.

Maybe it's the night or the frustration between us, or maybe I'm just that goddamned good, because the silver on his belt flashes in the light as he flicks it open.

Holy shit.

Then his hand is inside. He starts again, slower.

The expression on his face...

It's the hottest fucking thing I've seen in my life.

I'm a live wire now, my skin prickling as heat rushes over me.

My core throbs. On stage, I can't slide a hand between my thighs without being seen, but I want to rub on Harrison, on my own fingers, on anything.

This club is more than a third wheel in this transaction. It's part of both of us, one we won't ever give up.

For the next song, I split my attention between the partiers and Harrison. If I stare up too long, someone will figure out what's happening.

That the most fully dressed man in this place is stone-cold sober and fucking his hand.

Every movement of his arm, his jacket, feels like he's tugging on a string wrapped around my core. I'm so fucking turned on in this moment, I think I might come for real.

His jaw is tight, his hand working his cock like he's my dream fantasy come to life. I'm breathless, my reckless smile impossible to hold in when I pick up the pace of the track.

His gaze narrows, but he does the same with his strokes.

The music moves every person in this club, but he's moving me.

I can tell when he's getting close. I can't look away.

I want to watch him come.

I want to *feel* it.

His head tips back.

He's close.

His hips jerk. Once. Twice. Then he groans—I can't hear it over the pounding bass, but I see it.

When he comes, I *do* fucking feel it. The wave grips me, and I reach for the desk in front of me to steady myself as if I'm coming too.

His unsteady breathing is mine.

When confetti rains down from the ceiling, I realize this is the best time I've had in a long time. Maybe ever.

It's because of Harrison, but also because of this place. It does feel like home.

The crowd is chill and happy, content to take selfies at Debajo with me, with each other. Then the crowd parts, and my breath catches.

Harrison King walks toward me, his tuxedo jacket unbuttoned and his mouth pressed in a hard line.

When he reaches me, I say, "I thought it wasn't a good idea to be seen together in public."

"It's not, which is why you're in trouble."

He's cool, cold even, as he gestures for me to go ahead and follow security. I head down the hall toward the VIP room. Leni's there, along with the bartender. Harrison shuts the door before turning to face us.

"Whose bright idea was this?" His voice is deadly calm.

"I called her," Leni admits. "We had a cancellation last minute. And Cam's a terrible fucking DJ."

The bartender ducks his head.

"Cam?" I call. "Mr. King could use a whisky."

He fixes one immediately, bringing the glass over. His gaze slides to my legs, and his throat bobs.

Harrison sends the guy scurrying away with a look.

"Cam, I'll drink the whisky." I cross to the bar and take it from him before sipping the golden liquid.

Harrison paces the room. "Mischa isn't supposed to know we're talking. Tonight you all but announced it."

"We announced that Debajo had an opening," Leni cuts in, "and a former DJ in residence picked up the slack for an impromptu—

and a fucking fantastic, might I add—show."

Adrenaline surges through me again. It was fantastic.

"You're the one making this worse by marching her down here," Leni goes on.

Harrison's gaze finds mine.

If Leni knew that her boss had jerked off to me upstairs…

"To be fair," I say, the whisky heating my stomach, "it probably looked as if you were marching me here to chew me out. Which is apparently what's happening."

"There's a car for you out front," Harrison says.

My breath hitches. He's sending me away? I told him to back off, but after what happened upstairs, it feels like a slap in the face.

Without a word, I turn to leave.

I make my way through the halls and out to the parking lot. A sleek, black limo is waiting. I get in, and the car pulls away. I half expect it to circle the block and return for Harrison or do some other covert maneuver. But I'm disappointed when it continues straight down the road.

A few minutes later, it turns the opposite direction of my hotel.

"Excuse me, where are we going?"

The man doesn't answer.

Nerves dial up, and I pull out my phone to call Harrison. But before the ringtone sounds, I realize where we're headed.

The car parks at the beach, and I get out. The familiar sound of waves crashing along the shore greets me. I scan the nearly empty parking area for Harrison's car, the knot in my chest loosening when I spot it.

He's already there.

On the beach.

I take off my shoes at the edge of the beach and walk to him, the sand slipping between my toes. He meets me halfway. He's barefoot, his waistcoat unbuttoned. The breeze blows his hair, and his eyes glow like blue coals in the dark.

I spot a piece of confetti stuck to his jacket sleeve.

"Classy," I murmur as I pick it off.

I barely have time to look back up before he drags me against his hard body.

"I know you went to see Mischa. *Again*."

I drop the shoes and my bag to fold my arms in the little space between us. "And I know you fucked your hand until you popped like a bottle of Dom at a bachelorette in the middle of Debajo. So, we all have secrets."

He shakes me hard, anger and fear clouding another emotion in his eyes. "I'm tempted to tie you to my damn bed just to keep you safe."

We're so close that his lips rub across mine when he bites out the words.

"Is that the only reason?" I murmur.

He hauls my lips to his. It's possessive and desperate, and I want to fight him, but not as much as I want to hold him close.

He backs me across the sand. His hands cup my face, the initial demand giving in to something earnest and full of longing. I jerk in surprise when my heels hit the water and the waves lick at my ankles.

He pulls back an inch. His eyes are as deep as the sea, every bit as tortured. "I won't let you pretend this is all I want from you."

I swallow, my heart racing as I grip his wrists. "What do you want?"

"That first night I arrived," he mutters, his voice oddly rough, "I didn't ask Sebastian if he fucked you. I asked him if he loved you."

Shock slams into me, tickling starting deep in my stomach like the tickling from the waves against my legs as he continues.

"I couldn't bear the idea. When I saw the photo of you two at the event, it destroyed me. I tried to tell myself I would stay away if he was what you wanted."

His thumb strokes the tattoo on the inside of my wrist. His words course through my veins, leave me shuddering. We're up to our hips now, the water tugging at the fabric of his tuxedo pants. Harrison doesn't notice, or if he does, he doesn't care.

"Because I love you. I loved you first. And no matter what happens, dammit, I'll love you last."

I've seen Harrison King ruthless. I've seen him angry.

I've never seen him desperate.

I'm a different woman than I was a year ago. I'm stronger and weaker. I hurt more and I love more. I didn't think it was possible to be both of those things.

He taught me how.

We're connected in a way that will never end. Out here, where I feel as if I met the real Harrison King for the first time, I can't deny it.

I shove off his jacket and toss it toward the shore.

"You missed," he murmurs against my open mouth.

"Did not."

I wind my arms around his neck as he reaches beneath the water to cup my ass, molding me to the hardness between his thighs.

His mouth closes over mine. It's hungry and powerful, and he pulls my bottom lip between his teeth and bites down until I gasp.

I slip my hand under the water, and when I close it around that blazing hot hardness, he groans. The sound is primal and raw and goes straight to my core. I massage him, lifting up on my toes to get a better angle, and his hold on my ass tightens.

The sea tries to drag us away, but Harrison is my anchor. Steady. Relentless.

"Tell me you love me," he rasps against my ear.

Before I met him, I never let anyone in. It wasn't living, not really. But the way I felt about him, I was open. Raw.

"I loved you once. More than I thought I could love another person." The words stick in my throat, and his fingers still on the zipper at the back of my bodysuit.

"Then love me again." He leans his forehead against mine.

My heart squeezes. "Harrison…"

I understand why he left the way he did. That doesn't mean I'm ready to start down this path once more. I have the career I want, friends I care about, a life I built myself. When he vanished from it last year, I realized how deep in me he'd been.

I could say that I want to love him, but the world is fucked up. That while I'll stand shoulder to shoulder with him and stare down the devil, I'm afraid to do that with my heart on a string attached to his.

I can be brave, but not when everything I am is tangled up in him.

His jaw clenches. "Until you do, I'll love enough for both of us."

He's holding out hope. I don't know if it's well founded or completely foolish, but I can't help admiring him for it.

I reach for his pants.

He exhales his frustration but presses aside the panel of my outfit. The water tickles my bare skin, and I gasp as he brushes his fingers where I'm already hot and wet.

"I want you in my bed," he murmurs, playing with my slickness. "I want you in my life."

My nails dig into the muscles of his shoulders, the shirt spattered with drops of spray. He presses a finger inside me, and I moan into his mouth.

All my resolve flees, chased away by his words and the rhythm of his finger. I'm get wetter, even under the cold water.

His touch, his words, it all hurts in a way that's so damn good. Because I can't deny it, just like I couldn't deny it a year ago.

This is coming home.

The realization flips a switch, and suddenly, I'm the demanding one.

Every second he's not inside me is too long.

I reach into his underwear for his cock, thick and hard. I wrap my fingers around him, rub my thumb over his crown.

"Raegan… fuck."

He lifts me effortlessly, and I hitch my legs around his hips. His cock presses where I'm aching. I take a breath, change the angle, and he slides inside in an endless stroke.

He's everywhere. His big hands hold me, his cock fills me. His mouth finds mine, and it's like he's finally home, too. There's nothing gentle about what we're doing, and I drag my nails across his skin, mark him.

For tonight, he's mine. I want him to know it.

He moves fast, our mouths still pressed together. The world is spinning around us, the faintest hint of dawn teasing the sky.

He's me. We're inseparable. There's nothing but us and the water washing over our slick skin.

His rough breathing falls on my lips. "Only you. Always you."

His conviction has my heart swelling against my ribs.

The ocean ebbs and flows around us, but Harrison sets his own pace. One for us.

When we come, the sea trembles.

CHAPTER 16
Harrison

It's possible to fall in love anywhere. But here, in the dark, I understand why it's possible to fall here.

She's floating on her back, and I'm holding her by the hand, both of us swaying gently with the waves.

I keep touching her, but it's leisurely and not desperate like before.

I could touch her forever. The curves of her body, its secrets.

When I saw her tonight, I was pissed. And proud.

She's stronger than I ever gave her credit for. This past year, she's gotten stronger still.

My Queen.

I understand why she's wary with her heart. She was before I met her, and now she has reason to be. I gave her reason to be.

"I realized something tonight." My voice cuts through the rhythmic sounds of the beach.

Rae turns toward me, shifting so her feet are rooted in the sand once again.

I tuck a wet piece of hair gently behind her ear. "If Mischa keeps us apart, he's already won. I don't want to keep you at a distance."

She exhales but doesn't answer.

The water flows around us, between us.

"I found my mother's wedding ring the other day. Sebastian and I did, technically. It says, 'Through everything.'" I don't know what they went through, what choices they made. But God, did they love one another."

"You envy them," she reads.

"I respect them. Because I know how fucking hard it is," I admit, threading my fingers through hers. "Last year, my entire past was called into question. If my parents weren't good people, why the fuck should I be? I didn't deserve more. I didn't deserve you. After Kings burned, the only thing I could see a path to was vengeance. I thought I was doing the right thing, the noble thing. I thought I could win you back when it was over. But in trying to save our future, I gave it away before it had begun."

Her troubled eyes search mine. "Your past can only define you if you let it. If there's a chance for us—if," she goes on as if she can feel my jaded heart leap, "we need to be equals, Harrison. You can't make decisions without me."

She presses up on her toes, her full lips coaxing mine. I taste her, the faintest hint of my favorite whisky, but under it is strength. Resolution.

When I pull back, I murmur, "You're a force."

"So are you. Unafraid of jerking off in a tux with a club full of witnesses."

My lips curve to match hers. "You enjoyed that."

I recall how she looked on stage, daring me with her eyes, full lips parting with appreciation when I started.

"Not nearly as much as you did." Her teeth flash white in the dark.

My laughter rumbles through my chest. God, I love this woman. More than I knew I could love anything.

"A cottage," she says.

My brows rise. "A cottage?"

"Somewhere quiet. With a lake. No paparazzi. No work. That's where we'll go when this is all over."

"Ahhh," I say, getting into the possibility. "No internet either."

"But how will you watch *Great British Bake Off*?"

"Unnecessary," I contend as I stroke the back of her hand. "We'll pack our bags—"

"I own *one*—"

"Which I'll buy to replace the god-awful one you have. We can walk Barney in the mornings—"

"Mornings?"

I splash her, and she laughs in protest.

"Early afternoon," I concede when her laughter dies. "Though you won't be playing any late gigs, so you won't need to sleep in."

"I see. And what will I be doing?"

"Swimming. Reading. Me."

Her dark eyes search mine. "It's one thing to fantasize about it, another thing to do it."

I have a ton of work to do to win back her trust. I dug myself a deeper hole than I knew, but she's worth it. She's worth everything.

"I'm taking you on a date," I decide. "Dinner tomorrow. I might not find a taco truck, but it'll be the next best thing. I'll answer anything you ask me. We can talk about the future. And I want you to move back in with me," I go on as her brows pull together. "I'll line up additional security. I hate knowing you're on my island and under some other man's roof."

She trails a hand along the surface of the water, lips curving. "Maybe it's *my* island now."

Fuck. She's a different woman than the one I fell in love with. An even stronger, more fascinating one.

"Come back to me, Raegan. Nothing is the same without you."

It's a minute, an eternity, as I wait her out.

"We can try."

The knot in my chest loosens a degree. But when she starts toward the shore, I catch her hand.

"I need to go back to the hotel tonight," she says.

"Not yet. One more time."

Raegan's the one to run her fingers through my wet hair and rub her swollen lips on mine.

This time when I drag her against me, I'm not thinking of yesterday.

I'm thinking of tomorrow.

CHAPTER 17
Harrison

A shadow falls over me as I hang up my call.

"You look awfully cheerful this morning."

I look up from my café table down at the marina and gesture to the chair opposite. Sebastian drops into it.

"My roommate came home around five this morning," he goes on. "Know anything about that?"

I stretch out my legs, picturing Raegan crawling into her bed sore after the night we had at the beach. "A gentleman never tells."

"Right. I trust from the phone call that you were ordering new testicles to replace the ones Raegan's been carrying in her pocket."

"I was arranging additional security for Raegan and myself." Two for Raegan, two for me.

"Where's my security?"

"Even I can't afford what it would take to have trained ex-military mind your arse once they realized how irritating you are," I gripe.

He rolls his eyes. "Well, I'm glad things are going well between you."

"Some things are still unresolved." She's guarding her heart, and as frustrating as it is, I can't blame her. "But I will do whatever it takes to keep her with me."

Starting with a date tonight, where I will prove how committed I am to our future.

The waitress delivers my coffee, and I gesture to Ash, who orders one too.

A notification buzzes on my phone—a shipment notification for Sawyer's AI. One is destined for London, one for Tokyo, and the third for Debajo here in Ibiza.

I hold up the phone so my brother can see it.

"Nightclub robots?" he demands. "Do they twerk?"

"You're in a good mood too," I observe. It's rare that we can have such a mild conversation, and I'm not foolish enough to believe one heart-to-heart over our dead parents' things erased years of tension. "You sleep like the dead. Which means if you were up when Raegan returned, you had company. Who is she?"

His smile fades. Sebastian flexes his hand on the table. "It wasn't a she."

The waitress returns with his coffee, giving me a few beats to study him. When she leaves, he takes a slow sip, holding my gaze over the rim.

It's a surprise, and also not. I had a suspicion my brother wasn't as enthusiastic about the opposite sex as I was, but he's never said as much, and I've never made it my duty to pry. Perhaps I should've.

Perhaps this was part of why his teenage years were so hellish to suffer through alone.

"Who is he?" I ask evenly.

My brother shifts in his seat, scanning the street behind me. "Another bloke from my club. It was a tough season. Gavin was there for me when I let my team down, reminding me I'm not defined by my performance on any given day. It's easy to forget when you're hounded by management and fans, every mistake hung out for everyone to see."

"Is he good enough for you?"

Sebastian's brows shoot up. "That's not the first question I expected from you."

"Well, it's the one I have."

He shakes his head. "Trust me. He's good. We were still up when Raegan got back..." Then he looks guilty, as if questioning what he should say in front of me.

"I didn't mean in bed."

He rubs a hand over his neck. "I don't know what it is or isn't. We haven't put labels on it. But until we do, the team can't know."

I stare out over the pedestrians strolling the street. I wish he'd confided in me sooner. "If you decide it's something, you'll tell the team?"

He frowns. "I don't know, Harry. People will talk."

"People will always talk."

He shifts forward, rising, and I lay a hand on his arm before he can. I can't help feeling protective of him.

"I don't want them talking about you, but if they do? I'll put them right."

"Send an army of twerking robots after them," he replies, deadpan.

I laugh, and he joins in after a moment.

We'll get through this. I feel that possibility for the first time.

A call comes in, and the name lifts my spirits more.

"Hello, love," I say when I answer. "My brother is with me. Thought I'd let you know before you start talking about how good I was last night."

It's Sebastian's turn to snort.

"So, please, don't be shy. Let's set the record straight on which King is the best lover. I'll even put you on speaker." I hit the button, grinning, but there's nothing at the other end.

Finally, Raegan's voice comes over the phone. "Harrison, the woman we took from Bliss to the hospital after she overdosed? I asked the doctors to let me know if her condition changed, but hadn't heard anything, so I went by the hospital. I figured we could find out if she saw anything that would help us."

I don't love the idea of her playing investigator, but I go with it. "And?"

"Her condition changed. She's dead."

Rae

After playing Debajo and spending the rest of the night with Harrison, I was riding a high until I got word of the woman's death.

She was a stranger, but Harrison's fury and grief over her death proves how far he's come since I met him. I can't picture the man he is now turning his back on people, even ones he has no responsibility for.

But when Harrison called a meeting for Leni, Ash, himself,

and me at the villa, he was in control once again.

"He's getting reckless, pushing bad supply through clubs that don't even belong to him," Harrison says, seated at the head of the table. "I want you all to be careful."

Leni devours the spread Natalia fixed for us on short notice—fresh sandwiches on ciabatta with pastries for dessert. Plus wine, which Ash avoids looking at.

"Fine. So we lie low," Leni says. "All I care about is that Mischa stays away from your venues. But what are you going to do?"

"Find a way to stop him. I spoke with Christian," Harrison says. "He's out of the game, and even he won't cross Mischa. But there has to be someone who'll talk. We just haven't found them yet."

Harrison rises from his chair and crosses behind mine. His strong hands move my hair before going to work on the knot of tension between my shoulders. It feels way too good, and I swallow the groan.

"Am I the only person who's not worried about what we do next?" Ash tears into his sandwich, and a few crumbs fall to the floor.

Harrison's hands still on my shoulders. "If this conversation bores you, then you can leave."

"That's not what I meant. I'm worried about what *he'll* do next." Ash leans his elbows on the table, his jaw tightening. "If Interpol raided his club in London, even if they found nothing, you think he doesn't know? You think he's not pissed?"

Silence falls over the room.

Until a phone ringing makes us all jump.

Leni holds up a hand. "Right back. It's Debajo." She lifts the phone to her ear and heads for the living room.

Ash rises with his glass, bound for the kitchen.

A low whining from the floor has me looking under the table. Barney licks crumbs off his nose. His brown eyes shine with hope. I take a piece of meat off the platter, offering it to him.

"Sucker," Harrison murmurs so only I can hear.

My hand closes over his, my fingers stroking his palm as I tilt my head back to peer up at him behind me. "He's your dog."

Harrison's expression softens, his mouth curving up despite the weight of the day. He bends closer, his nose bumping my chin as he kisses me. My fingers thread into his hair, holding him to me when he starts to pull back, and I deepen the kiss.

Something shifted between us last night at the beach. He apologized for leaving, explained why he did, and I believe he wants to be better. I'm not throwing my heart in just yet, but for the first time in a long time, I have hope for us.

The coffee machine starts in the kitchen. "Anyone want…" Ash starts, but trails off when he spots us. "Yeah."

"Never kissed a woman upside down before," Harrison murmurs against my lips.

"Don't worry. You'll get better with practice." I move my hands down his shoulders, not letting him back off as I smirk.

Harrison's soft groan is tight.

A huff of breath and pressure on my thighs has me looking down. Barney's planted his face between my legs, staring up.

Harrison chuckles. "I knew I was doomed the second my dog fell for you."

"Really? That was early days."

"You ruined my favorite jacket. I couldn't very well ignore you."

"You tried, though."

"Mmm. Hard to ignore a woman who takes center stage at your club and flips you off like it's her job."

He crosses the room away from me, and I twist in my seat to watch him. "Pretty sure it was in the contract."

He laughs. "I know we have a ways to go, but I will prove I'm the man you need. And I have something I hope you'll wear." He tosses me a secretive smile over his shoulder as he heads upstairs.

A dress?

A moment later, Harrison returns with a small box. He hands it to me, and I open the lid.

"My bracelet." I lift the cuff, my heart skipping. I'd left it with him before we parted ways. "You were keeping it for your next girlfriend?"

"I'm never buying jewelry for a woman who's not you again."

My chest tightens as I look at him.

"I haven't forgotten our date tonight. In fact, I've got a private location at one of my favorite restaurants."

"Private because you want to eat me rather than the food?" I taunt lightly.

"Private because I want the world to fuck off while I focus everything I am on you."

He fastens the cuff around my wrist, but I can't look away from his face.

The ball of emotion in my throat threatens to overtake me.

"So, I'm going to have to babysit the manager tonight," Leni calls, rejoining us from the other room and pocketing her phone.

Ash returns from the kitchen, his coffee half-consumed, as if he's decided it's safe.

"Sebastian's probably right. Mischa will retaliate," Harrison says at last.

"And we don't know how," Ash presses.

The cuff glints against the black of my tattoo, its cool weight grounding me as I rise from my chair. "We can get through it together."

I say it firmly enough even I believe it.

CHAPTER 18

Rae

That afternoon, I'm busy with work, but I take some time to go shopping.

When I show up for dinner, I'm feeling more relaxed despite the awful news this morning and the tense conversation at the villa after.

The restaurant is exclusive, and when I check in at the front, they immediately show me past the other patrons, up the stairs, and out to a lone table on the roof.

My breath catches. The scene is beautiful and romantic. Tiny fairy lights drape around the single slim railing that would keep patrons from falling off, if there was anyone up here but me.

Any man can be the grand-gesture type, but this is a precise gesture. A place that sets the stage for a meaningful conversation, not one so grand as to stifle it.

"Would señorita like a drink?"

"Thank you." I opt for a glass of wine to take the edge off.

I'm waiting a while, self-conscious in the silver dress I bought today that dips low in the back and ends partway down my thighs. Ash promised it was a ten when I sent him a picture, but now I smooth a hand down my straightened hair and hope Harrison likes what he sees.

I'm starting to get nervous when a throat clearing behind me makes me turn.

Harrison's there, tall and imposing in a dark suit, his shirt open at the collar.

His nostrils flare as he takes in my appearance, his gaze dragging down to my wedge sandals and back up over every curve to linger on my face. "You're stunning."

I blow out a breath. "And if you were any other guy, I'd say you took your time getting ready. But this is faster than pulling on a T-shirt."

He walks to me, tipping my chin up and brushing a soft kiss over my lips that leaves me tingling. "I thought about the T-shirt. I'm saving it for our anniversary."

My heart skips. "Our what?"

"Mhmm. Last year, you tried to paint a picture of what our future could be. I walked away." His expression clouds. "This time, I will make it up to you."

"With incentives?" I tease, off balance.

"Correct. This, in a way, is our one-year anniversary. On our second, I'll accompany you in a T-shirt—"

"That's not much of a promise."

"—to the Casino de Monte-Carlo in Monaco."

"They have a dress code."

"I'll break it."

I suck in a breath. That does sound promising.

He shows me to the table, holding my chair while I take a seat.

The waiter brings our menus, and I read down the list, freezing.

Sandwiches, like the one I made him on his mother's birthday after he got drunk the first night we bonded.

Tacos, like we had on the beach in LA.

Paella, like we made after I lost a gig.

"I can't believe you even remembered all of these."

He sets his menu on the table, staring calmly at me. "Raegan, I remember everything."

I've been the subject of Harrison's intention and intensity. He's seduced me with his will, but this is new.

Every piece of tonight, every look he gives me, feels as if it's without his typical agenda.

He's not beating at my walls. Instead, he's wearing them down, like season after season of rain and erosion. Relentless. Unstoppable.

I want to let him in because I've never had anyone love me like he has.

I've also never had anyone hurt me like he has, and as much as I want to believe he's more committed to me than to his vengeance, a few gestures can't make me forget months of aching for him.

I opt for paella because it feels like a crime to order tacos or sandwiches at this great restaurant.

"So, what do you have planned for these other anniversaries?" I can't resist asking after the waiter takes our order.

"Not telling."

Impatience tugs at me. "Not even one?"

"No. But I have them planned for a good long time."

"Three years? Five?"

He shakes his head. "More. You'll have to stay with me to find out."

I'm stunned silent. We both know that's longer than I've stuck around anywhere.

"But we'll start small. Your birthday."

"I have birthday plans."

"As long as they include me."

I take a long drink, eyeing him over the rim.

"Relationship isn't all big gestures, Harrison. It's the day-to-day."

"Alright. Let's talk about today."

I stiffen, thinking he's going to segue into Mischa, but he surprises me.

"Sebastian told me about the man he's seeing."

"He did?"

His gaze narrows. "You knew?"

"He tells me lots of things."

Harrison frowns as if the idea of Ash is confiding in me disturbs him.

"He wants to be close to you."

"That's not why I'm bothered. It's because he's been able to contact you all year. He had this relationship with you I couldn't have."

"You could've," I point out. "It was your choice to leave."

"I thought it was for the best," he says softly.

Our dinner comes, and the conversation shifts back to Ash. Harrison tells stories about them growing up. It's clear he adored his little brother.

"We should've been closer after our parents' deaths, but he blamed me. I protected him from the worst of it. Ensured he had the best schooling. Kept him away from the media, the legal side of things."

I take another bite of delicious paella, feeling the night breeze whisper over my skin before I reach for my wine.

"Maybe you should've stayed with him instead of trying to bubble-wrap him," I murmur.

He flinches. "I thought I did the right thing. It feels like the right thing is obvious, but when you look back, sometimes it seems there were only many wrong ones."

We sip in silence.

"I know you thought you were doing the right thing by leaving LA," I start when I set my glass down. "But it wasn't. Not because you left, but because you treated me like my opinion didn't matter." I lean forward, my cuff clinking against the table. "You called me your queen and then treated me like a pawn."

"I'm sorry I ever made you think that."

"Why is Mischa so set on chasing after you? You said you never considered working for his parents."

"I did one gig for them." My brows shoot up in surprise. "Then when I learned my parents weren't the people I thought, it reinforced that about me."

"You're a good man. Not because of what you've built. Because of what's in here." I reach over and tap his shirt under the edge of his jacket.

He presses my palm to his chest, and the steady thud of his heart beneath my hand is so warm and real it's a wonder I don't melt into him.

We finish our dinner, and he rises from his chair, motioning to me.

His hand on my back, he moves us to the ledge and leans both elbows over it to look out at the lights of the city, the black ocean beyond.

"Tourists come to Ibiza for the crowd. But when you lift your gaze past the party, we're surrounded by stillness. It's easy to forget there's a whole world out there."

"I'm sure your executive team in London reminds you that you have a business to run."

"It doesn't matter." He turns toward me. "When I'm with you, I feel that calm. I don't need to be on an island to feel it anymore."

My heart skips. "Where should we go? You might have an empire, but this girl needs to work."

He reaches for my hand, threads his fingers through mine. "Where would you like to work?"

Emotions collide in my chest. "I was working on some options back in the US." I feel him turn toward me. "I don't want to say it in case it doesn't work out. But the past couple of months, all I could think about is playing La Mer."

"You won't play La Mer." There's a finality to his words that would make me argue, but it's moot anyway.

"It might belong to Mischa, but it has nothing to do with him. It existed before him, and it will exist after." I shake my head. "I was still hoping he'd rethink it."

But when he hears I played Debajo, there's no way he will. He'll find out I'm with Harrison—assuming he doesn't know already...

"I'm sorry."

I cock my head. "You're not."

"I am because you want it, and I want you to have everything you want."

Damn, it sounds as if he means it. My fingers curl around his.

"After your final gig in Ibiza—at Bliss or somewhere else—I'll take you somewhere scenic, and we'll laugh about this. But until then… dance with me."

He offers a hand as music starts from somewhere in the distance. Not club music, but strings.

"Ditch the jacket."

He obliges with a boyish grin, tossing it over the chair before pulling me close.

My lips brush his shirt.

"Since the first time I held you at La Mer, nothing has ever felt the same," he confesses. "When I set foot inside the warehouse in LA, I didn't picture you on stage. It was you dancing with me."

"My dancing is mostly hips. You probably know how to ballroom dance."

He shrugs a shoulder. "Only the basics. Waltz, foxtrot, rumba…"

"Of course you do," I murmur, laughing. "I tried to take a class at school. I could barely shuffle. But I'm done apologizing for it," I declare.

That's the biggest difference in the last year. No more pretending to be something I'm not.

Harrison brushes his lips across my temple, surprising me. "Good. Because I'd rather shuffle with you for the rest of my life than waltz with anyone else."

CHAPTER 19
Rae

Bliss is full, but I'm on edge, scanning the crowd as I mix.

I'm still thinking of my date with Harrison last night. Dinner was a dream. We went back to his villa and stayed up on the patio until the early hours of the morning, where he laid a blanket down on the grass and we talked and touched under the stars.

It's not as if everything is resolved between us, but he certainly wants to try. And he seems like a changed man.

Now, I'm back to the reality of playing the club where a woman died when it could have been prevented.

Which means there's something I need to do.

As I finish, I catch sight of the owner.

After a few selfies, I wave off the crowd of fans and cut straight for the bar. The bartender pours me a drink, and the owner nods at me. I lift my glass to him, taking a long drink. "A woman died outside. A customer from last week."

His eyes widen. "I don't know anything about that."

"You should. Mischa's drugs killed her. And you let him in."

His gaze cuts past my shoulder. When I follow the owner's

eyes, a hulking security guard nods to me.

"Go with him," the owner says.

I stiffen. "Where?"

He doesn't answer.

The hairs on my neck lift in warning, but I want to know where this leads. Maybe he's decided he'll talk to me after all.

I follow the security guard, my hand tightening on my phone to signal my own security.

We're heading through the halls, and it's quieter after the door to the club closes behind us. When we reach another door—a VIP room I remember from my tour when I arrived—the security guard opens it and holds it wide. I have no choice but to step inside.

The room is the size of a hotel suite, velvet furniture and curtains. A booth is along the far end, a bar on the wall nearest, but it's the man at the center that draws all of my attention.

Mischa sprawls along the largest couch, wearing black trousers and a white shirt. His legs stretch in front of him, and there's a woman on either side of him. If they're not twins, they're doing a damned good impression. One is completely naked, the other topless. They're brunettes, unlike his fiancée.

Armed security watches from either corner of the room. They're not club guards either. These men look hard, and they don't move except for their eyes.

"Miss Madani." Mischa's lips curl.

My breath is shallow as I stop in front of the coffee table littered with pills and powder.

"If I'd known you were coming to my show, I would've played something for you."

"Believe me, I was more than affected." His eyes are blue, but gray-blue, like a dead sky.

I wonder what he sees. What he thinks about that makes him treat people like commodities.

"It's a great club," I say.

"That's why I'm buying it."

I whirl around to see the owner by the door. His face is downcast.

Mischa rises, ignoring the hands of the women trying to drag him back, and steps around the table.

"You've been moonlighting. At Harrison King's club no less."

Of course he knows about Debajo. It was all over social media, and though there are no new photos of us, there are conversations online speculating about Harrison and me getting back together.

If Mischa brought me here to hurt me, or to use me against Harrison, I wish he'd get the hell on with it.

"He made me an offer. Besides, my contract isn't exclusive. I play where I want. If that means you're not interested anymore—"

"On the contrary. You were glowing. I can't imagine a single woman in that filthy basement didn't want to be you or that a single man didn't want to own you," the Russian says smoothly.

He stops inches away. Close enough I smell his cologne.

"Meaning what?" I force the words through my tight throat.

The first time I met him, he hit me. I have no doubt he'll do that again, or worse, if it suits him.

We're not in Harrison's club anymore. This isn't even neutral ground—security is his, and the man by the door won't stop Mischa from doing anything he wants.

He brushes my hair behind my shoulder. Every inch of me tenses when he leans in, but I refuse to tremble.

"You, my Little Queen, will play for me. La Mer," he whispers, and my head snaps up in shock. "One month from tonight."

Harrison

There's a chance. Not a good one, but a sliver.

I've been reviewing documents for Kings—the ones I shelved months ago—to see if there's a hope of reviving it.

Because the fire marshal won't say for certain that I didn't set fire to the club myself, the latest reports suggest insurance will cover only a small portion of the damages. But I could leverage capital from other projects and put it back together.

It feels worth hoping for.

My date with Raegan only solidified my convictions.

Once, I wanted revenge. Now, I want it done with so I can have a future with her.

Which is why I've compiled all the intel I've gathered on Ivanov and sent it to the authorities, including the inside information I didn't trust them to use effectively.

I have enough resources to protect everyone I care about from Mischa until they figure out how to bring him down.

It's the early hours of the morning, and I'm finishing a drink when I hear the car I sent for Raegan pull up the driveway.

Barney lifts his head from where he's lying on the floor of my office. I rise from my chair and start for the door. When Raegan is around, I'm more eager than the damn dog.

She refused to have my security in her venue, so they waited outside, a call away.

I'm halfway down the hall when the villa door opens and she steps inside. My footsteps on the stairs have her looking up.

Her costume is intact, black leather shorts with a bodysuit beneath, showing off her long, curvy legs. The blond hair spills in waves over her shoulder, contrasting with her dark, lined eyes.

"You waited up," she murmurs, stepping out of her heeled sandals.

I cross the floor to her, and the knot in my chest eases with each step. "Barney wouldn't sleep until you returned," I say.

Her eyes search mine, relief filling them. "You raid Sebastian's closet?" she murmurs, taking in my appearance.

I'm barefoot in shorts and a polo, and I chuckle.

"Dry cleaning day," I contend, unable to resist reaching for her. My hands thread into her hair as I claim her full mouth.

Her hand finds my chest, pressing over my heart. She lets me part her lips with my tongue, moans when I take the kiss deeper.

I want everything deeper with her. I've always been the one to push, and she's been the one to hold me at a distance. But she's not holding me at a distance now. She grabs the back of my shirt, then strokes up my back. Her touch heats my skin instantly.

We're alone in this house. I want to fold her over the kitchen table, take her until she's gripping the sides and groaning into the wood. Then carry her upstairs and love her in my bed.

Before I can, she pries her lips from mine.

"What's wrong?" I demand.

Her eyes turn glassy, and alarm sets in my gut. "Mischa wants me to play La Mer."

I grip her arms, hard enough she flinches. *No.*

"He came to my show and—"

"He spoke to you. In person."

She nods.

My heart accelerates, a horrid thudding that sounds like my past and my future colliding.

If he laid a hand on her, I would drive to him this second and rip every limb from his body.

"Did he touch—"

"Just my hair. I wanted to get the owner to turn on Mischa. But we were too late, if we ever had a chance at all. He's selling." She takes a slow breath. "The only thing I could think is Mischa saw me play at Debajo, and rather than turning him off, it made him…"

"Angry?"

"I was going to say jealous."

Mischa pursued Eva because she was mine. Eva was beautiful and ambitious, though I now see she was a glittering facsimile of a gem.

Raegan is a different kind of jewel. The real kind. The rare kind.

Mischa is ruthless and arrogant, but he's not stupid.

I knew he wanted to hurt Raegan in order to hurt me. But if there's a chance that's changed, and he wants her…

That's a million times more dangerous.

I reach for the pins holding her hair in place. "You told him no?"

I finish unpinning her hair and drop the blond wig on the table with the pile of pins. I want to burn the wig. If Mischa breathed on it, I want it gone.

I turn back to the woman I love. I thread my fingers into her thick, silky hair, spreading it over her shoulders.

Still, she doesn't answer.

The hairs on my arms lift. "Tell me you didn't say yes."

"This club is my dream."

I grab her arms hard enough she flinches. "He's doing it to fuck with me."

"Not everything is about you." The edge in her voice sets me back.

"This is," I insist, thinking of the boy who hated me in school, the one who failed to recruit me to his cause, the man who's never forgotten it. "You're not playing for him."

Her brows pull together, but she doesn't try to move away. "What happened to you not making unilateral decisions?"

My laugh is humorless. "You've got to be kidding. I assumed you'd see the reason in not playing for a madman. One who knows you're with me."

"It's the world's most famous club, Harrison. I'll be on stage. There's nowhere safer." Her chin juts out at me.

My abs clench, and the next breath I take is ragged. "I won't sit idly by and watch you risk yourself for your career," I whisper against her throat.

Raegan pulls back to look in my eyes. "You do it every day."

That's a low blow. A reminder there's a double standard.

But I inherited this rivalry—she didn't.

Last year, she was never in danger. Now, not only is she in Ibiza and playing for a monster, but he knows she's mine. And there's nothing the man lives for more than taking away what's mine.

Minutes ago, I was handing this off to law enforcement and looking at our future. But I need to finish this first, and our timeline just shortened. I won't let Rae play La Mer, not as long as that man owns it.

I can't change her mind. I see it in the tilt of her chin, the warning in her eyes.

She's the one forcing my hand.

Raegan starts to pull away, hurt. I don't let her.

I lean in and thread my fingers into her hair, pressing my lips to her forehead. After a beat, her arms go around me.

I breathe her in, my heart a thudding against my ribs.

I will end him. I swear to God.

CHAPTER 20
Rae

"Flying solo again?"

Ash's comment has me looking up from where I'm working on the villa patio in a lounge chair.

I shift my legs to one side, and Ash drops onto the end.

"It's been a week." My fingers flex on my notebook, and I set it on the table next to the lounger. "Harrison barely eats. Toro won't say where they go. Natalia's worried."

Ash sighs, scratching his chin. "He's single-minded. Especially when he thinks you're being threatened. He's probably tearing his hair out at the thought of you playing La Mer."

"Harrison's turning into someone I barely know." I stroke the bangle on my wrist and stare at the crown beneath, emotions clashing in my chest.

I can't kick my excitement to play there. I've been thinking about my set every second. My publicist has been busy since I confirmed the offer, working with La Mer's team on graphics and promotions. I told Callie I'm about to play the biggest gig of my career, leaving out the part about Mischa.

I want the man to be brought to justice—more than ever after seeing that poor woman die.

But this performance isn't about Mischa. It's everything I've worked for, and I'm not going to let him ruin my chance to do what I love.

I'm over letting men with their own agendas shape my life.

"Harry's lost everyone who mattered to him," Ash says.

"He hasn't. You're here. Leni's here. Natalia and Toro and me." I shake my head. "Today he's in London doing God knows what. Secret meetings."

Ash cocks a brow. "You're not…" His gaze flicks to his brother's bedroom window. "If my brother's not delivering, the offer always stands."

His slow smile has me rolling my eyes.

"That's what Beck says. You're into girls too?"

Ash shifts off the chair. "Nah, not really. I dated a couple. But this boy in boarding school made it perfectly clear what I want."

"Dicks."

"So many dicks, Raegan." His blue eyes dance. "Do you know what you can do with a perfect dick?"

"I have a few ideas."

Last night, I stopped by Harrison's office after one in the morning.

I told him, "I'll be in bed if you want to join me."

His eyes swept over me, glassy and unfocused.

"If you don't, I'll take care of myself."

In my bedroom, I undressed, then waited ten minutes before I started going through with it, and I didn't hold back. Seconds after the first moan drifted from my lips, the door opened wide. He dragged off his shirt before kneeling between my thighs, yanking my ankles wide, and pinning me to the bed.

"Impatient woman," he murmured as his mouth lowered toward my hips.

Then all my words were gone as his tongue and lips wreaked sweet havoc on my body.

But immediately after we finished, he crept back down the hall to his office to wage war on a man who isn't under our roof but feels as if he's in every inch of our lives.

I force my attention back to Ash. "How's your guy?"

They've been staying together at the hotel.

Harrison's brother's smile is irrepressible. "He had a call with his lawyers yesterday. Said the arrangement's going well."

Gavin and the girl I met at the club event aren't married, but they have a child together. Ash said Gavin has told his girlfriend he's gay and that the relationship is over, but they're working through the logistics of custody and their belongings.

It must be difficult, but I still wish Ash had more to go on. I don't trust the guy after how he treated Ash before.

"Have you been in touch with the team?"

"Yeah. They want me to come back early next month to train." He frowns.

"Your contract's not at risk, right?"

"I'm secured another year. They can't turn me loose without cause. And missing a few too many penalty kicks doesn't count."

It still sounds like a lot of pressure on Ash. I feel for him.

"There's this place we're planning to go to tonight," he continues, leaning in. "Las Puertas Del Cielo. 'Heaven's Gate.' It's a lookout near Santa Inés."

"Sounds beautiful."

His smile fades a few watts. "We're not flying off to Hawaii to say I do. But it helps when the person you're into isn't living with someone else."

My chest tightens, and he kicks my shin lightly.

"Don't let my situation drag you down. Or yours. My gloomy brother isn't a reason to ruin a perfectly good day in Ibiza."

"You're right."

He grabs my arm and drags me toward the door. "Grab your bathing suit. We're going swimming at the hotel. We need to go somewhere to have fun."

After swimming at the hotel with Ash, I do feel better. I change and stop by a café in town before swinging by Debajo with treats for the staff.

"Dibs on that coffee," Leni says, swooping in to grab it when I carry the tray through the doors. "Thanks, Rae. Things have been rough."

"Because of Mischa?"

"Because of Harrison."

I set the rest of the treats on the bar, and the day staff descends on it.

Leni nods across the room, and I follow, folding my arms. She lowers her voice.

"This week, he bought more vodka than we would use in two months of high season so Mischa would run short. He paid staff not to work there. One of Ivanov's Paris clubs had to shut down temporarily, supposedly due to a rodent infestation."

"Harrison is personally sabotaging Mischa?" Things have escalated more than I expected. "Would that even put a dent in Ivanov's business?"

"Maybe. But more than that, he wants to force Mischa to fuck up and show his hand, ideally before your show." She sighs. "But in the meantime, he's causing more problems for Echo Entertainment than for Ivanov."

"He was in London today for meetings," I prod.

"Damage control because he forgot to sign a lease renewal for one of his clubs, and Ivanov swooped in and made a better offer."

Shit. This has gone further than I realized. Harrison's taking his eye off his own business. He's been so caught up in sabotage he's hurt himself.

"Forgetting to renew the lease was a mistake," she says as if reading my thoughts, "but he's always known what's best."

I want to have the same faith as Leni that Harrison has things under control, but I can't. He's wielding his power recklessly, escalating what's between him and Mischa when I had hoped he would back down.

I squeeze my wrist, a habit, and glance down when I feel only skin and not the cool metal I've gotten used to again these past few weeks.

My bracelet.

I had it on earlier, but now, it's gone.

CHAPTER 21

Rae

I'm still agitated from the conversation with Leni when I try calling Ash but get no answer.

So, I head directly to the hotel, speaking to the staff by the pool in case anyone found my bracelet.

No luck.

I head upstairs and quietly let myself into Ash's suite with the key he insisted I keep in case something came up.

There's no sign of the jewelry in the kitchen or living room or bathroom, the only spots I was in when I was here.

But something else is off.

Ash's door is open a crack, but there's no sound from within. Not even his light snoring. Alarm bells go off in my head.

I throw open the door of Ash's room, see his stuff still there. No Ash. No Gavin. In fact, I don't see anything to indicate anyone other than Ash has been sleeping in this room.

But on the bedside table…

There's a collection of bags and pills.

No. Shit. Shit, shit. Has he been using the whole time?

I try Ash again. Still no answer.

Next, I hit a contact on speed dial.

"Harrison, it's me," I bite into the voicemail. "Ash is gone. Something's wrong."

I head downstairs and get into the car with my driver and security.

"Where to?" the driver asks.

That's when I realize I have no idea.

"Where would he go?" I mutter, thinking back to the room. There were no suitcases. No shoes belonging to anyone but Ash.

I know what happened. "Where is Heaven's Gate?"

"It's difficult to get to."

"I don't care. We're going."

When we arrive, the driver stays in the car while security accompanies me through the pine forest to the secluded lookout. Tripping over roots, I second-guess this idea more than once.

"Ash!" I call through the dense brush.

I curse as I scrape my knee. Once I emerge from the trees, I find a hunched form sitting near the edge of the lookout.

I wave off security, motioning for them to stay back.

My racing pulse steadies a few beats as I approach him.

"It's a hell of a view," I comment.

Ash turns. "That's why people come here. Americans. Brits. Everyone. They say they come for the party, but they come for this. To feel free."

He's high. Dangerously so.

I sit next to him. "Is that how you feel?"

His shoulders tighten. "Not so much, Raegan."

The heaviness in him breaks my heart. "He left, didn't he?"

There's no answer for a few minutes. All I hear are the waves far below, the insects in the forest.

"His girlfriend showed up. He left with her."

The raw anguish in his voice rips me up inside. Emotion rises up my throat, and I swallow it back down.

Ash inches closer to the edge, and I grab his arm. "Let's stay back."

"But you can see better the closer you are. It's like you could fly off into heaven."

"It's not so bad here. People love you and need you. The rest of your team. Me. Harry."

"He's here?" Ash turns quickly, as if hoping for his brother's presence.

"Not right now."

I wish he were here. For me, for his brother.

But he's in London. Not because of something important—because no matter what he promised me about focus on our future, his vendetta is once again taking priority.

"Come on," I say. "Let's go back to the villa."

After I get Ash to the car, I check my phone. Still nothing from Harrison.

I send off a text.

> **Rae: We need you at the villa. This is not a fucking drill.**

Harrison

"My hands are tied, Mr. King." The man across the conference table in the London boardroom taps a pen on the desk. "Ivanov offered us a better price, and the deal has been inked."

My efforts to interrupt Mischa's operations the past few days have been mildly entertaining, if not even wholly satisfying. The rats in his Paris club were especially vindictive. But yesterday, my efforts caught up to me when I learned my real estate team was waiting on a signature to renew a major lease and couldn't reach me.

Because of it, I lost my lease on a fucking club.

Now I'm negotiating to ensure one of my more profitable venues—one of a handful of which I don't own outright—continues.

There's no way I'm giving it up.

I survey the executive at the property management company. He might be responsible for billions in real estate, but so am I.

"What if I tell you Ivanov won't be in any business in a few months?"

"Forgive me if that's hard to believe."

The windows in the historic building let in filtered light, and I shift out of my chair to cross to one, getting a view of the street below and the park on the far side.

"You don't have to believe it, but know this—it's easy for you to review paperwork and file deals and cut checks, but when you sign on to work with Ivanov, he's not interested in those things. He's a gravedigger."

"And he'll fall into one of his own graves by mistake?"

"No. The next one he digs could be yours."

Whatever he sees on my face has him blanching.

"Tell him," I start, "that you were mistaken about the dates on Echo's contract. The venue is no longer available. For your inconvenience, I'll ensure your son's tuition is covered at Eton next year."

He extends a hand and we shake.

I leave the boardroom grimly satisfied.

On impulse, I pick up my phone and leave a voicemail as I head down the hall.

"You can't beat me. Whatever you do, I will watch you. And cover you. I won't forget what you did."

I click off and take the three flights of stairs down to the main level.

It feels good to stretch my legs after a day of travel. The past week has been hell, but I'm on my way back to Ibiza, where I can hold Raegan in my arms.

The limo is waiting at the curb to take me to the airport. But before I shift inside, I pull up.

The rear tire is flat.

I knock on the driver's window and motion him over.

He rounds to my side, hand curling at his hip when he sees the damage.

"I'm so sorry, sir. I don't know what could've happened."

There's a slice as long as my thumb clean through the rubber. "I do."

It's twilight, and I need to get on a plane for Spain, but while the driver promises to call me another car, I'm already tuned out.

Up the block, another black car is idling.

The back window is shaded, so I stare in the front for a second. Two.

I cross to the park on the other side of the street, sinking onto a stone bench with a view of pigeons playing in a fountain.

Less than a minute later, a man is out of the back and approaching me.

"I trust you heard I got the lease back," I say as he shifts onto the other end of the bench.

Mischa's mouth twists. "Never like to deal with landlords. Better to own property. Your parents always said that."

"Before you killed them."

He lifts a hand as if I'm the one being unreasonable. "I didn't kill them. They indulged."

"That's bullshit."

"Remember when we did that job together? We made a strong team." Mischa stretches his legs out, and it's like we're two old men reminiscing about good times.

If the good times were trafficking narcotics.

It was the first and last thing I did for his parents, back when he was trying to convince me to work for them.

"No. We were never a team. You never had a chance at recruiting me."

"That's what I told my parents." He sounds almost sad.

I don't know what they did to him for his failure.

I can't find it in me to care.

"Congratulations," I say, thinking of his engagement. "I'm sure you'll be very happy."

He grins. "I have plans for her. You won't miss her? I used to prefer blondes, but lately it's brunettes. Strange to have preferences change after decades."

My gut twists.

He's not talking about Eva. He's talking about Rae.

I lean across the bench, ignoring a pack of schoolchildren that runs past, and grab his collar. "You will never have her."

The children are barely past when two men—no, three—start to close in on us from around the park.

I didn't bring security to London, preferring to leave them with Raegan.

Now, I realize that was either wise or foolish as Mischa rises, dragging me with him. He produces a knife, holding it at my stomach, hidden from prying eyes by my jacket.

Despite the public setting, the blade is an unyielding promise against my abs.

Bloodshed is a crass way to get what you want. I prefer deals with wits and money. But adrenaline and rage pound in my veins.

"Coward's way out," I rasp. "You always took it, even in school."

"Would you do it?" He wraps my hand around his, flipping the knife so it's against his stomach. "You say you're not like me. Let's find out."

I could do it, could end this for all of us.

My phone jumps in my pocket. I ignore it, but he grins.

The next second, he's gone, turning and slipping into the stream of pedestrians along the sidewalk that borders the park.

I'm not a killer like he is. But I wish I were.

It's not until I'm in my new car and on the way to the airport that I check my phone.

A slew of messages and notifications fills the screen, and one in particular grabs my attention.

Rae: We need you at the villa. This is not a fucking drill.

I call her.

No answer.

I hang up and try again.

Midway back on my flight, she finally answers.

"What's wrong? Are you hurt? Did Ivanov—"

"It's your brother. He had a bad day, and he's really upset, and it messed with his head."

My eyes squeeze shut. "Thank fuck it's nothing serious. I'll be home in ninety minutes."

There's a long pause. "No. Not 'thank fuck,' Harrison." Her voice trembles, with sadness or rage—I can't tell which. "Not everything wrong in the world is caused by a single man."

She hangs up on me, and I'm left staring at the phone, frustrated and angry myself.

The plane lands, and I waste no time getting back to the house.

"Raegan!" I call when I barge in.

Leni's the one who appears, looking tired and wary. She tilts her head toward the patio.

I stalk through the house and find Sebastian lying on the table. Confusion grips me as I watch him point at the sky, stabbing his finger in the air as he murmurs words I can't hear.

Unreal. I hurried home with a gut full of panic only to find my own flesh and blood has indulged in some kind of party drug.

"What did he take?" I demand.

"Not sure. Rae found him. We're waiting for him to come down."

My jaw clenches. I cross to my brother and grab him by the shirt collar.

His glazed eyes find mine. "Harry—"

"Don't," I bite out, my grip tightening as I lift him to sitting.

Sebastian's hands close around my wrists, trying to pry me off him.

"I've been trying to bring down the man responsible for all our problems, and you're getting high?"

"What the fuck are you doing?" Rae's voice at my back has me spinning.

"This is what you called me back for?" I demand. "My brother went on a trip?"

Her eyes flash. "You don't know what you're talking about."

"What I know is my brother fucked himself up. I don't tolerate drugs. It's the only thing I can't abide."

Rae grabs my wrist and stalks into the house. "He had a rough night," she says under her breath. "I went to find him."

"He doesn't need a keeper. He's an adult."

"And he fucked up, like we all do. That's why we have friends and family. You showed me that. How you take care of people. It's one of the things that made me love you."

"I'm too much of a damned bleeding heart, and it's going to stop."

Shock collides with hurt on her face. "I know you've been dealt some shitty hands in this life, but I won't watch you destroy your family"—her gaze cuts toward the patio, toward my brother—"or yourself."

Low laughter comes from Sebastian. It cuts off the second I level my gaze on him.

I nod to Rae. "Let's go upstairs."

But she steps back. "No." Disbelief slams into me as she tilts her head at my brother. "Come on, Ash."

"You're going with him?" I demand.

"He needs help. You have no idea what happened to him, and you don't want to. That's how I know this isn't you."

Her eyes shine with more emotions than I can name. If I weren't overtired and bewildered, I'd make her stay until I could tease them apart, have her explain each one to me until I understood.

She piles him into the car while I watch. I'm helpless and furious. A terrible fucking combination.

I call out to her, "You owe me a favor."

Rae freezes and turns. She crosses back to me. "What did you say?"

My heart starts beating again. I'm not sure when it stopped, except everything in me seems synced to her.

"When you first came here last year, we made a deal that included three favors," I go on, threading my hands into her hair. "You gave me two."

Her lips part. "Harrison…"

"Don't," I mutter, leaning in to press my lips to her hair as my fingers tangle in the strands. "Don't walk out on me."

She's not going to, I realize as she lets me hold her.

But when she pulls back, it's to brush her lips over mine, cool and fleeting. "I am doing you a favor, but you have to see that."

Those are the last words before she disappears into the dark and I'm alone.

CHAPTER 22
Harrison

"How do you like it?" Sawyer drawls over the video call.

I tap the controls behind the bar to watch the thing skim along a ceiling track and descend down a column on the other side.

"The photographer bots are even bigger, sales-wise," he goes on.

I scan the club, empty except for a skeleton crew preparing for tonight's show.

Since Rae walked out on me last night, I've needed to prove I'm not coming unhinged. Which is why I'm at Debajo, running my business.

I hang up with Sawyer, and the robot comes down the track across the ceiling, bringing a Post-it note.

Apologize, it says.

"Don't tell me I hurt your feelings last night," I toss at my second-in-command as Leni rises from behind the bar.

"Hardly. Your brother and girlfriend on the other hand..." With a cloth, she wipes down the surface. "What's between you and your family is your business. But you can't afford to cut your own clubs off at the knees indefinitely."

The steel edge under Leni's voice makes me blink. She's always been a friend and an advisor. But right now, she doesn't get how close we are to blowing this all up.

The door opens, letting in heated conversation exchanged between security and someone outside.

"What is it?" Leni demands.

"Some guys out back in the parking lot thinking they can sell," security replies.

I stomp for the door, but the security guard clears his throat. "He's gone, Mr. King."

Lucky for him. God knows what I would've done in my current mood.

"Ivanov doesn't sell at Debajo again," I tell Leni. "If one of our patrons buys so much as a pill on my property, I swear to God I will fire everyone in that establishment. Do whatever it takes to stop it from happening."

She hesitates before nodding. "On it."

Two hours later, I'm back at the villa, cursing my brother and wondering whether Raegan's lying in bed without me, when the call comes in from Debajo security.

"Señor King, it's about Leni," the man says. "They were waiting for her. She tried to stop them..."

I'm in my Ferrari and tearing down the driveway. I don't look back to see if my personal security is following in their car.

The person who's stood by me for the last decade is bleeding on a table in the emergency room.

When I arrive at the hospital, I barge in the doors and demand to see her.

"She sustained multiple wounds. She's in surgery," a doctor informs me.

The blood drains from my head. "Call me the fucking second she's out," I command.

I head out the front doors, kicking a garbage bin on the way.

It's my fault Leni felt she needed to defend Debajo with the same fierceness I'd defend it with. To stop a deal in progress in the alley, not noticing she was outnumbered or thinking it might be a trap. But she's not me. And Debajo isn't hers.

An ambulance pulls up, so I round the corner of the building, more to avoid their eyes than to give them space. There's a garden, and I grab a tall plant with red flowers by the stalk. I tear it out of the soil.

Another.

"Señor—"

I whirl to face a janitor with his cart. Whatever he sees on my face has him backing down, hands lifting as he disappears toward the parking lot.

Sweat beads at my brow, my neck.

My jacket is the next victim. I drag it off, then throw it in the dirt.

My knees buckle as I brace against the side of the building.

I yank my phone out of my pocket and stare at a picture of the four of us at the villa. Leni, Ash, Raegan, and me. Plus Barney's head stuck between Rae's legs.

I've hurt them all by knowing them. They've all stood by me.

Until Raegan's words last night.

"I am doing you a favor."

In my quest to punish the man who caused me pain, I've punished everyone I love. I wanted to protect them, and I hurt them instead.

My eyes burn.

An object on the ground glints at my feet. I bend to pick it up.

My mother's ring.

I've been carrying it around. *Through everything.*

Those words inscribe themselves on my heart with a blade duller than the one Mischa used back in boarding school.

I thought I was doing the right thing. Maybe she did too. Maybe they both did. They thought they were doing right by Ash and me. By people who worked for them.

I need to fix this. If I lose everything I've built, every damn penny, I need to make it right.

I hope it's not too late.

I pull out my phone and type out a text because I can't speak.

Harrison: Leni's hurt. Someone attacked her outside Debajo. At the hospital now.

The ring back in my pocket, I stare at the photo once more. The woman I love looks at the camera with an amused smile. Before we took the picture, she asked if this was some kind of family portrait.

Leni said, "It's as close as we're going to get."

It is.

Once, I knew how to look after my own. Raegan was my most stubborn challenge—she wouldn't let me love her, wouldn't trust me or rely on me. Somehow, I was given the most exquisite fucking gift of being the man by her side while she figured that out.

Now, she's the person who called me out when I stopped being that man.

I've never prayed, but my gaze finds the sky.

Forget destruction. I need redemption.

I will do anything to make this right. Leni, Ash, Raegan. Everything.

CHAPTER 23

Rae

I hated fighting with Harrison last night. But when his text comes through, the churning feeling in my gut is replaced with a block of ice.

I grab Ash and run downstairs and into the backseat of the car driven by security that stubbornly clung to me after I left the villa.

"Did he say what happened?" Ash demands as we lean forward, willing the driver to go faster.

"Nothing more than his text."

At the hospital, we leap out of the vehicle and bolt inside.

The woman at the nursing station tells us Leni's in the operating room.

"Did anyone come in with her?" I demand.

She gestures to the hall, where one of the security guards from Debajo paces, another slumped in a chair.

I race over to them, Ash at my heels. One of them says, "Mischa's men. She went out to chase them off."

My stomach drops, time stopping. "Where's Harrison?"

Right now, all that matters is he's alive. I'm terrified by the possibility that he was there too.

"I'm here."

The two words make me spin so fast I nearly trip.

Harrison King fills the hallway. His shirt is rumpled and stained, his hands covered in dirt.

My heart stops beating. I rush toward him, scanning the dark stains on his white shirt.

"I'm alright," he rasps. "This was intentional. They went after her as retaliation for my actions this week."

My fingers thread through his, and Harrison's expression fills with guilt and disgust as he stares at my clean hands and his dirty ones.

A doctor emerges from the double doors, stopping in front of us. "Are you her family?"

"Yes," Harrison says immediately.

The doctor eyes him up and down. "Husband? Brother—"

"We're everything she has."

The doctor relents, tucking a clipboard under his arm. "She has suffered significant blood loss, but her condition is stable."

Next to me, Harrison exhales hard. "I want her transported to my villa as soon as it's safe for her to be transported."

"She should remain under observation for forty-eight hours. That requires staff, equipment—"

"Fine. I'll take it all. Spare no expense." He cuts a look toward the door, then back at me. "I don't want her alone here."

"We could have security stay—"

"No. It's not enough."

The grim look on his face makes me realize how agonizing this is for him. He's pale, his lips thinned, eyes haunted. He knows this is bad, and could've been worse.

"I want to see her." Harrison looks past the doctor toward the doors, seeming to think better of charging through without permission. "Can I?"

"In a few minutes. I'll show you to her recovery room."

It's midafternoon by the time Harrison sees Leni and makes arrangements to have her transported back to the villa later today.

Ash heads for the car, Harrison heading for his Ferrari.

I hold up a finger to tell my security to wait for me as I cross to Harrison.

"Should you drive?" I ask, leaning in the driver's window.

He lifts his gaze to mine. "Yes. I'm all right."

I nod, but before I can pull back, he lays his hand over mine. "Thank you. For being here."

I swallow hard. "Of course."

"No, not 'of course.' You've been keeping an eye on my family. All my family," he goes on, meaning Leni.

I pull my fingers away. "What can I say? They grew on me."

Our gazes hold as if neither of us wants to pull back from this shared connection. I'm not sure who needs it more.

Finally, I turn back and slide into the backseat of the car next to Ash.

This time when security asks where we're headed, I say, "The villa."

Ash cocks his head. "You want me to go another round with my brother?"

"You were barely conscious for the last one," I point out. "And yes, you're coming."

His normally dancing blue eyes are dull, but he squeezes my shoulder. "I've had worse."

We follow the Ferrari through the streets and up the driveway. When we get to the house, Ash tells me, "Think I'll go crash for a bit."

Harrison and I follow him inside, where a worried Barney greets us with a whimper. I scratch his head as Natalia emerges from the kitchen, looking equally concerned.

Harrison fills her in, and Natalia bustles off to get a room ready for Leni, and it's just the two of us.

His sharp jaw is as stubborn as ever, his mouth pressed in a firm line, but his square shoulders are slumped as he crosses to the kitchen for water, pouring me one too. I take it and sip, my gaze lingering on the streaks of dirt caked on Harrison's hands as he braces himself against the sink.

"Leni was always up for anything," he mutters, "including a bar fight. I didn't learn until later she was shy growing up. One of her friends from summer camp said she used to be timid. Wouldn't play in the dirt for fear of staining her clothes." His exhale is half laugh. "Can you believe it?"

I fold my arms across my chest. I want to go to him, but I can't. Not yet.

"I led her to this, Raegan," he whispers. "I blame my parents for what they did, but I'm no better."

The agony in his voice guts me.

"You can choose to be better," I say.

"My top employee is bleeding in the hospital. My brother is doing drugs from the same man who killed our parents. It's my fucking fault."

God, the blood and dirt on him is getting to me, almost as much as the way he's speaking. "Come on."

He looks up in surprise as I take his hand. I lead him upstairs and down the hall into his bedroom, tugging the door closed behind us.

I pull him into the en suite. Then I reach for the buttons on his shirt.

His blue gaze searches mine, perplexed. "You don't have to—"

"Shut up."

I start running a bath and strip him down. He stops me only once—to set his phone on the counter, along with a gold ring that makes my breath catch.

I'm curious about it, but I don't ask as he steps into the bath.

When I start to scrub him clean, he stops me. "You don't need to take care of me."

"We all need taking care of sometimes. I learned that from you." I sneak a look at him as I wash his hands, the dirt under his nails.

He sinks back in the tub, watching me with half-lidded eyes. "I won't be responsible for any more people I care about being hurt."

"You'll stop going after Mischa, then? Because that's the price."

He studies me while I switch to the other hand.

"I can't succeed," he says. "Not if the people I love are hurt in the process. Without them, I have nothing."

"Leni and Ash know they're important to you," I say softly.

His throat bobs. "Without *you*, I am nothing."

The painful balloon stretching my chest expands more. "It's not enough for you to put me on some pedestal I never asked for.

To do reckless shit to protect me and anyone else. Any decisions we make, we make together. That's the deal."

I'm willing to put my heart on the line for him, but we can't be together unless he does this.

His mouth tips up at one corner. "You're right. That's how we'll do things."

A wave of emotion washes over me. "You mean it?"

His slow nod makes the block of ice in my stomach start to melt.

He stands and surveys me. A hard, dripping god in a rare moment of vulnerability.

"You're wet," I murmur.

He reaches an arm around my waist and tugs me toward him. I step over the edge of the bathtub, my bare foot finding grip on the bottom as the water rises to my calves.

"What are you doing?" I ask.

"I want you with me."

"I'm here."

"Not close enough."

Before I can decide whether to strip out of my clothes or try to coax him out of the bath, he tugs me down into the water. I'm soaked. My denim shorts are plastered to my hips, my tank top sticking to every inch of my breasts and heaving stomach. He strips the shirt over my head before getting to work on my shorts.

"Good luck getting them off."

"Challenge accepted." The glint in his eyes is the first hint of humor I've seen him show in a week, and I didn't realize I was starved for it until now.

He works the shorts off my hips, though I slide and send a

sheet of water cascading over the side of the tub in the process. We're both breathless when he drags my hips to straddle his, the impressive erection pressing against my wet panties.

"I succeeded." The rumble of his voice strokes along my skin. "I'm claiming my prize."

The tension is as thick as the steam around us. I skim a finger across his muscled bicep, trace the scars on his chest.

"I don't have anything for a king," I murmur. "I can't sleep. I can't stay in one place. I'm just a girl from Orange County."

"Then I'll stay up with you all night. And in the morning, I'll follow you anywhere."

He crushes my lips to his, his grip on the back of my neck desperate. As if he needs this to keep breathing.

In this moment, I need him too.

I know what it's like to lose him. This past week, I was losing him all over again before my eyes. I tried to keep doing my job, to appreciate everything I've built for myself, but nothing felt the same without having this man to talk to, to laugh with, even argue with.

"Make me yours," I murmur against his mouth.

His hands slick down my back to my hips. He grinds against the panel of my panties, where my wetness mingles with the bath.

Harrison's touch slips under my bra to squeeze my breast. I arch into the pressure, tortured by his rough palm and the pinch of his fingers on my pebbled nipple.

Every ridge and plane under my touch is perfect. I stroke down to brush his cock, the silky hardness of him. He catches my hand, forcing my exploratory touch to still. Then he threads his fingers through my hair.

The intensity on his face overwhelms me. Emotions so vivid I never thought I'd see them on this man.

Regret.

Devotion.

Love.

He drags my underwear to the side to position his cock. The first stroke makes me gasp. He fills me so tightly, rubbing against that magical place. I'm drenched.

My hips buck into his, seeking more friction. He grabs my waist and grinds in a slow circle. The intensity of his gaze makes my blood pound.

My hands slip as I try to grab the side of the bath. I fall forward, braced against his hard chest. My knees wedge themselves on either side of his torso, squeezing as he fills me with a long, deep thrust.

He's attuned to every breath, every twitch I make. All the emotions of the past week, the frustration and worry, evaporate in the steam. His humility is still there, but it's twined with determination. Conviction that he can give us both what we need.

We're making a mess of the bathroom.

I don't care.

I cup his face, soaking up his look of devotion before I kiss him hard. Harrison lets me take control of his lips, his tongue. Below, he's driving the rhythm of our coupling.

My knuckles dig into his shoulders as he fucks me, as I meet him stroke for stroke.

His hands knead my ass, building the pressure inside. His fingers drift between my cheeks, my breath hitches. When one presses behind where we're joined inside, I gasp into his mouth.

Nerve endings light up my entire body. It's surprisingly intense but feels so good. It's not something we've done before, but I can feel his need to assure himself I'm his, all of me.

"You okay?" he murmurs, pulling back to assess my reaction.

"Yeah." I'm breathless and dazed by the rush of sensation. "I want to know what this feels like."

Harrison rubs me in slow circles, a look of satisfaction and fascination on his face. The pleasure builds until I can't catch my breath, and when he adds more pressure, his finger slipping inside, I gasp against his lips.

I can't believe I'm allowing this. I can't believe I'm enjoying it.

He strokes my ass, adding a second finger which only makes me clench around him harder.

"Oh my God."

He slants his mouth over mine, curving his tongue to suit my silent demands. His hips roll, his hands knead, and the pressure within me builds. I sink my teeth into his lower lip, plundering his mouth, devouring him again and again.

His speed picks up, and I rock back, riding his cock and his fingers.

The eyes I love are so dark they're indigo, the sea on the blackest night. "Beautiful. My fucking beautiful queen."

His words, defiant and reverent, are more than I can take.

A shudder racks through me, lifting my body as I come. He tenses, staying inside me, catching me as I fall apart. He shudders again and I can feel his release, pulsing into me.

The tension deep in my core tears, sending ripples outward as I cry out.

A few strokes later, Harrison's jaw tightens. His gaze cuts between my face and where we're joined. The sight of him coming makes me want to come again too. He sees it and fucks me through it until I do.

After, he helps me out of the bath and dries both of us with huge, fluffy towels.

I'm wrapping a towel around me and knotting it at my breasts when he says, "You trusted me, and I let you down. I won't do it again."

I catch his eye in the mirror. "You will."

He stiffens.

"I want your word that we'll figure it out when you do." I collect my soaked clothes and hang them on the bathtub before starting out into his bedroom.

"Through everything," he says.

I glance over my shoulder and see him standing naked by the closet, turning over the ring in his fingers.

"This was my mother's," he says. "Found it in the guest room with Ash the other day. She always wore it."

I take it from him, admire the inscription.

I wish I'd met them. No matter their flaws, they created something beautiful in this world—Harrison and his brother. Made two boys who turned into the kind of men any parents would be proud of.

"You can choose to believe in them," I say, passing the ring back. "It doesn't make you weak or wrong."

His throat bobs as he sets it on the vanity again with a nod.

Harrison reaches into his closet and riffles through dress shirts until he chooses a navy-blue one. Ever the discerning customer, even in his own collection. Instead of putting it on, he motions at me to turn.

I hold out my arms and he helps me into the shirt. The bottom reaches halfway to my knees, and I cock my head up at him. He fastens the buttons from the bottom up, deciding to leave the top two open.

The doorbell rings downstairs, and we both straighten.

I don't give a thought to what I'm wearing. Harrison tugs on pants and tucks his phone in his pocket before following me down the hall.

Ash sticks his head out of the guest room. "Did you hear something?"

"Probably the hospital staff bringing Leni's equipment," I suggest.

But as Harrison reaches for the door and pulls it wide, Ash and I flanking him, we realize our mistake.

It's not the hospital staff.

CHAPTER 24
Harrison

O f all the people I expect to visit me on a given day, Eva is the least likely.

Her blond hair is limp around her face. Makeup cakes her cheeks and forehead. Her aqua-blue jumpsuit is pressed, but her posture is cowed.

Her gaze darts past my shoulder. "Harrison. I need help."

I don't believe her for a second. "You made your allegiances perfectly clear."

"Let her in," Sebastian says.

I shut the door in her face before starting to tell my brother how stupid this idea is when Raegan cuts me off.

"I agree with Ash."

"You want Mischa's fiancée in my house?" Disbelief drips from every word.

Rae blinks at me. "I want to give a woman in obvious distress a chance to explain herself."

Fuck.

I jerk the door open. "If it were up to me, you'd be gone."

"Harrison King taking orders. That's a new one."

I pull the door shut behind me so it's the two of us on the step. "If you so much as look at Raegan, I'll have you delivered back to him with a full account of where you've been."

Fear flashes across her face, blinding and real, before she follows me inside.

Sebastian's sitting at the dining table, and Raegan's in the kitchen making tea. Still wearing my shirt.

Eva's gaze lingers on Raegan an extra beat before she remembers what I said and looks away.

Rae comes over with a teapot and cups, then pours into each cup.

Eva accepts the tea from Rae and takes a sip. Her engagement ring blinks in the light. "He's not the man I thought."

I cough. "Who did you think you were marrying? A saint?"

"No. But he was constant in one thing—wanting me. At least until recently." She sneaks another look at Rae.

I turn to my brother and Raegan. "Could you give us a moment?"

Rae finishes pouring tea and drops into a seat at the other end of the table. "No."

I swallow a groan. *Please*, I implore her silently.

A stubborn jerk of her chin. *Fuck no.*

Damn it. I called her a queen, and she is one now.

In full.

"He doesn't want me anymore. I called him out on it, and he got physical." Eva angles her head, and in the light, it's impossible not to see the shadow beneath her cheekbone. She turns her cup in her hands, lips pressing together. "At first, it was exciting. It felt as if he needed me in a way you never did."

When her gaze lands on me, I see accusation and sadness mixed together.

"You want protection," I guess.

"Why not go to the police?" Sebastian asks.

Eva's gaze narrows on Sebastian. "With the amount I've spent on skincare, I'd like to continue looking twenty-five for another few decades. Which is hard to do when you're dead."

"What are you offering?" I ask.

"Harrison…" Rae says. "This shouldn't be a negotiation."

I'm struck by the contrast between the two women.

Eva is willing to do anything to save her own skin.

Rae is pragmatic enough to know how the world works but idealistic enough to try to make it better, even for people who don't deserve it.

"I'll tell you anything you want to know." Eva's voice trembles at the edges.

My phone buzzes in my pocket, and I pull it out.

Christian: Don't say I never gave you anything.

"Excuse me." I brush Rae's cheek with my knuckle on my way past her to the steps upstairs—a simple gesture to let her know I'm still here with her.

I hit the contact, and he answers on the second ring.

"This was you?" I demand as I reach for a shirt, shrugging into it.

"She didn't know where to go. I steered her your way."

I step out of my room, peering over the railing at the three of them seated at the table below.

"I don't want her," I say under my breath as I fasten the buttons on my shirt.

"A woman who knows Mischa's habits and secrets? You can't use that?"

A day ago, I would've cut off my own arm for this type of information. But I promised Raegan I'd let it go.

I hang up and walk down the stairs. At the bottom, Rae rises from her chair and reads my expression. She jerks her head toward the kitchen and I follow.

When we're out of earshot, I explain about Christian's text. "Eva has enough information to take him down a dozen times over. But," I go on as she stiffens, "I promised you I wouldn't. That I'd lay it down. We can send her packing. Pretend this never happened."

Rae sighs. I wish I could hear the thoughts running through her head, could find out if they're the same as mine.

She's probably thinking it's not worth risking.

"One chance to hear her out," she says. "Whatever we learn goes to the police."

I nod, pressing my lips to her forehead. I would stay there forever if I could.

We make our way back out to the dining area, my hand laced with Raegan's. "I want everything."

Eva fidgets in her seat.

"Won't he know she's been here?" Sebastian asks.

"No. Because she's going back to him."

"Harrison..." Rae says.

Eva's expression fills with dread. "I can't."

"You will, or there's no deal." I can have her surveilled to ensure she's protected, though I'm not about to tell her now. "You won't tell him about our agreement because if he finds out you've been here, he'll end you."

Rae

Harrison's jaw hasn't unclenched for the last hour while Eva's discussed what she knows about Mischa's activities. Some of it we'd figured already—that he's running drugs through the clubs. That the money from that is bigger than the legitimate business.

"What about the bad drugs?" Harrison demands.

Eva picks at an invisible piece of lint on her jumpsuit. "I don't know anything about that. But I do know the cost of staying one step ahead of you is eating into his profit."

"You've seen the books?" Ash asks.

"I've seen his face. The one thing that pisses him off as much as losing is losing money." The room is quiet for a moment before Eva adds, "Something big is going down soon. I overheard him talking about next week on Sunday, but I could convince him we have plans that day and see if he'd move it to Saturday."

"Why Saturday?" Ash asks.

Eva's gaze settles on me.

"Absolutely fucking not." Harrison's voice is commanding. "You are not encouraging him to do a deal while Raegan is in that venue."

"He'd be distracted," Eva says smoothly. "He likes you."

The way she says it leaves no question as to what he likes about me.

She wouldn't care if I was sacrificed in all this. Hell, she'd probably love it.

My hand finds Harrison's arm, the muscles corded and angry under my touch. "There's nowhere safer than the middle of the stage. He won't risk his business to catch you."

Harrison exhales slowly. "I want to know the layout of the club."

I push a tray of tea cookies Natalia must've left on the counter earlier toward Eva, and she balks. "I haven't eaten a carbohydrate in ten years."

I take two cookies and lay them on the table at opposite ends. "This is the stage. And this is the front door. The dance floor is here." I wave my hand over the space in the middle. "Where's Mischa's office?"

If Harrison's going to tell the police, it would help to have as much detail as possible.

Eva shifts forward and takes a wafer. "Here." She sets it down between the two cookies and off to the side. "There's a hallway here with offices and a couple meeting rooms, plus inventory to stock the bar." She takes another three cookies, turning toward the other side of the table. "This half is VIPs. They're serviced by their own bar."

"Is that where he does business?" I ask.

"No. He might entertain in a VIP, but everything is decided in his office."

"Are there any entrances near there? There must be one for inventory," Harrison says.

Eva considers. "Loading dock services the stock room."

Another cookie goes down, this one close to Mischa's office.

My heart thuds. "So, if the police can get in while he's doing that deal…"

"They can bring him down," Harrison says.

Eva takes another cookie, and we wait for her to place it.

"Well?" Harrison prods, clearly impatient.

Eva nibbles the corner. "Well, what?"

Harrison rises. "You need to go back to him before he suspects anything. We'll let you know when we need you."

"You still have my number?" she asks as she follows him.

"Someone will be in touch."

She flinches at the dismissal. It's deluded, but I feel for her, so I walk with them to the door.

"We didn't offer you ice," I realize when she turns outside on the landing.

"Oh. This is a day old." Her full lips press together, blue eyes shifting over mine. "It wasn't an easy decision to come here."

I think of my decision to hide my assault, how some of the women my cousin helps with her charity are victims of assault by their partners. Eva isn't someone I'd empathize with, but seeing her like this, it's impossible not to.

She's halfway to her car when I chase after her, lowering my voice so only she can hear. "I know Harrison said we'd call you, but if you need help—"

"He loves you." Her voice is wistful. Then her eyes narrow, the faintest smirk marring her pretty features. "Good luck with that."

She might not betray Harrison, either out of loyalty or pragmatism.

But she'll fuck me over if she gets the chance.

CHAPTER 25

Rae

"When were you going to tell me about La Mer?" Annie demands over FaceTime when I call her on the weekend. "You're playing the biggest club in the world, and I had to find out from social?!"

"It's been a crazy time."

My final show at Bliss last night was bittersweet.

I played some new stuff I've been working on, but with the shadow of what we're about to do hanging over my head, I couldn't relax into it.

"How are you and Harry?"

I think of the texts he sent me last night.

Harrison: Play me a song.

Rae: Something you can fuck your hand to later?

Harrison: Something I can fuck you to later.

"He's Harrison," I say at last.

"So, you're back together."

I roll my eyes. "It's a work in progress. Our relationship has some... extra pressure points."

"I'm glad you guys found each other. I had a hard time picturing the perfect guy for you. If I'm honest, I wouldn't have picked him."

"Smug, gorgeous, rich as sin with a reputation to match?"

"Yeah. But you're sarcastic, unselfconscious, and anti-materialistic. He's perfect for you."

Since I moved in, Harrison's been consolidating what we learned from Eva and communicating with the police. He's spent time down at the local station and on calls with Interpol.

Still, he's here, and he's more attentive than a week ago.

I haven't told him about the feeling I have about Eva. I'm not going to. I can't make him more concerned.

Though concerned Harrison isn't all bad.

Last night, he was tracing my palm with his thumb from the moment he picked me up in his car.

On the steps to the house, his hands were squeezing my ass.

By the time Ash shut the door to his room, Harrison had his hand up my dress and his hard mouth whispering filthy things in my ear.

He kept me up all night.

He's also bought me gifts. When I ordered a custom outfit for my gig at La Mer from a designer in Barcelona, Harrison swooped in and paid for it before I could.

He also found my bracelet under the bed.

What a fucking domestic thing.

I haven't taken it off since.

Even though there's a real chance something could go wrong at La Mer, I need to believe there's good on the other side.

"I'm ready for a vacation. It's mathematically impossible that one tiny person can create more havoc than an entire Broadway crew pulling eight shows a week, or an international rock tour hitting twenty countries, but she manages to do it." Annie's voice brings me back.

"You guys should get away somewhere while you have the time off. Get Beck to go with you. I'm sure he'd watch the baby. Or Jax and Haley." I think of her semiretired rock-star dad and coder-genius stepmom, their own kids about six and two.

"An A-list nanny," Annie muses, her smile teasing and intrigued at once. "That's a good idea. Maybe I can talk Dad into it. He's been working on bringing Wicked back from the dead." The label he and Tyler bought as an investment last year wasn't only a business deal—it was personal. "He'd never say he's ready for a break, but when I talked to Haley the other night, she told me she caught him scribbling on organizational charts and muttering about restructuring. Of course, he's chewed his nails down to the nubs too."

I laugh, picturing the former biggest rock star in the world trying to do Harrison-like things. "Jax Jamieson's always going to crush the music part. Sounds like he needs help with the 'running the company' part."

"He does, though he won't admit it. And he doesn't trust anyone left over from the old management."

"He should call Harrison. Harrison might not have experience running a label, but he knows how to grow a company. And he definitely knows how to deal with the unexpected."

"That's a great idea. I'll tell Dad and Tyler. They might take him up on that. Anyway… What are you doing for this huge, career-capping show?"

I glance at my computer, anticipation surging through me. "I'm working on a few things."

I sound casual, but I've had ideas for this set for years. A file on my computer. Things I swap out with new tracks from time to time. Thanks to that, preparing should be simple, but it's not.

I picture the open-air venue packed from wall to wall. The thrill of imagining it for years doesn't match the reality now that it's so close. I'm nervous, and it's not only about Mischa. It's about me.

I've worked toward this my entire life, and I want to do it justice.

"Go all out. Don't save anything for next time. I knew which show on Broadway would be my last before having this baby, and I'm grateful. Because if I hadn't..." She shakes her head.

"Take no prisoners," I murmur. "You're a really good friend. You and Beck both."

Her eyes widen. "Wow. Rae Madani going emo. There must be an apocalypse I don't know about."

I force a shrug. "Just the usual. Guys. Gigs. Grudges."

Harrison

"You're not supposed to be here."

Leni looks up from a lounge chair locked into its most upright position on the patio. She's wearing a pink robe that hides her bandages and holding a copy of *Little Women*. "It's been days. I'm supposed to sit around and get fat on Natalia's baking? My keeper let me out."

I picture the nurse in my hallway who gave me a frustrated

look on my way out here.

"You need to heal."

"Fresh air. Look it up. I even grabbed some classic literature. I wanted something lowbrow but couldn't find anything in your office." She waves the book. "This Laurie dude has it going on. Loaded, big family house, bunch of girls who worship him… Speaking of healing," she goes on as I stop in front of the chair, "you cleared the air with your brother yet over the way you acted?"

I narrow my eyes at her. "We have more important things to deal with."

"Urgent, maybe. That's not the same thing."

I shove my hands in the pockets of my trousers. I haven't been wearing a jacket. The feeling of constriction in my chest is enough without the added weight of another layer of clothing.

Sebastian and I don't need a heart-to-heart. The few moments this summer when he's opened up were surprising.

Still, I feel shitty about what went down the night I returned from London. Probably because Raegan planted this seed of an idea that I should've been here for him and I wasn't. And my damn brain weighs everything she says.

"Tell me about these urgent things." Leni's voice drags me back.

"They're above your pay grade. You're here to relax."

"Because some asshole stabbed me."

I shift onto the next chair. "We took Eva's evidence to law enforcement. They didn't want to disclose anything or budge on their own plans, but when they heard the detail we had from Eva, they realized this was a rare chance to capture him in a major deal."

I hope to God it protects Raegan rather than puts her in more danger. Because if this goes off the way it's supposed to, the police will be inside before a single one of Mischa's staff is tipped off.

"So, you put all your faith in the cops?" Leni cocks her head. "That's not the Harrison King I know."

I shake my head. "I'm trying to find a better way to monitor the situation. To have eyes not only on Raegan, but this deal." To make sure the two don't happen anywhere near one another.

I've been keeping my composure. In the moments it starts to waver, I remind myself that in a week, Mischa could be in custody and we could be free to live our own lives.

I've never wanted anything more. But I'm afraid to hope for it with everything hanging over our heads.

Raegan wants to go to London.

I'd take her to Machu Picchu if she wanted. Hike the damn jungle in boots and cargo shorts just to see her smirk. I'd suffer it all knowing at the end of the day she's mine.

Through everything.

"What about the robots?" Leni asks.

"The bartending robots Sawyer sent?" I frown. Maybe she hasn't been taking her medication. I should get the nurse…

"He has photographer robots," she says pointedly. "Ones you could station anywhere there are patrons, right? Plus Sawyer's company gets access to the data coming in. If the robots were installed at Mischa's club, Sawyer could theoretically see whatever they see and pass it on to law enforcement. But you can't order them for La Mer."

Leni shifts forward, wincing. She drops the book, her hand going to her stomach as she takes a few wheezing breaths.

"No." I retrieve the book from the patio, the wheels in my

mind turning. "But I can order them for Debajo. Or be seen to be ordering them for Debajo. A lot of them."

"If Mischa finds out, he'll want them too," she finishes.

Yes. It's one thing I can do to take back some piece of control.

"This would need to happen fast."

Leni holds out a hand for the book. "I'll let you get at it, then."

CHAPTER 26

Rae

La Mer is shaking. The booth. The floor.

I'm in the middle of my set when a cracking sound from beneath makes me look down.

The stage is splitting between my feet, the gap widening with every thump of the bassline.

I drop to my knees and try to drag the halves back together with sweaty hands.

Instead, a piece of the stage falls into the chasm, and I fall with it.

Alice in Wonderland–style, I fall and fall.

Mischa's face appears, threatening, and he shoots out a hand to grip my throat. "I've got you."

I can't breathe.

"I've got you."

Before I pass out, the voice changes.

"Raegan. Love. I've got you."

I force myself back to consciousness. It's hard to breathe, but I focus every part of my attention on making my lungs expand, and reality comes rushing back.

When I blink my eyes open, Harrison's over me, expression alert and concerned. We're in his bedroom at the villa, light filtering in across the floor.

"Bad dream," he murmurs.

I exhale, wiping a hand over my sweaty forehead. "What makes you say that?"

The sheet is tangled in my legs, and he reaches down to unwrap me. Strong hands linger on my naked calves. In fact, I'm naked everywhere and so is he, but I can't shake the images behind my eyes.

"Everyone has nightmares before a big gig," I say, willing my heart to stop racing.

It doesn't have to be a sign of bad things to come. But the pit in my stomach disagrees.

Harrison tugs me into his lap, his hard body curving around mine. "My biggest regret today is that I can't watch you."

I wish he could watch me too. But he's staying somewhere he can keep an eye on all the happenings tonight, not only me.

"Someone will stream it on social."

"I can't get a personal reenactment?" A brow lifts, a smirk playing at his beautiful lips.

Insolent bastard.

"This is your problem. You've always thought you should get special treatment because you're Harrison fucking K—"

His head drops to my shoulder, running soft, devastating kisses down to my breasts. "Treat me however you want, Raegan." He looks up at me, and his expression steals my breath. "I'll come back for more."

When his mouth claims mine, I meet him.

It's urgent for reasons I don't want to name.

My hands stroke down his chest, linger on the scars covering his pec. It doesn't feel like a childhood prank. It's a warning. A promise that the man my lover calls his rival will stop at nothing to destroy him.

And after what Eva said… possibly me too.

If my dream comes true and I fall down a hole tonight—if the deal doesn't go down, or if Mischa learns we've helped the police—I could lose this man forever.

Harrison slips between my thighs, fills me with a familiar need I want to memorize. I'm torn between losing myself in this moment and imprinting it on my mind, my body, for fear it will never happen again.

When we separate after, my eyes drift closed. I feel him shift across the bed, reaching for pants.

"We need to get up." His lips tickle my ear.

"Mmmm."

He rubs my tattooed wrist, a habit that makes me smile. "When I met you, I tried to treat you like other women. I wanted to buy you gifts. I wanted to show you the world. But you don't like anything I buy—"

"I loved the yacht, mostly because it made you sick. Plus the headphones—"

"As for the world, you've already seen it." His touch skims up my palm.

"But I haven't seen it with you." My body is tingling from what we just did, and my heart is full of him. "I want to see where you grew up. Find a beach food truck on every continent and watch you eat from it like it's got a Michelin star."

"Hike in cargo shorts at Machu Picchu?" My breath hitches as I blink my eyes open. "Is that on the table?"

He chuckles. "I have a gift for you." He reaches for the bedside table and pulls out a box.

"More jewelry?"

I open it to find a tiny camera, smaller than my fingernail.

"So you can capture what it feels like to be up there tonight and relive it whenever you want. Because today is about you. And I won't let you forget it."

My eyes burn. I love that he sees me, that even if he doesn't agree with my choice to play, he'll support me anyway.

"It's going to work," I say. "Mischa ordered the robot cameras for La Mer."

A tight nod. "Sawyer will see what they see, and he's patched the police into the feed. I'm patched in too."

Of course he is.

He'll be watching the stage, but more than that, the hallways and any rooms with public access.

He can't see inside Mischa's office, but he wants to ensure I'm as far from harm as possible.

It hits me for the first time, the possibility that I've made this harder on him.

I shift onto my elbows, the sheet bunched over my breasts.

"Don't do anything crazy," I whisper, and his brows lift. "For me or anyone else. Whatever happens today, promise we'll still be here."

He presses his lips to my forehead before pulling away, fastening his pants as he heads for the door.

I spring out of bed. "I mean it. I can't lose you over this." My heart rate accelerates, and this time it has nothing to do with the nightmare.

Barney sneaks through the crack and accosts me, delighted to find me running and naked. I go back and grab the sheet off the bed, wrapping it around me as I dodge the dog in pursuit of his owner.

"Hey!" I grab Harrison's arm halfway down the hall.

His face is a mask of tension when he turns back. "I'm not a good man," he murmurs. "But I will protect the people I love."

I run my fingers up his face, thumbs brushing the tight lines around his mouth.

I love you. I feel it in every inch of me, a raw, aching truth that's been part of me for longer than I knew.

God, if I lose him today…

I shift up on my toes and press my forehead to his. "Let's get out of here," I whisper. "Fuck all of this, Harrison. I don't need La Mer. Let's just leave."

His eyes crinkle at the corners. There's no bloodlust in them now. Only commitment. Responsibility. Devotion.

"There's a woman—a queen—and her stage is waiting."

He gently pushes my hands away, and when he starts down the stairs, I feel like the ground has split wide and I'm falling again.

My costume was intended to be daring.

A black silk tuxedo jacket, custom made for me by a designer in Barcelona. One side has gold threads woven through it. Underneath, I have black silk pants that hug my hips, gather around my ankles.

The white vest, once it's fastened, dips low between my breasts.

At the moment, it's lower than intended. A button came off, and if I wear it like this, Harrison will start a riot.

I'm straddling a dining room chair and sewing the button back on, a needle in my teeth, when the tiny camera with a battery pack on the table catches my eye. Harrison suggested I stick it to my phone and set that somewhere on the desk in front of me when I mix.

But I can do better.

Five minutes later, I pull the last thread tight. The button is secured once more, the lens on the outside of my vest and the tiny battery secured with thread against the lining.

My phone rings.

Annie.

"Are you excited for your show?" she demands. My friend is a dark shadow, the sun at her back.

I take the needle from my mouth. "Excited doesn't begin to describe it," I admit.

There's a knock at the front door, and Natalia bustles toward it. She shoots me a frown on the way—she doesn't understand why I wouldn't let her fix the costume. To be honest, I needed to keep busy.

"We're about to find out."

I barely hear Annie's words over the phone because there's a squeal from the doorway and my phone at once.

"Fuck." I drop the vest, the button, and the phone.

"We came to see your show!" Annie cheers.

"Who's 'we'?"

Tyler's behind her with the baby. Plus Beck and Elle.

My shock and joy are overshadowed by dismay. Tonight, something thrilling is going down, but if we do our jobs, something dangerous will follow. "You guys can't be here."

"I get it, the club is sold out. I can get us in," Beck says, smirking.

"As usual, Hollywood misses the point."

I turn to see Ash jog down the stairs.

"Ash! Tell them they can't be here."

He cocks his head at me. "Well, they are." He cuts a look at my friends. "Quiz: What would stop you from seeing Raegan's show tonight? Warning from a mysterious oracle?"

Annie shakes her head, Elle snorts, Tyler frowns, and Beck lifts a brow.

"How about plague of locusts? Pestilence? Nothing?" Ash grins, grabbing my shoulder before I shove him off. "Sounds like they're staying."

CHAPTER 27

Rae

By the time I head to La Mer, I'm so amped up I could explode.

"Don't worry about us," Annie insists. "The nanny is looking after the baby here. We'll be over in a car closer to the start time of your show."

I hug each of my friends in turn.

Toro insists on driving me, and Harrison holds the back door.

"What are you doing?" I ask as he shifts inside.

"Going with you."

I'm grateful to have his presence.

We drive over in silence. There's so much to be said, but given the amount of our relationship devoted to banter and argument, the quiet is too precious to break.

When we arrive, Harrison kisses me hard. I don't think he's going to let me go, but finally he pulls back.

"I've got your back. We all do," he murmurs against my lips.

I nod.

At the back entrance, I get out. My security followed us in another car, and they come with me.

I've always wanted to be here, and now I am. The club is huge and empty, but as we wind through the halls, it occurs to me that tonight it's mine.

Not Mischa's, not even Harrison's.

You can't buy a feeling. Can't own an emotion.

No matter what happens beyond the dance floor, I can give the people on it everything I am.

The prep is a blur. I catch Eva's eye once, in the hall outside the green room, but don't see Mischa.

I get on stage as the lighting tech cuts everything to black.

There's nothing but the energy of the crowd. A pulsing, throbbing beat.

It's my heart.

When I lift my headphones onto my ears, I focus on what I can do—my set.

From the first chords of my opening track of the night, the crowd erupts. The lights come up, and they see me and I see them.

This is what I wanted, and nothing can take tonight away from me.

It's my job to hold them in my hands. To take them on a journey, to keep them safe and entertained and away from whatever's going on behind closed doors.

I lose myself.

It's the end of my set when my phone lights up.

Harrison: There's a problem. The deal's supposed to be going down, but the cameras haven't shown Mischa setting foot near his office.

Shit.

I scan the venue from my bird's-eye view on stage. Nothing.

Rae: Maybe it's not happening tonight.

Harrison: She said it was.

"She" meaning Eva.

Did she cross us? I could see her fucking with me, but not Harrison.

If she did…

My blood runs cold.

Rae: He has to be around.

My set wraps up, and I head back to the green room, muttering to security about needing to unwind in private. Then I call a number.

A few minutes later, the blond woman slips into my room. I whirl to face her.

"You set us up. Where is he?" I demand.

Eva cuts a look down the hall. "VIP. The deal moved."

"The cameras didn't show him going in there."

"There's another entrance."

"Did you tell the police? Harrison?"

"No."

I hit Harrison's number.

"It's in the VIP room," I bite out when he answers.

He exhales tightly. "They won't move without visual confirmation of what's happening in there. Sawyer's cameras don't include the VIP."

This is bad. There's no way to get eyes into that room. If they don't act now, who knows when there will be another chance.

I press a hand to my stomach, sweat still sticking my clothes to my skin. My fingers brush the smooth buttons of my tailored vest. One is smooth. One has a slight bump.

I glance down at the camera. "Harrison? Did Sawyer get the feed from my show?"

"I'll check." Pause. "Yes. Why?"

I look at Eva. Her pretty face has healed from what Mischa did to it, but I can't forget how the bruises looked under her skin.

I know what it is to have someone take from me in a way that's unforgivable. To not only violate me but make me question myself. The doubt, the fear, the need to get out of my own skin because it doesn't feel safe.

This time, I know where the danger lies. And it's more imminent, more treacherous, than any I've walked into before.

But on the other side is safety for the people like the woman who died at Bliss, the ones who would be harmed by Mischa's empire. It's for the people I love, the ones who'd do anything for me.

I never used to believe in that kind of loyalty and devotion.

Now, I do. I'm not afraid of it.

The phone at my ear, I say to Eva, "Get me into the VIP room."

"I can get you in, but I can't get you out," Eva says.

I don't trust her for a second. But I trust the man on the other end of the phone. And my friends.

"Harrison..." I murmur into the microphone.

"Raegan, don't even fucking think about it." The panic in his voice makes me swallow hard.

"I need to tell you—"

"We have to go." Eva grabs the phone and clicks off.

As I follow Eva to the hall, blood pounding in my ears, all I can think is I hope he knows I love him.

CHAPTER 28

Rae

Eva's knock on the door of the VIP room is crisp. She's close enough her perfume hangs in the air. I breathe through my mouth and count the seconds, half hoping the door doesn't open.

I reach seven before the door swings wide, revealing a huge security guard with a tattooed face.

"I brought entertainment for my fiancé."

If Eva's nervous, she doesn't sound it. Her choice of words makes the hairs on my arms lift under the tuxedo jacket.

The guard's gaze rolls down my body. I fold my arms to hide the camera, and his attention stops on my breasts.

"Turn. Arms out," he states.

Shit. I'm really wishing my security hadn't been detained at the other end of this long hall at the insistence of Mischa's men that only Eva and I could pass.

I face away, my gaze locking with Eva's. Now she's nervous too.

He starts at my ankles, hands lingering on my calves, my thighs.

"Don't damage his property," Eva says lightly. "He'll be angry if you do."

"Hey!" The bark has the man freezing, casting a look over his shoulder. "Bring her here."

Security steps back to reveal four men—two guards and two seated men in suits.

Mischa Ivanov is impossible to miss even reclined on the couch. His suit is crisp, a red handkerchief sticking out of his breast pocket. Cold blue eyes see into me, through me. I feel for the camera, making sure it's still unblocked. Hopefully, it still works.

"You're excused," Mischa instructs his fiancée.

What? No.

Her presence might keep things from getting ugly.

But Eva doesn't protest, just nods without looking at me and closes the door silently behind her.

Didn't plan on being alone with the madman. Figured I could get in, provide Harrison and the police the visual confirmation they needed to take action.

Please take some damned action.

"Miss Madani," Mischa drawls, interrupting my thoughts. "I understand your set was tremendous."

"It was. I wanted to thank you for the opportunity."

He spreads his hands. "So, thank me."

I lift my chin. "I just did."

One of the guards, who is on his phone, hangs up and taps Mischa on the shoulder. "Third loading dock. In the kegs."

I straighten. That must be where they're moving the drugs.

Did my camera pick up the audio? It must have.

Mischa nods to the guard but speaks to me. "A woman who brings Harrison King to his knees. Perhaps I should be thanking you. He's been distracted enough I was able to sweep this place out from under him."

My heart kicks, the hard ball of tension in my stomach giving a degree.

"My empire is expanding," he goes on, and I can't resist taking a shot.

"Through cheap drugs that kill people?"

His smile freezes. "Every war has collateral damage, Miss Madani."

"You can't call it collateral damage when you're planning a delivery of the same drugs tonight."

Mischa's eyes flash. I've made a mistake. Maybe he'll drag Eva back in here. Or he thinks I've figured this out on my own.

Armed police will be here any minute.

He shifts off the couch, adjusting his cuffs. "I can call it whatever the fuck I want. I'm more interested in talking about you. You are quite appealing, though you don't try to be. It's that attribute that makes you desirable."

Smug son of a bitch. I'm vulnerable here, but there's a part of me that won't be silenced. The assumption that women exist to attract men, that we're pawns to be desired and manipulated.

"I thought it was the fact that I'm with Harrison. I mean, that seems to be what gets you off. Going after what he has. His parents. His brother. His fiancée." I glance back at the door, toward wherever Eva's gone.

But instead of looking angry, Mischa laughs. "I've never seen him so captivated by someone. You gave him something his entire corporation never could."

"What's that?"

"Hope. And now we're going to take it away from him."

Sweat rolls between my shoulders.

Where are the police?

The truth washes over me in a sickening wave.

They're not coming.

Either they can't, or they're not seeing what's happening. If they could, they would've been here by now.

"What are you waiting for?" Mischa drawls. "You're a beautiful woman. Entertain us."

The guard behind me steps closer, and something hard bumps my lower back.

When cold metal slips under my jacket and presses against my skin, it's worse than my nightmare. At least if I fell forever, I wouldn't hit the ground.

Ivanov's cruel grin and the gun in my back say I'm about to do just that.

CHAPTER 29
Harrison

From the second Rae entered that VIP room, I've been ripped in two.

"Go in," I snap for the third time from the car outside, even though no one can hear me.

Watching her in that room with Ivanov, I'm dying a slow death. Sawyer got me a link to the feed when we figured out Rae's plan and patched it through to the police too.

It kills me the audio on her camera isn't working. I'll ream Sawyer out for this later, assuming there is a later for all of us.

If she gets hurt in there, I'll never forgive myself.

I should've stopped her. Should've taken her up on her suggestion this morning to walk away from all of it.

I rue the day I so much as uttered Ivanov's name in her presence because if I hadn't, we wouldn't be here. Now the woman I love is risking herself to bring him down.

The second the asshole gets off the couch and crosses to her, I'm cursing. Then the camera swings wildly before settling again at a new angle, one that shows a security guard but not her.

She took off the vest.

Or someone ripped it off her.

I'm out of the car.

A plainclothes officer emerges from an unmarked vehicle. "Mr. King, do not go in there."

I wrench away from him. "If you won't, I will."

I head inside, trying to wade through the crowd, but La Mer is packed. Raegan stirred them into a damned frenzy, and the afterparty is going strong.

This is taking too long.

I pick up my phone and hit a contact. Tyler answers over the din.

"I'm trying to get to Raegan," I holler. "I need crowd control. Everyone near the stage and out of the halls."

I don't want anyone in the way of what could happen.

He hangs up, and I think he's been cut off until the DJ changes to something else and I hear Tyler singing over it.

The crowd erupts, flooding the stage. A few people are in the halls still, and I shove past, reaching for my phone. I switch a few settings on it before sticking it upside down in my jacket pocket.

There's no sign of Raegan's security, or Mischa's.

But when I reach the VIP door, it's locked.

I throw my shoulder at it. Nothing.

A fire extinguisher is nearby, and I smash open the glass and retrieve it, then swing it at the door handle until it gives, and I fall inside. When I right myself and survey the scene, my stomach lurches.

Mischa is standing in front of the couch. Raegan's next to him in her trousers, heels, and a bra, her eyes wide.

Her jacket is gone, her white vest lying across the arm of the couch. Her headphones lie on the floor, the cord twisting along the carpet.

Rage and protectiveness unfurl from somewhere deep and dark in my gut.

"Are you all right?" I demand of Raegan.

She doesn't answer.

It could have been minutes at most since I left the car. I hate to think what he could've done in that time.

If he touched her...

I start to reach for her, but then I hear the click of a gun hammer behind me. The next second, my arms are caught behind my back, twisted painfully high.

Mischa grins. "You should've stayed with the Ivanov business. Your parents too. They might still be here. Loyalty is repaid. Those who work with us are compensated generously. It's everything we learned in business school, Harrison."

He's fucking nuts.

"I tried things your way," I say evenly, as if my heart isn't thudding against my ribs. "It wouldn't have worked out."

"You were too good for what I offered. Now, I have your attention."

Mischa crosses to me, flicking open a knife from his pocket.

He rips open my shirt, satisfaction glinting in his eyes as he sees the scar still there.

"I've been thinking about this for the past twenty years. This artwork is not nearly completed."

He doesn't want to kill me. He wants to fuck me up.

I tell myself that as the knife comes up, the blade hovering over my scar.

As it presses into my flesh, the searing pain making me bite down hard.

I don't have to look down to see blood trickle across my skin. I can feel it.

I can smell it.

"Stop!" Rae shouts.

Miraculously, Mischa does, turning to take her in.

Rae folds her arms. "Men are fickle. Five minutes ago, you wanted me."

What the fuck is she playing at?

I want to tell her to stop talking. Almost as much as I want to drag her behind me.

"It's true," Mischa purrs. "You have other redeeming qualities. Ones we'll get to once we've finished catching up."

She gestures to the other men. "This is some fucked-up boys' game, isn't it? Harrison rejected you twenty years ago, and you're still hurt over it. There're no drugs—you're just rich assholes fighting over your egos."

His face tics in irritation. "You're no queen. You're a child. And the deal going down in this building tonight is bigger than you can imagine."

He's supremely confident, and that's what she wants—to push him.

I inch toward her.

"Where are you going?" The guard twists my arm harder, stopping my progress and sending fiery pain from my shoulder socket down my spine.

I look down at my pocket. The phone is still there, mic tilted up. I pray to God the connection hasn't been severed.

Rae's lips curve. "What I imagine is that you're a scared boy who's ashamed he couldn't do what his parents wanted by recruiting one single employee." Dark brows draw together as she shifts onto the arm of the couch and crosses her legs. "And who had a weirdly personal thing for my boyfriend in high school—"

Mischa backhands her.

I wrench against the man holding me, the pain in my shoulder nothing compared to the panic in my chest. *No.*

Rae's facedown on the couch until he grabs her hair and drags her up.

"It's justice I want," Mischa spits in her face. "The pound of flesh I'm owed."

"You'll take it from me," I bark.

It's enough of an interruption that he turns slowly. "Or from her, while you watch."

Fear turns my gut into a block of ice before I can stop it. My breath is a shallow rasp echoing in my ears as I strain against my captor.

"On your knees." Mischa's words are for Raegan.

"Do you know how much these pants cost?" She's bluffing, but I can hear the edge of fear in her voice.

Because I know her.

And I love her.

"You won't be wearing them again," he promises. "You won't be wearing anything soon, and the only thing you'll care about is saying my name when I fucking tell you to. If I let you breathe long enough to say it."

He reaches for the buckle on his pants.

This room is squeezing the life out of me. I barely hear the crackle in my pocket because I've been reduced to watching the woman I love face down a villain she never should have met.

Raegan backs away from him, realizing his intention.

But she collides with a security guard, who forces her forward again.

"My patience is wearing thin," Mischa gripes, turning to me. "You'll get on your knees, and you'll tell him to watch."

Ideas of good and bad blur together. Of justice and vindication.

I hate him. But what comes through that hate is something bigger.

Love.

I love her, and it's not about possession or control. It's about the way she teaches me to see the world. Revenge is worth nothing—there's no reason to fight for the past, but there's every reason to fight for the future.

I'm going to get us out of this.

I'll tear out of the security guard's grip, lunge for Mischa.

But the men with the guns will get to me first.

Don't care. I need to protect her.

"Harrison." Her voice is steady, and I can hate everything in this room except those three fucking syllables from her perfect lips.

She's held my gaze across a hundred rooms. I've always felt the strength of that connection, even if she was fighting me.

I'm coming, I say. *I'm going to get us out of here.*

But Raegan's the one who opens her mouth and whispers, "Watch."

I can't make sense of the word until she shifts off the couch onto her knees.

No. No, this isn't happening.

With a chuckle, Mischa works the zipper on his pants. He's hard, and I want to throw up.

But her eyes are on me, and as I calculate my odds of kicking the guard behind me in the balls and making it out of here alive, her expression stops me.

I'm not watching. I'm listening.

Trust me.

We do this together.

It takes everything in me to stop fighting.

She reaches for his pants and drags them down to his ankles.

He grabs her hair, yanking her face back up to meet his gaze. "Faster."

"Since you asked nicely."

I hear something—the sound of voices in the hall.

Then the room erupts.

Rae's hands move fast, and Mischa bellows in pain. Blood streams from his thigh, where Raegan's buried the knife from his pocket.

I wrench out of the surprised guard's hold, fighting the sickening pain in my shoulder, and lunge across the carpet.

I grab Mischa by the collar and hurl him toward the floor.

Mischa's head cracks against the side of the coffee table, but it's the gunfire behind me that splits the room.

I'm already diving to cover the woman kneeling on the floor.

CHAPTER 30

Rae

The noise is deafening.

Not like a high-decibel sound system, machines made to produce music. This is the sound of machines made to produce destruction.

I can't count the shots—five, at least. Some from the doorway and some from deeper in the room. Harrison grips my arms, covering every part of me with his body, pressing my cheek against the coarse carpet.

It's too loud one second, too quiet the next.

I sneak a look between Harrison's chin and shoulder and see men with badges and guns stream in.

They speak to one another in rapid-fire Spanish, and in my state, I only get one of every few words.

"We got the delivery," an officer says in English to Harrison. "At the loading dock, hidden inside kegs of beer."

The weight on me lifts. I can breathe again, though my lungs are slow to expand.

Harrison shoves himself to standing and holds out a hand. I rise to shaky feet and turn in a circle.

One of the security guards is down. The other is on his knees, being handcuffed by a man with a badge and a gun.

The other officers stand over two crumpled forms.

The peek of a red handkerchief matching the blood seeping into the carpet is enough to confirm it's Mischa.

He's not moving. Neither of them are.

My hands are covered in blood. I should be horrified, but all I feel is a grim numbness.

"Are you all right?" The familiar voice makes me flinch. "Raegan…"

Hands grip my arms. Harrison looks as if he was the one shot. His brows are a tight line, blue eyes stormy as he searches my face. I wrap my arms around myself, fingers sliding on the sheen of cold sweat.

He slips off his jacket, wincing, and slings it around me. My gaze shifts back to the lifeless forms.

An officer appears next to us. "The camera was brave. Or stupid. We couldn't tell what was being said." He turns to Harrison. "Good thing you had your cell phone on you. Audio was muffled, but between that and the video, we had enough to move."

My gaze lifts to Harrison's, but the officer continues. "We're going to need statements from both of you. Ivanov might not be talking again, but based on what we got tonight, we should have enough evidence to implicate other senior people in his organization."

"We'll give statements at the station," Harrison says. The officer appears ready to argue, but Harrison continues. "We have some things to resolve first."

I head toward the door. In the hall, officers are directing upset patrons out of the venue. Fortunately, they seem in a hurry to leave.

"Raegan..." Harrison's voice at my back has me stiffening.

I don't want to talk right now. I can't.

"We need to find Tyler and Annie and Beck and Ash." I press through the thinning crowd, pulling out my phone and hitting a contact. Annie answers on the fourth ring.

"Where are you?" she shouts.

"Heading from the VIP rooms."

"Are you okay? We heard gunshots."

I cut a look over my shoulder to see Harrison's grim face. "We're not hurt." Because that's easier than telling her we're not okay. "Where are you?"

"Backstage."

"Wait, what?"

I'm pressed to the wall, moving in the opposite direction of traffic. I nearly get to one set of the double doors thrown wide to the open-air dance floor when a hand grabs my shoulder. I spin to find Eva, eyes wide.

"Where is he?" she asks.

"He's dead."

Her hands drop away. "Thank you." Her hand rests on her flat stomach, and a piece clicks into place.

She's pregnant.

I guess she decided enough was enough—if not for her, then for the family she could have. Her child doesn't need to follow in his father's footsteps.

The dance floor is wide open. It's easy to cross to the stage, and by the time I reach the halfway point, I can spot the figures on stage.

"Annie?" I call.

My friend waves. Her husband stands next to her.

"What happened?" I ask.

"Harrison wanted a distraction to keep the crowd on the dance floor." Elle drops off the stage. "So, Tyler took the mic to keep everyone here."

The numbness around my heart thaws a little.

"Beck said he'd steer everyone out of the hall. Last I saw, there were dozens of people running his way. I haven't seen him since," Annie says.

Shit. The crowds tonight were thick. It's one thing to be on stage, but Beck alone, trying to get attention without security… It could have been dangerous.

I try calling Beck's number but get voicemail. I send off a text.

Rae: Are you okay? You went AWOL.

Dots appear.

Beck: I'm safe.

I heave a sigh of relief.

"Where's my brother?" Harrison demands.

We all look at one another.

Rae: Ash is missing.

Harrison grunts. "I'll call—"

I hold up a hand as dots appear again. The seconds tick by. When the response comes, it's shorter than I expected.

Beck: He's here too.

My brows rise, but I show Harrison the message.

"You guys," Annie calls before I can decide how to respond. We all turn to find her holding up her phone. "I know it's been a long night, but before we leave… Group photo? I haven't gotten out in months."

CHAPTER 31
Harrison

When I woke yesterday morning, my chest was tight with dread and Raegan was in my arms.

Today, the dread is gone. But so is she.

I'm in the guest bedroom, and I roll to one side, exhaling hard as I hit my shoulder, which hurts like someone ripped it from its socket.

Last night comes back to me in a rush.

Our friends headed directly back to their hotel from La Mer, but Raegan and I were at the police station until after five.

We answered questions independently. Somewhere along the line, a medic put five stitches in the cut in my chest and reset the shoulder that had been dislocated before my dive across the room.

After the police released us, Raegan and I drove home in near silence. Raegan took a shower in the guest bathroom, and I washed off in the en suite. After, I padded out to the hall to see if she was still in the bathroom—only to see the guest bedroom door closed.

I opened the door to find her lying in bed, staring up at the ceiling. I crawled in next to her, pulling her body to mine.

She hasn't talked about what happened in that room. The way she kept her cool to gain the upper hand on Mischa in a way I couldn't have was amazing. It might've given me a heart attack, but I respect her even more than before.

But as I lay next to her, I wondered…

How sure was she that someone was coming? Did she think we'd left her?

I'm relieved Mischa is dead. But witnessing her at his mercy, knowing I won't forget it for a long fucking time, is a parting gift he would've appreciated.

The ache in my shoulder is nothing compared to how it felt to see her helpless in that room. That will linger on my soul.

Now, the door nudges wide.

I shift up on an elbow, hoping it's her, but the top of Barney's head and furry back appear as he pads to the bed. He noses at my hand and lifts hopeful eyes to my face.

Fuck, it's impossible to be a dick to a dog.

After stroking his head, I get up and pad out into the hall.

The shower's on—second one in twelve hours.

I want to talk to her, but accosting her while she scrubs extra blood from under her nails isn't the right time.

I head down the hall to my room for clean clothes. Barney follows, and after, we head downstairs together.

My brother is already drinking coffee and reading a newspaper.

"How was your evening?" I ask.

Ash frowns. "Uneventful. Boring even."

My brows lift.

"Relatively," he adds.

I take the paper from him.

He's not as pale as he was last week. Instead of being lethargic, his voice is light. His reactions are quick and irritated.

"I was a dick about you using," I say.

He shifts an arm over the back of the next chair. "Is this some kind of 'near death experience' remorse?"

I grimace. "It should've been me helping you. Not Leni or Raegan."

Sebastian studies me a long moment, then holds out a hand. "Don't worry about it. I want to get my shit together. I will," he vows.

I clasp his forearm.

"Brunch is at two down at the marina," he says. "Tyler and Annie are bringing the baby."

"Is Beck coming?" I ask.

An exasperated sigh. "How the fuck should I know?"

Natalia appears with a coffee, and I thank her as I drop into a chair. "Raegan's upset. What happened in that room… I don't blame her."

"What did happen?" Sebastian asks.

I don't want to talk it out, but I need to tell someone because it's burning a hole in my gut. So, I tell him everything, struggling to get through a few parts.

"That's intense." He blows out a breath.

"I wanted to save her." I pause, my coffee halfway to my lips, then set the cup back down. "It felt like I was the one on my knees."

Noises behind us have Ash looking over my shoulder. "Morning, sunshine."

I turn as Rae comes down the stairs wearing a T-shirt and

denim shorts. I rise and hold a chair for her. She sinks into it.

"You were on fire last night," Ash comments. "Have you checked out social yet?"

"Been busy." But her lips twitch, and I'm grateful to my brother for reassuring me it's still possible for her to smile.

Natalia brings her coffee and biscotti, and Raegan murmurs her thanks. My gaze runs over the bruise on her cheek as she breaks off a piece of cookie and holds it out to Barney, who devours it and eyes her like she's the sun, moon, and stars.

Get in line.

Ash rises from his seat. "Brunch this afternoon. With everyone down by the port. If you're up to it." Her gaze flits to mine, then away again.

Raegan doesn't answer, and my brother shifts out of his seat and heads toward the door.

I can't stand the distance between us. But when I cover her hand with mine, she flinches.

"How's your shoulder?" she asks.

"It's nothing."

Not compared to what happened to her.

She looks away, and I grab her chair and drag it toward mine until she can't avoid my gaze.

"It hurts, love. Is that what you want to hear? It aches, but the only thing I cared about last night, the only thing I care about *now*, is you." I try to put my agony into words. "When I saw you in that room, I've never been so terrified in my life. I did everything I could to protect you. But underneath… I felt helpless. If he wasn't dead already, I'd have killed him for touching you. The second I got free." I grimace. "I didn't expect *you* to be the one to do something fucking crazy. It took everything in me to hold back."

Her gaze softens with compassion. "You waited?"

"You asked me to. And I told you, we're a team, love." I smooth back her hair from her face. "You're brave and beautiful, and you came into my life like a storm and wouldn't leave. You taught me there's more to life than a list of assets bearing my name or a team of people in my employ.

"You reminded me that damaged people can still love. You tried to take down a Russian drug dealer. Unassisted. *Fuck.* If you need space after last night, I will give it to you. But I won't pretend I want to be anywhere other than where you are. I won't tell you I'm not jealous Barney got to lick your hand just now."

Her eyes glaze over, her lips parting. Every second she's silent leaves me ripped in two.

"You want to lick my hand?" she asks at last.

I exhale a half laugh. "I want to lick you everywhere." My heart hammers against my ribs. "How was it? Your set, I mean."

There's a spark behind her eyes, signs of life returning. "Incredible. The crowd was so into it. I felt like a priestess, Harrison. At the altar of the most awe-inspiring ceremony."

My chest tightens. "The way you wanted to play La Mer... That's how I want you. The way you felt on that stage... That's how I feel when I'm with you. You make me glad I'm alive, like there's some purpose outside of me. I don't want to live in a world where I don't get to feel that."

Her head lifts, and her dark gaze searches mine. I can't dare to name the emotions there for fear I'm wrong.

"I love you too." She holds out a hand, and my heart kicks.

I grab her hand before she can think twice and press my lips to her palm. The feel of her, warm and real and here, soothes the ache in my gut.

That's not enough, so I cup her face and tug her toward me. When I crush her lips under mine, she meets me.

"Raegan," I murmur against her skin, unwilling to pull back. "I want to be with you. Tell me you want that, too."

Her phone rings and she yanks it out of her pocket. I want to hurl the thing across the room, but she looks torn. "I have to take this."

She's out of the room before I can respond.

Rae

Ash claims the back seat when Harrison drives us to brunch. It's our first time without security in weeks. Harrison's hand rests on my thigh, his fingers brushing the skin exposed by my shorts.

The phone call I took an hour ago echoes in my head. I feel better than I did this morning, but the events of last night still weigh on me. My cheek hurts, and I resist the urge to brush it.

The way you felt on that stage... That's how I feel when I'm with you.

Harrison's words meant everything. I love him with parts of me I didn't know could love.

There's no chance of going halfway with Harrison King—not emotionally, anyway.

Since last night, my social media's blown up. But I don't know how to tell Harrison about the phone call I got earlier.

Harrison finds parking, and we get out at the port. The restaurant is open air, with jaunty blue-and-white-striped umbrellas mimicking the sea. Our friends are already at a table, and my chest expands.

The last time I went through hell, I was alone.

I'm not anymore.

"Good morning, superstar." Annie passes the baby to Tyler so she can rise and hug me. "Or should I say afternoon?"

"Late night," I say as Harrison pulls out my chair and claims one on the other side.

"About that…" Tyler starts, and I stiffen. I don't want to rehash it again.

Beck leans in. "Yeah. Let's hear it." He looks around the table. "How'd the set feel?"

The knot in my chest loosens. "Amazing. I have a dozen messages from my publicist I haven't returned with requests for interviews, even a documentary."

"That's so great!" Annie gushes, and even Elle bobs her head.

Beck snorts. "And you didn't want to be on my TV show."

"I didn't say yes to the documentary." I sneak a look at Harrison. *Because there might be something bigger.*

The waitress comes to get our drink order.

"What's next for everyone?" Elle asks, looking around the circle of us. "We brought down Harrison's nemesis, right?"

Tyler nods. "Paid you back for saving my life."

"You never told me what happened," Annie prods.

Harrison and Tyler exchange a look before Tyler says, "I was driving in London. Wrong side of the road. I got messed up and drove into a fountain."

"You're joking. I pictured it as something crazy or sexy or dramatic," Annie says.

"It was dramatic," Harrison weighs in. "The man drove into a stone angel. Water was spurting from her navel."

Tyler winces. "It wasn't pretty."

"You should save that kind of drama for my show," Beck goads.

"I'm not going on your show."

Beck shifts an arm over the back of Tyler's seat. "It's one of the top ten streaming shows, and we're only in the first season."

"People are bored and stupid if they want to watch you fuck around," Ash drawls.

"My fucking around," Beck says, "is charming."

The baby fusses, and Beck motions to Tyler, who passes her over.

Within moments, Rose quiets.

"What about you?" Annie asks Harrison.

"It'll take time for Mischa's estate to be worked out, but as the investigation unfolds, many of his assets will be repossessed and sold off. I'll be first in line." His gaze meets mine.

I squeeze his hand. He's always wanted that club, and I can't expect that to change now.

More than that, I want him to have it.

"You could be back playing there sooner than you think," he murmurs.

I shift in my chair. "I got a call this morning from DJ Maxx. This guy I used to work with. I never liked him, but he's put in a word for me about a residency in Vegas."

Everyone gasps and gushes, but Harrison goes still next to me.

"When would this residency commence?" he murmurs when the waitress brings our drinks.

"Four months." He doesn't answer, so I add, "I've been traveling forever. Maybe it's time to put down roots. I want more than living out of a suitcase. I could buy a place. Hell, I could be a grownup. Even get my own espresso maker." I try to joke, but he doesn't smile.

"An espresso maker in Vegas."

I lift a shoulder.

I can picture it. Crowds there to see me, a club to call my own. The familiarity was one of the things I loved about Debajo, but I've outgrown it. I want a new challenge.

But I don't want it without him.

Harrison's hand resting on my knee withdraws. His ocean-blue eyes I love cloud, and he rises abruptly from his seat, tossing his napkin on the table before addressing the table. "Excuse me. I'm afraid I can't stay."

Before I can say a word, he's halfway to his car.

"Harrison?" I call into the house.

There's no answer, but Barney peers through the railing upstairs.

I hung out with my friends over lunch before they had to fly back, pretending the man I love more than anything didn't walk out on us and take my heart with him.

When I return to the villa, I'm resolved.

I want Harrison. The rest we'll figure out.

I step out of my sandals and head across the room, taking the stairs in bare feet. I pause at the top.

There's movement in Harrison's room, a shadow falling across the open doorway.

"I know I sprung the Vegas thing on you, but I want a future. And I want it with…"

When I step inside, he's waiting.

My attention drifts to the matching set of Louis Vuitton luggage on the bed. I reach for one and open it, finding it full of my belongings. "What is this?"

"Proper bags. For more than a handful of items. You said you wanted to settle down. Doesn't mean you won't travel occasionally, but this will get you started."

His thoughtfulness slices through the knot in my stomach.

"This is a lot of luggage. What could possibly be in…" I unzip the second bag, and the silver appliance glints up at me. "The espresso machine?" My jaw drops.

"I bought it for you," he murmurs from behind me.

"You're insane."

"Only since I met you. You're impossible to please."

"That's because there's nothing you could give me that would make me happy."

Because what I want is you.

He frowns, nodding to the next suitcase. "Look anyway."

I roll my eyes but open the top.

The contents have my hand dropping to my side.

Rows of folded, pressed dress shirts stare up at me. Neatly looped belts. Folded slacks.

The window is open, but there's not enough air in the room. My throat works for a moment before I can make a sound.

"Your things?" I force my gaze to meet his, and when I do, it's full of so much emotion I'm tingling everywhere.

"Consider me newly acquired baggage. I love you. You're not going anywhere without me."

Hope surges through me. I want to so badly. I know he usually leaves Ibiza at the end of the season, but for London. The last time he was in the US, it was for Kings, which is a pile of rubble. I can't quite believe this man would drop everything to follow me.

"Even Vegas?"

He nods. "I made a call. We have a penthouse at the Wynn."

My slow smile won't stop. "God, you're arrogant. I haven't even invited you."

Harrison drags me against him, his hard body warm through our clothes. "You owe me one favor—"

"Keep it," I interrupt, breathless. "This time, you're doing me one."

His eyes warm with love and desire, and he drags me up to his lips. My hands fall to his chest as he kisses me. In this moment, I have everything—a home, a family, someone I adore who loves me back, when I want him to and when I don't.

"What will you even do in Vegas?" I pant, pulling away an inch.

He brushes his thumb across my lips. "It's close to LA. I can run my business from there."

"And La Mer?"

He shrugs. "I'll put in an offer when it comes up. Leni would love to take it on and find the right person to run it."

I shake my head, disbelieving. "I can't believe this."

"Worked out well for me too." His quick grin is sexy as hell. "This way, you still owe me a favor."

"There's an expiry date on those."

"No such thing."

Harrison lifts me into his arms, and my legs go around him.

He tastes like sun and sand and man, and when he claims my mouth, my arms wind around his neck without permission.

I kiss him back, with relief and love and the kind of hope I never thought I'd feel.

Barney barks, and we reluctantly part. I frown, reaching for his collar. It matches the luggage.

"Barney's coming?" I demand.

"Charter leaves tomorrow. If you'd rather avoid a man you hate, you can fly commercial."

I grin. "How terrible."

He kisses me again, pushing me back toward the bed, and we find a spot between the luggage. I kick at one of the bags, and there's a loud bang as it crashes to the floor.

The espresso maker.

I look guiltily up at Harrison.

"Oh, you're in trouble now," he murmurs before his mouth descends.

EPILOGUE
Rae

The crowd is amazing.

From my raised platform, I get a look over the top of the dance floor to the booths circling the floor at the Vegas club.

In the two months since my residency started, each time I take the stage, my mind is blown again.

Still, tonight is special.

I take a sip of the vodka soda in front of me, the buzz going to my head. I spent my life keeping secrets, but suddenly I have news, and I can't wait to share it.

The nearest booth is occupied by half a dozen execs in suits with Harrison in the center.

I take advantage of my angle and drink him in. His sharp jaw and nose, firm mouth, muscled shoulders and chest beneath the custom suit.

I send a text quickly after a transition.

Rae: Charm them yet?

He glances at his phone, typing with a smirk.

Harrison: That's your job.

He shoots me a hot look and pockets the device before returning to his conversation.

This isn't his club, but he came to see me, and brought some prospective partners to discuss collaborating on a new project. While he didn't give me all the details, I'm praying it works out.

Harrison likes Vegas. It suits him, its flash and flair with an edge beneath the surface.

He has zero problem getting businesspeople to come here to see him, and I've been pleasantly surprised how little he's traveled since we arrived here.

I don't hate it either.

While we spend most of our time living at our penthouse at the Wynn, we do days off in LA and we've been to London twice to see Ash.

The only wrinkle is that a top DJ is normally travelling two hundred nights a year or more, something we knew we'd have to take a hard look at once my residency was up.

I can tell Harrison would rather stay put. But it hasn't been clear how long we can make that work.

I refocus on my set, and the crowd is lost in the music, in me.

At one point, I see the execs shake hands like they've done a deal.

I dash off a text.

Rae: Looks like my magic worked.

This time, Harrison looks my way in an instant. His expression, full of love and admiration, steals my breath.

He lifts a hand, and I think he's going to flip me off. My heart kicks as I think of our old Ibiza tradition.

Instead, he blows me an air kiss.

Fuck me.

I'm grinning like a moron, and I don't even care.

His gaze stripped me bare when I dressed for tonight, my mermaid-inspired getup an homage to the water-themed club, with a cropped, lilac lace top that leaves my navel exposed and green pants that hug my hips and butt.

My body tingles with anticipation because after my set, I have more to go home to than a hot bath and a sleepless night.

I have a man who loves me.

Two years ago, all I wanted was to play La Mer, but I didn't realize who I'd become in making that dream come true.

Now, I'm in love with the man who owns it.

A trustee in charge of Mischa's business assets until Eva's unborn child can inherit decided La Mer was too huge to run effectively and should be sold to an attractive buyer.

Good thing an attractive buyer was available.

Very attractive, if I may say so. But I'm biased because every night, he wraps those very attractive arms around me.

I wrap my set to screams and applause and head out of the

booth. After, I'm lingering with fans to take selfies when my phone buzzes.

Harrison: Come find me.

I shake my head, typing back with a grin.

Rae: A little busy. Why don't you come find me?

A few moments later, there's a response.

Harrison: Because if I come find you, I'll drag you into the nearest corner and fuck you senseless. I don't care who's watching.

I'm already damp with sweat, but now my panties are sticking even more.

When I'm good and ready, I weave my way toward his booth.

As if he feels my presence, he turns and reaches for my hand.

"Gentlemen," he says. "This is Raegan Madani. My..."

He trails off, and I look up, arching a brow.

He typically introduces me as his girlfriend. Though we think of ourselves as partners, it's a possessive thing for him, and I don't hate it.

But now, he doesn't say anything.

I'm spared overthinking it when men whisper-shout compliments on the show.

A booth girl shows up and begins pouring Dom, handing out

glasses starting with me.

"Raegan"—Harrison takes his own glass and lifts it—"these gentlemen have agreed to invest in an expansion of Echo Entertainment in America." He pauses, and I see the emotion behind his eyes. "We're going to rebuild Kings."

My heart kicks hard in my chest as he clinks his glass to mine.

I ignore the champagne and press up on my toes to kiss him hard. "Hell yes," I tell him with a grin.

When he tugs me against his side, stroking a hand down my back to my ass where they can't see, my happiness is overtaken by a sudden jolt of arousal.

"Perhaps we can talk her into an exclusive partnership next year," another man suggests.

I raise a brow. "Unfortunately, that's going to be impossible."

Harrison's hand on my ass stills. While I like playing for him once in a while, we've learned it's best if I keep my work separate, but he's noticed my firm words. "Why is that?"

I think of the news that's been bubbling in my chest all night.

"Because I've committed to playing here for another six months."

Harrison's mouth parts in surprise. "Since fucking when?"

I bite my cheek. "This afternoon. I had a meeting with the owner, and we discussed it."

Six months in one place. The penthouse Harrison found personally. Our luggage stored in the closet, Barney lounging on the carpet.

I can't tell if he's upset I didn't let him in on it or simply stunned. At least not until he threads a hand into my hair and jerks me toward him, taking the kiss I planted on him before and raising it to straight-up tongue-fucking, audience or no.

The fact that I matter more to him than work makes me move into his lips, the invitation of his body, the way his arms drag me closer.

When we come up for air, he's only looking at me.

"I didn't mean to interrupt your business," I pant, innocent. I flick a glance to the men who've started talking amongst themselves given the awkwardness.

Harrison's eyes flash. "Business is over. I'm taking you home."

"You want to wrestle for the good side of the bed?"

Harrison leans in to whisper against my ear. "You can have it. After I fuck you in it until you're too sore to move."

Harrison

When we get back to our penthouse at the Wynn, Barney's passed out on the carpet. He lifts his head as we enter, ears twitching while Raegan sets her bag on a hook, then flops back down.

"I'd say he's adjusted rather well," I comment, stretching my neck.

Rae steps out of her heels, groaning a little when her feet hit the carpet. "Why not? It feels like home."

Some days I can't believe she's here—in front of me, beside me, under me. She is every bit the queen I never knew I wanted.

No, needed.

I shrug out of my jacket and toss it on the hall table without looking.

"When were you going to tell me you decided you wanted to stay?" I ask.

We'd talked about it as a possibility, but I didn't want to pressure her. While we're becoming more comfortable together with our routines as a couple, her career means being available to play to crowds all over the world.

It's part of the job, and part of the thrill.

"Just recently. Everything I want is here."

This is good news. I drag her against me. "Dinner at Picasso?" I think of the restaurant at the Bellagio.

"And shopping," she deadpans breathily against my lips.

"But mostly..."

"...Barney," she says.

The dog perks up once again.

For that, I toss her over my shoulder. "You're in trouble."

"Put me down! Being British doesn't make this any less caveman."

"No, but it means I can stare down my nose at you imperiously when I decide to drop you."

I flick the lights by the door with my free hand, and the soft glow from behind the dark wood headboard brings our bedroom into focus.

I toss Raegan on the bed, taking a moment to appreciate the view from here.

Her costume is sexy, a joke and a provocation at once, like only the woman I love can pull off. Her curves are decadent, but it's the confidence beneath, the ownership of who she is, that's most attractive.

"This outfit is ridiculous," I rasp.

Rae angles her chin up, offering me full lips and knowing eyes in the semidarkness. "And here I figured you'd like it. Seeing as how you're the clothes whore."

I'm already hard in my pants.

I take my time stripping her out of her obscenely sexy costume and tossing it on the floor.

The lingerie beneath is lace, matching the color of her skin. As I shift over her, I imagine it darkening when it's wet from my tongue, her slickness.

Her fingers thread through mine, and I drag her hands over her head, pinning them against the headboard.

"Save your breath, love," I murmur. "The only thing you'll be calling me in a moment is a god."

She grins, and I go to work making it so.

I touch every curve, following my hands with my mouth, until she's moaning and incoherent. Then she helps strip my shirt and trousers off, and when I turn her over and yank up her hips to slip inside her bare, my gaze locks on the floor-to-ceiling mirror across from the bed. Watching her take me, arching her back while I grip her ass and sink deeper with every stroke, is the hottest thing I've ever seen.

"Oh shit," she groans.

"You like how fucking deep I am, love?"

"Yes, more."

"More," I agree, thrusting in until my balls slap up against her, and she's grabbing fistfuls of sheets while I indulge in one of my favorite fantasies and fuck her from behind.

Every day, her fans worship her.

Every night, I do.

When I let my hand drift up between her legs to circle her clit, she explodes, clenching on my cock so hard I come with a jolt. I grind against her, turning her chin to catch her moan of completion in a deep kiss as I follow her over.

The second time I take her, she's on top and we're face-to-face. Her nails rake my back, and I'm lost.

Turns out having someone brand you is fucking perfect, if it's the right someone.

I want this forever. Me, planning the next stage of my business—one that's no longer tethered to the past, but free to expand in the future. Her, triumphing in the club or working on a track. After, both of us coming together like this.

"I love you," I say after, pulling her toward me.

She traces the outline of my face, my jaw. "I love you too."

We lie across the satiny sheets, the glow from the headboard the only light in the bedroom. Behind the blackout curtains, the city throbs with its own nighttime energy.

"But...?" I prompt.

She's wearing that look, the one that says she's thinking hard about something.

"Tonight, you started to call me your girlfriend but didn't."

I can't stop the chuckle. "That's what you're worried about?"

"Not worried. Curious."

I stare her down until she starts to shift away, but I drag her back and tilt her chin up to me.

"I like you curious," I murmur against her neck.

"Go to sleep," she retorts, but she's smiling.

"And leave you awake to spin in that beautiful head of yours?

Never."

One thing that hasn't changed is that it takes her awhile to wind down after a gig.

I brush my fingers through her hair.

"Not spinning. Thinking about your birthday next weekend," she says. "I have plans."

"You can't because I have plans."

"That's not how birthdays work." But her protest is softer, her breaths longer and slower.

I stroke down her arm and thread my fingers through hers, rubbing my thumb across each of her bare knuckles and memorizing the feel.

"It is now. I've been working on something too," I murmur.

But she's already asleep.

I smile.

EPILOGUE TWO

Rae

"**Y**ou're joking," I blurt.

"I'm quite serious."

My hair blows around my face, and I brush it away to look around the deck of the yacht. "You *wanted* a boat for your birthday? Why the hell?"

Harrison follows my gaze, the wind tugging at his half-unbuttoned shirt. "Fond memories," is all he says, his mouth twitching in a cryptic smile as he takes my hand.

"You guys going to come and get drinks or what?" Beck calls.

Because, yeah, our friends came too. With Tyler and Annie, a one-year-old Rose, Elle and Beck, it feels more like my birthday than Harrison's.

When Ash showed up, I knew this was a big deal. He flew over from the UK for only a couple of nights, arriving at the port thirty minutes after the rest of us given traffic from LAX.

Interestingly, Beck gave Ash more than his share of shit—probably because Ash did the same to Beck on my birthday when he'd been late. But as soon as they started sparring, it was impossible to stop them.

Something's up. I only found out we were going on an overnight trip when Harrison told me to pack a bag and then drove us to the port at Long Beach this morning.

I don't have a chance to press him as we set out to Catalina for the day, exploring the island together on bikes and on foot.

Harrison doesn't seem to be feeling any ill effects from the yacht—or maybe he's okay because we've spent more time on land than at sea.

After exploring Avalon and the Catalina Casino, we come back to the anchored yacht for a delicious chef-prepared dinner of swordfish, followed by cake.

"How fucking old do you think I am?" Harrison demands, taking in the dozens of candles interspersed with real flowers on the beautiful white cake.

"Don't blame me," Ash retorts, lifting a brow. "They know when you were born."

Annie, Elle, and I crack up. Even Rose gurgles, half-asleep in Annie's arms.

"You think this innocent act is gonna work forever?" Beck's arm leans across the back of Elle's chair, but his smirk is focused on Harrison's brother.

Ash leans over the table. "Not an act, Hollywood. What you see is what you get."

"The baker didn't want us to put candles on it, but we insisted," Tyler says, bringing the attention back to the cake.

Harrison shakes his head at me. But he's grinning.

I shift my chair closer to his.

"Wait. You have to make a wish, remember?" I prompt before he can blow out the candles. "And it'll only come true if you get them all in one breath."

He cocks his head. "You never told me what yours was."

I feel the flush crawling up my cheeks. "Maybe someday I will."

"In that case, I'll tell you mine when you tell me yours."

He blows, and every tiny flame extinguishes.

I wake up to a gentle rocking motion.

It takes a moment to recognize the stateroom in the dark.

The bed next to me is empty, and I frown. It can't be that long since we came down here.

After long looks over cake and drinks, we didn't even make it to the bed before Harrison lifted me up against the door and pressed inside me, his scent making my head spin while his hot breath fanned my throat.

But when we lay down together, me soaking in the perfection of this day, he seemed like the one locked in his head.

Now, sliding out from between the sheets, I tug on a shirt and shorts and head above deck, trying to be quiet so as not to wake Annie and Tyler or Rose or Elle or Beck.

At the top, the moonlight kisses the boat. The lights of Catalina are glittering jewels on the horizon.

Harrison leans over the railing, shirtless and in drawstring pants.

I take a moment to admire the view—of our surroundings, but equally, of him.

"Thinking of jumping off?" I tease, wrapping my arms around me against the breeze as I cross the deck to him.

He turns at the sound of my voice, chuckling. "Not seasick, love."

"Right." I lean over the railing next to him, staring down at the waves lapping against the yacht. "Men like you charter yachts to fuck on them," I tease. Hard to believe it was more than a year and a half ago we had that conversation.

"It's not the only reason."

I sigh out a breath, relaxing into the evening.

He shifts off the railing, and it's only moments before I miss his company.

"Where did you…"

When I turn back, my words dry up.

Harrison's not standing behind me.

He's on one knee.

My heart stops. "Um. What are you doing?"

I grip the hem of my shirt, twisting it nervously in my fist.

I want to look around to see if this is some joke, but can't tear my eyes from him.

"Making my birthday wish come true," he replies.

He pulls out a small box and lifts the lid.

The blue-diamond teardrop, surrounded with white diamonds, sparkles back at me.

"I lived by my own rules until I met you. You were impossible and stubborn and…"

My eyebrows rise further.

"And I never want to live a day without you by my side." The breeze ruffles his hair, his throat bobbing with emotion. "You're already my queen, Reagan. Be my wife."

Holy shit.

I never thought of myself as the kind of girl to be swept off her feet, but there's no deck. No earth. Nothing stable to hold on to, except the commitment in his eyes.

I reach for the ring, lifting it out of the case and turning it in my fingers. The blue diamond is the size of my fingertip. He knew it was huge when he bought it. He probably doesn't know it's the same color as his eyes when he's inside me.

The band is wide enough for an inscription on the inside.

Through everything.

My throat tightens.

"Not because I merely want to survive what life throws at us," he murmurs, noticing me reading. "Because every day with you is an experience I will never take for granted."

I press my lips together.

"I want you with me always," he finishes.

I never thought much about a ceremony, but the idea of marrying him feels so damn right.

He's still larger than life, but maybe I am too. And it's the quiet moments with him I love the most—the teasing, the appreciating where we've come from, what we've been through together. When he tugs me against him at night.

"Well?" he prompts, looking agitated.

I take a breath. "Yes."

His grin flashes in the dark before he rises, towering over me again in a heartbeat. I'm already overwhelmed before he slips the ring on my finger, the cool metal feeling strange against my skin.

He pulls my lips up to his and kisses me with so much devotion and love and happiness that I'm speechless when he pulls back.

A noise has me looking up.

"Did it work?" Annie's head sticks up from the stairs that go belowdecks.

My jaw drops. "You were in on this?"

She tries to look innocent and fails.

"The best birthday gift," Harrison calls, loud enough for her to hear.

"You didn't like the bookcase?" I protest lightly, and he winks at me.

"It was stunning"—I had the custom furniture made to display his books in our place at the Wynn—"but this is even more beautiful and rare. And while that was something I didn't know I needed, you are quite simply someone I cannot live without."

Damn.

Suddenly our friends pour out of the stairway, surrounding us with love and congratulations. Elle carries a tray of bubbling champagne flutes while Ash claps his brother on the back and messes up my hair with a grin.

My heart is so full I can barely breathe.

"How are you guys going to do this?" Beck demands.

"Huge wedding," Harrison murmurs, wrapping an arm around me.

"Hell no," I retort, even as I rub my thumb over the inside of my ring to get used to the feel of it.

"We'll sell rights to *People* magazine," Beck promises.

"I'll sell your balls to them first." My eyes narrow. "If this is all some trick to get me to agree to honor and obey you—"

"I don't need that."

"Because I love you?"

He strokes a thumb along my jaw, reverent and possessive.

"That. And I still have a favor."

THANK YOU

Thank you for reading *Enemies*! I hope you loved Harrison and Rae's love story as much as I do.

If you're not ready to let go of these characters…

Scan the code below to join my VIP newsletter for an exclusive Harrison and Rae bonus scene.

So many readers have asked what's next for this ruthless billionaire and the woman who tamed him. I'm excited to share that they're getting a happily-ever-after book!

To find out what surprises are still in store as they make their life together, grab BEAUTIFUL SALVATION.

PSST! Did you know that Sawyer Redmond, Harrison's mysterious friend, is the hero in a hot forbidden romance?

Forced into exile after falling from grace, reckless Sawyer has one chance to redeem himself by teaching at his former college. But when he meets a woman he craves like nothing else, will he risk his future to claim her?

Find out in Crave.

ACKNOWLEDGMENTS

Harrison and Rae lived in my head for almost two years before I typed a single word. Back when I was writing Tyler and Annie, these two kept tugging at my heart.

This story wouldn't have happened without the support of my awesome readers, including my ARC team. You ladies provide endless enthusiasm, cheerleading, and help spreading the word. I could NOT do it without you, and it would be a lot less fun to try.

Becca Mysoor, thank you for your story genius. Cassie Robertson and Devon Burke, thank you for questioning, polishing, and catching all the little things.

Nina Grinstead, thank you for your sage advice and for helping my stories find their way to the right readers.

Kate Tilton, thank you for helping me not only dream up new ideas but actually get them done. Annette Brignac, thank you for your kindness, enthusiasm, and unwavering support. Don't ever leave me.

Love,

Piper

WICKED WORLD ROMANCES BY PIPER LAWSON

WICKED SERIES
Jax and Haley
Good Girl
Bad Girl
Wicked Girl
Forever Wicked

RIVALS SERIES
Tyler and Annie
Love Notes
A Love Song for Liars
A Love Song for Rebels
A Love Song for Dreamers
A Love Song for Always

ENEMIES SERIES
Harrison and Rae
Beautiful Enemy
Beautiful Sins
Beautiful Ruin
Beautiful Salvation

Scan the code to read the books:

ABOUT THE AUTHOR

Piper Lawson is a WSJ and USA Today bestselling author of smart and steamy romance.

She writes women who follow their dreams, best friends who know your dirty secrets and love you anyway, and complex heroes you'll fall hard for.

Piper lives in Canada with her tall and brilliant husband. She's a sucker for dark eyes, dark coffee, and dark chocolate.

Here's where to find her and talk books:

- www.piperlawsonbooks.com
- www.piperlawsonbooks.com/subscribe
- www.facebook.com/piperlawsonbooks
- www.instagram.com/piperlawsonbooks
- www.goodreads.com/author/show/13680088